OMEGA REQUIRED

DESSA LUX

❀ Created with Vellum

CHAPTER 1

*S*oon-to-be-Doctor Beau Jeffries was doing his best not to show it, but he could hardly believe he was walking around the campus of the Rochester Clinic as a possible future resident. The interview for the residency program was actually an entire day of interviews, interspersed with meals and other "casual" events that Beau knew were no less crucial to the impression he was making.

He needed to make an *impeccable* impression. Beau was the only werewolf being considered for a residency at Rochester.

Even with excellent grades and stellar recommendations, securing a place in a residency program focused on human medicine was going to be an uphill battle.

When he was shown to the waiting area outside the program director's office, the administrative assistant gave a little smile and he tried to return it with the same intensity. "Dr. Aster will be with you in just a moment."

"No problem," Beau said, moving to sit in the chairs she had waved toward. She nodded and retreated to her desk.

Like virtually every human, which was to say every *person*, he'd met at Rochester, she didn't seem at all frightened of him or even unduly curious. He'd even noticed werewolves around the place, working as security guards and maybe orderlies. He hadn't been introduced to any of them, and hadn't given them away by showing that he'd noticed, but they were there, working with these humans, accepted by them. It was just one more thing—aside from it being *the Rochester Clinic*—that had him mentally ranking this program as his first choice before he'd even finished his interview.

Beau had been the only werewolf med student at all the other interviews he'd gone on as well. There were a handful of others in his graduating class, but he'd chosen Northwestern because it was one of the few medical schools in the country with openly lycanthropic students. There weren't many werewolves in medicine, and Beau was the only one he knew of who wanted to treat humans, instead of advancing the brand new fields opening up in lycanthropic research.

There was plenty of good to be done there, of course. Beau was as curious as anyone to know how his own kind really ticked. But werewolves had gotten along for centuries before the Revelation without modern medicine, because werewolves were pretty damn hard to kill. The Supreme Court decision handed down the same year Beau graduated high school, ruling that werewolves were people and killing them was homicide, had done more to improve werewolves' life expectancy than the entire medical profession ever could.

Humans, on the other hand, could be killed by all sorts of things. Beau was becoming a doctor because he wanted to save people—and that meant being a doctor for the people who needed saving.

He'd dreamed of working at Rochester since long before he got into med school. Rochester was the last resort for a lot of sick humans; the world-renowned clinic specialized in difficult cases. If Beau wanted to prove that a werewolf's senses, combined with a proper medical education, could save lives through improved diagnosis, this was the place to do it.

So he really, really had to stop grinning like an idiot every time he saw another sign, or piece of stationery, or *employee badge* with the Rochester Clinic emblem on it. He was here to be considered for a residency, not to ask for a medical institution's autograph.

He kept his gaze down as he waited, and couldn't help looking at his own visitor's badge. It had his picture on it, duplicated from the headshot he'd sent with his application; he had spent a great deal of effort getting his smile right, a warm expression that countered the appearance of a dark-haired, dark-eyed alpha werewolf. He was well over six feet tall with the broad, muscular alpha build that could make humans edge away from him even before they knew what he was, if he didn't take care to look friendly and non-threatening.

It reminded him to try to look like that, amiable and approachable and not beaming with idiotic delight.

"Mr. Jeffries?"

The director herself came to the door of her office, and Beau popped to his feet maybe a little too fast. She and her assistant both showed brief indications of being startled, but nothing more. Beau smiled and smoothed down his shirt. He stepped forward slowly as Dr. Aster's expression settled into a professional smile.

This interview was his last of the day, and it was only scheduled for about fifteen minutes, not really time for anything in-depth. Beau figured it was just a handshake and a little chat—a formality.

That idea lasted for about two minutes while he exchanged pleasantries with Dr. Aster, and then she said, "Now, I don't want to ignore the elephant in the room, here. You're unlike any other med student we're interviewing."

Beau nodded, guarding his expression. He'd gotten variously blunt questions about lycanthropy several times in his interviews so far. He had come up with pretty smooth answers to all of them.

"If accepted," the director went on, "it follows that you would have needs that would be different from any other resident's, and so we are trying to get a handle on what that would involve. This is our draft policy on werewolves in the residency program here at Rochester. I'd like you to just take a look at it and tell me what you think, or ask me any questions that occur to you right away."

Beau stared at her for a few seconds before he forced himself to take the papers from her hand. He kept his face schooled to a neutral expression, his hands steady, but he could barely read the words in front of him, all the extra rules they were going to make him follow to make up for being what he was.

A provision near the top leaped out at him.

Werewolf residents will be expected to demonstrate strong and continuing support from other werewolves (with pack of origin, local pack fostering, and/or a mate/spouse).

Beau couldn't even pretend to look at any other words on the page; his throat was tight and his heart racing as he stared at the paper, which was suddenly a wall coming down between him and everything he'd spent the last decade working toward.

"I..." Beau forced himself to look up, to meet the human's politely concerned gaze. "I'm not a member of a pack."

They couldn't, technically, force him to disclose anything about his pack membership if he didn't have one, but if they asked him what had happened with the pack he was born to, why he had left, he would have to answer. Lying would damn him, and the truth was something he'd been walking away from for a long time. He didn't want to have to spill all of that here, but if he had to, if that was the price...

Dr. Aster didn't press that point, though. "I take it the fact that you didn't bring a partner to last night's dinner is not just the two-body problem in scheduling, then?"

Beau shook his head slightly. He hadn't had time to date since he was sixteen, and before then he'd never gotten past having a crush. Since he left home, every bit of time and effort had been focused on surviving without a pack, putting himself through college and then med school.

The werewolves among the med students sometimes called themselves a pack, but it came nowhere near meeting the legal definition. Given that everyone in it was either still in med school or in a residency, even if they *were* a legitimate pack they still wouldn't be any use as a support network, and no one here would believe him if he tried to claim they were.

"There are some local packs in the area that we've touched base with," Dr. Aster said tentatively. "There are at least two who seem open to taking on a temporary or permanent new member, and I gather from what they said when we discussed it that that kind of support really would be crucial. It wouldn't be safe for you or anyone else for you to try to complete a program as demanding as our residency without some support."

Here it was, more baldly stated than anywhere else he'd interviewed. *We can't have you going crazy and biting patients.* He wondered if there was some provision in the policy for having extra security on hand for his shifts, ready to take him down if he went wild, or if they wouldn't consider that any of his business.

He thought of the other werewolves he'd noticed around, and realized that they must all be keeping the secret somehow; surely Rochester wouldn't trust werewolf security guards more than a werewolf medical resident. He couldn't risk compromising others by showing that he knew; if he came here he could never acknowledge any of them, even if they were set the ironic task of keeping him under control.

Beau plastered on a self-deprecating smile and made himself look up, ignoring the strangling feeling of claustrophobia that came with the idea of returning to such terrible secrecy in the guise of openness. "I understand. It would mean some extra adjustments, but obviously I would do everything I could to abide by the program's policy if matched here."

Dr. Aster smiled. Beau didn't know her remotely well enough to have any special insight into the meaning of her scent or her heartbeat, but she seemed calm, settled. Not angry or afraid, not inflicting this from cruelty, but determined that it was the best course.

Beau made his way through the rest of the interview on autopilot, but he already wanted to be back in Chicago, away from the false promise of this place. There was no way he was going to be putting the Rochester Clinic on his list of possible matches. No matter how neat and tidy they made it sound, he wasn't going to sign up to have his private life dictated to him by *humans*.

❧

Six weeks later, Beau had ordered and re-ordered his list of residency programs about a thousand times. The deadline for submitting his prioritized choices was only hours away, and he knew that swapping his seventh and eighth place choices yet again wasn't really what he was worried about.

He only had nine programs on his list.

He had interviewed at twelve, and the two he'd visited after the Rochester Clinic had both been absolutely clear *no*'s. Everyone had been polite, but he'd gotten incredibly bad feelings about both places, unable to connect even tentatively with any of the doctors or residents he met. There had been no werewolf security guards, nothing but humans.

Did that matter? Had he just been hypersensitive after Rochester? He didn't know, but he felt hair standing up on his neck and a growl vibrating at the base of his throat when he thought about putting either of them on his list.

The irony was that he still remembered how happy he'd felt at Rochester, right until the end. Every time he thought about it, he couldn't remember anything but that sunny, suburban campus. He'd spent nearly eleven years in the city in Chicago and he was ready to be somewhere that wasn't quite so hard on a wolf's senses. No residency program was going to be anything like where he'd grown up, but Rochester was one of the smaller cities he'd visited, and it was surrounded by vast sweeps of state and national parks. It was *Minnesota*.

He could be happy there, if it wasn't for...

He shook his head. No. He wasn't going to let his residency program force him into a pack, to make himself subject to some strange alpha's decisions; it couldn't possibly turn out any better than it had the first time. And he certainly wasn't going to be rushed into a

6

mating. He couldn't, not like this. Not to satisfy humans who would probably never be satisfied that he wasn't some time bomb of lycanthropic aggression, straight out of some distorted sensational news story about another werewolf killed by a human in so-called self-defense.

But that meant he still only had nine choices on his list. They had been told, time and again, as they applied and interviewed, that if they put down ten or more choices, they had a better than 90 percent chance of being matched.

But those were the statistics for *human* med students, of course. Dr. Pavlyuchenko, who served as a semi-official adviser for all the werewolf students at Northwestern, had told him flatly that ten was the bare minimum if he hoped to be matched.

The matching between applicants and residency programs was done nationally; every fourth-year med student would find out on the same day whether they had matched and then, a few days later, where they were going. If he didn't match, he'd have to scramble to find a program that would take him.

If he could find any spot at all, at that point, it would be in werewolf medicine, not human. If he spent two or three years doing a residency in a lycanthropic specialty, he could kiss his chances of ever getting board-certified in a human specialty goodbye.

So he had to match. He had to match one of the twelve programs he'd managed to get an interview with, or it was all for nothing.

It wasn't like Rochester would take him anyway, probably, given how they clearly felt about werewolves. And if it got down to his tenth choice...

Beau gritted his teeth and typed in *Rochester Clinic* at the bottom of his list. He hit *Submit* before he could second-guess himself. He had ten programs on his list. He would be happy at nine of them. He still had his final semester to get through, and he couldn't waste any more time thinking about where he might match. It was out of his hands now.

CHAPTER 2

"Mr. Lea? You can keep going if you want, but I'm just going to turn off the timer."

Roland squeezed his eyes shut, pressing his knuckles to his forehead as if he could push back the searing pain of his headache. It also gave him a little cover from the gentle, patient gaze of Susan, his case worker at the North Chicago Omega Refuge.

Susan was an omega, too, and she would certainly be able to tell if he actually let a tear fall, but if he hid his face she wouldn't acknowledge it out loud. Probably.

He heard her take a few tentative steps closer to his end of the table, and Roland used his other arm to cover the test booklet he'd been staring into without writing down a single answer for... he had no idea how long. Long enough that Susan had given up on him making any kind of progress on the practice test within the time limit.

"Don't," Roland managed to say, his throat constricted almost too tightly even for that. "Don't look. Please."

Susan stayed where she was, and then he heard her backing away. "I won't look at your test. But maybe you'd like to go and wash your face, and then we can talk about this. About where you'd like to go from here."

Roland nodded against his fist, latching on immediately to the escape offered in her suggestion. He grabbed the test booklet as he stood, his shoulders hunched up as he turned away without looking in Susan's direction. He hurried out of the little meeting room toward the nearest bathroom and locked himself in, then pressed his flaming face to the metal door.

He didn't know what was shaking his body, making him feel hot and weak all over, even beyond the shame and rage of his latest, most obvious failure. He'd been feeling like this for weeks, even before he'd come to the refuge. It felt a little like heat coming on—that uncomfortable, achy almost-fever, but worse, ugly and painful.

And he certainly wasn't coming into heat. The suppressants he kept hidden away in his locker protected him from that. He took them faithfully, every day, and guarded the bottle more fiercely than any of his other meager possessions.

He wasn't going to be helpless like that again, mindless like that. Not ever. No one was going to use him like that ever again.

That was the decision he'd made, when he finally got his shit together enough to realize that, whether or not there was anything better to hope for, he had to get away from Martin. It was the one thing he'd stayed certain of through his struggles to survive before he found the refuge. He wasn't doing any of that again.

But he had to do *something*. Without a shitbag alpha boyfriend, let alone a real mate or pack, Roland had to find a way to support himself. If he stayed on the suppressants, his heats wouldn't get in the way of finding a job. He'd even be able to pass among humans again. He could have a life, or something resembling one. He might be lonely and cold, but he would be his own.

All he had to do was find a job, despite the fact that he'd never finished high school, never held a real job, and...

Roland opened his eyes and pushed back from the door, using both hands to spread out the test booklet against the metal surface. He stared fiercely at the page he'd been on when Susan broke the silence in the study room, but it was no different here, alone. The words blurred into illegible smears as he looked at them, and when he did decipher one he couldn't place it within a sentence, forgetting it by the time he had wrestled through the next.

He was broken. Sometime in the last eight years, when he wasn't paying attention—and the moon knew, he had worked hard enough at not paying attention—he had lost the ability to even fucking *read*. To even *think* properly. He hadn't taken a bit of wolfsbane since he came to the refuge, where he had a safe place to sleep and food to eat, but the shivery weakness hadn't let up, and neither had this.

Roland turned away from the door and staggered to the sink to splash water on his face. He looked at himself in the mirror, trying not to flinch from the sight. His pale green eyes stared back at him, the color looking lurid next to the bloodshot whites of his eyes. He was gaunt, his color sickly pale. He'd shaved off his hair at one of the shelters he'd stayed at before he found the refuge because it had started to fall out in patches; his head sported a few hints of pale stubble among the stretches of naked skin, even paler than his face. The vivid, unhealed silver burns peeked out of the collar of his shirt, and Roland rearranged the out-of-season scarf he wore to cover them, using one end to mop his damp face.

No one was going to hire him looking like this, and he wasn't good for anything anyway. He couldn't go back to school, and he was in no condition to do the kinds of heavy labor that a lot of alphas and betas excelled at, with werewolf strength and healing. The refuge was big on all the omegas who lived here having a *plan*, a *goal*. Roland had been telling Susan that this was his, to finish the education he'd missed out on when he ran away at sixteen with an older alpha who promised to take good care of him.

If he didn't have a plan, would they kick him out? Would he have to go back to the human shelters? Back to begging on street corners, sleeping cold and hungry in doorways when human strangers' pity didn't keep him fed?

Roland squeezed his eyes shut. "Fuck. *Fuck.*"

There was a gentle tap on the door. "Mr. Lea?"

Susan. Of course. Susan was kind, and patient, and *relentless*. She wasn't going to let him hide in this bathroom forever.

Roland shoved the test booklet into the trash, deep under the damp paper towels and used tissues. He rinsed his hands and dried them, and then opened the door.

"Are you going to kick me out?"

Susan blinked at him. She was at least sixty, though soft living and werewolf genetics made it hard to tell; she never talked about herself, her own life, but Roland had her pegged as a grandmother from some nice suburb, doing Good Works among the fallen omegas at the refuge.

She was still a wolf, though. She still had teeth. She didn't flinch from him, and if it came time for him to go he had no doubt she'd escort him to the gate and put him out personally.

"No," she said after a moment. "That's not what we do here. But I think we need to reconsider your options."

As if he still had options. But if they weren't kicking him out, that was something, and he owed it to this place to go through whatever motions were required.

"Okay," Roland said, making himself let go of the doorframe. "Sure, let's reconsider."

Susan led him away from the bathroom, not back to the study room, which must reek of his desperation and despair, but to a quiet little sitting room. She shut the door firmly, but the windows were open, looking out at the refuge's courtyard. There were a few little green shoots poking out of the ground, the first brave flowers of the spring.

"So," Susan said. "I'm not going to tell you by any means to give up on finishing high school, but it seems like that may be a longer-term project for you."

Roland stared down at his hands, clamped around each other until his bony knuckles were bloodless. Susan was always like this, pretending he had a future, that he could do things normal people did, as if his past was really just past.

"I think you need more individual support than the refuge is able to give you," she went on. "I know you've said there's no pack or family who you want to get in contact with, and I don't really want to push you toward joining a pack on your own at this point."

She fell silent there. Roland thought that did sound like they wanted to kick him out, or send him to some even-more-institutional institution, because what the hell did that leave?

He raised his head to look at her, and Susan was holding a pamphlet now. Even he could read the two linked symbols on the cover: *alpha* and *omega*.

Roland stared at it for a moment, and then looked up at Susan's gentle expression. He buried his face in his hands and started to laugh, wildly and a little painfully. "You—what—"

Susan was as unperturbed as ever. "It's an agency that helps to connect single alphas and omegas, and they work with us sometimes to find suitable mates for omegas here. You haven't met Eric yet, I don't think, but he's one of our volunteers and a former resident—he found his mate through them. They wouldn't force anything, but they could help you to find a mate who'd support you, in every sense."

Roland forced himself to stop laughing before it turned into something else. He breathed for a little while, still keeping his face hidden, and then sat back in his chair, mopping his face with the end of his scarf. He tugged it out of place when he was done and dragged down the collar of his shirt, letting Susan really see the silver burns that still marred his neck in ugly, raised red patches, blistered around the edges.

Her eyes widened slightly. "Roland! That's—"

"They don't heal," Roland said, tucking the scarf back in place and looking away. "I've been to the clinic, I put the salve on it twice a day, but... they don't heal. And that's... that's not even everything."

He gritted his teeth, pushing away the memory of the pain in his belly and between his legs, the midwife's strong hands, his alpha's sneer. *Who'd want you now? You're only good for one thing.*

"Trust me, I'm not mating material. No alpha's going to want me. Or if they did, what they want me for is..." Roland shook his head and stared out the window again.

"I'll grant you, it would have to be someone very special," Susan said. "But there's every chance the alpha for you could be out there somewhere, Mr. Lea. Registering with the agency doesn't commit you to anything beyond meeting prospective alphas. If you aren't comfortable with anyone they introduce you to, you say no and that's that. But if you think it's possible that there could be someone you'd say yes to, I really want you to consider it."

Then he would have a plan, wouldn't he? Then he could say he was trying. They would let him stay here at the refuge, and he could keep trying to heal. Maybe he could read again if he just had more time to recover, and then he could change his plan.

No one was going to choose him, and he was pretty confident in his ability to spot scumbags who wanted to use him like Martin had, so he could always say no. They'd probably let him say no a few times before they decided he wasn't trying, and how many alphas would really ask for someone like him?

Roland sighed, letting Susan see him give in. "Okay, yeah. What do I have to do to register?"

CHAPTER 3

*M*atch Day, like a lot of occasions that were supposed to be happy and exciting, was mostly filled with stress. Beau had gotten the email a few days earlier notifying him that he did indeed *have* a match, so that part of the suspense was over, but the ensuing seventy-two hours had been filled with worrying over which program he was going to end up at.

"Congratulations," the dean said, smiling his big, careless human smile as Beau accepted his envelope, on stage in front of his class-mates. "With your specialty, I was worried you'd break our perfect record of matching our lycanthropic students, but you've done it!"

Beau smiled back, feeling sick. He managed to keep the smile in place, and his envelope in hand, while he shook another half-dozen hands. He skirted around the microphone where he could, if he were an entirely different person, have opened his envelope and read the contents to those of his classmates who were still sitting and waiting for their own matches. Instead he got off the stage as quickly as possible and headed straight out of the auditorium toward the rendezvous point he and the other werewolf students had pre-arranged with Dr. Pavlyuchenko.

Lauren was waiting at the door of the stairwell, a little red-eyed but smiling. He raised an eyebrow, but she just waved him inside, where he would have a modicum of privacy and Lauren standing guard for him. Touching his envelope to his heart in silent thanks, Beau ducked through the door and sat down immediately on the first step.

His knees wouldn't carry him any farther.

He ripped open the envelope, scanning hastily past his name and the name of his med school to...

Rochester Clinic, Residency in Internal Medicine

For a moment he couldn't move, or breathe. He'd had this exact nightmare a dozen times already.

But it just kept being real, no matter how many times he opened and closed his eyes and looked around to be sure the walls were all solid. He even sniffed the paper, grounding himself in the bitter tang of the ink. There was no denying it.

Rochester, and their prejudice, and their demands, and all those seemingly-friendly people who he'd thought he might be able to like before they showed their hand. *Rochester.*

Beau dropped the paper and put his face in his hands. He didn't raise his head when he heard familiar footsteps coming up from the level below, a werewolf he had known for four years now.

Dr. Pavlyuchenko put one hand on Beau's knee as he crouched beside him, close enough to read the paper.

"Ah," he said. "Well, that's hardly surprising, is it? Considering the lengths they went to for you?"

Beau jerked upright at that. "What *lengths*—"

He couldn't even speak; he just stared while Dr. Pavlyuchenko looked down at him imperturbably. He'd told Dr. Pavlyuchenko about the werewolf policy they'd shown him, and he had raised his eyebrows, nodding, and said nothing. Beau had been perfectly clear about not intending to list them, but...

But Dr. Pavlyuchenko had reminded him that he really did need ten choices on his list.

"What..." Beau's voice came out as a thin croak that time.

"Beau," Dr. Pavlyuchenko said gently. "They *wrote a policy.* They *reached out to their local werewolf packs,* and that means they somehow successfully convinced one or more local packs to speak to people from a human medical institution. They were very, very serious about having you there, and they continue to be very, very serious about wanting you to succeed."

Beau opened and closed his mouth a few times, but he'd learned to listen to Dr. Pavlyuchenko on stuff like this, all the social-political maneuvering that he'd never been good at. He couldn't even really manage the way werewolves did that stuff—his departure from his first pack proved that beyond a doubt—let alone humans.

For a second, he entertained the idea of rejecting the match, but he had an idea of how badly that would turn out for him, and probably for a lot of other werewolves after him. Especially if Rochester's policy really was a sign that they wanted to train werewolves.

"So, I, what?" Beau said helplessly. "I take time out from my last semester of med school to *find myself a mate?*"

Dr. Pavlyuchenko squeezed his knee and gave him a considering look before he moved to sit on the step at Beau's side. "Well, I'm sure you know these things *can* move rather quickly, once you find the right person. If you need pointers on the right sort of place to meet someone..."

Beau grimaced at the thought. He knew there were werewolf clubs, places where werewolves of every gender and aspect prowled for mates, every one of them hunting in competition with every other. Beau knew for a fact that he would end up in some corner, trying to stay out of the whole thing, which would get him nowhere. Anyway, if he needed a mate, any mate, that badly, he might as well just...

"Actually," Beau said, recalling a few half-despairing late-night searches he'd done, years ago now, when the loneliness was acute and he hadn't yet learned to control it like any other craving, "I think I know where to go."

"Do you?" Dr. Pavlyuchenko looked a little amused, and faintly skeptical.

"There's an agency," Beau said. "Probably more than one, really, but... for matching alphas with omegas, all organized, up front. If I need a mate, that's probably the quickest way. Don't you think?"

"Mm," Dr. Pavlyuchenko said, not looking less skeptical but not telling him it wouldn't work either. "It certainly is a straightforward approach. You might want to contact them soon, though, just in case the process takes some time."

Beau nodded, trying to remember if the website he'd looked at had said how long it took. There were probably background checks and things, to make sure everything was on the up-and-up. Which could be a problem, maybe, considering his particular motivations.

"Anyway, congratulations on your match, hey?"

Beau nodded, and leaned down to pick up the paper. He thought again about what Dr. Pavlyuchenko had said, and the fact that he'd listed Rochester tenth out of ten in his own preferences.

"The other programs I interviewed with. None of them had a policy. Does that mean..."

"Don't think about that now," Dr. Pavlyuchenko said firmly, which definitely meant, *Yes, they never meant to take you.* "You're going to Rochester! It's the best program for what you want to do. Now go take over guarding the door for Lauren. Adam will be here soon."

Beau nodded and heaved himself up off the step. He'd had plenty of practice, in med school and long before, at pushing himself onward to deal with what needed to be done right now. Never mind fatigue, never mind loneliness, never mind fear or anger or uncertainty. Do the job.

So he tucked his match paper into his pocket and went out to where Lauren was waiting.

She hugged him without speaking, and he hugged her back, pressing his cheek against her curly red hair and breathing in the familiar almost-packmate scent of her.

She didn't ask him where he was going—she had to have heard every word he and Dr. Pavlyuchenko had exchanged, but like any well-brought-up werewolf she wouldn't acknowledge it until he did. She didn't linger for him to ask where she was going, either, just turned away and walked down the hall with her hands in her pockets.

Soon enough Adam came striding up, looking grimly determined, which was probably not really called for. Adam wanted to do were-wolf research and had only applied to programs that already had significant percentages of werewolf residents. But that didn't mean Beau really knew the first thing about what was worrying Adam—they might be the only two alphas among the werewolves in their year, but that had by no means made them close friends. Beau just stepped aside from the door and let him go through.

~

"I don't really want a mate."

Beau had meant to say something a little more diplomatic when first meeting the facilitator from the alpha-omega mate-matching agency. He'd already paid the deposit for their services and he'd given them all sorts of information, weeks ago, and waited and waited for this appointment; he couldn't screw it up now, with so little time left.

But she had introduced herself—Ellen Dawson, mated omega, the collar of her shirt high enough to hide the scar of a bite-bond or the absence of it, very modern and liberated—and said, "Tell me, honestly, what are you looking for? What do you want in a mate?"

And. Well. If he was being honest...

"Ah," Ms. Dawson said, raising her eyebrows slightly. "What *do* you want, then?"

Beau huffed and ran a hand through his hair. "I want to be a doctor. For humans. I just graduated med school—as I'm sure you're aware—and my residency is going to require me to *demonstrate stable bonds with other werewolves*, so..."

"So you came to us." Ms. Dawson sat back in her own seat, eyeing him thoughtfully. "Do you think these humans are wrong to require this of you? Are you angry about that?"

Beau sighed, but searched himself to be sure he was answering the question honestly; whether she acknowledged it out loud or not, he knew Ms. Dawson would be observing every slightest sign of his reactions to take his measure. There was no point being less than truthful now that he'd started down this road.

"No, I'm not angry. It's frustrating, but I know they mean well. And it would—will—be easier to have someone there with me to help with things, another werewolf to talk to when I'm spending all my work time with humans. And there'll be a lot of socializing outside of work; I'm not great at that. I just..."

Beau shrugged stiffly and looked down. "I wanted to do this differently, I guess. Not, you know, have my pack alpha just choose someone and say, here, this is your mate, and have it all be decided for me, or go to some club and latch on to the first person who smells right, and then get dragged into whatever pack *they're* attached to, sight unseen. I'd like to meet someone, get to know them, get to know their life, their family. Fall in love. That kind of thing."

Ms. Dawson nodded, her expression unreadable. Well, she wouldn't be in the business she was if she was stuck on the idea of people falling in love without being pushed into it.

"I just don't have *time* for anything like that," Beau went on. "I never have. Med school is crazy. Residency's going to be worse. I'm not going to be great to be around for the next three years. How do I ask some total stranger to sign up for that?"

Ms. Dawson didn't say anything for a moment; he heard the soft tap of her fingers on glass, and looked up to see her frowning at a tablet propped on her knee.

"Are you thinking of something temporary?"

Beau opened his mouth and closed it again. He hadn't been thinking anything like that—three years was an awfully long time to just walk away at the end of it—but committing to three years was asking less than committing to *forever*, wasn't it? Maybe even just one year would be enough. If he could get through the first year, prove himself, show he was trying... If after that it just didn't work out, Rochester couldn't blame him for that, could they?

"I could," Beau said slowly. "That could work. But how, uh..."

Werewolves didn't mate for life as easily and irrevocably as humans and movies might think, but it was difficult to disentangle a true mate bond. He wasn't sure why an omega was suggesting it.

"Pre-nuptial agreement, legal marriage," Ms. Dawson said briskly. "You commit to a certain settlement and promise not to contest divorce under certain conditions—within a particular time frame, and as long as there are no children, no bite-sealed bond, that sort of thing."

Children. Beau's entire brain locked up for a moment at the very idea, and he shook it off. "Definitely... definitely no children. I wouldn't... if it's going to be temporary, then I wouldn't... and of course I wouldn't require..."

"Sex optional," Ms. Dawson summed up for him, still tapping at her tablet. "Heats are an issue, of course. You'd be willing to provide a secure, private space, with suitable amenities?"

Beau nodded, dazed, even while he thought of the floorplans of the houses he'd looked at, considering which would be most appropriate.

This all sounded much more *real* than he'd been prepared for when he walked through the door. Only now did he recognize that he'd expected Ms. Dawson to reject him out of hand for coming here with improper intentions. But she seemed to be taking him seriously, and to believe that she could find an omega who would have him under these conditions.

"The best thing for you—the thing that I would advise for your personal well-being and success—would be to choose an omega who happens to be without strong pack ties holding them here and who could be a good, supportive partner."

Ms. Dawson met his eyes again, and the weight of her attention made him lean forward, instinctively pushing back against a challenge. "You'll need, at minimum, someone to look after the household and smooth the way for you socially with other doctors' spouses. It would not be impossible to find someone who would be qualified for that, willing to be a non-romantic companion, and willing to relocate with you in—what's the timeframe?"

Beau flushed. "The residency program starts next month."

Ms. Dawson's lips tightened slightly, but she nodded. "Well, it may take some searching, but we can likely find someone who is suited to be supportive."

Beau's eyes narrowed. "Or?"

Ms. Dawson tilted her head and said nothing, but Beau thought he detected a faint change in her scent and heartbeat, a motion around her eyes that meant he'd just made the right move, or at least an interesting one. She didn't say anything out loud.

"That would be the best thing for *me*," Beau prodded. "For my success. But is there something else to consider?"

"You don't like this," Ms. Dawson said, shrugging, her posture relaxing into an attitude of careless frankness. "Your background checks out, you meet all our standards on paper, but you don't like the whole idea of making this match. And I find that pushing alphas to do something they don't like rarely works out well for omegas in their vicinity."

Beau winced at the implication, but he knew enough of the kind of thing she meant to keep his mouth shut.

Her expression turned stern anyway. "We are not in the business of providing convenient warm bodies for alphas, Mr. Jeffries. We are in the business of making mutually successful matches. And I think the best odds of success would reside in turning this situation into something you *do* want. Not the least-objectionable omega, but one you will genuinely want to take home with you."

Beau looked away as his jaw tightened. He was long-practiced at pushing down his own reaction to having his hackles put up, but it had been a long time since he'd been faced with an omega doing it with such surgical precision.

He forced his gaze back to Ms. Dawson. He felt a little whiplash at being angry with her for telling him exactly what he'd expected her to tell him, that he was doing this wrong, that she couldn't match him with an omega when he didn't want a mate. But there had been that moment when it had seemed solvable, possible...

"Do you have an idea of how to make *that* work?" His voice came out with only the faintest growl under it.

Ms. Dawson merely smiled. "I do, in fact. Just a hunch about you, so maybe I'm wrong. But... instead of focusing on which omega would be best for you, we could think about which omega *you* would be best for."

"I'm not—"

"For instance," Ms. Dawson went on, as if he hadn't spoken. "Some of our omegas are in very, very difficult personal circumstances. We work with the North Chicago Omega Refuge, a shelter for homeless omegas. By definition, all of them are without the protection of a pack. Most are fleeing abusive or exploitive relationships, and would not regard relocation as a drawback."

Beau scowled at the very thought that such a place was needed. "And you want to take them out of a safe place like that and push them to mate again? After whatever they've been through?"

"Signing up with us is the omega's choice, Mr. Jeffries, and we certainly don't match them with just any alpha. An omega like that would need an alpha who could be trusted to be kind and patient, to not make demands they wouldn't be comfortable with. An alpha who might be willing to let them move on, if they realize they want something other than a mate. So that whatever they've been through need not be the end, but can become the start of a new stage of their lives."

Beau's lips parted and he sat back, thinking of it. An omega who needed a safe place, who needed him to keep some distance. Who would be *glad* to have an alpha who didn't want those intimacies with a stranger, who wouldn't want children. Who would agree to let them go after a year, or three at the outside.

"Your temporary arrangement could give an omega who's been through a serious trauma time to heal, time to consider their options. Perhaps to go back to school or gain some job training and preparation before they embark on a truly independent life."

Beau smiled a little. "You want me to run a one-omega halfway house?"

Ms. Dawson gave him a knowing look. "Would you rather spend three years with a perfectly nice omega who needs nothing from you?"

The thought of someone he could *help*—someone who *needed* the temporary home he could provide—turned the whole problem on its head. It wasn't a duty, a hoop to jump through. It was an opportunity to give something back to his own kind, even though he meant to spend his career helping humans.

"Yes," he said. "Yes, I'd like to help someone. You're right, I'd be glad to do that."

"Excellent," Ms. Dawson said. "I had someone in mind—did you have a gender preference?"

Beau shrugged and shook his head, curling his fingers into his palms to keep from reaching for the tablet. "I lean toward male omegas, but not strictly. Any omega's fine, if—if they're in a bad place, like you said. If I can help."

Ms. Dawson nodded and turned the tablet. "This is Roland Lea. He's been at the Refuge for a couple of months now."

Beau frowned. "Did they take this picture when he first arrived?"

"I took it myself, just this week. We like to be sure that what you see is what you get."

Beau sat back, crossing his arms over his chest. "I see an active wolfsbane addict who's going to fatally overdose sometime soon. They allow that in this refuge?"

Ms. Dawson frowned, seeming a little wrong-footed for the first time, but she said, "No. No intoxicants are allowed. And I met with Mr. Lea myself; he had a problem before coming to the refuge, but I assure you, he's sober now."

"He can't—" Beau leaned in, peering at the tablet, and reached for it without thinking. Ms. Dawson handed it over, and Beau touched the screen to enlarge the high-resolution image, studying every detail of Roland Lea's appearance.

He was clearly malnourished, despite being at this refuge for weeks before the picture was taken, which had to mean something was very wrong. There weren't many diseases that could produce these effects in a werewolf, and if he did have one of them he'd have died or infected someone else by now, which surely would have been noticed.

Beau glanced at Ms. Dawson again, but she seemed to be the picture of health. "Do any other omegas at the refuge look like this?"

She shook her head slowly. "His case worker is aware that there's something wrong, but... he's been through a great deal, and his emotional state has not been the best. She thought... lone-sickness, or a sundered mate bond."

Beau snorted and looked down again. *Lone-sickness.* Might as well say he was dying of an excess of black humors, like this was the dark ages. Not that they were by any means out of the dark ages when it came to werewolf medicine, but there had to be something organic at work.

Beau enlarged the image on Roland Lea's bloodshot eyes, more ivory than properly white, then his scalp, half-shaved, half-hairless. He scrolled down to the lowest edge of the image, which barely extended past his sharp chin. Scrolling further took him to Lea's profile, and he glimpsed *unknown number of past sexual partners* before hastily looking away from information he wasn't supposed to have.

"Is there a midwife at the refuge?"

"Yes, but Mr. Lea certainly isn't pregnant, or in any danger of going into heat, given his—"

Beau pinched the bridge of his nose as the certainty of what was wrong with Roland Lea formed in his head. Just as obviously, Ms. Dawson didn't know. Probably no one knew, which meant Beau couldn't just go blurting out this omega's secrets to people who controlled whether he had a safe place to live.

"I need to talk to him. Today. I'll take him, I'll agree to whatever—just, I need to talk to him right now, because he's in terrible danger."

CHAPTER 4

*R*oland was sitting outside on a bench, breathing in the green smell of the grass and the flowers growing. It was nearly summer, and summer had never smelled like this since he came to the city.

He could taste something bitter in his mouth, and he could feel fever crawling along his bones, a worsening ache in his belly. He didn't know what was happening to him, but he didn't think he was going to live long enough to have to reject many suitors.

"Mr. Lea?"

Roland opened his eyes and watched Susan come toward him. He could smell her, which was good, because his vision was getting worse; it wasn't just when he tried to read now. He hadn't told anyone that part. He didn't want the midwife here poking at him and asking questions, or for anyone to know what was happening to him while he could still hide it.

Susan was smiling, he realized as she perched at the end of the bench. He smiled back reflexively, keeping his mouth closed so that there was less chance of her smelling anything on his breath that would give away how sick he was.

"I have wonderful news, Roland," Susan said.

Roland could feel the way she wanted to touch him when she said it, to share that basic comfort and connection. Roland tucked his hands—always cold, even in this early-summer sunshine—more firmly under his arms.

Susan's smile dimmed slightly, but she went on. "Ms. Dawson from the agency is here for you. With an alpha! He's very excited to meet you; she said he couldn't wait. I know it's quite irregular, but if you're willing to meet him, this could be something really wonderful for you."

Roland looked away so that he could take a few quick, sharp breaths without her seeing his face.

Well, he had known he might have to say no a few times, and any alpha who was *that* excited to meet him was probably going to be someone he definitely wanted to say no to.

Probably not someone who would be *easy* to say no to, though.

"Will you stay with me?" Roland looked cautiously over at Susan again.

Susan's expression melted, just for an instant, and she reached toward him and then drew back without touching. "Of course, Roland. We're not going to just throw you in with him sight unseen. Would you like to have Ms. Dawson bring him out here, or go into one of the sitting rooms?"

"Here," Roland said at once. No need for Susan to watch how long it would take him to make his way inside, and no need to be in a confined, scent-trapping space with an alpha who wanted him.

"Just a minute, then." Susan tapped at something on her phone.

Roland breathed in and out and focused on holding his head exactly level—not baring his throat, nor the back of his neck—while he watched the way Susan had come. It was less than a minute when he saw two more blurred shapes approaching. One was a slim, middle-height figure who matched his memory of Ms. Dawson from the agency; the other, tall and broad with dark hair, must be the alpha.

It took a few more seconds for Roland to recognize that the alpha was wearing a suit, which shook a few of his half-formed expectations. If he'd been fucked by an alpha who even *owned* a suit in the last eight years, he hadn't known it.

Of course, he didn't know much about plenty of the alphas who'd fucked him in the last eight years. For an awful second he wondered if this was one of them, but then Roland caught his scent. It was blessedly unfamiliar, beyond the base notes of *werewolf* and *male* and *alpha*. He couldn't tell if he liked or hated it, but he didn't know it.

The alpha's expression, when it came into focus, was also unfamiliar: he looked intent, almost concerned, and his gaze didn't stray from Roland's face.

He stopped on the path, far enough away that he wasn't looming over Roland. It occurred to Roland that he was probably supposed to stand up or something.

He didn't.

"Roland, you remember Ms. Dawson," Susan said, "and this is Beau Jeffries, the alpha who wanted so much to meet you. Mr. Jeffries, Mr. Lea."

Beau Jeffries actually *bowed* a little, keeping his hands at his sides, his gaze still intent on Roland. "Hello, Mr. Lea. I'm glad to meet you. How are you doing today?"

Mr. Jeffries' voice was deep and warm, pleasant to listen to, but the question was not quite a pleasantry. Roland's heart began to beat faster.

He knows.

Roland had told the agency mostly the truth, though, and it wasn't like he wasn't obviously unwell, from his shaved head to the fact that he was in an omega refuge. He couldn't help reaching up to tuck his scarf more firmly around his throat as he nodded to Mr. Jeffries.

"Fine, thanks. Um. You?"

Mr. Jeffries smiled a little, his gaze still not wavering from Roland, and something warm blossomed in the pit of his stomach. Oh, no. He wasn't supposed to *like* the alpha. He was supposed to have finally learned better than to fall for one again.

"I'm well," Mr. Jeffries said. "But nervous, because I'm about to propose marriage to a stranger, and I'm not at all sure that he'll be interested in what I have to offer. And I really, really want him to say yes."

Roland squinted at that, looking Mr. Jeffries up and down. He looked to be perfectly fit, and fairly well off. His hands looked soft and clean, matching his nice suit, and he didn't have the hardness that Roland had long since learned to recognize in werewolves who lived or worked on the streets. How could he possibly doubt that any omega would want him?

"You see," Mr. Jeffries took a step closer and then crouched down, so he was looking up at Roland where he sat on the bench. "I've just graduated from medical school."

He probably owned more than one suit, then, and had absolutely no reason to be slumming with a broken thing like Roland.

But he had said *marriage*, and said it in front of witnesses.

Marriage was human, legal. You got proper papers and everything with that. Roland was still waiting to see if the letters the shelter had sent on his behalf would be enough testimony of his identity to get him a copy of his own birth certificate; no one in the last several years had ever offered to even add him to the lease when he lived someplace nice enough for there to be paperwork.

"What, uh," Roland swallowed hard, trying to think of how to talk to someone like that. A *doctor*. "What... specialty?"

Dr. Jeffries smiled slightly wider. "That's the tricky part, actually. I want to treat humans, not werewolves. I think that—with patients' permission, of course—I could do a lot of good as a diagnostician."

He didn't ask Roland if he understood what that word meant. He was watching Roland for his reaction, and Roland knew he didn't hide it.

He knows, he knows, he knows.

Roland struggled to find his voice. He couldn't look away from Dr. Jeffries' eyes. They were almost black, but not quite; he could just barely make out the coffee-colored irises surrounding the dark centers. "And you think they'll give permission if you're married?"

Dr. Jeffries shook his head, solemn and intent. "Well, no, I don't think it will help much with the patients. But I also have to do three years of training—my residency—and the program there, *they* want me to be married. I didn't want to be pushed into that, but Ms. Dawson suggested that I could find somebody who I can help while they're helping me, somebody who needs a safe place to live and would like to move away from Chicago. It wouldn't have to be forever. I would agree in advance that they could leave after a certain time. We'd have a pre-nuptial agreement. And when Ms. Dawson showed me your profile, I knew I had to meet you."

Roland's heart was beating so fast it hurt, and he could barely take in all the implications of what Dr. Jeffries said beyond the one that kept thundering in his brain.

He knows. He knows. He knows.

Roland pushed up to his feet without thinking about what he was doing; Dr. Jeffries stood too, taking a step back as he did, so that Roland didn't have to get too close to him to step around the bench and walk away across the grass. He kept his arms wrapped around his middle and his eyes on the ground, walking as fast as he could. For a moment he couldn't feel anything but the lightness in his head, couldn't hear anything but the thunder of his own heart.

He walked just to the other side of the big, shady tree that grew in the middle of the courtyard, and then he put his back against it and covered his face with his hands. He panted for breath, trying to think, trying to imagine what this meant, why Dr. Jeffries was really here, what he was doing, when he had to *know.*

"Mr. Lea?"

Dr. Jeffries' voice came from just on the other side of the tree. Roland flattened his hands against the bark on either side and leaned around cautiously, looking over his shoulder.

Dr. Jeffries stood facing him, with the tree mostly between them. Susan and Ms. Dawson were blurs back by the bench.

Well, he didn't really want a chaperone for this part.

"I'm sorry," Dr. Jeffries said quietly. "I didn't want to frighten you, or embarrass you, and I meant everything I said. The offer is absolutely sincere. But I'm also very, very worried about you. Is it—are you taking suppressants?"

Roland's jaw dropped a little and he settled back against the tree, squeezing his eyes shut. What did *suppressants* have to do with it? He shouldn't even be in season now anyway.

"Has your health gotten better since you came to the refuge?" Dr. Jeffries asked softly, in a prompting tone. "Or has it continued to get worse, even though you're off the wolfsbane and have a safe place to rest and food to eat?"

Roland's fingers dug into the bark, but he didn't say anything. Maybe he didn't have to.

"I don't think whatever you're taking was prescribed by the midwife here," Dr. Jeffries went on quietly. "And that can be really dangerous, Mr. Lea. It's not my area of specialty, but from what I remember happening in my pack when I was young and from what I see and smell on you... There's a reason midwives are careful about giving them out. They're fundamentally toxic. One of the midwives I knew theorized that they stop heats by keeping you just unwell enough not to be fit to reproduce. They're poison, carefully calibrated for a specific patient. But if you're taking something on your own, if you've been taking it for a long time..."

"I need it," Roland whispered. "I can't—I won't. I *won't.*"

He couldn't even imagine saying more to this nice, suit-wearing alpha with his soft hands, dragging up all of his shame. All he could do was repeat, "I need them. I *won't.*"

"If you went off them now, you would still be far from well enough to go into heat," Dr. Jeffries said, still quietly, still staying where Roland didn't have to see or smell him, where there was no danger of touch. "And summer heats are rare, although obviously if you've been on suppressants a long time your cycle will probably be erratic for a while. But the alternative is getting sicker and sicker, Mr. Lea. Please, even if you don't want to trust me for anything else, *please* go off them, just for a few days, a week, whatever you can bear. You're safe here, even if you did—"

Roland's knees gave way at the mere thought of that fever swamping his body, stealing his mind, stealing his control, leaving him without even coherent memories of what had been done to him while his heat raged.

"*I can't.*" It was only a whisper, mostly lost in the sound of him sliding down the tree to huddle at its base, his knees folded up to his chest.

"Please." From the sound of his voice, Dr. Jeffries was kneeling too, probably getting grass stains on his nice suit. "Mr. Lea—Roland—I don't want to have to tell anyone else about this, but I'm a doctor. I can't just let you die without doing something to help. If you came with me, I'd make sure you had your own space for heats, doors to lock me out, anything you need. I'd never force you, never—"

Even through his own terror, Roland could hear the ragged edge of desperation in Dr. Jeffries' voice. He really meant it. He had done all this, put on his suit, come to this refuge, because he thought he knew why Roland was sick and he needed to stop it.

A sudden memory of his mother flashed through Roland's mind, the desperate sincerity in her voice. *I tried, baby, I swear, I asked them, I begged them, but they said no way.*

"Is that—" his voice was almost soundless, and Roland swallowed and started again. "Is that why—if they're poison, they won't—wouldn't—the midwife said I was too young, when my mom asked."

"Yeah," Dr. Jeffries said quietly. "Yeah, in my pack they wouldn't until after high school, or until you were over a certain height and weight, I think. Strain on the body, stunts growth, all that."

Roland let out a shaky breath. No one had ever told him *why*. Not that it would have helped to know, really, but no one had ever told him why, until now. Until this alpha.

He pressed the heels of his hands to his eyes and said, "I can't... I can't decide anything right now. Can you..."

"I'll come back tomorrow," Dr. Jeffries said quietly. "All right? I have a few weeks of wiggle room, I can give you some time. But please, Mr. Lea, think about what I said."

He wasn't going to be able to think of anything else, Roland was sure. And he wasn't going to be able to stop thinking about how much he'd rather Dr. Jeffries had called him *Roland* again instead of *Mr. Lea*.

CHAPTER 5

*B*eau's apartment, when he returned to it, seemed like foreign territory. He was half packed to leave, and now everything was up in the air in a whole new way.

Roland—*Mr. Lea*, he was still all but a stranger—hadn't said no, only *I can't decide anything*. Had that been an omega's instinctive equivocation, placating a pushy alpha? Would Beau be turned away at the door tomorrow?

Or would he be greeted by something worse? Mr. Lea had been really distressed, really frightened, and he was already so weakened.

Beau couldn't do anything about that. Mr. Lea's case worker had seemed attentive and kind, and the refuge in general seemed like a good place. Surely they would see Mr. Lea's distress and look after him accordingly.

Beau just had to be ready to go back tomorrow, to show Mr. Lea that he meant to follow through on everything he'd promised. He grabbed his computer and a notepad and sat down among his stacks of textbooks to make lists of everything he needed to research: available houses in Rochester, pre-nuptial agreements, exactly what he would need in terms of money and paperwork to marry as soon as possible, anything anyone knew about suppressants...

He thought for a moment of Adam, his former classmate and fellow alpha. He'd been planning to leave immediately after graduation to start his research program, though he hadn't told anyone exactly what or where it was. Beau knew Adam was interested in omega health—they'd even talked about suppressants once. Adam agreed with the toxicity hypothesis, but he got *angry* about it in a way that put Beau off from ever raising the topic again.

Adam got angry about most things relating to omegas. Beau had wondered for a while now if he had an omega sibling he felt protective of, but he'd never been able to think of a way to ask without it sounding like he wanted to *date* Adam's hypothetical omega sibling. It wasn't the kind of thing one alpha could ask another without inviting a fight, and Adam always seemed to be on the verge of one anyway.

On second thought, maybe Adam was exactly the wrong person to ask for advice about the sick, scared omega Beau was hustling into marrying him. It didn't matter, anyway. Beau could see what was going on with Roland, and Roland was all he was really concerned with right now.

He hadn't slept, but he did shower, and eat, and put on fresh clothes. He slid his laptop into his bag, along with the folder of things he'd printed out, his lucky exam pen hooked to the top.

On his way to the refuge, he checked his watch half a dozen times to remind himself that the moon was still on the wane, the full moon's influence days past. The itchy, anxious feeling, the pull he felt, wasn't the moon: it was Mr. Lea, and the need to know he was safe, whether or not he was willing to be Beau's.

Temporarily. For their mutual, legally delineated, benefit.

By the time he reached his destination, the urge to shift was as strong as Beau had felt it since he left his pack. He had to stop down the street from the refuge and take several deep breaths to pull himself under control.

That lasted only until he caught a hint of Mr. Lea's scent on the air,

OMEGA REQUIRED

sickly-sweet and blood-tinged, and then he was running up the steps to ring the bell.

"Ah, yes," the omega who answered the door said. This one was nearly as tall as Beau, decidedly male. "Mr. Lea's caller? He's waiting in the courtyard for you. Come with me."

Beau struggled to remain a half-step behind the unfamiliar omega as they walked through the public areas of the refuge to the courtyard door.

Once the door opened, he wasn't really aware of anything but Roland, pacing back and forth by the bench he'd been sitting on the day before. His steps were painfully slow and shaky. He stopped when Beau stepped into the courtyard, looking anxiously in his direction with an expression of not-quite-recognition on his face, as if the handful of yards between them were too far for him to see clearly.

As Beau hurried toward him, he saw the instant when Roland recognized him with certainty, immediately followed by Roland turning and walking determinedly away toward the tree he'd hidden behind the day before.

Beau made his own steps as slow as Roland's, carefully not chasing him. Just following where he led.

Roland was already sitting against the tree's base by the time Beau reached him, and Beau took the chance and walked around to that side before sitting down on the grass facing him. Roland had his arms wrapped around himself, his head ducked down so his face was half-hidden in the soft knit scarf he wore, wildly out of season.

"Hi," Beau said softly, not knowing where to begin.

Roland clutched himself tighter and said into his scarf, "I couldn't. I tried, but I... I couldn't. I'm sorry, I just—I couldn't skip them. I couldn't."

Beau kept his breathing and heartbeat even. He must not frighten Roland. "You took your suppressants again today, you mean?"

Roland nodded stiffly. "I—I couldn't—"

"It's okay." It wasn't okay, but saying so wouldn't help when Roland was already this wound up, and Beau wanted to actually help,

37

not just be correct in his diagnosis. "Thinking about it is a good start. Does that mean you believe me, what I told you yesterday?"

Roland shrugged, then nodded jerkily. "It makes sense. I crushed one of the pills and then I could tell there's some kind of wolfsbane in it. Even the fun blends of wolfsbane are... I mean, it says *toxic* right in *intoxicated*."

Beau didn't let himself look too impressed, though he hadn't expected Roland to make that connection. Plenty of people didn't understand that getting high was always a matter of poisoning yourself somehow.

"You're right," Beau said quietly. "Wolfsbane won't be doing you any favors. You look..." He looked worse, more than Beau would have thought could happen in a day. It was probably the anxiety, but his skin also had a more pronounced yellow tinge to it than it had the day before.

Beau's alpha instincts, which had been jittering all over the place on the way here, were now perfectly focused: all he wanted in life was to gather Roland into his arms and hold him and make this better somehow.

"Would you..." Roland looked at him for the first time, not lifting his face out of his scarf but looking up through his eyelashes at Beau. "If I came with you. Would you let me keep taking them?"

It was tempting to soften it, but Beau said a flat, "No."

Roland looked like that was the answer he had expected, nodding slightly and still not looking up.

"But I would also never, ever force you to spend a heat with me," Beau said, leaning forward a little. "And once you recovered, I would find a midwife who could help you find a safe dose, or a better formulation, so that you wouldn't need to have heats if you didn't want them. I swear to you, Roland, I would never force any of that on you. *Never*."

"I can't," Roland looked down again, and he loosened one arm from clutching himself to touch low on his belly, a careful gesture that spoke of pain. "I'm broken inside. So I can never... no matter how many heats, no matter what, I can't ever have children. But if you only wanted me for a while, maybe that's better?"

Beau couldn't answer for a moment, choking on grief for the loss Roland's curl of fingers spoke to, and rage for whoever had hurt him so. *Broken*, he said, and Beau could hear the echo of painful memory in his voice. That was no mere theoretical diagnosis.

"It doesn't change my mind," Beau finally managed to say evenly. "I'd like to help you. I'd like you to marry me."

"Really marry?" Roland's eyes came up again. "With papers and everything, and witnesses? And the—pre-nup, you said? Right?"

"Yes," Beau said, slinging his bag down onto the grass and yanking it open. "Yes, I printed one up, you can take a look."

He pulled the papers from the folder and offered them, but Roland tucked both of his hands out of sight and dropped his face lower into his scarf. "I can't, uh—"

Beau was starting to feel actual pain every time he heard Roland say *I can't*. His hand faltered, but he set the papers down between them, and Roland's eyes followed them down before rising to meet Beau's again.

"Is it like—poison, can it mess with your vision? Because with wolfsbane, sometimes things got blurry, or everything had halos, or..."

He really hadn't been able to recognize Beau from five yards away. He couldn't read the words of the agreement.

"Yeah," Beau said, swallowing to smooth the first roughness from his voice. "Yeah. Blurred vision, especially, is a symptom of... several kinds of poisoning."

Also several kinds of *organ failure*, which he was pretty sure Roland was on the verge of. It could happen so fast now, and Beau would have no right to do anything to help if he couldn't persuade Roland to give him that right.

Roland moved, tugging something out from under his shirt—a still-sealed envelope. He dropped it on top of the papers and said, "Can you...? I think that's something I was waiting for."

Beau picked it up and saw that it was from the State of Wisconsin, the Department of Health. He carefully tore open the envelope, and withdrew a birth certificate.

Roland Michael Lea. Moon above, he was only twenty-four years old. Beau would have guessed he was ten years past that from his appearance. He'd been born in a hospital, in some Wisconsin town whose name Beau didn't recognize, which only meant it wasn't Milwaukee or Madison.

"Your birth certificate," Beau said, setting it down very carefully on top of the draft pre-nup. "It's got a seal in the corner and everything, you can feel it. You're all proper and legal now."

"So I can get married, right?" Roland said quietly, reaching out with an almost believably casual movement to run his fingers across the paper until he found the raised seal. "Seems like a sign, almost. If you really meant it, about doing it like that. Proper and legal."

"I swear," Beau repeated. "I swear to you, Roland."

"And then it's just you and me, right? You don't share me, because I'm just yours. That's the legal way."

"*Yes,*" Beau choked out, fighting down rage all over again. "Yes, I would never—"

"Okay," Roland interrupted. It might have been no more than Roland not wanting to hear Beau's protestations anymore, but he tugged down his scarf and tilted his head, baring his throat.

It was ringed in ugly, shiny-red burns, probably from silver exposure. Someone had *collared* him, for a long fucking time, preventing him from shifting or fighting back, but there was no sign of a mating bite. And now he was offering himself to Beau. Trusting him, or just too far gone to resist anymore.

"Roland," Beau said helplessly, reaching out. He touched his fingers to the whole skin just under Roland's jaw, sliding them back toward his nape, where he could settle his hand flat against Roland's skin. "I— I'm not going to bite you, not... Not yet. That's part of the agreement, actually, we won't bond like that. That way..."

Roland's eyes were closed, and his voice was quiet, almost dreamy, when he said, "My family used to call me Rory, when I..." He swallowed, then went on, "You could. If you wanted. If I'm gonna be yours for a while."

When I had a family, was that what he hadn't said? But he had to have lost everyone who truly cared for him, to wind up here like this.

"You'll be mine," Beau said, and he scooted closer on the grass until he could draw Roland, *Rory,* into his arms. The omega felt so frail, so horribly pliant. Beau tucked the scarf around his throat and nuzzled against his bare scalp, focusing on the quick, fragile motions of Rory's breathing. "As long as you want to be mine, Rory, you will be. And you should call me Beau."

Rory nodded against his shoulder, and murmured obediently, "Okay. Beau."

CHAPTER 6

*R*oland knew he probably ought to be scared, or at least properly wary, but he was too tired to care.

It wasn't like being scared would make a difference. He'd made his mind up to put himself in this alpha's hands, and he wasn't going to be able to protect himself from Beau any more than he ever had from any other alpha he'd made this mistake with. Being scared had never helped.

This time, maybe he'd chosen right, or at least chosen less wrong. Beau hadn't bitten him, but he was still promising to marry him. Susan had promised, when they talked it over last night, that she would keep in touch with Rory, check on him. If things went bad, she would help him get away from Beau and back to the refuge.

So there was no point in caution anymore. Even if he wanted to be careful, he was too exhausted to do a good job of it, after a sleepless night and hours in the grip of panic as he stared at the bottle of pills— of *poison*—and still couldn't resist taking another one. His belly felt worse than ever, and he ached everywhere, and the bad taste in his mouth was getting stronger.

But Beau's arms around him felt good. Whatever it cost him later, it felt so good to have an alpha holding him, telling him he would handle things.

There was a *reason* he'd made the mistake of trusting alphas so many times before. There were good parts sometimes, like this. This was good.

After a while, Beau murmured, "Have you eaten anything today? Rory?"

Roland's mouth twitched up a little at the deliberate, awkward way Beau tacked on his nickname, like it was a question of its own. He liked the sound of it in Beau's mouth, though. He'd never told any other alpha to call him that; no one had, not since the last time he saw his mom, and even she'd been mostly calling him Roland by then.

"Anything to drink, even?" Beau prompted.

Roland shrugged a little. "Some water? My stomach isn't... feeling good."

"Do you take your suppressants with water?"

Roland winced. "S'posed to. But lately..."

"Your stomach's empty, and you already feel sick, and too much water makes you feel sicker," Beau said, as if he could see it all laid out. "So you haven't been drinking much water with your pills. Or at all?"

Roland nodded against his shoulder.

"Okay," Beau said. "So, dehydrated, and low blood sugar, and your stomach's upset, and probably irritated by the pills without enough water to buffer it. How about..."

He tightened one arm around Roland and took the other away, rummaging in the backpack he'd brought with him.

Like a kid with a schoolbag, Roland thought fondly, but then Beau had only just finished school, hadn't he? Medical school, but they probably didn't carry all their books and things in black doctor bags just because it was that kind of school.

Something crinkled in Beau's hand, and he brought it around to his own mouth, tugging at a plastic wrapper with his teeth. It released a spicy smell, just a little sweet, that made Roland's mouth water.

"It's ginger candy, real ginger," Beau explained, and touched it to

Roland's lips. "It can be a little intense when you're not used to it, just give it a lick and see what you think."

Roland obediently licked it, and the hot-sharp-sweet taste of it almost prevented him from noticing that he also licked Beau's fingertips in the process. The taste seemed to scour the sickness and stale panic from his mouth, and he nodded and opened his mouth for Beau to pop the piece of candy inside.

"Kinda confuses your scent, too, if some wolf in your vicinity's being rude and sniffing you to try to figure out what's wrong with you."

Roland tipped his head back to meet Beau's eyes, and Beau winked.

Roland's mouth tipped up toward a smile, his insides feeling funny in an entirely new way. It was a good thing he'd already thoroughly made this mistake, because it would have been so much more embarrassing to get lured in by candy and a little gentle teasing.

He closed his eyes and focused on the candy in his mouth, letting all his senses be swallowed up in the slight sharp burn of it, the tinge of sweetness. He couldn't hear anything else, could hardly smell anything else. He wondered if Beau liked these candies because they confused his scent, or because they helped him ignore everyone else's. Or did he just forget to eat and have stomachaches? Med school was hard, and busy; Roland did know that much.

"Here come the chaperones," Beau murmured, and Roland opened his eyes to see shapes he guessed were Susan and Ms. Dawson coming across the lawn. "I'm gonna bet they want to talk to you alone, so I'll go find you something warm to drink, and then we can see about getting to the clerk's office."

Beau's grip on him tightened for another few seconds, and then Beau stood, letting Roland lean on him until he was steady on his own feet. Beau kept one hand firmly on Roland's elbow while he bent to pick up the papers with the other, offering them just as the other omegas walked up. "Roland has agreed to marry me, but I'm sure you'd like to go over the pre-nup with him? Please do ask him about each point, see if there's anything he wants to change. I think he's apt to trust me too much. I'm happy to make adjustments."

Susan took the papers, but Beau took the top sheet back, sliding the birth certificate carefully back into its envelope before he pressed it into Roland's hand. "You can hang on to that, it's not being negotiated."

Roland nodded, squeezing Beau's arm where he was still holding it, and made himself let go.

~

By the time they'd finished going over the papers with him, Roland was pretty sure that despite Beau's efforts they realized he couldn't read it himself. But they didn't say anything about that, only made sure to go over the wording of each line with him, so that he understood properly.

It wasn't actually very complicated. Roland was allowed to request a divorce at any time, and would receive money automatically from Beau if they did divorce, more if he stayed a year, and twice as much if he stayed for three years. Beau acknowledged in writing that they might not ever have sex, and it wasn't grounds for Beau to request a divorce or change any part of the agreement.

Beau had promised not to force him, promised that if Roland did have to have heats he wouldn't have to spend them with Beau or anyone else. Beau knew he was broken, even if he didn't know how he'd been made that way; Beau had seen the scars of his collaring. And Beau was still giving him all this, and ginger candy, and a cup of sweet peppermint tea that he had set down by Roland's elbow before slipping quietly away again.

When Susan asked Roland again if he was *absolutely sure* this was what he wanted, he laughed and nodded, swiping the back of his hand across his eyes. He wasn't going to get a better offer than this, and no matter how it turned out, it would be better than getting sicker and sicker here alone.

"Well, then," Susan said. "We need to get you looking presentable for the clerk, don't we?"

Roland agreed cautiously, and soon found himself being hustled through a shower and then more primping than he had ever experienced before in his life. There was nothing to be done about his hair, but he submitted to three different kinds of eye drops, makeup, and more attention than he'd ever paid to his fingernails, before Susan and Ms. Dawson brought out a set of clean, new clothes for him to wear.

"Don't you dare cry," Susan said, dabbing at her own eyes with the backs of her fingers as Roland stared at himself in the mirror. "If you smudge that makeup we'll have to redo twenty minutes of contouring."

He looked... alive. Healthy, compared to what he'd seen in the mirror for months or years now. It felt like a mask, or a glimpse of some alternate version of himself, and felt all the stranger since he was sure his smell would still betray him, and his body inside the fine new clothes felt as painful and unsteady as ever. He knew even the makeup wouldn't look as convincing to a healthy werewolf as it did to him—but it would be enough for a human, he supposed. The clerk would probably be human.

He tugged nervously at the collar of the white shirt, with its narrow stripes of pink and purple. It mostly concealed the burns around the base of his neck, but if it gapped open, or if one of them got irritated by the stiff cloth and began to seep...

"Can't I wear my scarf?" He glanced toward it longingly, although even he could see that the dark cranberry and navy stripes and the thick knit were out of place with his fancy new clothes. It looked drab and faintly grimy despite the rich color that had drawn him to choose it from the free-clothes bin at one of the human shelters where he'd stayed before the refuge. He'd worn it almost non-stop for months, so that was no surprise.

"It's June, honey," Susan said, resting one hand gently on his shoulder. "You can't be wearing a scarf in June. Just keep your collar straight—you won't be in front of the clerk for long anyway."

Roland closed his hands into fists, wanting to just pick up the scarf and take it with him. "It's... it's still mine, though, isn't it? You won't give it to someone else?"

Susan shook her head, folding the scarf and setting it down firmly on top of his locker. "It's yours, Mr. Lea. It'll be here waiting for you when we get back from the clerk's office. Now let's go find that alpha of yours."

Roland nodded, and let them usher him out of his little solitary room back toward the public areas of the refuge. He didn't know what Beau would think of him all done up like this. Maybe he wouldn't like it. Maybe he would like it too much, and want Roland to wear this mask all the time, to cover his scars and his bare head and be pretty for him, even though they would both know it was a lie.

Then Roland stepped through a doorway and Beau was standing there, a piece of navy-and-white striped cloth in one hand, his phone in the other. He looked Roland up and down, nodding and giving him a crooked smile. "Maybe you won't need this at all, then. I thought you might like a cravat with your shirt? It sits inside your collar, not like a tie, so it'd be soft against your skin..."

Roland's throat was too tight to speak; he could barely breathe, and only managed a tight, jerky nod.

"I've just been looking up how to tie it," Beau explained, stepping closer. "I was too embarrassed to say at the store that I had no idea. I could...?"

Roland nodded, raising shaky hands to undo the top buttons of his shirt, giving Beau room to tug his collar away from his neck and settle the soft cloth against his skin.

"There's a tiny bit of that red like your scarf in it," Beau murmured, his hands moving deftly, pulling the cloth against his throat, snug but not choking. "But mostly navy and white, that seemed good for summer? You could wear it more like a scarf for casual stuff—I could get some more in different colors if you like it, make it a whole personal style thing."

Beau fussed at Roland's shirt collar a little, and then took a half-step back, so Roland could raise his own hands to touch the simple shape of the cloth around his neck. It definitely hid the burns and cushioned them from his shirt, but felt more like a tie than a scarf.

"Thank you," he managed, a tiny whisper.

Beau just nodded, squeezing Roland's shoulder with one big hand. "Thank *you*, for all of this. For trusting me."

Roland looked away as all the awful things he'd just been thinking about Beau rushed through his mind. He didn't deserve this alpha, and sooner or later Beau would realize it; a good man like him wouldn't want to keep an omega around who was constantly waiting for him to turn out like all the rest.

But for now, Beau didn't know. Roland hadn't ruined it yet. He forced himself to meet Beau's eyes again, summoning up a little smile.

Beau smiled back and tugged him closer, curling one arm around him so Roland could lean into him, enveloped in his strong scent. He'd worked up a bit of a sweat while Roland was occupied—rushing off to some snooty store where they made him feel embarrassed, just to get something silk-soft for Roland to wear.

"Ready?" Beau said softly.

Roland nodded, and Beau guided him out the front doors to Ms. Dawson's waiting car.

The clerk was human, and seemed supremely bored by the entire transaction; the trickiest part was when Roland presented his crisp new birth certificate along with the letter the head of the refuge had written as his identification. The letter stated that the refuge acted *in loco gentis* and was therefore the equivalent of a pack membership document, which was supposed to be accepted as identification. It got a lot of squinting and *hmm*ing and there were several minutes while the clerk just walked away with all of Roland's papers before it was abruptly accepted.

Only at the end, sliding an official-looking piece of paper across the counter, did the clerk finally smile. "Congratulations, gentlemen. Good luck with the wedding."

There was a second when Roland was thinking, *Wait, what? I thought this was the wedding.*

He could feel Beau at his side, also frozen, and then the alpha smiled widely, curling one arm around Roland and taking possession of the paper with his other hand. "Thank you."

Roland let himself be turned aside, back toward where Susan and Ms. Dawson were waiting for them. Only when he heard the clerk call for the next person waiting did he dare whisper to Beau, "But when do we get married?"

"Soon," Beau said firmly, squeezing Roland a little tighter against his side. Roland touched his fingers gingerly to his cravat, and then Susan and Ms. Dawson were congratulating them on, as it turned out, obtaining their marriage license, but not... actually getting married.

It wasn't until they were in the car again that he saw Beau tapping at his phone, and felt him sigh.

"I didn't think to look it up before," Beau murmured. "I didn't realize. The license can't be used until tomorrow."

Roland curled his hands into fists, hidden against his belly. Another day. Just one more day.

One more day when he would have to decide whether to take poison or dare not to. One more day without an alpha to take charge and protect him. Without *Beau*.

"You may find," Susan said from the front seat, "that we're taking a very, very long route back to the refuge. It may take hours. I wouldn't be surprised if it's after midnight when we get there."

Susan twisted around to wink as Roland struggled for a few frozen seconds to take that in, and then he ducked his head to hide his smile. Of course they had it all worked out. They would know that an alpha wouldn't want to wait like a human before claiming the omega he'd chosen.

They didn't need to know that it was Roland who couldn't bear to wait, or why.

Beau squeezed him closer and murmured, "Why don't you just close your eyes, then. Might as well get some rest, if it's gonna be such a long drive."

Roland tilted his head back against Beau's arm, nestling as close as he dared without smearing makeup on Beau's suit. He kept his eyes closed and breathed in Beau's scent, thick in the close confines of the car. *My alpha. He'll take me home, he'll help me get well. He promised. Really promised, on paper and everything.*

He did sleep a little, or at least his thoughts drifted into quiet blankness for a while. He came back to himself when the car's front doors closed, leaving only him and Beau inside. Roland opened his eyes to find Beau's face closer than he expected.

Close enough to kiss.

His breath caught, and he felt that dangerous little thrill of anticipation, when he should have known better, should have been far past wanting anything like that ever again.

Beau just smiled. "Ready for our wedding day?"

Roland looked toward the window, and beyond it, the uninformative front of the refuge. "They didn't... *plan* something, did they? It's not gonna be, like..."

A tumble of images played through his head, mostly human weddings he'd seen on TV and in movies, elaborate and protracted events that always involved someone being terribly humiliated or disappointed or otherwise reduced to tears.

"I think they know you well enough to know you won't want anything huge and exhausting," Beau said quietly. "I suspect there's going to be cake, though. You think you might be able to eat a little cake?"

Roland bit his lip, and his stomach squirmed uneasily. "Do you have any more of those ginger candies?"

Beau smiled and brought one out of his pocket, unwrapping it before holding the candy to Roland's lips. He closed his eyes and opened his mouth for it, and the first sharp bite of the ginger made his mouth water alarmingly and his eyes sting. Beau stayed steady at his side, keeping one arm around him all the time, and after another moment Roland said, "I guess we have to get out of the car eventually."

"Not really where I'd pictured us living for the next few years," Beau agreed, but he didn't make any move to get Roland out of the car until Roland picked his head up and twisted toward the door.

When they got inside there *was* cake, and Susan and Ms. Dawson and Dr. Hanek who ran the refuge and was, as it turned out, both a registered officiant for weddings and a notary public. He had Beau and Roland sign the pre-nup first, getting it notarized and witnessed across several copies.

Which meant Roland had to write his name when he couldn't read it.

"It's okay, take your time," Beau murmured, and laid his finger down on the page. "Right along there. Right above my finger. When you're ready."

Roland took a few breaths, trying to make his fingers fit comfortably around the pen, to remember the motions of signing his name. He couldn't remember when he'd ever done it that meant anything, but it couldn't be that hard. He'd learned cursive in school. He knew how to write his own name, and that was all it was, really. His own name, in cursive, saying that he agreed to be married to Beau with all these conditions.

He squinted at it when he was done; it looked a little crooked and wobbly, but that seemed to be his name. *Roland Lea*. He'd done it.

And then he had to do it three more times.

"I'll put one of these on file here," Dr. Hanek explained, "and send one to the state Omega Rights Initiative. They hold a lot of these types of documents, just to be on the safe side."

"Of course," Beau said easily. "And Roland will have his own copy to keep as well."

One was duly put into an envelope for him, and Roland held it, along with his birth certificate, while they did the rest of the wedding formalities. It was all so calm and matter of fact, just sitting on a loveseat beside Beau in one of the refuge sitting rooms, with Susan and Ms. Dawson and Dr. Hanek gathered around on other chairs. Roland barely realized the questions he was answering were his wedding vows, even when he automatically responded, "I do."

But then there was a tiny round of applause, and Roland turned to meet Beau's eyes.

Beau raised his eyebrows, asking some silent question, and Roland nodded a little, and then—*oh, oh*—Beau dipped his head and touched his lips to Roland's, soft and chaste. A kiss. Their first kiss.

They were married.

There was another paper to sign for that, but Beau let Roland sign along his finger again, and his hand didn't shake any worse than the first four times.

"Excellent. We'll put the appropriate date on this and send it in tomorrow to be filed, but you are now officially married. Congratulations, both of you."

"Thanks," Roland murmured, and then looked up at Beau, who squeezed him a little closer.

"We'll eat some cake first," Beau said. "Then we'll figure out everything else."

CHAPTER 7

*A*ll of Rory's things fit into a single paper shopping bag, which was horrible, but simplified the problem of moving him out of the refuge and into Beau's tiny apartment. Rory's hands shook as he moved one particular plastic-bag-wrapped item into the shopping bag with a muffled rattling sound, and Beau didn't have to ask to know what was inside. He didn't ask Rory to hand that over—not yet, not here.

Beau shouldered his own backpack, with his own copies of their brand new paperwork safely inside, and kept his arm around Rory as they walked out of the refuge to the cab waiting on the street. The sun was still shining; it was the middle of the afternoon. It had barely been twenty-four hours since he first saw Rory's picture, and they were married, and he was taking Rory home with him. To his half-packed studio apartment.

Well, Beau thought, fighting down hysteria, *at least he won't mind that I don't have any food in the fridge.*

Rory seemed to be dozing, in fact, by the time they got to Beau's apartment. Beau paid for the ride, jostling Rory enough in the process to make him pick his head up and look around. He seemed to shrink in on himself, and Beau curled his arm around Rory again as soon as he could, guiding him out of the cab and onto the sidewalk.

Rory was quiet at his side as he unlocked the front door, but he winced when Beau turned him toward the stairs. "What floor are you on?"

Beau's heart sank painfully at the smallness of his voice, the determined calmness of the question. He'd *seen* how slowly Rory walked even on flat ground; it was obvious what an effort it cost him.

"The fourth," Beau admitted. "Sorry, I didn't think..."

"It's okay," Rory said firmly. "I can, I'm just slow."

Beau wanted to argue, but Rory was already gripping the banister and making his way up the first few stairs. Beau followed him a couple of steps behind, leaving one side of the narrow staircase for anyone coming down. It was painful to watch Rory struggling up the first flight of stairs, and worse on the second. Halfway up the third, he stumbled, and Beau barely managed to catch him from behind before he went down.

Rory was gasping for breath, almost completely limp in Beau's hold, his head hanging. "I'm sorry, I—"

"No, I'm sorry," Beau said. "Baby, please, let me carry you the rest of the way. *Please.*"

Rory's rough breathing hitched, and Beau saw the redness of his face, glimpsed a tear falling—as much frustration and embarrassment as anything else, Beau thought.

"Please. It's wedding tradition, right? Carrying you inside for the first time? Please, Rory, I know you can do it if you need to, and I will let you take all the time you need if that's what you want to do, but please let me help."

Rory sniffed and then nodded, still not raising his head to look at Beau, and Beau moved to gather him up against his chest.

He was terrifyingly light. It was like holding a CPR dummy or one of the training mannequins from med school. Rory felt as fragile as a model skeleton in Beau's arms, and he was holding himself stiffly, keeping his face away from Beau's shoulder.

"Relax, I've got you," Beau said, trying to tilt Rory in toward his chest.

Rory shook his head. "I've got stuff on my face, it'll get on your suit."

"It washes off," Beau said firmly. "Please, you're harder to carry when you're farther from my center of gravity."

That argument made Rory fold, and Beau hated it a little but couldn't regret it when Rory finally relaxed against him, his cheek tucked against Beau's shoulder. He hadn't let go of his shopping bag, and it rested now in his lap, rustling against Beau's chest.

"Okay," Beau said, and then he was hurrying up the stairs, trying to keep his motions smooth without sacrificing time. Beau had to let Rory's feet down to dig out his keys and unlock the door, and Rory leaned bonelessly against him, hardly seeming to notice the change in position. He did keep a firm grip on his shopping bag, though.

He stirred enough to make a little protesting noise when Beau picked him up again to carry him through the door, but Beau said, "No, hey, this is the threshold part, it's tradition."

Rory picked his head up as Beau kicked the door closed behind them, and this time when Beau let his feet down he stood on his own, looking around.

Beau ran a hand through his hair, wondering what the small space and the piles of cardboard boxes would look like to a stranger.

It looked cozy, to Beau. He'd moved in to this shoebox of an apartment as soon as he could more or less afford his own place, about six months after he came to Chicago. It hadn't been especially convenient when he transferred from the city college to Loyola to finish undergrad, or during med school, but it was familiar: his own little den in this crowded, noisy, human city. He hadn't wanted to leave it before he absolutely had to.

It was just a rectangular box of a room, with a kitchenette along the left-hand wall and a bathroom to the right, but he'd slept in that bed for the last nine years, the bookshelves positioned to half-enclose it. He'd studied at the little table he'd assembled himself and eaten countless meals there.

This was home. He knew it was objectively kind of shitty, and it didn't even matter if Rory didn't like it because they'd be leaving within days, to a house Beau could afford in part because he'd scrimped and saved by living in a tiny shoebox for nine years, but he didn't want Rory to think badly of it. Of him, for bringing him home to this.

"It smells like you," Rory finally said, still not looking at Beau. "It feels... safe."

"It is safe," Beau said, swallowing down any other reaction. "You're safe here, Rory."

Rory nodded, looking around. "I'm just gonna go wash my face."

He was still holding the paper bag as he turned toward the bathroom, and Beau reached out and touched that hand. Rory froze.

"You need to give me the suppressants," Beau said softly. "That was the deal. I'm your alpha now, we're married, and you give them to me. When you're healthy I'll find a replacement for you."

Rory tensed, his jaw clenching.

Beau was glad to see that little hint of resistance, since it meant that Rory still, deep down, had a little bit of self-protective instinct left. But he couldn't let Rory keep taking the suppressants; he would force the issue if he had to, to give Rory a fighting chance to recover, but it wasn't exactly how he wanted to kick off their wedding night.

"As soon as it's safe," Beau coaxed softly. "As soon as you're strong enough, I swear, I'll get you back on them at a safe dose. I know you don't want to have heats, and I know you aren't going to be spending them with me if you do. But for right now I need that bottle."

Rory nodded stiffly. It took another moment before he plunged his hand into the paper bag, rummaged through the plastic-bag-wrapped bundles, and came up with the one Beau recognized.

Beau took it from his hand rather than force Rory to reach out and give it to him, and said, without much change of tone to make it a big deal, "Thank you. I'm going to order some takeout, is there anything that sounds better or worse to you right now?"

Rory shrugged and shook his head and turned away. There was a little hitch in his step as he did it, more than just his slowness. He was waiting to see what Beau would do to him for walking away without giving a satisfactory answer. Without being dismissed.

Beau stuffed the plastic bag and the bottle inside into his pocket. He walked over to the windows, putting his back to Rory, and leaned his forehead against the glass while he pulled up the delivery app and requested a couple of gallons of chicken soup and loaves of bread from the kosher deli he liked best. He'd never set foot in the actual deli, but he'd been ordering their soups for years; everything they made tasted like real food, not chemicals and preservatives.

Behind him, he heard the bathroom sink tap turn on. He'd rarely heard the noises the pipes made while the sink was running from this angle; it was distracting for a moment, as if the apartment itself had rotated ninety degrees.

But it wasn't the apartment that had gone sideways. It was Beau's entire life.

He looked around the small space of the apartment to figure out where to dispose of the suppressants; he wanted them gone before Rory came out of the bathroom, but he didn't want to leave, even to go as far as the trash chute. He brought the wrapped bottle out of his pocket and unwound the plastic bag, revealing a glass bottle with a plastic twist top. He could see the shapes of the pills inside, small spheres of slightly varied sizes and shapes. Definitely homemade by some midwife. The bottle was only a quarter full, but from the size of the pills, it might have been a year's worth or more originally.

Judging by the effects on Rory, it might be enough to kill a were-wolf—or human—if taken all at once. He couldn't leave it intact for anyone to find.

He went to the kitchen sink and turned the tap on full blast, running cold, before he grabbed a bottle of vinegar from the cupboard underneath. He uncapped the jar of pills and poured them into the disposal, turning it on once they were all dumped in, and chased it with half the bottle of vinegar, to be sure that no scent lingered in the sink. Then he sealed the empty jar and wrapped it back in the plastic bag and stuffed it in the trash, where Rory would be able to see and smell it if he went looking.

If Rory had recognized the sound of the garbage disposal running, he gave no sign of knowing what it meant. Beau heard the toilet flush as he finalized the food order, then switched apps to find the fastest way he could get his hands on a couple of pounds of those ginger candies and a good peppermint tea. He meant to be calm and casual when Rory emerged from the bathroom, but as soon as he glanced up he dropped his phone on the counter and hurried toward the omega.

He'd known that the new clothes, the makeup, were all just masking Rory's condition. He *knew* that. He'd seen Rory au naturel before he was whisked off to be made up.

Somehow the contrast of it, with a few more hours of stress and exhaustion piled on, made Rory's appearance shocking all over again. He looked starved, his skin so pale it was almost gray, except for the sickly yellow tinge. He'd taken off the cravat and the new collared shirt both, so his unhealed burns were visible. He was holding his left hand against his belly, which was concave behind the thin t-shirt he was wearing; Beau could just about count his ribs, and restrained the urge to palpate his liver.

"Come lie down," Beau said, curling an arm around Rory. "I ordered food, you can rest until it gets here. Okay?"

Rory nodded wearily and mumbled, "Water?"

"Yeah, of course." Beau maneuvered him to the bed and laid him down. He could just about feel his wolf's pleased, possessive rumble when Rory nestled right into the tangle of pillows and blankets that all bore Beau's scent. He tugged a blanket up and went to fill a water bottle, so Rory wouldn't have to sit up to drink, and he grabbed the soft winter scarf Rory usually had around his neck.

Rory already seemed to be asleep when Beau returned to him, but he roused enough to take a few sips when Beau touched the nozzle of the water bottle to his mouth. When Beau tucked the scarf over his neck, he smiled a little, but his eyes didn't open.

Beau sat down on the foot of the bed to watch over him until the food arrived, listening to the slightly erratic beating of his heart and wondering what the hell he was going to do if it slowed any further.

It wouldn't. Surely it wouldn't. Once Rory was off the suppressants he would start to bounce back. He had to. He was here, alive, sleeping in Beau's bed. Beau couldn't have been too late.

CHAPTER 8

*R*ory's world turned into a series of dim, confused awakenings only partially breaking the blank heaviness of sleep.

His alpha's scent was always there, even when it was cut with something sharper. Chicken and onions and carrots; ginger; peppermint. His alpha crooned and coaxed, holding a spoon or cup to his lips with one warm arm wrapped around Rory's shoulders, and he did his best to do what his alpha asked, if only so he could stay.

He just wanted to stay.

Once he dreamed of waking, making his own stumbling way to a bathroom that wasn't where it should have been to piss for what felt like a very long time. He drank some water when he staggered out, and then looked around for his things, sniffing for the harsh medicine smell of his suppressants. He found his bag of stuff, which bore a lingering trace of the scent, but the bottle wasn't there. He had to find it, he had to.

His alpha was there, holding him, bearing him back to the bed and shushing him when he tried to pull away. Rory didn't want to make him angry, but he had to make him understand.

"I need it, I need my—my medicine," Rory insisted, struggling against his alpha's grip. "I need to, I have to, so I can go home, I just want to go home. *Please*, I can be normal if I have it, I just want to go *home.*"

He was crying, and the dream was a smothering mix of dread and grief. He already knew it was too late, and yet he still felt the frantic urgency of fixing it. Fixing himself.

"You are home, Rory," his alpha said, holding him tighter. "You are normal, baby, you're just not feeling good right now. You just need to get some more rest. But you're already home. You're safe here, I promise."

"I want my—my—" *Medicine*, that was the word, but it wouldn't come out, and he couldn't move, and he couldn't think. The dream was already turning foggy and vague.

"Want my dad," he whispered, or maybe *mom*, or maybe he only said *wanna go home.*

"I've got you," his alpha was murmuring, rocking him like he was a child. "I've got you, Rory, you're home already. Just close your eyes. Close your eyes, baby, you need to rest."

Rory wound his fingers into his alpha's shirt, so he couldn't send Rory away yet. The dream disappeared into another dark, featureless stretch of sleep.

He woke in the dark and knew he was awake. He could smell his own sour sweat and thought about showering it off, but as soon as he moved he breathed in the smell of his alpha—*Beau*, his *husband*, if that hadn't all been a particularly vivid dream.

Beau smelled unwashed and exhausted, and Rory groped toward the soft sound of his breathing and found him. Beau was leaning against the side of the bed, dozing with his head tipped against the mattress.

His alpha was sitting on the floor in the middle of the night, leaving the bed to Rory.

As soon as Rory's questing fingers brushed his dark hair, Beau picked his head up. His voice was clear and decisive, his eyes opening fully. "What do you need? Are you hungry?"

Rory was, a little, which was a strange sensation, but he didn't want to eat more than he wanted something other than himself to smell in this wide, clean bed.

He tried to speak and coughed; instantly Beau was kneeling up, offering a water bottle. Rory sipped enough to wet his throat and then pushed it back at Beau. "Just come to bed, that's all."

"No, hey, you don't have to—"

"Not to fuck," Rory cut in. "Just come lie down flat to sleep. You haven't been sleeping."

He flinched a little even as the words popped out of his mouth; it was a rude thing to say to a stranger, revealing what he could tell from their scent. Any other alpha he'd been this close to would probably have hit him for daring to tell them what they needed. Or that they weren't going to fuck.

But Beau had been sitting beside the bed, waiting for him to need something. Rory dared to reach for him, tugging lightly at the hem of his shirt. "Please?"

"You don't have to say please," Beau murmured, which definitely wasn't the way he'd been about to finish that sentence before. "Okay, I'll—if that's—"

Rory just tugged at his shirt again, since Beau didn't want him to say please.

Beau said, "I'll sleep harder if I'm lying down, but wake me up if you need anything, okay? Anything."

Rory nodded and tugged again. Beau let out a sigh and then climbed up onto the bed, crawling right over Rory to take the space by the wall.

Not making a show of protecting him from the door. Not hemming him in. Beau didn't even touch him, didn't even look, rolling away to face the wall and snagging a corner of a pillow and half a tangled blanket.

"Okay?" Beau murmured. His heartbeat was already slowing, his scent warming with sleep, and his words were slurred with drowsiness.

"Okay," Rory whispered, and rolled over to face his alpha's broad back.

When he was sure Beau was asleep, Rory scooted a little closer, and then a little closer again, until he could lean his forehead against Beau's spine. He breathed in his alpha's scent, basked in his warmth, and slept again within a minute.

～

Rory woke up to the smell of oatmeal and spent a few minutes drowsily wondering if he had to go to school today or if maybe he could stay home sick, or if it was even a school day. June, wasn't it June? The angle of the morning light against his eyelids, the artificial coolness of the room...

Rory turned his face down toward the pillow and the scent woke his memory. He stayed perfectly still for an instant, and then did his best imitation of a still-half-asleep turn in the bed, twisting so that his face angled toward the scent of oatmeal and the sound of another werewolf's heartbeat.

Beau, his alpha, his husband. Beau, soon to be a doctor for humans, who told him his suppressants were poison and convinced him to give them up. He remembered, dimly, some confused dream where he begged Beau, or his mother, or... someone else... for the suppressants, so he could go home. Go back to school, and his parents' house, and oatmeal on chilly mornings.

Rory opened one eye and looked at Beau, who was dressed in pajama pants and a soft, faded navy t-shirt with some kind of logo on the chest, maybe cross-shaped. Fire department?

Rory's stomach growled audibly, and Beau looked over, meeting his half-hidden gaze.

Beau just smiled. "Hungry?"

Rory nodded against the pillow and pushed himself upright, clutching the sheets as his head swam. "How long did I..."

"Three days," Beau said casually. "If you want to wash up first, feel free, this still needs a few more minutes."

Rory nodded cautiously as the dizziness faded. He pushed himself carefully up to his feet, scanning for any new or different or worse pain.

He felt sore and achy all over, but that had been with him for a long time now. His stomach ached a little, but he thought that was hunger, and nothing more dire. His mouth tasted like he hadn't brushed his teeth or had anything to drink in a while, but it didn't taste like sickness or anything worse.

His ass didn't hurt at all, nor did anything lower down in his belly. He was wearing his own pajamas from the refuge, flannel pants and a long-sleeved shirt; they both felt and smelled like he'd been wearing them for at least three days, but they hadn't picked up any scent of sex, only sweat and sickness. He didn't have that crawling, dark feeling that had accompanied him back to wakefulness so many times in the last several years—the awareness that *something* had happened that he couldn't remember.

He stretched cautiously, then extravagantly. His spine popped, and he groaned at the weird relief of the sensation. He sensed movement and froze, his eyes flashing open as Beau froze in mid-step, one hand outstretched, eyes wide.

He'd thought it was a pain noise, Rory realized. And now he knew that it definitely hadn't been.

Rory just stood there for a moment, arms still outstretched, and then Beau smiled a little sheepishly and said, "Sorry, you've got this. Yell if you need anything?"

Rory nodded, and Beau's voice echoed in his ears. *Wake me up if you need anything.* Beau had slept beside him... last night? At some point.

He belatedly dropped his hands to his sides and walked to the bathroom, picking up his bag along the way. Once he was boxed in with the scent of himself it didn't take long to decide that he absolutely needed an actual shower. He hurried through it as best he could, not only because he would be making Beau wait but because he tended to get dizzy in the steamy heat of a shower if he lingered too long. He did have to keep one hand against the shower wall most of the time, but he got himself clean, his own sickly stink replaced with the clean scent of Beau's soap.

He was half tempted to rub Beau's shampoo over his scalp, just to complete the scent profile, but then Beau would know he had shampooed his nonexistent hair. Rory settled for taking a sniff of the bottle before he shut the water off.

He dried off, and it was only then that he realized that the sting of hot water against his neck hadn't been nearly as bad as he was used to. He probed at the burns with his fingers, wincing when he found that they still stung plenty when he poked them. He went back to drying off then, habitually avoiding the sight of himself in the mirror. He was a little curious to see whether the burns were improving, but he didn't want to face the rest. Not now, with Beau waiting for him outside.

He took out clean boxers and a long-sleeved t-shirt from his bag of possessions, which was taking up half the tiny bathroom counter. He brought it back out with him when he emerged from the small space of the bathroom, unsure of what else to put on. The nice pants from his wedding day, which he hadn't seen anywhere in the bathroom? The sweat-reeking sleep pants he'd just taken off?

His eyes went to the stove first when he stepped out of the bathroom; the pot of oatmeal was there, still steaming, though it was sitting on a cool burner now. Rory looked for Beau next; he was half-hidden behind cardboard boxes, digging through a trash bag that smelled nothing like trash.

He looked up with a smile when Rory took a hesitant step toward him.

"Hey, I was just looking—I thought these might fit you. I had this crazy growth spurt right after I moved in here, so I never had a chance to wear 'em out, but they, uh, they still smelled familiar and Chicago didn't yet, so I kept them." Beau stood up, holding two folded pairs of dark-wash jeans. He set them on a cardboard box and shook one pair out, holding them up in Rory's direction.

"Maybe a little long, but I was skinny as hell, so they probably won't fall off? Or, I mean, we can get you new stuff," Beau amended, lowering the jeans and looking uncertain as Rory stayed silent, frozen in bewilderment. "I just hate buying new stuff, personally, it's a hassle to make it smell like home. And hopefully you'll be gaining enough weight once you're feeling better that you'd just have to buy stuff all over again, so for now I thought it'd be easier..."

Rory finally managed to give a jerky nod. "Yeah, that's, I'll—"

He set down his bag of stuff in the middle of the room and held out his hand, and Beau took the two steps to bring the pair of pants to him.

They felt soft under his hand—all cotton, he knew at a touch, a sturdy well-dyed denim weave. No tags, no labels, but a small design in red and yellow had been stitched in the center of the waistband at the back, and one in white at the right hip. Well-wishes, traditional charms.

These had been homemade for Beau. Pack-made. Of course he'd kept them when he came to a strange place—but now he was offering them to Rory.

He swallowed hard, remembering the last surviving sweater his mother had given him. It had been too small, worn practically transparent, and finally it had gotten a hole in it that he couldn't mend. Even when he couldn't wear it he'd kept it as long as he could, tucked away in a drawer. One day it was just gone, and Martin had said it looked like junk so he got rid of it. Couldn't have his omega going around in rags, could he? And then Roland had had to be grateful when he wanted to cry for the loss, and being grateful only ever meant one thing.

Rory felt a little sick at the memory, his skin crawling; he flinched when Beau's hand moved to cup his elbow, and Beau jerked back.

"I'll just—" Rory grabbed his shopping bag and hurried into the bathroom, shutting the door firmly behind him.

He sat down on the lid of the toilet, folding down over his lap as he tried to steady himself. When he'd caught his breath he couldn't help thinking, *Stupid, stupid, what are you doing.*

Why had he brought his things back in here? Why was he hiding in here himself? He could have sat down on the bed, or a chair at the table, if he couldn't bear to have Beau steady him while he pulled on a pair of pants.

He made himself sit up enough to shake out the jeans, which smelled clean and like Beau's apartment. There were a few thinning spots at the hems and knees, but otherwise they were in good shape, much nicer than anything in the donation boxes Rory was used to digging through for clothes. And these didn't smell like a stranger, or aggressive detergents, or the weird nothing-smell of heavy duty scent-neutralizers. They smelled like they belonged to Beau—just like Rory.

He stood and tugged them on. They did puddle over his feet, but they hung only a little loose on his hips and felt as soft and comfortable as anything he could remember wearing. He tugged his t-shirt down to hide how they were still too big, grabbed his bag and stepped out of the bathroom again, offering a tentative smile in Beau's direction.

Beau grinned immediately. He was at the table now, filling up two bowls with oatmeal. There was brown sugar and a honey bear on the table, plus maple syrup, a plastic bag of walnuts, a glass shaker for cinnamon, and a carton of soy milk.

"Looks good," Beau said. "We can get 'em hemmed, there's a place a couple blocks down that does quick work."

"Oh, no, I can just..." Rory set down his shopping bag again and shuffled over to the table, not picking his feet up enough to risk tripping.

"Well let me cuff 'em up for you, at least," Beau said, and waved Rory toward one of the two chairs. He sat, eyeing the bowl of oatmeal set out for him, and then Beau was kneeling at his feet, quickly folding up the hems of the jeans.

"We can get you some suspenders, maybe," Beau said, smiling up at him. "Make it a whole hipster thing, huh? Maybe some flannel shirts?"

Rory didn't know how to answer any of that. He couldn't quite imagine himself as the sort of person who could plausibly claim to be a hipster rather than *wearing ill-fitting clothes because he was homeless,* but he didn't want to contradict Beau, or risking dampening this bright, friendly mood.

Beau didn't seem to require an answer anyway. He returned to his seat and said, "I hope you don't mind oatmeal? I figured it wouldn't be too hard on your stomach. The milk's soy, is that—do you have any allergies? I should've asked that sooner."

Rory opened and closed his mouth a few times and then said, "My mouth and ears feel weird when I eat bananas."

"Oh, that's," Beau wagged his finger vaguely at Rory, but the gesture didn't seem scolding at all. His eyes were on his oatmeal as he spooned in brown sugar and then a handful of walnuts. "I've heard of allergies like that, it's a protein your body reacts to on contact, not a real food sensitivity."

Rory bit his lip and added a spoonful of brown sugar to his oatmeal, then a few walnuts, dropping them in one by one.

"Your ears because of your Eustachian tubes," Beau added. "They run down your throat, so they can get irritated, feel kind of itchy, maybe? Anyway—no bananas, got it."

Rory looked up from stirring the brown sugar into his oatmeal, trying to keep the walnuts evenly distributed. Beau was just shoving a big spoonful of oatmeal into his mouth. "But... you just said. It's not a real allergy."

Beau shrugged, chewing. He nodded toward Rory's bowl, and pushed the bag of walnuts toward him. Rory added a few more, stirred, and took a cautious bite.

"I mean, if you like 'em that much, I promise to only hover over you with an EpiPen from a polite distance," Beau said. "But it kind of sounds like they wouldn't be fun to eat, if they make your mouth itch."

"They, um," Rory stared down into his oatmeal and shrugged stiffly. "They're... sometimes I just really want fruit, you know?"

"Yeah, that's a vitamin deficiency—oh, hey, I got some vitamins," Beau went and got a brightly colored bottle from a cupboard, showing it to Rory as he sat down again. Rory could recognize Fred Flintstone on the label, if not the words around him, which was enough to know they were meant for kids.

Beau opened the bottle, tipped out two, and popped them into his own mouth. "You want? Two's for adults, and these are 'Lycan Formula' so they don't actually taste awful and at least claim to have a pretty good nutrient balance for us."

"Claim?" Rory held out his hand. Beau had taken them, and they were Flintstones vitamins. What harm could it do? Beau tipped two vitamins into Rory's hand—not hard little pellets as he expected, but puffy gummy things.

He chewed them, and Beau was right; they didn't taste too awful, not like... he pushed that thought away. He didn't need to remember things right now. He needed to listen to his alpha.

"Mm, well, vitamins," Beau said, making a rocking gesture with one hand. "They're not regulated like actual medicines, so it's hard to know what's actually in there; they don't even get tested for any particular efficacy. But a formulation like this probably isn't gonna do any harm, and, especially if you haven't been getting a lot of fruits and veggies lately, probably could be some help. Do you like oranges? Berries?"

Rory was feeling a little dizzy from the way this conversation kept veering from what he expected. Finally he said, "Oranges, yeah. Berries... are so expensive."

Bananas were cheap, which was why he kept eating them even though he occasionally wondered if one day his throat would close up after he did. And bananas always tasted pretty much exactly like a banana.

"Yeah, and the berries you get at the regular grocery stores are garbage, at least eleven months out of the year," Beau agreed absently, even though Rory hadn't dared to say it. "We could see about getting some nice ones, though—there's gotta be a farmer's market or something this weekend. When we get to Rochester, that's probably pick-your-own country. Have to see if there's a CSA around, but I don't know if you can get in on those in the middle of the season."

"Oh," Rory said faintly. That all sounded like a lot more effort than he would expect anyone to put into getting some raspberries that were worth eating, but... Beau was going to be a doctor. Doctors usually had nice things. Would Beau expect Rory to go out shopping for local produce? Cook for him? Keep a fancy, magazine-worthy house?

Beau had cooked for him. Rory had been asleep for three days, and Beau had looked after him while he was useless, helpless.

Rory hastily shoved another spoonful of oatmeal into his mouth, and after he swallowed he added, "Thank you for making breakfast. It's very good."

Beau smiled. "Hard to screw up oatmeal. I mean, I guess I could have burned it easier than reheating takeout soup, but I thought I should draw the line at feeding that to you nine meals in a row."

Rory licked his lips, the memory of the taste coming back to him—salty, fatty broth and bright carrots. "Chicken noodle?"

Beau grinned. "I thought you were kinda awake sometimes. Yeah, it's good stuff."

Rory looked down into his oatmeal, made himself take another small bite. He was still hungry, but also... everything else.

"Thank you," he said again, quietly. "I'll do the dishes."

"Okay," Beau said, giving no hint of whether that was the right answer, or if there *was* a right answer. "If you feel up to it. If not, it's no trouble. I'm used to looking after myself, and two don't make many more dishes than one."

"I'd like to," Rory said in a small voice, and across the table Beau just nodded, like that was all there was to it. Beau served himself more oatmeal, with a dash of soy milk, honey, and cinnamon this time. Rory kept taking smaller and smaller bites of his.

He was hungry, or he had been, and Beau had made this for him, served it to him, supplied him with good things to add to it, but his stomach ached and he was starting to sweat down his spine as he struggled to make himself take another bite. His bowl was nowhere near empty.

"Rory?"

Rory looked up sharply, bracing for things to finally go the way he expected.

"Maybe I gave you more than you're ready for," Beau said gently.

"You haven't eaten a whole lot of solid food in the last three days, your stomach's probably not ready for a great big bowl of oatmeal. It's okay if you can't finish it, or if you don't want to."

Rory ducked his head, his eyes prickling with gratitude and a disorientation more profound than dizziness. Beau just kept being *kind*, and Rory was torn between being angry with himself for forgetting that Beau was a good guy and still being unable to believe that any alpha really could be.

"Go ahead and dump it out if you want," Beau said, and Rory held his breath to keep from sobbing at that kind tone. "Oatmeal's cheap, there's plenty. We can make more. You can try it again—or something else—later."

Rory nodded, taking the opportunity to turn his back. He stood up carefully from the table, wary of getting dizzy again, but his head stayed firmly attached. It was only a couple of steps to the sink, and a brief investigation revealed that it had a garbage disposal, so he could wash the oatmeal down the drain instead of putting it in the trash, where the scent would linger and remind him of his failure to eat. Instead of keeping it in the fridge and forcing himself to try again and again to eat it while it grew less appetizing each time but at least wasn't *wasted*.

He scraped the bowl clean, ran the disposal, and then scrubbed his bowl and spoon. While he was doing that, Beau came back, scraped the last of the oatmeal from the pot into his own bowl, and set the pot and wooden spoon in the sink. Rory mumbled thanks and scrubbed at those, too.

He tried to ignore the ache in his hands and arms as he worked, the way he wanted to brace his elbows against the edge of the sink. He was leaning lower and lower, absorbed in trying to get every last speck of oatmeal out of the pot, and then every last trace of soap rinsed away from it, and then...

Then Beau's arm was around him, and the dripping pot was taken from his hand and set on the counter as Beau said, "Leave something for me to do, baby. I'll dry that, you just sit down a minute."

Rory nodded—wouldn't do to tell his alpha no. He started to turn toward the table, to sit at a chair, but Beau steered him firmly back to the bed. He squirmed a little in Beau's grip, not resisting but not liking the idea either. He could smell his own sickly scent rising off the sheets.

"Okay," Beau said. "Here, just sit down a minute."

Rory's legs went out from under him and he was sitting at the foot of the bed, elbows braced on his knees, face in his hands.

He felt and heard Beau moving around him, but he couldn't smell anything but the lingering sharpness of dish soap on his hands. Then Beau touched his shoulder, guiding him to tip over onto the bed, and Rory was too tired to resist.

His eyes flashed open when his cheek met a pillow covered in a fresh, cool sheet, smelling of Beau and laundry soap, but only faintly of himself. As he watched, Beau guided his legs into place on the fresh sheet, then finished pulling the old one out of the way and tucking the new one in.

"They teach you that in med school?"

Beau looked up at him, smiling a little. "Nah, but I worked as a hospital orderly for a few months one time, when I needed a break from riding the ambulances."

Rory frowned, squinting at Beau's t-shirt, the logo he couldn't quite make out. "Is that..."

Beau came and sat down beside him, drawing Rory's finger up to trace the design on his chest. "Chicago Fire Department. I put myself through college working as an EMT, then a paramedic once I qualified."

Rory let his eyes close, flattening his hand against Beau's chest and the soft, warm t-shirt. "Thought those were the same."

"Nope," Beau said. He ran a hand over Rory's bare head, and it felt warm but made him shiver. Beau let his hand rest at the back of Rory's neck. "Paramedic's another three semesters of school and another round of qualifying exams. And then another job interview, even though I'd been an EMT with them for over a year by then."

EMT, paramedic, med school. Doctor for humans. "Always saving people, huh," Rory muttered.

"Well, I try," Beau murmured, and squeezed gently on the back of Rory's neck. "Get some sleep, baby, I'll wake you up when it's time for lunch."

CHAPTER 9

*B*eau absolutely did not sit and stare at Rory for the rest of the morning. He took delivery of their clean laundry and dry cleaning, hanging up Rory's khakis and button-down shirt beside his own suits in the closet. He exchanged a carefully even-toned phone call with his realtor in Minnesota, then filled out some forms to scan and send back. He did some online shopping, marking lots of things but not actually buying any; he'd had to choose the house without asking Rory's opinion on it, but he didn't want to make any more choices for him if he could help it.

That only left him maybe ten minutes of every thirty to sit and watch Rory's sleeping face.

He was looking better already; proper hydration and the food Beau had managed to get into him so far meant his face looked much less gaunt, and the dangerous tinge of jaundice was barely evident at all. The livid burns on his neck were starting to change, the blisters fading away and the red fading toward pink. His eyes weren't so discolored, either, and whenever he looked at Beau, during the hour or so he'd been awake, he had seemed to be focusing without effort, really seeing him.

Beau knew it wasn't much, objectively, compared to the way werewolves normally healed. Still, it was enough to make him certain that Rory just needed time, and safety, and the absence of those suppressants, in order to heal.

That only reminded him of Rory's heartbreaking pleas, the last time he'd seemed to wake up. *I need my medicine. I can be normal.* When Beau first told him the suppressants were dangerous, the day they met, he'd said, *The midwife said I was too young when my mom asked.*

He'd been born in a hospital, in a middle-sized town not far from Milwaukee. Not exactly pack country—and Beau had never heard of an omega giving birth in a hospital. Their anatomy would give too much away to human doctors.

Rory's mother wasn't an omega, then. But Rory was. The only way Beau could make sense of that was that Rory must have been bitten, and manifested as an omega when he changed; that was rare, but Beau was pretty sure he'd heard of it happening.

No wonder Rory wanted suppressants; no wonder he wanted to *be normal.* To go home, to a life he could never really return to. He wanted to be human, to live a human life.

Beau would help him get as close as he could, at least, in whatever time he had before Rory decided to leave him. Because if Rory didn't want to be an omega, he definitely wasn't going to want to stay married to an alpha. Beau's presence might comfort him on some unwilling, instinctive level right now, but this couldn't be what Rory really wanted.

It was good to know that right away, Beau told himself. He just had to keep from forgetting it. He just had to resist the urge to sit and watch the sunlight shifting over the sharp planes of Rory's face, remembering that he had woken up this morning with his omega in his arms, sleeping sweetly and peacefully. That for one moment, he had felt like he was home, that he had everything he could ever need. For just a moment, he wasn't alone.

It was instinct, he repeated to himself, looking around for something else to do while Rory slept. Instinct was a lot, for werewolves— but that didn't mean it would ever be enough for someone who didn't want to be an omega to begin with. Beau just had to keep his own instincts under control, keep Rory safe, and let him go when the time came.

~

Rory snapped awake as soon as Beau said his name, pushing up on one elbow and looking around.

Beau tried to keep his smile only friendly, and didn't reach out for him. "Lunchtime, like I said. Do you want chicken soup? Or a sandwich?"

Rory blinked a few times and finally ran one hand over his eyes. "I, uh. Soup, please? I can..."

"Take your time," Beau said, and went to the fridge to pour refrigerated soup into a saucepan.

Rory visited the bathroom and then came to perch on the edge of a chair at the kitchen table. The soup didn't really need to be supervised, but Beau stayed by the stove, watching bits of solidified fat melt into the broth.

"When I was a little kid," Rory said, and then stopped.

Beau stared intently into the soup, remembering his own deductions from earlier, and how different Rory's childhood must have been from his own. He made a small, encouraging noise and didn't look directly at him, giving him space to decide whether he wanted to talk.

Rory fidgeted in Beau's peripheral vision for a few seconds, then went on. "I came home from school one day when I was maybe six or seven, and I asked my mom why we didn't have a microwave. Everybody had a microwave, they were so *fast*. Why'd she have to heat stuff up on the stove?"

Beau stared down at the soup, trying not to let his confusion show. That sounded like...

"She tried to explain it to me, but I got all wound up, yelling about how it wasn't fair, and I got my sister yelling too. After a while she put us both in the car and drove us to the gas station. It had one of those convenience-store microwaves, you know?"

Beau grimaced and nodded, knowing how this story had to end and wondering how he could have gotten everything so wrong.

"My mom set it for a minute and told us that if we could both stand by the microwave with our hands by our sides until it finished, we could go straight to a store and buy one." In Beau's peripheral vision Rory shook his gleaming head, lips tilting up in a tiny smile. "I lasted *eight seconds*, and then I covered my ears. Georgie—she's a year older than me, always looked out for me—she grabbed my arm and hauled us both out of there, and my mom was about a half second behind us."

The particular nails-on-a-chalkboard whine of a microwave was as much a sensation as a sound, imperceptible to humans as far as Beau could tell; even dogs didn't seem disturbed by it. Beau had spent more than one late-night study session debating what the hell it actually was with Lauren and Adam and the others. It was another question that someone would have to research someday. *Can werewolves hear or feel microwave radiation itself, and if so, how?*

Of course, to research it, you'd have to get werewolves to consent to being exposed to the torturous noise/sensation of a microwave. It would probably run into IRB problems even before anyone started trying to recruit subjects.

"So you, uh..." It was obvious that he hadn't been bitten, that his mother and sister were werewolves. Beau didn't dare trample over the first thing that Rory had chosen, of his own free will, to tell Beau about his past. "You didn't grow up in a pack, then?"

Rory shook his head. "I grew up in the *suburbs*. Or, well, Waukesha, it's kind of its own town? But, yeah, my—"

Beau remembered the lost, tiny whisper. *I want my dad.*

"My mom left her pack when she got married, so she had all of us in the hospital," Rory said. "My d—her husband was human. My sister and I were both born wolves, but our baby brother was born human."

Beau couldn't help looking over at Rory then. If his father was human *and* his mother wasn't an omega...

But he hadn't said that. He had corrected himself when he almost said that. Because the man he'd grown up with couldn't have been his dad, not biologically. Not if he was human and Rory was an omega.

Rory glanced up at him, nodded faintly, and dropped his gaze again. "I had no idea, until I started feeling really weird during full moons when I was thirteen. By then we were into the Revelation. People were starting to really know that we existed. A kid having his first heats..."

He would have endangered his family, his mother and sister, his apparently-not-father, his baby brother. Living alone like that among humans who now knew that werewolves existed, in those early days, when the idea was going around that werewolves were a threat waiting to launch into action, like sleeper cells, and it wasn't yet even definitely illegal to kill them as monsters... They would have been in far more danger than an entire pack living together, and Beau knew very well how much the danger of exposure had weighed on traditional packs.

To say nothing of the fact that Rory was living evidence that his mother must have deceived her husband—revealed more than thirteen years after the fact.

"My mom sent me to live with her pack, where she grew up, way up north," Rory said. "I, uh... I didn't last through high school before I met some alpha ten years older who told me we could live like humans in the city, and I was an idiot kid, so..."

Beau looked down into the pan. The soup was bubbling now. He stirred it.

"I grew up in a big pack," Beau offered. "But... oddly enough, no one there was supportive of my ambitions, so I left before I quite got myself driven out, as soon as I turned eighteen. Moved out of state, changed my name. Haven't heard a word from any of them since."

Rory was staring at him, looking oddly stunned. "So you—I mean, obviously you want to be called Beau now, but is that—"

Rory's childhood nickname was precious to him; he obviously didn't like the thought that Beau might be deprived of his.

Beau shook his head. "I was always called Beau, it's all right. It was a nickname when I was a kid, from my middle name. John Beaumont.

My dad was already Johnny, and *his* dad was Jack. The pack's Alpha, from as early as I can remember. Nobody could ever remember calling *his* dad anything but Alpha, or *sir*. So they always called me Beau. Didn't make any difference, changing it, except to take their name off my back."

He heard Rory rubbing his palms over the thighs of the jeans he was wearing. Beau's great-aunt had made those for him during his senior year of high school, when he was already decidedly on his way out, living on barely civil sufferance from the pack when he wasn't picking fights and getting himself punished. He'd kept those jeans, even when he'd grown another six inches and packed on another sixty pounds, because they smelled like home, like pack, and had the familiar protection-charms stitched into them.

If anybody could call bullshit on his show of indifference, it was Rory, but Rory said nothing. He just let his hand brush against Beau's when Beau set down the bowl of reheated soup.

When Beau started public school, he'd come home once and asked his mother why there were no microwaves anywhere on the pack land. He'd heard about them from classmates, heard they were so much faster. She hadn't shown him the reason; she'd just told him, *Sometimes it's better to do things slowly.*

Years later, when he was sixteen and they were telling him to be patient, to let things unfold, he'd hated that advice worse than anything else anyone in the pack said to him. But now, sitting at the table and watching Rory eat in tiny, cautious bites, he thought maybe his mother had been on to something after all.

Rory did the dishes again after lunch, and made it through all of them this time; when he finished he looked tired but triumphant, and still had some color in his face.

Beau grinned and waved him back to his seat at the table. "Here, I've got something for you. I meant to give it to you sooner, but you crashed pretty hard."

Rory's heart started beating faster; his posture straightened up, and an eager expression appeared on his face, but there was something about him that was still braced for trouble. Beau mentally penciled in a little more of what Rory hadn't said about the missing years between high school and now, that older alpha who'd swept him off his feet and right into a downward spiral.

Clearly gifts were dangerous. Beau was intensely glad he hadn't wrapped it or even put it back into the box.

He unplugged the new phone, the largest size that was still mostly a phone and not a tablet, screen zoom already turned all the way up and all the accessibility features activated, and brought it over without making any more of a fuss. "I didn't know what kind of case you'd like —mine are always pretty boring—but we can get one whenever."

He put the phone, already powered up, in Rory's hands, and Rory just blinked down at it for a moment, and then said, "It's. Thank you, I—I'll—"

"Hey, no need to thank me." Beau crouched down so he could look up into Rory's face and not tower over him. "And if you still can't read the screen too well, you can use the voice commands or I can—"

Rory was already swiping cautiously at the screen, and Beau shut up and let him. He stopped on a screen with just two icons on it, each taking up almost a sixth of the screen.

"That's Susan," Rory said after a second of staring down at the screen. "And that's you."

"Yep." Beau pulled out his own phone and waggled it. "I've been sending proof of life photos every time Susan demands one, but you can take that over when you're ready. She really wants to talk to you, make sure things are okay. I can go for a walk, give you some privacy."

Rory shook his head without looking up from the phone. He was blinking rapidly, but Beau could see the shine of tears gathering in his eyes. "Could you—I don't think I—not right now?"

"Okay," Beau said softly, setting one hand on Rory's knee. "It's fine. When you're ready, she'd just really like to hear your voice. But you can use your phone however you want. Set your own passcode on it, call anyone, download anything. That's yours. Only yours."

Rory's jaw tightened—had he heard that before, or did he not want to hear Beau's reassurances, knowing what Beau was thinking?—but after a moment he swallowed and said, "Thanks, Beau."

"No problem." Beau squeezed his knee. "Now, this is gonna feel pretty sudden, we didn't talk that much about it before, but... do you remember that I'm starting a residency program soon? In Minnesota?"

Rory blinked down at the phone, his grip on it tightening, and then he took a breath and raised his head, meeting Beau's gaze as he nodded. "We're moving, then?" He glanced around, his gaze touching on the boxes before returning to Beau. "Today?"

Beau blew out a breath, not letting himself think about how many sudden and chaotic changes of address Rory had made in the years Beau had spent digging in to this tiny apartment.

"No, not that sudden. We've got a few more days. My lease goes to the end of the month, technically, but I'd like to get us moved and have some time to settle in before the program starts. We'll be there before the empty moon, that way. But the new place is going to be a lot bigger, so we're going to need more furniture. I want to start ordering things now so we can get it all delivered as soon as we get there. Would you help me pick things out?"

Rory frowned a little, "I'm not... I don't..."

"It's just colors and stuff mostly," Beau said, squeezing Rory's knee. "I'll get my laptop, we can sit on the bed and look at things, okay?"

Rory nodded, obviously at a loss for how else to respond, and Beau wondered if he should have just done this all while he was sleeping, fait accompli. But Rory stood up when Beau did, and followed him over to the bed.

After a little coaxing, he betrayed a preference for rich jewel-toned colors and deep, soft upholstery; once they were in the rhythm of it, Beau even got him to pick out some more clothes and a phone case. His heart rate finally slowed to something like calm as he snuggled into Beau's side, and Beau settled one arm lightly around Rory and thought maybe he'd made the right call after all.

CHAPTER 10

*R*ory fell asleep tucked under Beau's arm and woke up stretched out alone in the bed, alone in the room. He sat up and looked around, stretching out his senses and still not finding the familiar steady beat of his alpha's heart.

He did, however, find a flattened cardboard box propped between the foot of the bed and the back of the bookshelf that walled it off. In thick red letters nearly a foot high, it said:

BACK SOON
  -BEAU

As if anyone else could or would have left that message for him. Still, Rory scooted down to the end of the bed, tracing his fingers over the letters he'd read almost without trying. His alpha's reassurance for him.

Moving made him aware of the solid shape in the pocket of his new jeans—his phone, bigger than one of his hands. *His*, Beau had insisted. His to use, his to lock. His to call anyone he liked. He pulled it out and touched the screen, which opened for him without any passcode required.

Maybe he'd ask Beau how to set one, or... maybe not.

For now, it opened up to the screen showing two pictures: Beau, and Susan.

Rory licked his lips and thought about calling Beau, just to check where he was, and how long it would be until he came back.

The familiar miserable calculations started up immediately. Was he *supposed* to call? Was he not supposed to call, because Beau had already left him a message? If he did call, would Beau tell him the truth about how long he was going to be gone, or come back early looking to surprise him? Or come back late, to make Rory wait for him?

He could feel the fear of it already coming on—the anticipation of getting caught doing something he shouldn't, even though he had no idea what he should or shouldn't be doing. The fear of Beau not coming back, or bringing home friends, or a prettier omega to flirt with in front of him, or...

Rory shook his head, pushing all those thoughts aside, and looked down at the screen again. With a shaky finger, he tapped on Susan's picture.

The phone rang twice, and then he heard Susan's voice in his ear, almost as clear as if she were right in the room with him. "Hello? Is this Mr. Lea?"

Rory's throat was almost too tight to speak, and then he said, "Yeah. I guess I didn't change my name."

Susan made a fond, amused noise, and Rory curled down into the blankets at the foot of the bed, hidden in the corner between wall and shelves and Beau's huge cardboard note. He kept the phone tucked tight to his ear and pulled a corner of blanket over his head and shoulders, hiding away with the sound of a familiar kind voice.

"Beau said you... you wanted me to call," Rory added hesitantly.

"Well, I did say I was going to stay in touch," Susan said briskly. "I can't make sure your alpha's treating you right if I don't talk to you, now can I? Is he there?"

She asked that last question in the same easy tone as she said the rest, but Rory knew what she meant by it. *Is he listening? Can you speak freely?*

"He went out," Rory said. "I was sleeping, but he left a note. He wrote it really big, so I could read it. It just says *back soon*, but he—he left it for me. So I would know."

Rory bit his lip after he trailed off. It really wasn't such a big thing; maybe Susan wouldn't understand what it meant, or how it felt, or why it mattered.

"Sounds like he didn't want you to worry," Susan said gently. "That seems like a kindness."

Rory nodded against the mattress. "I know it's only been a few days and I've been asleep for most of it, but he just... he's always... *kind*."

Not just *nice*—not polite and showing off his good date-manners, as good as a flashing neon sign to show what he was trying to con out of Rory. Niceness always carried with it the threat that the niceness would end, revealing the sharp teeth it had only half hidden.

Beau was *kind*, giving him just the things he needed, both actual *things* and...

"He slept on the floor," Rory blurted, when Susan stayed quiet. "He was sitting up next to the bed asleep, so I could sleep by myself. And even when I got him to come to bed, he didn't—but I just keep waiting for him to be like—"

Rory stopped again, pressing his knuckles to his mouth this time. He hadn't meant to say that. He *knew* Beau wasn't like that. That was why they had let him leave the refuge with Beau, let him marry him.

"Well, then you'll be ready if he shows any bad signs," Susan said simply. "But I think there's a chance you really did find a good one with him. It happens sometimes, though the moon's seen how long it can take us to trust again. I think I'd borne three children before I stopped expecting my alpha to use his claws on me if one of them cried or made a mess."

Rory made a tight little sound in his throat, not quite strangled back. She said it so matter-of-factly, so comfortably.

"Oh, yes," Susan snorted softly. "I know I don't look as if I could even remember anything other than Easy Street anymore, but believe me, if there'd been anything like the refuge when I was your age I'd have barricaded myself inside and never come out. I could see it in your eyes when you came to us, Mr. Lea. You were looking for a quiet place to die. I'm glad we could help you find something a little better than that."

"I..." Rory hid his face for a moment, struggling to steady his breathing. He'd thought no one knew. "Do you think he—you think this is really better? He doesn't—he hasn't touched me like that. He doesn't want to keep me."

And I can't have children, he didn't say. He couldn't confess it again, not yet.

"Still," Susan said. "Better than what you were thinking of before. And if he's not what he seems, well. I've learned a thing or two since the last time an alpha pushed me around. I've still got plenty of claws of my own, Mr. Lea. Just you say the word."

Rory swallowed, and remembered the echo of his mother's voice, and finally whispered, "Do you think you... would you call me Rory? Please?"

"Oh," Susan said, and he thought maybe she wanted to say *honey* or *sweetheart* from the sound of that one syllable, and it almost sounded like the same thing when she said, "Rory, of course."

He was sitting up at the kitchen table, painstakingly examining his phone, when Beau came back in. He could smell the warm sweetness of fresh berries as soon as Beau came through the door, and then, under it, the rich red scent of recently-slaughtered meat.

Beau grinned at the sight of him sitting up, and Rory swallowed awkwardly to get his watering mouth under control before he could smile back.

"Thought you might like something that wasn't chicken soup or oatmeal for dinner," Beau said. "You could use more protein anyway, huh?"

Rory nodded, adding, "Thank you," once he could speak. "For the note, too. And," Rory waggled his phone as Beau set the bags down on the table and started unloading everything. "I talked to Susan, she said she won't bother you again for a while."

"Hey, I knew what I was signing up for," Beau said. "Just glad you got a chance to talk to her. What do you like on your steak?"

Rory bit his lip, swallowing the reflexive answer—*whatever you like is fine*—and remembering what Susan had told him. *Try. Little things. Just try.* "I like... salt and pepper? Maybe butter?"

"Can do," Beau said agreeably, setting down salt and pepper next to an unlabeled seasoning jar.

Rory breathed for a couple of minutes and then said, "Can I do anything to help?"

He scrubbed potatoes while Beau started the oven and found a pan for them, and sat upright at the table for the whole time it took them to bake, letting Beau show him the features on his phone until it was time to start the steaks.

Rory wound up stuffing himself too full of steak and potatoes for more than a couple of raspberries, but Beau assured him they would keep for a day or two. Rory stretched out in bed, his full belly dragging him down into sleep again.

It was dark when he woke up to the sound of the bathroom tap running. Rory watched through half-lidded eyes as Beau emerged, obviously changed for bed already and accompanied by a waft of sharp toothpaste-smell. Rory reached over and patted the bed on the side toward the wall, and Beau stopped where he was and said, "Yeah?"

Rory nodded and repeated the motion. Beau came and climbed in, turning his face to the wall just like before. Rory rolled over to curl close to his back, his head barely touching Beau's shoulder, and he slept again.

~

The next few days were like that, meals and naps and the occasional sunny hour awake. Rory still tried to avoid the sight of himself in the mirror, but his neck stung less and less each time he showered, and he could almost forget the burns the rest of the time.

And then it was the morning before moving day. He ate his vitamins and a breakfast of eggs and toast and fruit, and afterward washed the dishes while wondering if he could help Beau pack up the last odds and ends to get ready for tomorrow. He turned toward Beau as he dried the frying pan, about to ask him if there was a box for it to go into.

He found Beau sitting at the kitchen table, utterly still, just watching him. Something in that look made Rory freeze. It wasn't predatory, wasn't frightening, but there was something that hadn't been there before. Something that made him feel pinned in place.

In the next second Beau's expression softened, his hands coming up placatingly like they did a half-dozen times a day. "No, no, it's not —come sit?"

Rory nodded and moved to sit at his usual place at the table, still holding the towel and frying pan. His hand tightened on the handle without thinking about it, and he found himself wondering how hard he could hit Beau with it—hard enough to get out the door?

No. *Stop.* It wasn't that kind of look. This was *Beau*, he wouldn't...

Beau's hand appeared in his field of view, slipping under the towel to touch Rory's hand. "Hey, it's... it's not a bad thing. You can say no if you're not ready, I won't mind, okay?"

Rory tried to remember to keep breathing, but he flinched from the touch and then froze when Beau cussed under his breath.

"No, no, that was at myself for making a big production of this."

Beau slid out of his chair, down onto his knees next to the table so he could look up into Rory's face. Rory shouldn't have made him do that, should have—he should—his knuckles ached from the tightness of his grip on the frying pan, and it shook a little in his lap.

"It's just a picnic," Beau said, looking up earnestly into his eyes. "Baby, it's just lunch outside by the lake, that's all. Getting some food and sitting by the water before we move away from it."

Rory stared at Beau, his ears full of the racing of his own heart. He'd understood the words, but... that couldn't be all of it, that couldn't...

"Just eating outside," Beau repeated, setting one hand gently against Rory's cheek. "It's okay, you don't have to. I can go myself, or I don't even have to. I'm not upset. It was just an idea. I just wasn't sure if you were ready, I thought maybe I shouldn't even ask you, but I thought you might like it. I'm gonna miss the lake, that's all. But it's not a big deal. You don't have to come."

Rory's whole face felt numb, but it was finally sinking in. Beau just wanted to know if Rory wanted to come to the lake with him, have a picnic. That was all, and Rory had—had—

He opened his hand abruptly, letting the frying pan fall into his lap and slide right off his knees. Beau's hand pulled away from his cheek to catch it, and Rory squeezed his eyes shut—stupid, stupid, overreacting, why had he freaked out like that, it was nothing. It was *nothing*, and he'd—and how could Beau ever take him anywhere if he was going to be like this? The whole point of him was to show that Beau had a spouse to look after him, to help him through his residency. Rory couldn't even be invited to a picnic without panicking.

Beau's hand came back, sliding around to the nape of his neck, finger and thumb squeezing at the base of his skull.

Rory gasped a deep breath at the sweet, hard pressure, and then he was sliding right off the chair, just like the frying pan. Beau caught him, too, pulling Rory into his lap before he sat down on the floor.

"It's okay," Beau was repeating, sounding a little hoarse. "Baby, it's okay, it's okay. I shouldn't have made it seem like a big thing. It's just a lake, it doesn't matter. It's okay."

Rory breathed in his scent for a little while, until Beau went quiet and just held him. Rory found himself shivering, shaking, the adrenaline of a fight that hadn't happened flooding his body.

"I'm sorry," Rory whispered, not daring to speak louder, "I'm sorry, I know you—I know."

He was clinging to Beau, unable to let him go even though it was Beau he'd been scared of—except it hadn't been, not really. He'd been scared of Martin, of the others before him—Sean, Greg, all of them, when the scales tipped and he realized they were all the same.

Not Beau. He wasn't scared of Beau. As long as he was with Beau, he was safe. Beau wasn't like any other alpha he'd ever been with.

"If you want," Rory managed. "I can, I'll—"

"Shh," Beau said. "Shh, don't worry about it, let's just go lie down, huh? Just let me hold you for a little while."

Beau's grip on him tightened, and Rory relaxed into it instinctively. Beau had never asked for that—to hold him. Other than occasionally helping him to bed, Beau had barely touched him since they got married; even at night, when Beau shared the bed, he kept his hands, and everything else, carefully to himself, always facing the wall.

But now he picked Rory up, arms steady and strong around him, and when he laid Rory down he didn't let go, stretching out with him. Rory pressed closer, hiding his face against Beau's chest, clinging tight to his shirt. He even dared to hook one ankle over Beau's leg.

"Shh, I've got you, I've got you," Beau murmured. "I'm here, baby, I'm not going anywhere. Not without you."

"You can," Rory tried to say, but he couldn't make himself loosen his grip.

Beau just kept shushing him and holding on, and Rory eventually fell into a heavy, blank sleep, every limb weighted down with exhaustion.

When he woke he was hungry, and the sunlight coming in had gone cool and indirect in the way that meant it had sunk behind the building across the alley. It was after six, then.

And Beau was lying half on top of him, pinning him to the bed.

Rory couldn't quite see his face, but he could feel real sleep in the weight of Beau's body on his, the particular warm scent rising off his skin. Beau had said he slept more deeply lying down than sitting up by the bed, but apparently even that was nothing to sleeping in his omega's arms. He was out like a light.

Rory looked up at the ceiling, at the *BACK SOON* note still propped at the foot of the bed, and didn't move. Clearly both of them had missed lunch, eaten outside or not; Rory was sure he would have awoken instantly if Beau had gotten out of bed. And Beau was obviously still in need of rest himself, or he wouldn't have passed out like this, even with Rory's influence.

This is good, Rory thought. He closed his eyes and tried to memorize this moment: the soft sound of Beau's breathing, the weight of Beau's body on his, the already-familiar mingled smell of them rising up from the sheets and their clothes, the lingering light of a summer evening.

When the thought finally occurred to him—*I could get up and he wouldn't even know*—it was only attached to the thought that he needed to pee. Even when he realized what he'd thought, and remembered all the other times he'd been lying in one bed or another, trying to decide if he dared squeeze out from under an alpha's hold, the panic didn't come back. He'd used it all this morning, maybe, or else spending eight hours held close to Beau had finally convinced his brain of something.

It just kept feeling good, having Beau's weight on him, Beau's scent filling his nose. It was enough to make something stir in his brain, in his body.

He couldn't remember the last time he'd wanted sex other than to scratch the mindless need of heat, or as a way to placate the nearest alpha, but he thought this feeling might be at least related to that. He'd like to have more of Beau's weight on him, more of Beau's touch, and... maybe another kiss like their first one. Maybe several kisses like that, and Beau's touch on the back of his neck, and Beau looking at him and calling him *baby* when he wasn't too panicked or sick to enjoy it.

He didn't get hard, or wet; they weren't quite those kind of thoughts, and his body didn't seem to do that outside of heat anyway. This new desire didn't root that low in his belly. But he thought he'd like Beau's touches, Beau's attention, and if it led to more, if Beau wanted more...

Beau wouldn't demand it; he'd promised that in writing, all official and legally binding. He'd probably be sweet, careful and kind, wanting Rory to like it. That was okay; Rory had a whole repertoire of ways to assure an alpha that he liked whatever was being done to him. It wouldn't be hard to assure Beau that he wanted whatever Beau wanted. He'd be able to give Beau something for all he'd given Rory, and earn more of this part, this touch and closeness.

Of course, that would depend on whether he could convince Beau to want him at all. Rory hadn't noticed any sign of that so far, but they'd hardly had any time together yet when one of them wasn't asleep, and Rory had made a strong first impression as someone next door to death. No alpha would be panting after that. But Beau wasn't disgusted by him, either, and he was a young, strong, healthy alpha. If he knew it was being offered, that Rory was healthy enough, he wasn't likely to say no.

He couldn't remember what it was like to invite before he was being taken, to offer when it wasn't already a foregone conclusion. Beau was kind and proper; he'd want it to be all sweet and normal. Maybe *romantic*.

Rory closed his eyes and snuggled into Beau's warmth, trying to remember what little he'd ever known about how regular people liked to flirt.

CHAPTER 11

*B*eau woke up knowing only that something was wrong. It took him a moment to realize what it was.

Rory was gone. He had to find Rory.

That was taken care of as soon as he stood up and looked. Rory was at the kitchen table, sitting next to an emptied plate. The frying pan was on the stove. The frying pan, that was. Something. Important.

"Are you okay?"

Rory looked up and smiled at him, sweet and happy, like something out of Beau's dreams. Had he been dreaming about Rory? "Yeah, sleepyhead. Are *you* okay?"

Beau blinked at him. That wasn't... Rory didn't have to worry about him. "What—what can I do?"

He had to fix it. There was something he had to fix. If he could fix it then he could go back to sleep.

Rory wasn't smiling anymore. "Are you hungry, Beau?"

Beau shook his head. "No, it's..."

He rubbed his face, finally aware that he wasn't really all the way awake, although he wasn't dreaming, either. He was caught in fuzzy half-awareness, like being sick. End-of-semester hibernation had finally hit him, his body trying to catch up all at once after months of stress and strain. He'd been hoping it would wait until Minnesota, or maybe be skipped altogether in the rush toward his residency and the urgency of taking care of Rory.

"I just..." Beau looked around and wound up staring at a clock, trying to make sense of the numbers and the light. "Are you okay? You were gone, and I... I had to find you. Did you eat? Do you feel okay?"

Rory stood up and stepped close, and Beau curled an arm around him automatically.

"You found me," Rory said, and Beau thought he might even be smiling, though he had his face turned down so Beau couldn't see. He felt warm, not fever-hot, against Beau's side, his breathing and heartbeat steady. "You want me to come back to bed so you'll know where I am? So you can go back to sleep?"

Beau nodded, holding Rory tighter, and Rory still didn't pull away or seem frightened. After a minute Rory did give him a little push. Beau nodded and turned them back toward the bed, bringing Rory with him every step of the way, until they were lying down together again.

He pressed his lips to the peach-fuzzy top of Rory's head and closed his eyes again. Rory was here with him. Everything was all right now.

$\sim$

Beau woke up and it was morning. Rory was leaning over him, smiling slightly.

Beau smiled back reflexively, even as he said, "What—what's—"

"Moving day," Rory said. "Can you wake up long enough to get us where we're going?"

Beau sat up, rubbing hard at his face. Of course he could. He could always do what had to be done, especially when he had Rory to look out for. No problem.

His stomach growled like there was an actual wolf in there, and Beau lowered his hand to look at Rory. "Did I just... sleep for an entire day?"

Rory was still smiling, and he shrugged now. "Your turn, I thought. Did you, um..." His smile shrank, his posture stiffening. "There isn't much left in the fridge, but..."

"Shh, no," Beau said immediately, squeezing Rory's shoulder. "I can go pick stuff up for breakfast, or we can go out if you're feeling up to it, and then I'll pick up the truck. Okay?"

Rory nodded, relaxing slightly under Beau's hand. The next second he tensed up again as he raised a hand to the collar of his t-shirt, just below the silver burns, then to his head, covered in stubble and bare patches just starting to fill in with fine, pale fuzz.

Still, he said determinedly, "I can go out. I mean, we have to start somewhere, right?"

Beau tried to see him like a stranger would, instead of only seeing how much better he looked than a week ago. Instead of only seeing *Rory* and *mine*.

"I washed your winter scarf," Beau offered, nodding toward the navy-and-red scarf draped over a few boxes where the sun fell on it in the afternoons. "Or you can wear your cravat? It's in the closet with your hanging clothes."

Rory darted a look toward the closed closet door, and something in the furtive glance told Beau without a doubt that Rory had never ventured to look in there. Maybe he hadn't even known where his other clothes had disappeared to.

"You're sure?" Rory said, his gaze moving to the soft, warm scarf he'd been wearing the day they met. "It's summer. It'll look weird."

"You wear what you want, baby," Beau said firmly. "I don't care what the other people at the diner think about your fashion sense. I just want you to be able to relax and eat breakfast, okay?"

Rory's gaze returned to him, and Rory offered another shy smile. "I could be a hipster, huh?"

"Absolutely," Beau agreed, as if he knew anything about hipsters. They wore flannel shirts, right? Why not a knitted scarf in summer?

There was also probably no way Rory was going to look anything but *direly ill* to the casual observer, given his thinness and his hair.

Most humans would have enough tact not to draw attention to anything strange he did that might somehow relate to that.

And if they didn't—if anyone at all was rude to Rory—then Beau would... deal with that.

Calmly, he told himself. Politely. Without frightening Rory or making a scene. Definitely without anyone calling the cops on a werewolf behaving threateningly; getting arrested would throw off the whole day, and possibly more than that, if word got back to the Rochester Clinic.

He kept repeating that plan to himself while he got dressed. It wouldn't do to forget.

Beau wound up bristling protectively in response to a few curious glances sent in Rory's direction, but that only earned him apologetic or sympathetic looks, not people getting alarmed or angry. After the third one Beau realized that no one thought they could be werewolves, because werewolves never got visibly sick. He didn't know how he felt about that bit of convenient social camouflage.

He tried to focus, instead, on the pleasure of watching Rory devour a three-egg omelet, toast, pancakes, and the garnish of fruit, without the least flicker of nausea or hesitation.

Beau scooted his own strawberry and orange slices toward Rory, and Rory did look a little shy then.

"I, uh," he ducked his head. "I guess I got my appetite back?"

"Good, I'm glad," Beau said, picking up the strawberry and holding it nearly to Rory's lips. Even as he did it, he knew this was different from feeding Rory for the last week, while he was sick and semiconscious and no one was watching, but he couldn't, wouldn't, take it back.

Rory looked up at him and then, with a smile that was almost playful under the shyness, he took a bite that left little more than the stem and some juice on Beau's fingers.

Beau dropped his gaze, suddenly struggling to control his own reaction. He felt his skin flushing, his heart wanting to race. He dropped the strawberry stem on his plate and licked his fingers clean, not thinking about Rory's healthily pink lips, the flash of his teeth.

It felt like the ground shifting under him, like something turning inside out in his brain as the paradigm shifted. Rory wasn't a person exhibiting a set of symptoms and a case history; he wasn't a patient who Beau had taken on in a somewhat irregular fashion. Rory was a person, *Beau's husband*, who happened to be getting over an illness which Beau had helped to nurse him through.

It didn't change anything, or at least it shouldn't. Rory needed a safe place to recover. He didn't need to worry about Beau wanting him, about what Beau might pressure him for. A lunch out had been enough to panic him yesterday; the moon knew what he'd do if he thought Beau might really have some kind of designs on him. And Beau certainly had no intention of demanding anything, just because... just because Rory was looking really much better today, and feeling playful, and his lips were very pink.

Rory's heart was beating a bit faster, but not ratcheting up toward panic just yet. Beau raised his eyes only to find that Rory was intently studying his own plate, his mouth hidden in the dark folds of his scarf, and... blushing. It wasn't the hectic flush of panic, just a pink tint across his cheeks and the tops of his ears. It made Beau want to put an arm around him, to press his lips to those spots to see how much warmer they felt.

Beau pushed that thought firmly away and focused on what he could see of Rory's expression and body language, which was... not afraid.

He was a little tense, which was Rory's default state, but not cowering or looking for an exit route. He might almost have been smiling, and then he snuck a look at Beau. When their eyes met, Rory did smile, and Beau couldn't help grinning.

They both looked away, barely meeting eyes or speaking for the rest of breakfast, but it wasn't an uncomfortable silence, or... not awkward, not worrying. It was like the silence of being in on some joke together, of not needing to say a word.

Beau knew he should be worrying about just what Rory was thinking, because he had no idea why Rory was taking this so calmly, but the feeling of being together on something was too good to spoil.

Stepping out of the diner broke the spell a little, returning them to the real world and the day's plans. Beau glanced at his watch, confirming that the rental place would be open now.

"I'll go pick up the truck," he said. "It's a long walk, you don't need to come with me for that. Here, take my keys. You have your phone?" Rory nodded, touching the pocket of his jeans where Beau could see the big rectangular outline.

Beau pulled out his wallet and extracted a few bills. "Here, you should have some walking-around money, if you think of anything you need. That store downstairs from our place is nicer than you'd think, and there's a bakery a couple of blocks the other way if you're still hungry, or a nice little park—" Beau gestured eastward. "If you want to just enjoy some fresh air or something. It'll probably take at least an hour to get the truck, and I'll call if it's going to take longer. Okay?"

Rory tucked the money into the opposite pocket from his phone, keeping the keys in his other hand. It was all of three blocks back to the apartment, and Beau had to give him a little space. Time to call Susan and beg for rescue, if it came to that. Rory would be fine.

"Okay," Rory said, when Beau just stood there staring at him like an idiot. "Um..."

He leaned in a little, going up on his tiptoes and tilting his chin up, and Beau recognized what he was silently offering, or maybe asking for. And, hell, they'd better get used to this kind of thing, or no one at Rochester was ever going to believe they were really married.

"Okay," Beau repeated, and he leaned in, curling one arm lightly around Rory to steady him as he pressed a soft little kiss to Rory's lips. "Okay. See you in an hour, baby."

Rory nodded, raking his teeth over his lower lip, and then he winked, smiling another small, shy smile, and turned away, slipping neatly out of Beau's grip.

Beau stood there and watched him walk away until he reached the corner and stopped to wait for the light. Beau turned on his heel and started walking before Rory could look back and catch him staring.

~

When Beau returned to the apartment, there was a white bakery bag on the kitchen table and Rory was just putting the last of the dishes into a box.

"Hey," Beau said, smiling. "Great. I'll start taking these down."

He grabbed a stack of boxes and headed straight back down the stairs, and for a little while it was just that, ferrying stuff down to the truck—first all the boxes and the trash bags, and then his little table and two chairs, and the bookshelves, and then he came back upstairs and found Rory had stripped the bed and was looking around for something to put the bedding in.

"Oh," Beau said. "Uh..."

He hadn't meant to bring the bed. It was old and not actually all that comfortable, or big enough for him to even stretch out on without his feet hanging off or head bumping the wall. He'd ordered beds to be delivered to the new place, but not until tomorrow. The empty moon was coming, and those new beds would smell all barren and lonely...

"Here," Beau said, grabbing another garbage bag and shaking it open for Rory to stuff the sheets and blankets inside, a concentrated scent-blast of the two of them sleeping. He was hit with the sudden body-memory of lying there with Rory in his arms, pressing Rory into the mattress with his own weight and holding him there.

Beau looked up to meet his eyes; Rory was blushing again, but he didn't look scared. He hadn't seemed scared at all. Beau couldn't have done anything wrong if Rory was acting like this. That had probably just been a dream, even if he could remember the jut of Rory's bones against him, and Rory's warm sleeping scent filling his nose.

"What about the towels?" Rory said, nodding toward the bathroom.

"We're getting new ones," Beau said, because he hadn't bought new towels anytime in the last nine years except on the occasions when he tore one in half drying himself—and even that had been a few years ago. The towels he thought of as new were nearly as threadbare and faded as the ones he thought of as old.

Still, Beau went and got a garbage bag and let Rory dump their thankfully dry used towels into it, along with the shower curtain. The liner went in the actual trash, and Beau started gathering up soap and shampoo and cleaning products into another box, cleaning out under the bathroom sink and then under the kitchen sink while Rory peeked into the closet.

In the end, it took barely more than an hour to empty the apartment, even with maneuvering the mattress and box spring down and into the truck. Rory's shopping bag had been changed out for one of Beau's old backpacks, and Rory carried it down to the truck himself, along with the bakery bag and a water bottle, which he set between them when he climbed into the passenger seat.

"Road snacks, huh?" Beau said, glancing down at the bag. He could smell chocolate and pastry, but he wasn't going to take anything if Rory didn't offer.

Rory nodded, smiling that shy smile again. "You've been working hard."

"You too," Beau said. He could see the tiredness starting to catch up with Rory, but he really had done fine with the trip to breakfast and helping out with the last burst of packing and cleaning. "We've both earned some sweets, huh?"

Rory nodded, opening up the bag. "You have to drive, though."

Beau raised his eyebrows, though it also reminded him that he actually *did* have to drive, so he checked the mirrors to see if he could safely pull out into the street. When he glanced back in Rory's direction, he was holding out a chocolate-frosted donut, biting his lip.

Beau grinned. "Thanks, baby."

He took a bite and made himself keep his eyes on the road as he got the truck in gear, instead of letting his attention drift toward Rory nibbling at his own donut. By the time they got to I-90, Rory had fed him an entire donut, a slice of crumb cake, and some kind of tart, and

Beau had almost entirely managed to avoid either licking Rory's fingers or watching Rory lick them. Rory had eaten a donut and a muffin himself, and still seemed calm and content. He drew up his knees to his chest and looked around as they rolled down the freeway, though there wasn't exactly any scenery. So far it was just billboards and the north side of the city.

It wasn't long before Rory was dozing with his head tucked awkwardly on his own knee. He had his scarf on, which made for a little pillow, but not much. Beau reached over with one hand, tugging gently on his shoulder, and Rory followed his hand, leaning against the seat back instead. That looked a little more comfortable, and Rory settled into a deeper sleep as they got clear of the worst traffic and picked up speed.

Beau considered stopping for lunch in Wisconsin, but Rory was still fast asleep in the passenger seat when he'd finished pumping gas, and Beau found that all he wanted to do was finish the drive as soon as possible. He let Rory sleep and got back on the road, driving into the afternoon, until he pulled into the double-width driveway and turned off the truck.

Rory startled awake as soon as the engine shut off, blinking at the house and then over at Beau.

"Hey, baby," Beau said, smiling. "We're home."

CHAPTER 12

*R*ory stared at Beau, and then at the house, and then Beau again. He'd known they were moving to a bigger place, of course, because the big couch and chair he'd helped Beau pick out wouldn't fit into another tiny studio. And Beau had promised him that he'd have his own room for heats, so of course that would mean having at least two bedrooms.

But this was... a *house*. A *big* house, bigger than the one he'd lived in as a kid, with a big, green yard around it. The trees were still small, and the house looked brand new, everything perfect, untouched. He couldn't imagine anything further from where he'd been living ever since he ran away to the city.

It looked like somebody's home.

"This?" Rory said, barely above a whisper. "We're..."

"Yeah," Beau said, squeezing his shoulder. "Yeah, this is us. I mean, unless you hate it, then I'm gonna need to make a lot of phone calls in a hurry and I don't even know what would happen with the mortgage, so we should probably go have a look around inside? See if it's okay?"

Rory could hear the gentle joking in the tone of Beau's voice, but he could hardly take in the words, still stuck on the house. Beau had done this, for him, for...

"Just... just us? This is just for you and me?" Rory finally managed to actually look at Beau, just in time to see his expression go all soft and warm.

"Yeah, baby," Beau said, in a low tone that made Rory want to shiver and push closer. "Just for us. And, I mean..." Beau wrinkled his nose. "Maybe a dinner party at some point? Or if you wanted to invite anybody over. But it's our place. We can den up here for empty moon, and you'll be safe here when—whenever you need to be safe at home."

When his heats came back. It occurred to him suddenly that whatever Beau did with that bottle of suppressants, they must have been left behind in Chicago now. Rory wouldn't know where to get more even if he wanted them, in this strange place. In Chicago he'd have had an idea where to find a midwife who wouldn't ask questions, but now...

Now he really was going to have to trust Beau.

"Okay," Rory said, though he didn't think Beau had really asked him a question. "Yeah, let's. Let's go inside."

The house was enormous and empty inside, cool and dim with the air conditioning on and the shades drawn over every one of the many windows. The front room, nearly the width of the house, had hardwood floors and a fireplace at the far end, and led through a wide archway into the kitchen, which was painted a sweet, sunny yellow and had plenty of room for a table and chairs by the sliding glass door to the back deck and the wide sweep of backyard beyond it. There was another room beyond that, tucked behind the garage, down a step from the kitchen and carpeted.

Everything smelled new, freshly painted and utterly clean, no lingering scent of former occupants.

"Was this... just built?" It couldn't have been built for them, there surely hadn't been time for that—though of course Beau must have known much earlier that he was coming to Minnesota; it needn't have had anything to do with Rory.

"Nah—they did some renovation, and I went through a wolf realtor who made sure the place was completely cleaned, repainted, and odor-scrubbed. They did a good job, huh? Do you want to see upstairs next, or down?"

He pointed to a door off the kitchen that must lead to the basement stairs, and Rory nodded and then led the way when Beau gestured for him to go ahead.

The basement was low-ceilinged, even cooler than the rest of the house. It smelled reassuringly dry. One big central area had a concrete floor painted gray, and the washer and dryer and a utility sink tucked under some high windows. But a finished wall sectioned off at least a third of the room, and Beau led the way toward it.

"There's a little... guest suite, they called it, down here," Beau said. "I thought... since we brought the old bed, maybe we could put it down here and sleep here for a few nights, until we've got the rest of the furniture and the moon is on the wax?"

The little bedroom beyond the door was small, surprisingly cozy and den-like. There was a soft, thick blue carpet covering the floor, and a couple more high windows letting in a dappled light that meant they were half-screened by bushes. The ceilings were lower than upstairs, and Rory had a feeling that the bedrooms on the second floor would be even bigger and airier.

This was... almost like being back in Beau's apartment in Chicago. Rory was pretty sure everything from the truck would fit into this room, though it might be a little more cramped than before.

He had a momentary vision of the rest of the house decorated like something out of a magazine while he and Beau lived just in this room, huddled together and hidden, secret and safe. Strangers would see a human façade, but they could have their den down here together.

At least for a little while.

"That sounds fine," Rory said, tucking himself close to Beau's side, and Beau put an arm around him and held him there, saying nothing about how much more they had to do to get settled in.

∾

The next several hours involved a lot of unpacking boxes and finding that Beau's possessions really did not fill up the echoing emptiness of the house at all: the few dishes and pans only made the kitchen cupboards look bigger and emptier, and the bookshelves in the front room only made it obvious how much nothing there was in the rest of the space.

Neither of them even went up to the second floor.

They ate pizza sitting in a square of sunlight on the kitchen floor before Beau left to return the truck, and Rory went back down to the basement bedroom to make up the bed and pick the tape off the scarred old dresser to free the drawers. Beau's suits were all hung up in the closet, and Rory's one pair of good pants and his wedding shirt, the cravat folded over the hanger, hung beside them, along with a sea-green shirt Rory had never seen before in the same size as his wedding shirt. It was almost the color of Rory's eyes.

He ran his fingers down the soft cotton of it and left it there. Beau must have thought he'd need another nice shirt for meeting people from the clinic, all the other spouses and the doctors Beau would be trained by. He'd have to look presentable, like a properly supportive husband.

For now, Rory set up the bedroom and tidied everything in it as best he could. Then he sat down on the floor at the foot of the bed and opened his backpack.

Everything inside was wrapped in plastic shopping bags, scrounged here and there over the years. He had three clean t-shirts and four changes of underwear, six pairs of socks—although three of them were gray with age and threadbare at the heels and toes.

He had a little bit of cash, including what was left of the money Beau had given him the other day. Bills and coins were carefully stored apart from each other—some tucked into his underwear, a few more bills hidden flat between the pages of a battered paperback copy of *I, Robot*, which Rory's dad—*his mother's husband*—had given him for his eighth birthday.

He'd been tempted to leave it behind when they sent him away, but somehow he had never managed to part with it. Never lost it, and was never less than careful to keep it safe. He hadn't even managed to hold on to a photo of his family, but he had this book that still, ever so faintly, if he pressed his nose to the middle pages, carried the scent of the house he'd grown up in.

He didn't open it now.

He looked around the room, which would be the safest place in this house, where he would be allowed to stay, had a *right* to stay. His and his husband's house, all legal and human, on paper.

He pulled up the fitted sheet to expose the cord handles on the mattress on the side closer to the wall, and tucked the book carefully through the handle, so it was held flush against the mattress. When he pulled the sheet back into place and smoothed down the cover, there was no sign of it there.

Rory stuffed everything else back into his backpack, tucked his backpack into the back corner of the closet, and then curled up on top of the neatly-made bed and fell asleep.

He woke when Beau came home. The summer sun was sinking, but the house was still bright, with no other buildings close enough to block the light. Beau had come back with a shiny blue rental car —"Just for now, we're going to have a lot of errands and I couldn't deal with buying a car today"—and its trunk was packed full of groceries. Rory helped him distribute them through the fridge and pantry.

When they were sitting at the counter sharing cookies from the grocery store bakery, Rory said, "What, um... what happens now? Not tomorrow, but after that?"

Tomorrow most of the furniture would be delivered; tomorrow night was the empty moon. Beau had offhandedly named a half-dozen errands that would have to be run—the bank, the DMV, more things to be bought for the house. But he hadn't said much about the actual reason they had come to Minnesota.

"Orientation starts Thursday," Beau said, sounding a little grim about the prospect. "I'll be gone all day Thursday and Friday. Saturday there's a barbecue for all of us plus families, so..."

"I'll wear that green shirt?" Rory offered, and Beau smiled at him.

"Sure, if you like it," Beau said. "With jeans, maybe?"

Rory nodded agreement, looking down at his cookie and letting himself imagine that it was because Beau wanted Rory to be wearing his clothes among all those strangers, and not because he had hardly any other clothes.

"I don't know about you," Beau said after another quiet moment, "but I'm feeling like empty moon's come early. All I want to do is go curl up where everything smells familiar."

Rory gave him a sideways look and said helpfully, "You probably still need to catch up on sleep. You did all that driving today and all the carrying, too."

"You carried your backpack, and your share of the groceries," Beau offered, smiling a little. Not annoyed with Rory for not pulling his weight properly. Not yet.

"Can we bring the cookies?" Rory asked. Beau actually laughed, and kissed his forehead.

Five minutes later they were curled up in the familiar bed together, the cookies already forgotten on the nightstand. Rory fell asleep with his nose tucked against Beau's chest, thinking, *This is what it feels like to have a home.*

Rory wasn't sure where the dream left off and reality started; even after he was sure he was awake, everything was warm and cozy and dimly lit. The sun and the empty moon were both just above the horizon, casting the light of a long summer's empty moon day and making him want to do nothing but push close to his mate and stay safe in their den together. He was already doing that, dreaming and waking.

He was wrapped up tight in Beau's arms, one of Beau's legs hooked over his to hold him, and Beau's mouth kept brushing softly over his, warm and faintly sleep-sour, already feeling familiar even though they hadn't kissed like this before.

Their mouths were open to each other, drowsy and easy, without the terrifying urgency of sex. This was just... as if there was nothing between them, as if they were one creature, passing breath and touch back and forth without the need to dominate or submit. There was no feeling of invasion when Beau licked into his mouth, any more than when his lungs expanded or his heart beat. Everything was just where it should be.

Even when he realized Beau's cock was hard against his belly, there was no feeling of fear, not even the dull resigned feeling of *here we go again*. Rory was as far from heat as he could be, wanting only the protective closeness of his mate's body wrapped around his, but this was a part of his mate, a part of the thing they made up together, no more a threat to him than his own teeth.

Rory wriggled helpfully against Beau, inviting him to move, to thrust. Beau's whole body jerked and stilled, shattering the sleepy ease and breaking them into two.

Rory bit his lip and dropped his gaze, staying as limp as he could while he waited for Beau's reaction. He didn't know what it was, but when he was actually thinking and not just caught up in whatever half-dreaming illusory thing that had been, he knew that sex was where people changed. Where *alphas* changed, especially. There was no knowing what exactly Beau would want, or how Rory would feel about any of it.

"Rory," Beau said, his voice rough and hoarse. "I'm sorry, I'll—I'll go and—"

Rory looked up then, startled enough to reach for Beau without thinking. "No, don't, don't go."

Beau didn't move, just looked at him, frowning worriedly, and Rory's brain caught up a little more at the sight. Beau was worried about *him*. Beau expected him not to want this, or to be upset about waking up like this.

Rory took his hand off Beau and fell back against the pillow, putting his hand to his own forehead. "Beau, I don't mind. You're an

111

alpha, friction feels good every day of the year for you. And we *are* married."

Beau blinked at him like Rory had said all of that in some foreign language, shook his head like he had to clear water from his ears. "You don't have to, that's—we agreed to that. I'm not going to demand anything. I don't..."

"Didn't feel very demanding," Rory said, smiling crookedly. "It felt nice. Like you liked it. I liked it."

Beau was still blinking at him, and his uncertainty was making Rory feel somewhere between bold and unmoored. Better to provoke *something* than to let his alpha get any further away from him—not today, not on an empty moon day in a strange place. Not when it had felt so good, so warm and safe, a couple of minutes ago.

"If you wanted to fuck me we'd probably want lube," Rory said, his cheeks heating though he tried to say it straightforwardly, like a condition he had a right to set, and not another way he was broken. "I, uh, I don't really get wet. Outside of heat. But my mouth's in pretty good shape, or..."

Beau squeezed his eyes shut. "Rory, you don't—"

"Please," Rory whispered, grabbing the side of his t-shirt. "Beau, please let me—"

"I've never," Beau said abruptly, sharp as a knife cutting off Rory's begging. He opened his eyes again, his cheeks reddening just like Rory's, his whole face tensed like *he* expected something here to hurt. "I was in med school, and before that there was never time, not since I was sixteen. So I've never done this. Any of this."

CHAPTER 13

*R*ory just stared at him, and Beau gritted his teeth against the stupid, searing shame of his failure to be a properly experienced alpha. It shouldn't have mattered, not with Rory. They really, really shouldn't be doing anything that even made it relevant anyway, but it wasn't something Beau confessed often.

He'd thought he could be good enough, could take good enough care of Rory, satisfy him, provide for him. He'd thought—

Rory moved all at once, surging forward to press himself against Beau, and Beau's flagging cock hardened again almost instantly. He held on by sheer reflex, responding to Rory's rough, hungry kiss without thought.

He couldn't smell or taste or feel anything but Rory, but he couldn't detect the faintest trace of pity or mockery, nor fear, nor resistance. There was just Rory in his arms, pressing close to him, kissing him.

"I know you deserve someone who..." Rory mumbled, pulling away just enough to speak. "But you can at least—you can practice with me, so when you meet—"

Beau cut that off with another kiss, not wanting to think about any other omega, about a time after this when Rory was gone. Not now, not with the empty moon rising in the sky, when they needed each other close and safe. He tried to tell Rory that in kisses and with his body, not grinding against him or pinning him in place, just holding him close and dipping in to taste him again and again.

Rory relaxed in his arms, pliant as if he were sleeping again and radiating welcome. Beau sighed against his lips and tilted their heads together, forehead to forehead.

"This isn't practice, Rory," Beau said softly. "This is you and me, however long we last, however long you choose to stay. This is real. No matter what we do or don't, this is—"

Beau's phone alarm started up a strident chirping that reminded him of exactly where they were. They'd be getting a stream of deliveries for hours, and Beau, at least, needed to be awake and dressed to receive them, starting within the next hour.

After several seconds Beau forced himself to let go of Rory enough to turn and shut the alarm off. He lay on his back in the quiet that followed, thinking of all they had to do today and tomorrow. And after that his residency was starting, throwing him among all those humans who would be looking at him and thinking *werewolf*, watching for signs of danger and instability.

"Beau?" Rory's voice was small, hesitant, and Beau quickly turned to face him, seeing the lost look in his eyes.

On top of everything else, it was the empty moon, when all any werewolf wanted was *home* and *pack* and the safety of a familiar den. Moon knew what that had been like for Rory for the last several years, but today wasn't going to be easy for him.

"I'm here," Beau said quietly. "I meant that, Rory, everything I said. I just think we shouldn't rush into anything. I want you to be sure that you know what you want, and that it's what *you* want. You don't owe me any of this, okay?"

Rory nodded, but he didn't relax again the way he had in Beau's arms, all sweet and melting. Beau could coax that response from him again, make him all happy and soft, but then what? It wouldn't do any good for either of them, not beyond the next five minutes.

"I'll go take a shower upstairs and get dressed," Beau said quietly. "I want to make sure I'm ready to meet anybody bringing deliveries by seven, just in case. You sleep as late as you want, I can handle things. Okay?"

Rory nodded, dropping his gaze. Beau wanted to press him for an answer, ask how he felt or what he was thinking, but this wasn't the time.

"Okay," Beau repeated quietly, and he leaned in to kiss Rory's forehead before he got out of bed.

~

When Beau came downstairs after showering, Rory was already in the kitchen. He was wearing Beau's old jeans and a long-sleeved shirt, and had his winter scarf wrapped around his neck, which Beau took to mean that he was braced to be seen by strangers.

Beau wanted, urgently, to unwind it from around his neck, to kiss the pale, undamaged skin above the healing burns, and carry him back to where it was safe for him to show himself.

Empty moon, he told himself. It was just the empty moon, and his alpha instincts, and a lot of other things that wouldn't help get the house furnished so Rory could have a couch to sit on and a table to eat at and a TV to watch while Beau left him alone here for sixteen hours of practically every day for the next three years.

Beau squeezed his eyes shut and ran a hand over his hair; when he looked again Rory was watching him, a little wary. "I thought... breakfast? I would've started, but..."

His voice trailed off into uncertainty. Beau thought he could see the ways Rory was braced against that going wrong: if he made something Beau didn't want, or made it badly, or if Beau got annoyed with him for cooking instead of taking the suggestion to sleep in, or who knew what else.

Beau smiled, as gently as he could, pushing down the other thoughts and worries. "It's fine, baby. You don't have to cook for me, but if you want to I'd be happy to eat whatever you feel like making."

Rory nodded slowly. "I was thinking, maybe pancakes? There's blueberries."

"Sounds good," Beau agreed. "I got syrup. And bacon."

Rory wrinkled his nose, then just as quickly smoothed his expression and said, "Okay."

Beau considered pressing him about which of those he didn't like —syrup and bacon both seemed like pretty essential pancake accompaniments to him, and he'd gotten good maple syrup, not that sticky fake stuff Rory had avoided at the diner the day before.

Beau came into the kitchen and started assembling pancake ingredients, and Rory didn't flinch from laying out bacon on a pan to cook in the oven, so apparently that wasn't the problem. He relaxed as they moved around each other in the kitchen, seeming almost at ease again by the time they sat down together to eat, and then, with a cautious look at Beau, he spread his pancakes with butter and nothing else.

"That's how you like them?" Beau asked. It occurred to him that Rory had sprinkled sugar over his pancakes at the diner, but he didn't have convenient sugar packets here. "Just butter?"

Rory shrugged. "Or with powdered sugar, or... whipped cream, if..."

Beau got his phone out and added powdered sugar and whipping cream to the shopping list. "Anything else you like that we don't have?"

Rory crammed a bite of pancakes into his mouth and shook his head, and Beau figured that just meant he'd have to keep an eye out for things Rory liked or wanted but wouldn't ask for. "I was thinking we should get grocery delivery so neither of us has to go out and do that. We'll look at the website later, see if it's something you'll be comfortable shopping on. If we can get that working, you'll be able to just add things whenever you think of them instead of having to go through me, okay?"

Rory's gaze stayed fixed on his plate, but he nodded. Beau turned his attention to his pancakes.

The first truck pulled up not long after they'd finished cleaning up. Rory froze like a deer, and Beau bit his tongue to keep from suggesting that he go downstairs. Rory had made his choice to be up here; he knew where the basement was. If he needed a break from the strangers in the house, he would be perfectly able to take one.

"Here we go," Beau said with a little smile, and Rory returned it, small and tense but determined.

Beau tried not to focus too much on Rory after that, just directing the parade of deliveries—couches, bedframes, mattresses, a dining table and chairs, boxes of pillows and bedding and so on.

Nearly all the people doing the deliveries were male werewolves; it was one of the jobs where werewolf strength made things faster and easier, and Beau hadn't gone through any of the delivery services that guaranteed only humans would enter a customer's home. Two of them—one of the pair delivering couches, and one of the ones bringing in the flatscreen TV a couple of hours later—were alphas. The first time, Beau stood casually in the archway to the kitchen while Rory unpacked and washed some of the new dishes, getting the packaging-smell off them.

The guys with the TV showed up while Beau was upstairs directing the placement of the newly-delivered beds. He went downstairs—he'd been meaning to have Rory come up and give an opinion on where he wanted the bed in the master suite anyway—and found Rory on his knees at one of the bookshelves, stalled in the middle of putting books away. The guys with the TV were standing frozen on the threshold, and the alpha werewolf was staring right at Rory.

Beau stamped down his first, violent impulse—it was obvious that the alpha was trying his best not to intrude on a mated omega's space. He went to Rory, kneeling down next to him and extending an arm to lay over his shoulders. "Hey, b—"

Rory whirled, slamming a textbook into his chest edge-on. Beau was startled enough to be knocked on his ass, and Rory stared at him for a second and then bolted to the basement, still clutching the heavy book.

Beau rubbed his chest with one hand and pointed with the other, not looking at the delivery guys. "On the stand there, please."

By the time they were done unboxing the TV and hooking everything up, the others were gone too; all the deliveries for the day were done. Beau went down to the lowest of the basement steps and, without setting foot on the concrete floor, called softly toward the closed door, "Rory? They're all gone now. I'm sorry I startled you. I'm not angry, I understand why you reacted that way."

He waited for a moment. He could hear Rory's heartbeat. It wasn't as frantically fast as it had been when he first retreated down here to hide, but nowhere near resting, either. He would hear every word Beau said; he had probably listened to every word Beau had said this entire time, searching for hints of what was going to happen next.

"You didn't hurt me," Beau tried. "I understand."

He didn't understand, not really. If he tried to imagine what would make an omega react like that to his own alpha, he was going to have to drive back to Chicago and kill someone. And even then, he wouldn't know what it was like to live that way, to feel that edge of danger forever under his feet.

"I'm going to go and run some errands," Beau offered, when Rory still didn't respond. "I'll be out for a couple of hours at least, so if you want to come upstairs and get something to eat, you won't have to see anyone. I'll lock all the doors before I go, so no one can come in and surprise you while I'm gone. I... I'll see you later."

Beau waited, and this time he did get the tiniest of muffled whispers in response. Somewhere in the basement bedroom, probably talking into his knees, Rory said, "Okay."

Beau sat down on the steps, his legs not wanting to support him at the sound of Rory's voice, so small and hoarse and scared.

"Okay," Beau echoed after a few minutes, and forced himself to leave Rory in peace.

It took an embarrassingly long time for Beau to realize that his growing sense of frustration at how long his errands were taking was because the empty moon was sinking in the sky along with the sun. The closer they got to the darkest of nights, with the moon following the sun under the earth, the stronger the pull to *pack* and *home*. He very nearly abandoned a cart full of lamps, light bulbs, and a toolkit when he worked it out, and he did take out his phone and touch the contact for Rory without stopping to second-guess himself.

"Hello?" Rory picked up almost before the first ring finished, his voice high and strained.

"It's me, baby, are you okay? I'm gonna be home pretty soon, I..." Beau didn't know what to say.

Rory knew what the empty moon was as well as he did, and he probably hadn't *forgotten it was happening*, which Beau managed to do at least one month out of three all through college and med school, though he'd never felt it this strongly before.

"I miss you," Rory whispered. "I'm sorry, Beau, I'm so sorry, please, just come home."

Beau glanced down at the cart and made an executive decision that everything in it could wait until tomorrow.

"I'm coming, Rory, I'm coming home right now, you just hang on a little bit longer for me."

Driving home was blessedly fast on Rochester's relatively-empty roads, nothing like the maddening constant traffic of Chicago. Before he quite believed possible, he was pulling into the driveway, and Rory was springing up from where he'd been sitting on the front porch with his arms wrapped around his knees. The light was slanting in from the west; the sun would be down in another hour or so, though the summer twilight would linger.

As soon as Beau was out of the car, breathing in Rory's scent and knowing he was home, the pull of the empty moon seemed to lose half its strength. When he had Rory in his arms, when the door was closed and locked behind him, he could almost forget it entirely. As long as he didn't let Rory go.

"I made sandwiches," Rory mumbled against his shoulder after a while.

Beau squeezed him. "Well, let's have dinner, then."

They ate together at the counter, ignoring all the new furniture. Every bite tasted better than anything Beau had ever eaten, but Beau was aware that that was the empty moon and the knowledge that his omega wanted to feed him. He didn't particularly care. Not now. They left the crumb-strewn plates in the sink and headed straight downstairs by silent mutual agreement, stripping down to underwear and crawling into bed together to cling to each other even tighter.

Rory went limp with sleep almost at once, his face tucked against Beau's chest, and Beau lay awake watching the light from outside fade. It was impossible not to think of the way the morning had started, right here, so much like this and so different.

If they hadn't been interrupted, if he'd said to hell with being perfectly punctual and drew Rory into another kiss...

He couldn't feel the way it had felt, the easy unfurling of pleasure and the warm, welcoming feel of Rory in his arms, the easy, trusting scent of him. But he thought it had been real, just as much as this was real now.

Except that there was a fading, bruised ache across his chest that reminded him the afternoon had been real, too. Everything that had happened to Rory was still real, even as the worst physical effects faded before Beau's eyes. The empty moon and a stressful day had helped bring it to the surface, but Beau couldn't forget the fear that Rory had lived with for so long.

Rory hadn't smelled *aroused* at all that morning, and he'd said— what was it? Something about alphas liking it all the time, which must mean he didn't. Couldn't? Didn't expect to, certainly, so whatever he was offering, the most he could get out of it was pleasing his alpha. Beau had no intention of being another alpha like *that* in Rory's life.

He didn't realize he'd tightened his grip until Rory squirmed against it, and then Beau had to tuck his head down and breathe in Rory's scent. It was only the moon, he knew, but clearly this was no time to think about letting Rory go.

"Sleep," Rory mumbled, pressing his lips against Beau's collarbone. "S'okay, honey, I'm here. Go to sleep."

Whether it was the moon or the warmth of Rory in his arms or that drowsily unhesitating command, Beau was powerless to resist.

CHAPTER 14

*R*ory woke up at the rising of the sun, the first hour of the day after the empty moon, while the moon was still down. Tonight, if the sky was clear, there might be a sliver of moon visible in the west after the sun set. A new waxing moon. A new start.

Beau was wrapped around him from behind, one arm resting heavily over his waist, and as soon as Rory was awake he knew that Beau was too. Beau nuzzled at the bare back of his head, and Rory shivered and squirmed a little.

Beau's hips jerked back, away from him, and Rory went still. The day before was abruptly clear in his mind, along with the way it had descended from promising beginnings into something he'd think of as a disaster if he didn't have much worse things to compare it to.

Rory reached behind him, grabbing a fold of Beau's t-shirt. He couldn't think of the words to say *don't go* or *I'm sorry* or *give me another chance* in a way Beau would believe. A way that would make him not think Rory was crazy, broken, too fragile to touch, or liable to explode at any moment.

Beau's grip on him changed, pushing and tugging gently at the same time, and Rory let Beau prod him to roll over and face him.

Beau looked worried, of course, because how else should Beau look at him? What else could Rory ever be but a worry to him?

"Do you want to talk about yesterday?" Beau asked, a little line appearing between his eyebrows. "Right now what I know is that I shouldn't touch you when you can't see me, and it makes you nervous to have strange alphas in our house. Or at least those are my best guesses. Is there something else I should know?"

Rory opened and closed his mouth, trying to fit that together with anything he'd been thinking, anything he'd ever expected. It was so... *Beau.*

"I like waking up with you," Rory said, which was maybe not what Beau meant. It was still what Rory wanted him to know. "I like you holding me while we sleep."

Beau's expression softened, and he tugged Rory closer. Rory closed the small space between them, nestling in.

"Yesterday morning," Beau said next to his ear. "What you offered... you don't have to do anything for me that isn't gonna be good for you too, okay? You can wake up with me without that."

It was supposed to be a relief, Rory knew. He was supposed to be glad Beau wouldn't demand, wouldn't push, that he could have the good parts without the rest. But something about it made him want to bristle, to push back.

He'd gotten good at swallowing that impulse, though. And Beau wasn't saying *never*, exactly. Rory could probably figure out a way around that, a way to convince Beau that he would like it even without being in heat. Maybe he'd even figure out why the hell he wanted to.

For now he nodded against Beau's shoulder and enjoyed his alpha's embrace.

～

Wednesday was a whole different kind of ordeal from the day before. Rory dressed carefully in his wedding clothes, and let Beau tuck the cravat around his neck. He wished for Susan to fix up his face, but there was no point wishing; he had to go out into the world with Beau and the face he had was just going to have to do.

"Tell me when you're tired," Beau said before they left. "Or if it's too much, or... anything. I'll do everything I can to make this as easy for you as I can."

Rory nodded, and summoned up a tiny smile. "It's traditional to look terrible in ID pictures anyway, isn't it?"

Beau smiled back and kissed his forehead, and didn't debate the point.

At the DMV, Beau did most of the talking, getting his application for a new driver's license and then explaining that Rory needed a state ID, passing Rory's papers across the desk to be scrutinized. They were able to sit together while they waited, but then their numbers were called at the same time. Beau looked worried, so there was nothing for Rory to do but gather up his own papers and march over to the window he'd been called to.

He slid everything across, and the clerk—human, naturally— glanced through it and nodded to herself, starting to type things on her computer. Rory glanced at the screen, blurry green on black, and looked away without trying to read anything.

He only nodded when she rattled off his and Beau's new address, and confirmed the spelling of his name.

"Eye color..." she looked at him, then back to her computer. "Green. Hair color?"

Rory raised a hand to his head, feeling the patchwork of stubble and... huh, fuzz, rather than the slick bare places he'd been expecting. He cleared his throat. "Blond?"

"Blond," she agreed. "Height and weight?"

Rory bit his lip. "Five... eight? One thirty?"

She snorted, but didn't argue with his overestimates. "Human or werewolf?"

"Wolf," Rory whispered.

She nodded, unperturbed, and typed it in. "Okay. Thirty-five dollars."

Rory panicked for a second—*money*, he hadn't thought about

money, how was he going to pay?—and then he remembered and stuck his hand in his pocket. Beau had given him "walking around" money again. Hopefully it was enough. He passed the bills blindly through the window. The clerk raised an eyebrow and pushed two back, then put two in the drawer and returned a five, along with a slip of paper. "Go on over to the photo line."

Rory nodded jerkily, shoving his remaining cash into his pocket and taking the paper. Beau was still at another window.

Rory wanted to go to him but didn't want to distract him, or annoy his clerk. After two different people nearly ran into him where he stood dithering between the seats and the service counter, he gritted his teeth and walked off to the photo line, labeled with a sign big enough for even Rory to read. It was where he was supposed to be, and it wasn't as if Beau wouldn't be able to find him. Beau would have to get a photo taken himself, so he would come to the same place. Eventually.

Beau did walk over, but only to say, "I have to go take the test to get my license—right over there. You can go out to the car when you're done or wait for me here."

Rory leaned into him for just a second—that was a benefit to not wearing makeup, at least he didn't have to worry about smearing it on Beau's shirt. "I'll wait here."

When Beau found him again he was sitting on a folding chair around the corner from the photo area. He'd stopped seeing spots, and if he closed one eye and squinted he could recognize his own face in the little picture, and make out the word MINNESOTA across the top of the card.

"Hey," Beau said, crouching down in front of him. "How'd it come out?"

Rory looked at Beau, and back down at the card. He hadn't ever had anything like it before, not a real one, with his own name and birthdate and even proclaiming *Werewolf* right next to his hair and eye colors.

"It's real," Rory said, looking down at the little card. "It's... I'm... real."

Beau hugged him and kissed the top of his head and didn't tell him that was silly.

~

Rory made it through a visit to a big warehouse store to pick up all the things Beau hadn't bought before coming home for the empty moon, and lunch, and a trip to the bank where he was added to all of Beau's accounts and signed up for a debit card, and then got his own accounts that weren't connected to Beau's. He didn't know where he was ever going to get money to put in them, except... except that Beau was supposed to pay him, once they got divorced. So the accounts were probably Beau's way of saying he could do that whenever he wanted.

Of course Beau wouldn't want to have sex with him, not when he was going to send Rory away. He wouldn't want to get tempted to bite him in the middle of things and then be stuck with him. He would save all of that for an omega he really wanted, one who could fill up their house with dark-eyed, round-cheeked babies, while Rory was off somewhere alone, living on the money Beau sent him.

Rory very carefully did not crumple up the paperwork when that occurred to him, just stared down at it on his lap.

"I think this has been plenty for today, don't you?" Beau said beside him. "Ready to head home?"

Rory nodded and closed his eyes, and didn't open them until they were in the driveway again.

~

"Well," Beau said, when they'd both changed into more comfortable clothes and had a snack. "I think the time has come to start breaking in the new stuff."

It would be hours yet until darkness, until the brief sliver of moon that meant it was waxing, but Rory's thoughts went immediately to the two wide beds in two separate bedrooms upstairs. The sheets were in a box on top of the washing machine in the basement, the pillows and blankets and all the rest piled up in their respective bedrooms.

Then Beau sat down on the big, navy couch in the living room, angling himself into a corner of it so his legs sprawled onto the middle cushion. He patted the cushion beside his thigh. "Come here, baby, let's just relax for a little while."

Rory exhaled and settled onto the couch, stretching his legs out and leaning against Beau's chest. Beau held him there, slouching down a little more, and Rory nestled in as close as he could. Beau might plan on sending him away someday, but there was still time. For now, Rory still had his alpha.

He fell asleep to the sound of Beau's heartbeat.

∽

They slept downstairs again that night, without discussing it at all.

"Tomorrow," Rory said, when they were snuggled together in their familiar bed. "Big day, huh? Dr. Jeffries?"

Beau blew out a breath. "Yeah. I mean, it's just orientation, but... yeah. Big day." He tightened his arm around Rory and added, "I'm... I'm glad you're here with me, Rory. I didn't like being told I needed someone, but being alone through the last few days would've been..."

He shook his head, then pressed a kiss to the back of Rory's.

Rory frowned, picturing it. If Beau hadn't brought him along... well, he probably wouldn't have gotten such a huge place, or bought so much new stuff to fill it up.

In fact, he probably would have moved into another tiny studio, so he wouldn't have had much to do at all for the last few days; he could have... relaxed, or explored his new town, or...

Somehow, all Rory could actually picture Beau doing was sleeping curled up in this bed, all alone through the empty moon with no one to hold, no one to help him make a strange place feel like home. Rory reached down to set his hand over Beau's where Beau was holding him, and interlaced their fingers. "I'm glad I'm here too."

~

He woke up briefly to Beau sitting down on the edge of the mattress beside him. He was wearing khakis and a polo shirt, smelling minty and clean.

"Time to go already?" Rory mumbled. The moon wasn't even up yet, though the sun was.

"Yeah, thought I might as well let you sleep. Call me anytime you want, I'll listen to my messages as soon as I have a chance. I'm not sure when I'll be home—the scheduled stuff runs until five, but there might be some official-unofficial stuff after, dinner or whatever. I'll call and let you know if it's going to be later than six, okay?"

Rory nodded, and when he reached out, Beau leaned down and kissed his cheek. Rory turned his head to kiss back, his mouth landing just at the corner of Beau's, and then Beau was smiling and tucking him back in.

When Rory woke up again, he knew for absolutely certain that he was alone in the house. It wasn't quite as awful as the day before yesterday, when Beau had gone off without him after Rory hit him and the empty moon was sinking toward the horizon, but it was still weird.

Before the last few days, Rory couldn't remember the last time he'd been this alone—not just alone in a room, but alone in an entire building, and with a big, empty margin all around it.

When he was alone in Beau's apartment, or in the refuge, or anywhere he'd lived before that, there were still other people somewhere in the building, or across the narrow firebreak in the next building, or walking or driving on the street within earshot. He could always hear voices, footsteps, car engines, all the clattering and banging of people getting on with their lives.

This was... quiet. He could hear the house itself creaking, water in the pipes... If he focused, letting himself hear farther than he'd trained himself to in order to survive in the city, there were neighbors, and cars on the main road a couple of blocks away. Dogs and cats and kids.

It sounded like being home. It sounded like being a kid in a subdivision not so different from this; letting himself hear at the level of the neighborhood felt strange and dangerous for a few seconds and then almost painfully familiar.

He got up and put the new sheets in the washer, to let the rushing and churning water fill up some of the silence in the house. He washed himself and put on clean clothes, making a little pile of his own dirty things to wash next.

That led to him sniffing out Beau's dirty laundry, which he found in a hamper in the upstairs bathroom. He scooped it up into his arms, inhaling Beau's scent, and then caught something he hadn't smelled on Beau before. It was just a trace, but...

Rory folded down to his knees and buried his face in Beau's laundry, including the boxers he'd taken off just a few hours ago, the boxers that carried a lingering trace of—not just arousal, but precome. They must have had a wet patch on them by the time Beau took them off.

Beau had left him sleeping and come upstairs to jerk off, then showered himself clean. He'd only come back to say goodbye to Rory when there was no hint of desire or completion left to smell on him.

It made him think of Beau sleeping sitting up on the floor, of Beau waking up confused and asking Rory if *he* was all right. It made him think of Beau alone on the empty moon—on how many empty moons in that studio apartment?—and what Beau had said about how long he'd been alone, how he'd never had sex with anyone.

He found himself thinking of Beau not as an alpha, but just... a person, a person who was alone and jerked off because he had no other options. It felt strange to think of an alpha, his alpha, that way. *Since I was sixteen*, Beau had said, and Rory looked down at his jeans, which had been Beau's jeans when he was about that age.

He thought of himself at sixteen. Of that hunger not to be alone, that constant urge to find someone who would understand him, who would want to keep him, not just in spite of what he was but because of it.

Rory used to jerk off a lot, back then. He'd get hard, get wet, at the touch of a stiff breeze. By sixteen he was pretty shameless when he did something about it, sliding his fingers into himself, using his own slick to jack himself. He'd thought all the time of how much better it would be when he wasn't alone, when it wasn't his own hands. When he had an alpha to fuck him, to satisfy the hunger inside him that was never filled.

Rory pressed his face more deliberately into Beau's clothes, remembering and imagining, and he felt the faint stir in his body. It wasn't exactly desire, definitely nothing like he'd felt when he was young and unbroken, but there was a possibility there, something waking up.

His hand shook a little as he unfastened his—*Beau's*—jeans and reached in to stroke his cock through his underwear. He wasn't hard, but maybe a little chubbed up, and then he thought of what it would be like if it was Beau's hand touching him. Beau's hand, just as gentle as his own, but bigger, stronger. Not his own trembling, uncertain touch but a firm stroke.

Rory whined softly into Beau's laundry and palmed himself, rubbing up and down as his cock firmed up.

It wouldn't be just Beau's hand; Beau would be holding him, wrapped around him, talking in his ear. Calling him *baby* and telling him...

This isn't practice, baby. This is real. You and me, this is real. You're mine. I'll take care of you.

Rory's breath was getting fast and shaky, and he pulled his hand out of his pants and shoved it back in, inside his underwear this time, to curl his fingers around his cock. Half-hard outside of heat, for the first time in ages.

For Beau. If Beau would just touch him, it would feel like this, but better. It would be good for him, and he would be good for Beau, if Beau would just—if Beau wanted—

The image fractured, taking his certainty with it, and that tentative spark of desire flickered and failed.

The only thing he knew for sure that Beau would do was leave him sleeping and jerk off alone in the shower. Beau had said *what we do is real*, but then he had made sure not to do anything at all with Rory. Even his kiss goodbye had been on Rory's cheek, and he'd pulled away before Rory could try for a better one.

This might be real, but it was temporary. Beau had obviously been willing to go right on being alone and looking after himself, if he hadn't had to bring Rory along to his residency. If he wanted to keep on waiting for someone better, someone he really wanted...

But he's the one I want, Rory thought. *I could wait all my life and I'd never find anyone better than him.*

Rory wiped his eyes on Beau's t-shirt, getting another breath of his scent.

Then I'll just have to try to be someone he could want.

He had three years to work on it. Three years to convince Beau to want him. That had to be enough time. Didn't it?

He pushed himself up to his feet, still holding on to Beau's laundry. Being someone who could do a few chores when Beau was working all day would probably be a good start.

CHAPTER 15

*B*eau had hoped that jerking off in the shower would make him *less* likely to spend his first day of residency orientation sexually frustrated and unable to stop thinking about Rory, but by fifteen minutes into the program director's opening remarks, it was obvious that he had miscalculated. Badly.

When he woke up, snuggled close to Rory and rock hard, he had known that he had to get out of bed as quickly as possible. He hadn't let himself hesitate. He had resolved just the night before not to start anything with Rory, and he especially didn't want Rory waking up like that, maybe not even remembering who he was with right away and reacting on instinct.

On the other hand, he couldn't leave without saying goodbye. But that meant that he'd left with the warm smell of a drowsy omega in his nose and clinging to his clothes for the rest of the day. When Rory had tried to make that goodbye peck into a real kiss...

Beau forced his attention back to the speaker just in time to hear her say, "The most diverse group of residents we've ever accepted."

Beau sat very still and tried to school his features to unconcerned calm, as though nothing she was saying had anything to do with him.

If she said his name, if the other fifty-one residents all turned to look around for the werewolf in their midst...

But she moved on into other platitudes, about how the program wanted to support them all and hoped they would support each other. Beau carefully didn't look around to see if any of them looked like they knew what she meant, what he was. He didn't intend to keep it a secret, but he hadn't contemplated being put on display to the rest of the residents.

No one did anything obvious, but that was almost worse. He spent the next couple of hours grimly attending to the overviews and introductions, increasingly aware of being *surrounded by humans*. He usually didn't notice that at all—he spent most of his time mostly surrounded by humans—but after the last several days spending nearly all his time alone with Rory, it was jarring. Even in med school, he'd at least had the other werewolf students and Dr. Pavlyuchenko. In this gathering of residents and administrators, there weren't even any werewolf security guards for him to carefully not acknowledge. He was on his own completely.

By lunchtime he didn't even bother trying to make himself sit among the other residents to eat, grabbing his box lunch from the long table and retreating out of the building to sit in the first shady spot he found where he could see and hear for a little way around. He pulled out his phone and was disappointed, and startled by his own disappointment, when he realized Rory hadn't called or texted at all.

It didn't mean anything; he'd been half asleep when Beau told him he could call, and Rory might be sleeping in, or getting settled into the house, or exploring the neighborhood, or...

Or wondering whether Beau's invitation to call had been an order to check in.

Beau hesitated another few seconds—would Rory think he *was* checking in if he called?—and then decided that knowing was better than not-knowing and tapped the button.

The phone went on ringing long enough that Beau realized they'd never set up Rory's voice mail, and then Rory picked up, sounding breathless. "Beau! Hi, sorry, I was just making up the beds and I left my phone downstairs, so I—I hope you weren't waiting long?"

"No," Beau said, his stomach sinking at the thought of those damn beds on the second floor, in their separate bedrooms, which Rory apparently intended to make ready to use by tonight. "No, I... it's no problem. I just wanted to hear your voice."

"Oh!" Beau listened to Rory's breathing evening out and wished he weren't limited to what the phone could pick up, that he could hear Rory's heartbeat and smell his scent, but even his breathing was familiar and comforting right now. "Um. Anything in particular you wanted to hear about?"

Tell me you need me, Beau thought. *Tell me you're scared and I need to come home right now.*

Beau shook off the thought, wondering if anyone would find it ironic that having an omega at home was bringing out the caveman-alpha instincts he'd spent his entire adult life learning to control, instead of making him more human-friendly and stable.

"Tell me..." Beau glanced down at his unappetizing lunch. "Tell me what you're going to have for lunch? Or did you eat already?"

"Oh," Rory said. "Hm, I guess... sandwiches, probably? I, uh, I'm not much of a cook. Maybe I should work on that, now that I've—we've—got this big kitchen. I have plenty of time, and you'll be too busy for it."

Beau wanted to say *you don't have to* but the thought of his omega at home, cooking, was too soothing to argue with. And he shouldn't discourage Rory from learning new things, anyway.

"You can try anything you want," Beau offered. "I promise not to mind if you burn everything as long as you don't hurt yourself doing it."

Rory made a small noise Beau couldn't interpret, and he felt the urge to be near him race through his whole body. He needed to see Rory's face, to hear his heartbeat, to smell his scent and feel the warmth of his skin. How else could he know what Rory meant by little sounds like that? How else could he know what Rory needed?

"I did manage to do the laundry without wrecking anything," Rory said, his voice gone flat and colorless. "Didn't even flood the basement."

Beau winced, realizing then what he'd implied about Rory burning things. "Of course, baby. I didn't mean... thanks for doing that, though. I appreciate it."

"No problem," Rory muttered. There was some expression back in his voice, but it was all unhappiness.

Beau had no idea how to fix this; he was blundering around in a minefield. Getting off the phone wouldn't be better, and... he just wanted to talk to Rory, to feel close to him and forget about all the humans he was going to have to face again when the lunch break was over.

"I..." Beau picked up the box lunch. "I have to eat my lunch, but if you don't mind listening to me chew, would you, um... tell me about your favorite thing to eat? Cooking aside, just... all-time favorite?"

It was something he should know about the omega he was married to, wasn't it?

"Oh, hmm." Rory sounded thoughtful, less unhappy. Beau unwrapped his lunch and took a bite of his sandwich, so Rory would know he wouldn't be interrupted and could take his time. "Well, I don't have much of a sweet tooth, I guess. I know it's usually like... cake or, or... something like that, something special, or... fancy."

Beau *mm*ed encouragingly, the best he could do with his mouth full.

Rory was quiet a little longer, while Beau grimly ate his lunch, and finally he said, tentatively, "Fried chicken, maybe? No, that's—"

"Hey, if you like it, you like it," Beau put in. "Tell me?"

"Well, it's just... It's always good, I guess? It's not like... my mom didn't have some secret family recipe or something. I can only remember her making it a few times, and I think she just used whatever Penzeys mix was in the cupboard—"

Beau didn't mean to interrupt again, but, "Penzeys mix?"

"Penzeys, you know, the... the spice store?" Rory offered hesitantly.

Beau still had absolutely no idea what he was talking about, but he just crammed down another bite of sandwich and waited for him to keep talking.

"It was... there were so many things to smell in there, Georgie and I would go kind of nuts. Mom always wound up sending us to wait outside. Even then every time the door opened you could smell more things on the air from inside. We would beg to go just about every time we drove by, and I think my mom only ever bought one tiny little jar at a time, but... I guess she must have liked it too," Rory said, his wistful tone turning thoughtful. "Huh, I never thought... but I guess if we liked getting to smell everything, she must have too, didn't she? She was just a little less, uh," Rory laughed softly. "Less hyper about it."

"Sounds like it," Beau dared to offer. "What else did she make with the spices from the store?"

"Oh," Rory said, huffing out a breath. "I mean... everything? There was one for barbecue, one for meatloaf, one for... well, like four or five different ones for muffins or cookies or cake..."

Beau's mouth watered at the thought of all that home-cooked food, and he used it to push himself through the rest of his lunch, letting the sound of Rory's voice soothe him until Rory abruptly said, "Beau, how long is your lunch break? I've been talking forever."

Beau forced his attention back inside the building, and heard the unmistakable sounds of humans settling back into the lecture hall. "Shit, yeah, I should go. But I—" *I would rather keep listening to you talk about anything at all.*

He wouldn't. He was here to learn, to train, to do the most important thing in the world. To save lives. It was just hard to remember that when he could hear Rory breathing on the other end of the line.

"Thank you," Beau said, standing up with the wrappers from his lunch in hand. "For keeping me company."

"Oh," Rory said, sounding surprised all over again. "Oh, you're—you're welcome, Beau. Of course." With a sliver of shy humor in his voice he added, "Anytime. My schedule is pretty flexible."

Beau felt a little more even-keeled with the echo of Rory's voice lingering in his ears, and the knowledge that he had managed to steer them—mostly, probably—back out of the ditch he'd run the conversation into to begin with. There were two more hours of lectures after lunch, and then they were turned loose in a large open hall to attend to various administrative tasks: getting their ID cards, filling out paperwork, and so on.

Beau listened to the conversations going on around him, his fellow new residents introducing themselves and comparing backgrounds. He should join in, he knew, but then he would have to decide whether he had to tell them what he was, or wonder if they already knew, or...

He kept his head down, pretending to be engrossed in his phone, and kept his body language uninviting. There would be time to meet people, to get to know them, and figure out how to let them get to know him. It didn't have to happen today, in this chaos.

Beau was waiting to get his ID card after having his picture taken. Something had gone wrong with the printer, and one of the staffers was cursing quietly at it and possibly sending a frantic message to IT, judging by the frantic pace of thumb-taps against touch-screen. Beau eased away to the edge of the group, putting himself a little farther away from the smell of stress verging on panic, and was wondering if he could get away with calling Rory again when he felt a touch on his arm.

Beau turned, looking to see whether he was in someone's way, and went carefully still at the sight of the man standing there. He wasn't physically imposing—he was about Rory's height and had a slim, wiry build, but he was white-haired, wearing wire-rimmed glasses. He had introduced himself earlier, during one of the first overview talks; he had seemed taller when he was up on stage.

His name was Dr. Evan Ross, and he was Beau's adviser for the next three years. Which meant it would be up to him to determine whether Beau was meeting the requirements of the residency.

"Dr. Ross," Beau said, trying to unfreeze, to assume some reasonably friendly expression. "I, ah..."

Meetings with advisers were scheduled tomorrow. Beau hadn't been ready for this yet.

Dr. Ross smiled and patted Beau's arm. "It's all right, you're not being graded just yet. But I thought, given your unique situation, we ought to chat a little before our scheduled meeting. If you have a moment?"

Beau nodded. There was clearly no other answer.

He followed Dr. Ross out of the huge echoing hall full of his fellow residents to a blessedly empty and quiet conference room. Dr. Ross took a seat near one end of the table, and at his casual-looking gesture, Beau took the seat across from him. Dr. Ross set down some folders in front of him, folding his hands atop them. Beau set down his own slim collection of papers, thankful that he hadn't collected his scrubs and white coat yet.

"So, elephant in the room: you're a werewolf, I'm not, no one in the administration here is that I'm aware of. I suppose you would know better than I?"

Beau elected to honor the breezy tone and echoed it as well as he could manage. "I suppose I might be able to tell, if I worked with someone. But unless they acknowledged themselves to me, I would not acknowledge them."

Dr. Pavlyuchenko, for instance, was treated as human by everyone at Northwestern. Beau honestly wasn't sure whether they knew why he took an interest in all the werewolf students and were turning a blind eye, or genuinely didn't care, or if he had actually managed to keep his own secret through the general Revelation. One did not ask.

Dr. Ross nodded amiable understanding. "Werewolves don't out each other."

Beau tilted his head. "It's not a matter of loyalty to each other. We don't... intrude upon others' privacy, despite what our senses allow. What is heard or smelled or sensed is treated as invisible until one is invited to notice; otherwise we would have a difficult time living with each other."

"Ah," Dr. Ross. "And this allows you not to be a perpetual walking violation of patient privacy?"

"I protect patients' privacy the same as any other health professional," Beau said carefully. "Anyone could see things, or overhear things, when working in a hospital or clinic."

Dr. Ross nodded. "But if I am not mistaken, you intend to make active use of your senses, for diagnostic purposes."

Beau nodded. "I believe—with training, and with some work to document the accuracy of my observations—that I could be a big help to diagnosis. Non-invasive, faster than lab tests—"

"Non-invasive as long as the vulnerable human patient doesn't consider being sniffed by a werewolf invasive," Dr. Ross interposed, in the same mild tone as before. "And prone to human—pardon me, mortal? personal?—error, in a way that lab tests are not."

"I have no objection to being referred to as human in that sense," Beau said, carefully even. "It's not offensive. And it's not as if lab tests have no margin for human error either. I'm not suggesting that I should personally replace all other diagnostic tests, I just—I want to help, the same as anyone becoming a doctor. And I have this special ability to help, and I want to learn to use it. Rochester seemed like the best possible place to do that."

Dr. Ross nodded, as if that was exactly the answer he expected. "Well, we shall certainly see. And in any case, you came highly recommended. Exemplary applicant, apart from being an unattached alpha werewolf."

Now they came to it. "No longer unattached, in fact. I brought my husband with me to Rochester."

Dr. Ross's eyebrows went up, and he sat back slightly; the little jump in his heart rate might have indicated some actual mild surprise. Beau did not speculate.

"Ah, well. Congratulations, of course. You married very recently, I take it?"

Beau did not react visibly. He was jumping through their hoop. He would not give them reason to believe he was some kind of half-feral lone-wolf menace. "Last week, in fact. But it's not unusual for werewolves to bond quickly."

Dr. Ross nodded slowly. "Yes, I... when discussing your situation with a few local werewolves, they did mention that. Once you met someone with whom you felt compatible, you were likely to move quickly."

Beau had to take a careful breath to steady himself, keeping his reaction invisible. "You... discussed me?"

"Yes, well, having assumed that you would need a bit of additional support from your adviser, and that your adviser would need a bit of advice himself on how best to supply it..." Dr. Ross opened a folder and withdrew a sheet of paper. Contact information.

Niemi pack. Jensen pack. Bryson pack. Fraser pack.

"Those are the individuals who were identified to me as appropriate to contact for a new werewolf in town looking to form a temporary alliance or join a pack. Obviously there's no knowing who you might be compatible with, or if you already have some family ties...?"

Beau honestly had no idea. He'd been an angry kid, and an alpha; for as much time as he'd hung around the pack's omega midwives trying to learn what little there was to know about the werewolf version of medical practice, he hadn't taken much interest in the other traditional omega concerns, like genealogy and the maintenance of pack connections. He might have cousins in any of these packs—hell, if things had gone differently, any of these packs might have been his intended destination for his exchange year.

But he'd turned his back on all of that in order to be here. And they had turned their backs on him. He wasn't signing up to go through that all over again.

Still, he knew the correct response. He manufactured a smile, and tucked the sheet into his own folder. "Thank you, sir. I'll take it under advisement."

After that came another hour of standing in a huge, echoing room surrounded by humans, humans he had to smile and speak politely to. He knew he should be making more effort to observe the people around him, to get a feel for his classmates and the staff. But it was all he could do to hold down the feeling of being utterly alone among strangers, among people who might hate him or fear him if they knew, and he couldn't help focusing his senses down to the tightest possible range.

On the bright side, his staggeringly unsociable behavior meant he wasn't roped into any of the shared meals or excursions for drinks he heard being organized. It was a relief, an escape, and still he found himself remembering his first year of medical school, being automatically and irresistibly included among the werewolf students.

At that point he'd already been on his own for six years, with only passing contact with other werewolves. He hadn't thought he needed them, had been prepared to resent their intrusions into his life, but they hadn't been that kind of pack, and now...

Now he had Rory waiting for him at home.

He found the rental car and started reversing his route from that morning. They really were going to need to go buy a car. Sunday? It would have to be Sunday. The barbecue was Saturday, and Beau had no idea how long it took to buy a car properly, but he had to guess it wasn't something he could run out and do before lunch on a Saturday.

He was exhaustedly turning over the logistics of it, and hoping that the local werewolf credit union would trust him with a car loan on top of his brand new mortgage, in between bouts of dreading the next day and the social gauntlet of the barbecue, when he pulled into the driveway of his house.

Beau just sat for a moment, staring at it. *I live here now. We live here.*

Rory wasn't waiting for him on the porch, and the front door didn't open as he sat there. He felt another lonely pang, and shoved the feeling away as soon as he recognized it. Rory was probably sleeping, or busy with something around the house.

But what if something was wrong? What if he was hurt, or he'd tried to hike off to the nearest grocery store, miles away, or—

Beau flung himself out of the car, leaving everything from orientation piled on the passenger seat, and hurried up to the front door, unlocking it and pushing through only to come to a sharp halt.

Rory looked up at him, blinking as though he was just awakening, or coming out of some trance. He was sitting in front of one of the bookshelves, all of Beau's battered old paperbacks piled around him, from when he used to have time to read. Rory was holding a book in his hands, open to page 43. *A Canticle for Leibowitz*, Beau recognized, as Rory kept staring at him.

"Rory? Are you—is everything—"

"I was just going to see if I could alphabetize them," Rory said, looking back down at the book. "And then I recognized this one and I... I just... started reading. I forgot what I was doing because I was reading."

Beau felt the entire day evaporate off his shoulders as he grinned, and he barely remembered to push the door shut behind him before he hurried over to Rory. He knelt down beside him and hugged him, book and all. "That's great, baby. That's so great."

Rory grabbed a fold of his shirt, hiding his face against Beau's shoulder, and Beau added lightly, "Plus, you have good taste. You've read that one before?"

"Yeah, my d—I mean, um. When I was a kid. We had tons of books. I liked thinking about what the werewolves were doing in this universe. I thought lots of us would've survived. Maybe some of the monks were werewolves."

Beau was grinning as he sat back. "Yeah, I thought about that too."

The post-apocalyptic monks had seemed like the furthest thing from his own pack, when Beau read this book the first time, the summer after he left Chicago. Dedicated to preserving knowledge, protecting it, not ignoring it all and punishing anyone who tried to—

Beau shook that thought off. Rory was looking down at the book again.

"Our house, when I was a kid," Rory said quietly. "I don't think I realized how much it smelled like books in our house until I opened up the boxes of books here."

My dad, Rory had almost said, talking about the book. And earlier, when he was telling Beau about that spice store, talking about his mom and his sister... he must have grown up in a house, and a town, more or less like this, somewhere in Wisconsin. Living like humans, until his heats betrayed him and revealed his mother's secret, and he was sent away. And then he'd left his mother's pack only a few years later, and apparently never looked back, even when the only safe place for him was the refuge.

"Do you..." Beau set a hand on Rory's knee. "Do you want to get in touch with them, Rory? Maybe just your mom, or your sister? I bet they'd like to know that you're okay."

CHAPTER 16

*R*ory stared at Beau in silence for a moment, barely understanding the question. He'd just been jerked out of so many different layers of escape—reading the book, feeling again like the kid who got lost in this book in a different sunny house on a summer day—and then realizing what he'd been doing, that he'd been able to read it—that for a second he didn't understand why anyone should be wondering where he was. It wasn't even dinnertime yet.

Then it hit him all at once: Beau was asking if he wanted to call his mom, or Georgie, and tell them that he was okay.

He looked around vaguely, considering the fact that for the first time in a very long time, he *was* okay. Safe. In a house. With his husband.

His mom and Georgie hadn't seen him get married.

His mom and Georgie *didn't know where he was.*

Beau's arms went around him suddenly, hauling him in tight to Beau's chest.

"Sorry, baby, I didn't mean—I didn't think. I know that's a lot, that's a big decision. I'm sorry."

Rory shook his head against Beau's chest, clutching at his shirt. "I just—I hadn't even thought, I—I was—"

Beau curled around him, tucking his nose against Rory's throat, "I am batting a fucking thousand for ruining things every time I talk to you today, huh? I'm so sorry. I'm so glad your eyes are better, Ror."

Georgie used to call him that. They'd drawn pictures of themselves as monsters: JOR and ROR, giggling at the red eyes and menacing fangs they gave themselves, at least until their mother snatched the crayon picture away, pale with horror or fury or both.

You're not monsters, she'd told them fiercely. *You may be different but you are not monsters. You don't hurt people. There's nothing wrong with you.*

His mother had been pale the last time he'd seen her, but the ferocity was long gone by then. She had seemed tired, and not just from the four-hour drive up north to visit him at the pack lands. She never spoke of her husband, though she would tell him about Georgie and his baby brother, Spencer, who was eight years old by then. She didn't bring him drawings from Spencer or notes from Georgie anymore. He had learned to stop asking if Georgie could come with her one day, or even stay with the pack for a while.

He had thought it would be a relief for her not to have to visit him anymore, to be able to forget. But she had held him as tightly as ever before she left, hugging him close. She had brought him a sweater; she knew how much colder it got up north. She had told him she loved him.

He still remembered the phone number of the house where he had grown up. If she still lived there, if the number hadn't changed—if she was the one to pick up the phone, and not...

"I was going to make dinner," he mumbled into Beau's shirt. "I was... I was going to make something."

"Yeah," Beau said, and pressed a kiss to the top of his head. "Well, now we can do it together."

~

By the time they made and ate dinner, it was obvious to Rory that Beau was exhausted. He was just about falling asleep with his eyes open as they washed the dishes together.

The beds upstairs were neatly made, with freshly washed sheets that had a faint, pleasant soap smell, nothing like plastic and strange places. And nothing like anything else, either. Nothing like either of them.

The smell of the food they had shared lingered in the kitchen, and Beau's books were filling up the shelves in the living room, but nothing upstairs smelled familiar. Rory didn't want to sleep up there, and he didn't want to send Beau to sleep alone there either, not unless Beau said it was what he wanted.

So far, Beau seemed to want to stay by Rory's side, even when he was dozing off on his feet.

"How was it today?" Rory asked, mostly just to make sure Beau would stay awake while he scrubbed out the pot. "Busy?"

"It, uh... yeah, I guess," Beau said.

Rory waited, wondering what filled all the blank, unknown time Beau had spent away from him, other than that phone call, when he had just wanted Rory to talk, not to tell Rory about anything that was happening.

"It was—" Beau yawned, and Rory ducked his head as he yawned too. "Uh, most of the day was just sitting in a lecture hall while fifteen different people welcomed us, and they talked generally about what we'll be doing, how things will work this year. And—oh, it's still out in the car, I should get that. I picked up scrubs and stuff for rotations, and got my ID, and—" Beau yawned again, "Met my adviser."

Beau's heartbeat changed a little, the scent of him going tense and unhappy, but he didn't explain beyond that.

"Did you... tell them about me? About..." That was why Rory was here, after all, to make sure they let Beau stay in his residency, to show that he wasn't alone or untrustworthy.

Beau nodded quickly, smiling at Rory and turning to lean against the counter. Rory returned his attention to pot-scrubbing.

"Yeah, he said that was good. He seemed kind of surprised, like they didn't think I would've found someone so soon, but we've got each other, huh? So we're all right."

Rory rinsed the pot and gave Beau a smile as he handed it over to be dried.

"Come on," he said, when they were all finished, "Let's break in another couch."

"Perfect," Beau said. "I'm just going to grab my stuff from the car, I need to look over some of it before tomorrow."

Rory went back to the living room, studying the pile of books, and then picked up *A Canticle for Leibowitz* again. Beau came back in with an armload of plastic-wrapped clothes and a stack of folders, and Rory took the clothes from him. "You don't have to wear these tomorrow, do you?"

Beau shook his head, looking confused.

"They're gonna smell awful," Rory pointed out. "I'll wash them before you need them. Now come on."

"Oh, I can," Beau started, but Rory just turned away to drop the pile of wrapped clothes on the dining table and continue into the family room. Beau followed him, and soon they were tucked together on the couch, their legs tangled together and Rory's head tipped against Beau's chest, the book propped on a pillow in front of him.

He let his eyes close instead of finding his place and trying to read again. He was a little afraid it wouldn't work now, but he also just... still had the things Beau had said rattling around in his head.

We've got each other, so we're all right.

I bet they'd like to know that you're okay.

Were there people who wanted to know that *Beau* was okay? Well, of course he was okay. He was an alpha, a doctor; he hadn't needed Rory in the same way Rory had needed him. To prove himself to humans, yes, but not to *survive*.

But Rory knew how hard it was to be alone. It wasn't like he'd never walked out on a shitty alpha, even before that last time when he finally found his way to the refuge. Even when he was still healthy, he hadn't found it easy to make ends meet on his own, but it was also just... *hard*. To see headlines and news stories about yet another werewolf shot by the cops, werewolves suspected of this or that violent crime, and wonder if you were hiding enough, if the humans around you suspected what you were. To spend empty moons alone, to have no safe place, no pack, no one to turn to who understood.

That was how he'd always wound up with another shitty alpha who treated him worse than the last. And he didn't think it was so completely different for alphas. Beau seemed dead on his feet after today—after all that time alone with strange humans who maybe didn't want him there, maybe didn't want him to succeed at this thing that was so important to him that he'd married Rory just for the chance to do it. He'd been alone such a long time, and now that he had someone, it was just... Rory. He could barely look after himself, and now he was all that someone else had. He could call Susan for advice, but still, it was only him that Beau would come home to, needing comfort and a safe place.

If Rory could call his mom—which was an awfully big if, considering everything that had happened before and since he left the pack —could Beau call his?

Beau didn't have anything to be ashamed of about the years he'd been alone; he'd been a paramedic, saving people. He'd put himself through college and med school so he could be a doctor and save even more lives. Who wouldn't be proud of him? Who wouldn't want to count him as part of their family, part of their pack?

He tried to remember exactly what Beau had said about how he ended up alone. His pack hadn't approved of him wanting to be a doctor, and they'd almost driven him out? That couldn't be the whole story, not for Beau to have been so utterly alone for so long.

And the other morning, in bed, he'd said he was alone—or at least, he hadn't dated—since he was sixteen. That was the age Rory had been when he'd run off with some sweet-talking alpha ten years older; Beau's pack should have still been taking care of him when he was sixteen, no matter how much they didn't like his career plans.

Rory curled closer to him, settling his ear right over Beau's heart, and Beau's arm tightened, holding him there, though he thought Beau had to be half asleep already. The folders he had brought in were all still on the floor beside the couch.

"Beau?" Rory said softly, not wanting to wake him if he was sleeping. "Can I ask you something?"

"Yeah, of course," Beau said drowsily, unconcerned. "Anything, baby, of course you can."

Rory's face flushed, and he was tempted for a second to ask something else entirely—about that morning, about why Beau had gone to shower upstairs while Rory was sleeping—but he stuck to his guns. "It's... you might not want to talk about it, I don't know."

He felt Beau wake up a little more under him, and he sounded more alert when he said, "I'll tell you if I can't, then. But I won't be upset with you for asking me a question. We're married, you have a right to know things about me that no one else does."

Rory squirmed a little, moving so he could rest his chin on Beau's chest; Beau was already looking down at him curiously.

Rory took as deep a breath as he could in that position and said, "What happened when you were sixteen?"

Beau frowned. "How did—did I say...?"

"When you said you..." Rory found himself blushing a little. "You said you'd been too busy to date, since you were sixteen."

"*Oh.*" Beau put one hand over his eyes and made a weary noise that wasn't quite laughter. "I forgot I said that. I've been thinking about it a lot today."

"It was something to do with you wanting to be a doctor?"

Beau took his hand from his eyes, studying Rory for a moment, and he nodded.

"You said your pack didn't want you to. And today was all about becoming a doctor, obviously, so."

"You, uh... you remembered that, huh? Yeah, it was... it was a lot of things that all kind of—" Beau gestured. "Wound up into one thing, you know? The Revelation was a few years in, so everyone was on edge about that, and... there was this boy at school."

Rory raised his eyebrows. "A human?"

Beau nodded. "I liked him a lot. I knew I couldn't... I knew I would be going away the next year on exchange to another pack, I knew I would really want an omega for my mate, but..."

Beau smiled a little, sad and fond at once as he looked back on the memory, "I liked him *so much*. I knew better than to try to date him, or anything like that, but I couldn't resist being his partner for projects, things like that. We couldn't work on them at my house, obviously, because I lived on the pack lands. But no one saw the harm in me going to his house. I was sixteen, I knew how to handle myself among humans."

Rory tightened his own grip on Beau, wanting to reach back to that boy and shield him, hold him back from whatever had happened to him to leave him all alone.

"He had a little sister," Beau said. "Just a little kid, in first grade, and..."

Beau moved then, tugging Rory up and turning on his side, so that his back was to the room, Rory tucked between Beau and the cushions. Rory pressed his face against Beau's shoulder, and Beau put his head down against Rory's.

"She smelled wrong," Beau whispered. "I'd never smelled anything like that. I didn't know what it was, but I knew it was bad. I couldn't pay too much attention to her without being weird, but I knew for sure, something was wrong. Cancer, I eventually figured out. Even that took weeks, while it was growing inside her, getting worse, and no one knew except me."

Rory wanted to tell him to stop; he already knew this story didn't, couldn't, end well, and he didn't want to know. But he couldn't tell Beau to keep quiet, not when he'd asked. Not when there was no one else Beau *could* tell.

"I couldn't tell my friend or his parents without revealing what I was—and if they knew about me, they would know about my family, my whole pack. Michigan was a hunter state, and the first federal ruling had gone against us—it wasn't until the next year that the Supreme Court ruled for us. But I couldn't believe that he or his family would want to hurt us, especially if I was helping their daughter.

"But I knew that it wasn't up to me. So I asked my parents, and when they wouldn't even listen, I tried to ask other people in the pack

—the midwives, and eventually the alpha. No one would listen. No one would even consider it. I was still visiting my friend's house, still seeing his little sister. I could tell she was getting sicker, and I couldn't disobey my pack, but I couldn't do nothing, either. I was going back and forth over how to let them know without giving myself away. I had gotten stuck on the idea that if she got hurt, the doctors would find the cancer, but I didn't want to hurt her. I didn't want my friend thinking that I..."

Rory hitched himself up a little and curled his hand around the back of Beau's neck, bringing their faces together. Beau's old, time-worn grief over this was so thick in the air between them that Rory was almost choking on it.

He found himself thinking of Spencer, his own human baby brother. If Spencer had ever gotten sick like that, his mother would have known at once.

What if he had? Rory wouldn't have the slightest idea. It had been a long time, and anything could happen to a little human kid, even if he had a werewolf mother and sister looking out for him. If Rory got in touch...

But he couldn't think about that now. He had to be here with Beau, to help him get out the words that he'd probably never spoken to anyone before.

"What happened?" Rory prompted softly.

Beau's grip on him tightened, and Beau made an awful little sound, half laugh and half sob.

"I didn't do anything at all," he said. "I didn't help anyone. She got sick enough for her parents to notice, and they took her to a doctor; it would all have ended there if I hadn't..."

Beau breathed raggedly, roughly for a moment, then went on.

"My friend told me his sister had been diagnosed with cancer, and it was—after all that time wondering, waiting, knowing and doing nothing, I couldn't hide what a relief it was. He was furious, hurt, thought I wasn't taking it seriously, and then, somehow... I tried to explain without giving myself away, but I'd probably let all kinds of things slip by then. I can't have been as subtle as I thought I was,

150

teenagers generally aren't. One way or another, he figured it out. What I was, and that I'd known and said nothing. Did nothing. Didn't help when I could have."

"It wasn't your fault," Rory said softly, but Beau didn't even seem to hear him.

"People, even some werewolves, talk about the wolf inside, the beast, as if it's the wolf in us that makes us capable of hurting, of being animals. But humans are animals too, when you push them far enough. That day, he... I think he would have killed me. Not because of what I was, but because of how I'd betrayed him. I couldn't even fight back; I knew I deserved it, I knew—"

"*No,*" Rory said, so sharply that Beau jerked away from him, looking worried. Worried for him, worried that he'd upset *Rory* somehow, when he was saying such awful things about *himself.*

"No," Rory repeated more softly, cupping one hand to Beau's cheek. "You didn't know that. You might've thought it, but you couldn't know it, because it was *never true.* You never deserved that."

Beau frowned a little, took a breath, and then half his mouth quirked up in a smile. "You're, uh... you're not going to like the rest of this story, then."

Rory snuggled down again, pulling Beau close. "I still like *you,* though. So tell me."

Beau sighed against his chest, tightening his grip on Rory again. "I... well, I thought I deserved it. I just let him hit me until I realized he wasn't going to stop, and then I ran away. Rushed home, to safety, to... I don't know what I thought would happen, exactly, but I had nowhere to go except back to my pack. I was so shaken, I couldn't even try to lie, or shade it, or... anything. So then I was... punished. By the Alpha. My grandfather, incidentally. It was only my parents begging him that kept me from being banished immediately."

Punished, said like that, could only mean that Beau had been beaten, badly enough to make an impression on a healthy young alpha werewolf who must have been near adult size by then.

Beau had been sixteen, in high school, having his first big crush on a boy. He had only wanted to save a child, and hadn't even disobeyed in the end. Only gave himself away by accident, because of all the worry his pack had put him through in forbidding him to help, and because he couldn't lie very well to the boy he liked so much.

"For the rest of my time in the pack, I lived in the guesthouse instead of with my parents," Beau said quietly. "Got fed by whoever was feeding strangers that night, clothed by whoever had something spare. I worked any job I could find, every hour they'd let me work. And my—the boy who had been my friend, he never spoke to me again, but he never told anyone else, either. His sister was still going through treatments when I turned eighteen, so I don't even know..."

Beau squeezed him tighter for a moment, then said, "So that's... that's what happened when I was sixteen. That's why I haven't..."

Rory caught the sharp whiff of something like shame rising from Beau's skin, and he pushed up to cut off his words with a kiss, rough and fierce. *No, no, no, you didn't do anything wrong.*

Beau let him for a moment, and for a moment Rory was afraid that he wouldn't respond at all, would just suffer Rory's kiss.

Then Beau took over, shifting his weight to press Rory into the cushions, breaking the kiss only to start it again. It was gentle this time, feather-light brushes of lips and the faintest, softest flick of Beau's tongue against Rory's open mouth. Rory sighed and felt himself melting, getting just a little wet, yielding to everything.

Yes, he thought, opening his hands to press his palms against Beau's neck and his back. *Yes, I'm yours, you don't ever have to be alone now. Yes, take me, yes.*

But after another moment Beau pushed back. He looked at Rory for a long, quiet moment, when it felt like everything was teetering. Rory thought that if he just knew the right word to say, the right way to ask, Beau would come back into his arms and be his for real, completely.

But he couldn't think of the words, and Beau's gaze dropped to the healing burns ringing Rory's throat.

"You didn't deserve what happened to you, either," Beau said softly, and then he stood up, bending to pick up his things while Rory just lay on the couch, staring helplessly at him.

"Thank you for... listening," Beau said, when he straightened up. "I... think I'll sleep upstairs tonight. Since you went to the trouble of making up the beds."

No, Rory wanted to say, *No, don't leave me, don't go off alone.*

Beau turned away before he could figure out the way to say it that would bring him back, that would make him believe Rory wasn't broken, wasn't ugly and scarred and good for nothing more than this.

Neither of them deserved what had happened to them, Rory thought, staring at the place where Beau had been. Neither of them deserved to be alone and still hurting now, when they could at least have the comfort of each other. Beau had just said it himself. *We have each other, so we're all right.*

But Rory didn't how to convince Beau of that and knew better than to throw an alpha's own words back at him.

After a while he dragged himself up the stairs to the vast, empty, nothing-smelling bed he'd made that morning. If he listened hard, he could hear the beating of Beau's heart in the room down the hall, and he had almost convinced himself that it was better than being completely alone before he finally fell asleep.

CHAPTER 17

*B*eau slipped out early the next morning, only letting himself linger in the upstairs hallway for a moment to listen to the sound of Rory sleeping. He'd woken over and over in the night, wanting to go find Rory, to make sure he was all right, but each time he'd managed to stay in his own bedroom and just listen for him. Rory had been awake sometimes, asleep others, but always nearby and perfectly safe.

Just not in Beau's arms. Not in his bed. Not all sweetly yielding, like he would let Beau have anything, because... what? Because he'd told Rory a sad story? Because he'd treated Rory the way any halfway decent person would?

Rory deserved better than this; Beau had *promised* him better than this. Not yet another alpha swooping in and taking over his life, taking advantage of the vulnerable position Rory had been in, and an omega's nature.

Rory deserved to have choices. He deserved his family back. He deserved *everything*.

And Beau had promised to let him go at the end of three years, so this was better. Letting him go a little bit at a time, never getting too close. Look at what happened the last time he got too attached to a boy he liked, after all.

In the meantime, Beau had another day full of humans ahead of him, and his reasons for doing this were all sharp and clear in his mind. He was allowed to help, at last. And if that meant he set himself apart from other werewolves... then that was what he would do. That was what he had to do.

He'd gotten good at doing what he had to do. He could keep it up until...

He couldn't think of when he would be able to stop, but that was life, wasn't it? He could keep it up. It wouldn't kill him.

That day when he got a break, instead of calling Rory again like he wanted to, Beau tapped out a brief email to Adam, who was off at whatever research post-doc he'd gotten out of med school. Beau had a hunch it would have something to do with omega health; even if it wasn't what he was formally working on, Beau didn't know anyone more passionately interested in that topic than Adam. If he couldn't answer Beau's questions, he would know who, if anyone, could.

Beau barely had time to take two bites from his box-lunch sandwich before his phone rang, Adam's name popping up on the screen.

Beau frowned as he swallowed. He hadn't meant to make it sound urgent, and he'd assumed Adam would be head-down in whatever he was doing. "Hello?"

"What *exactly* do you mean when you ask me how much I know about omega genetics?" Adam demanded, without preamble. Small talk was decidedly not Adam's style.

Beau leaned back, relaxing into the first conversation he'd had in days with someone he knew well, hiding no land mines—other than whatever was making Adam sound so very, very urgent about what Beau had posed as a very general question.

"Well," Beau said. "I... I got married, before I left for my residency."

"To an omega through some agency, yes, I'm still on the group text," Adam said impatiently. "What's going on with him? Is he all right? Is he—"

Beau frowned again. No one back at Northwestern had ever met Rory, and Beau's few mentions of him in sporadic texts with his former classmates had said nothing about Rory's state of health.

"He's fine," Beau said. "I mean... he'd been taking suppressants for too long when we met, but he's off them and doing better now."

Adam made a sound that was very nearly a growl; Beau could almost smell the warning scent of alpha rage that would be rising off him if they were in the same place. Since there was no danger of actually provoking a fight and Adam hadn't hung up yet, Beau kept talking.

"The reason I wanted to talk to you is that he's estranged from his family, more or less ever since he found out he was an omega."

"At puberty?" Adam guessed, sounding less angry and more intrigued. "When his heats started? Not an omega mother, then?"

Beau nodded slowly. "Right. He was born in a human hospital, grew up living among humans with his parents, an older werewolf sister, a younger human brother. Father is human, or—well, everyone seems to have thought he was Rory's father until they realized Rory was an omega, and then... it seemed like he couldn't be."

"*Ah.*" All sound of anger had vanished from Adam's voice now, leaving only scientific interest. "I couldn't say anything for certain without doing a genetic workup of both putative parents and, preferably, all three siblings. We've only sequenced DNA for a handful of omegas, it's worse than pulling teeth trying to get anyone to give up samples, and the ethics are a nightmare with most of the ones who are willing. If I could add at least your husband, if he were willing—and you, I suppose, as his *alpha*—that would add to my data set significantly."

There was a hint of a sneer in Adam's voice, as there nearly always was when he talked about alphas mated to omegas. Beau wasn't particularly sure he didn't deserve it, so he didn't argue, even though it always struck him as a bit hypocritical. Adam was an alpha himself, after all; he should know that most alphas would never mistreat an omega.

"I'll talk to him," Beau said. "But is it even possible? *Could* his father be human? How'd he wind up being an omega without an omega parent?"

"Y chromosome, probably," Adam said. "His father—if he is the biological father—and brother would make a really interesting case study. Do you have their contact information?"

"*Adam*," Beau snapped. "What about the Y chromosome?"

"Oh, well, it's probably what makes an omega an omega," Adam said, settling into a lecturing tone as he explained. "Seems pretty clear that omegas have them, regardless of their gender, so it makes sense that it's Y-linked. And they also have to be werewolves—there aren't any human omegas, which is why humans get so fucking weird about them, and why omegas face so much unique discrimination from humans as well as systematic oppression within werewolf communities—"

Beau took another bite of his sandwich, resigning himself to Adam veering off onto a rant about the plight of omegas. He actually got back to the point pretty quickly, though.

"But there are humans—cisgender male, XY chromosome humans —who become omegas when bitten. The bite doesn't change the human DNA, just introduces the Lycan bodies which facilitate the shift to wolf form, plus some epigenetic effects. But whatever makes a bitten werewolf into an omega has to already be in their DNA at that point, because it's there in the human form once they change."

Beau had entertained that theory about Rory, briefly, when he thought that Rory had been born human—that he must have become an omega after being bitten. But if he would have had to inherit even *that* from a parent, then the trait had to be out there in humans.

"Probably from a werewolf ancestor," Adam went on. "In the male line if I'm right about the Y chromosome. Your husband could've been fathered by a human who never found out about that because he was never bitten. But like I said, I'd need to see the entire family's DNA to be sure."

"I'll... see what I can do," Beau said, and hung up without bothering with any of the niceties Adam wouldn't care about anyway.

If Rory really *was* his father's biological child... it certainly wouldn't undo what had happened to him when he was thirteen, or everything since he was sixteen. But it might make it that much easier for him to reconcile with his family, to finally heal the rift created when he presented as an omega. He at least wouldn't have to flinch and correct himself every time he started to say something about his dad.

But then again, what if testing proved the opposite? What if Rory finally made contact with this long-lost family only to learn that everything they'd said when he was just a child was true, and stirred up all that bitterness again? Beau couldn't offer him this ray of hope only to have it demolished.

But he already knew Rory's sister's name, and what town they were from, so maybe there was a way to make sure first. *She always looked out for me*, Rory had said. Beau was willing to bet that hadn't changed.

~

That afternoon knocked everything else out of Beau's thoughts: they got their clinical and on-call schedules for the first month's rotations.

The block schedules for rotations had been sent out a couple of months earlier, so he'd already known he was going into four weeks of Pulmonary care. He'd been vaguely aware that he was going to have to worry about being on-call and overnight coverage shifts around the full and empty moons, but they'd already been told they wouldn't be scheduled for overnights in this first rotation.

He hadn't considered what would happen when they tried to accommodate their first werewolf.

His schedule was cleared, not only for the night of the full moon, now less than two weeks away, but also for the day before and after. He stared at that for a moment, thinking of having thirty-six straight

DESSA LUX

hours with nothing to do but stay at home, excruciatingly aware of the moon's effects on his own libido and Rory's.

Then his gaze slid down the page toward the end of the rotation, searching for where he was expected to make up the hours he was being given off, and... oh yes. Of course.

He was working two Saturday overnight shifts, the latter two Saturdays of the rotation. Including the night of the empty moon, just when he would be most desperate to be home with Rory, curled up in bed with him.

Well. It was probably better if he learned to resist that urge sooner rather than later; he ought to be grateful to be working during the empty moon, to train himself.

Even as he thought it, though, he wondered if he could pull it off. It was the one concession he'd made to his own nature throughout the past ten years, through ambulance shifts and night classes and all the challenges of med school. He'd let himself den up during the empty moon, even without anyone to share his home or his bed with. He'd let himself feel as safe as he could on the darkest of nights, when no wolf wanted to be alone among strangers.

He'd worked plenty of full moon nights, and wary as the humans around him usually were at first, they'd soon forgotten all about it. The full moon pulled at him, but it didn't force him to change, or make him run wild. Mostly it made him *awake*, eager to move, to pursue... something. A goal worked as well as a hunt. He was quicker on those nights, more in tune with his senses. Every life he'd ever saved on a full moon night was etched in his memory, bright and clear and triumphant.

"Jeffries? Everything all right with your schedule?"

Beau looked up to find Dr. Ross standing nearby, and realized that every resident around him was excitedly discussing their schedule or entering it into a calendar on their phone.

He also realized, looking at Dr. Ross's mildly expectant expression, that there was only one possible answer to the question.

He couldn't convince all these human strangers that he would be safe on the full moon. They would never forget that he was a were-

160

wolf, or where the full moon fell in the monthly schedules. This was the accommodation they were offering.

And he couldn't ask for even more time off, in order to be at home on the empty moon. Until they knew him, until he knew he could convince them to let him work during full moons, he couldn't make up the shifts to take the empty moon off—and certainly there was nothing to be done for this month, not without asking three other residents and who knew who else to rearrange *their* schedules on limited notice.

He wondered for a second whether anyone had consulted the local werewolf packs on *this*, or if they were just going on what all humans knew about werewolves. Almost no humans outside of werewolf packs knew there was any significance to the empty moon; even now, with all their legal protections in place and the first hysteria of the humans dying down in the fifteen years since the Revelation, were-wolves were reluctant to reveal when they were at their most vulnerable, when they were sure to be home and gathered in one place, easy to attack.

He didn't think he could say it himself, not to these humans. Maybe when he knew them better—when he'd at least begun to prove himself to them—and when he could make the request with a bit of lead time, so that he wasn't asking them to overhaul a schedule already completed. He could ask then. In the meantime, he would just have to handle it.

"Yes, sir," he said to Dr. Ross, opening up the calendar on his phone to start entering in his shifts. "Everything's fine."

CHAPTER 18

$\mathcal{R}$ ory couldn't have said which one of them was more tense as they walked into the official welcome barbecue that weekend. He hadn't been surrounded by people like this since before the refuge. Even then, he could hardly remember anything like this, where his goal was to seem normal, to be liked—not to avoid punishment, but just to be a part of something.

Beau, of course, *was* worried about avoiding punishment. It made Rory's heart ache a little, to think of Beau trying to placate the people in charge of his residency the same way Rory had had to placate his succession of shitty alphas. It was a skill you learned over time, and he didn't think Beau had ever had a need to learn it before. His pack clearly hadn't taught him that; he had walked away instead of giving in.

Rory didn't want him to have to learn it now.

Rory would just have to prove that Beau was doing everything right, everything they wanted, so they would leave him alone. So Beau would never have to experience the moment when the tension and fear snapped into *you're gonna get it.*

Rory tucked himself close to Beau's side, grateful for the excuse for skin contact. Beau had kept a careful distance from him ever since he'd bolted to bed alone after telling Rory what had happened with his pack. Last night Beau had kissed Rory's forehead and then gone off to bed alone again, and this morning had been no different. Beau wasn't angry or indifferent—Rory knew well how to read those signs—but he was being careful in a way Rory wished he wouldn't.

That had been when they were alone, though. In front of all these humans, they had to present a united front, and Rory wasn't above enjoying it a little, if that was what it took to have Beau close to him again.

Beau's arm went around him, and Rory doubted anyone just looking at them would feel how stiffly Beau held his arm. Rory honestly couldn't tell whether it was the humans making him nervous or if that was how Beau felt about having to touch Rory.

It didn't matter. They had to do this, and do it well.

"All right, strategy," Rory murmured, lips barely moving, too low for a human to have heard even if they were as close to him as Beau was. His eyes scanned the crowd, reading body language, posture, distances between bodies, to work out who was in charge, who were the other residents—and who were the spouses brought along to be showed off. At least all the children were self-explanatory.

"Do we pay our respects first, or start making friends with your classmates and let the alphas approach us?"

"My adviser, Dr. Ross, is at your two o'clock," Beau murmured. "Striped shirt, white hair. Looks like he's busy? We could get food?"

That was not an answer to his question. Rory had a feeling it meant that Beau had no idea how to answer his question.

Well, why should he? He was an alpha. He'd belonged to one pack all his life, until they cast him out, and then he'd simply gone it alone. He had never been the thirteen-year-old coming into a strange pack and trying to make himself fit. He'd never had to navigate the intricacies of being friendly-but-not-too-friendly to his alpha's friends.

"Sure," Rory said. "Let's get food."

He let Beau guide him over to the tables where food was already set out, listening intently to the snatches of conversation around them. Beau's first rotation was Pulmonary—that had been marked on the calendar, along with the names of the senior residents and attending physicians who Beau would report to. All Rory had to do was listen, and...

"—Dr. Lidstrom over there, and I don't see Dr. May yet, but she should be here—"

Rory filled his paper plate on autopilot—exchanging glances with Beau over the four different kinds of potato salad before both choosing the least mayo-ful one—and then tugged Beau in the direction of the voice he'd identified, coming from a black woman even shorter than Rory with her hair in braids twisted into a knot on top of her head. She was talking to a pair of people—the red-headed woman was attuned to her, listening seriously, while the blond man standing possessively close to her was eating and looking idly around.

The black woman might be the third attending, but from the tone of her voice as she named Dr. Lidstrom and Dr. May, she was probably a senior resident. The redhead would be one of Beau's fellow interns on the Pulmonary rotation and the blond guy was her husband, or partner, or whatever.

Not going to last, Rory silently diagnosed, as he strolled as slowly and seemingly-aimlessly as he could without losing any time. Beau was trailing a half-step behind him, looking around but not focusing on anything.

He wondered if people looked at them and thought, *Not going to last.*

Well, if they did, it wouldn't be because Rory didn't take any interest in his husband's concerns. He managed to time their approach so that they arrived near the little group of three at a lull in conversation. Rory hesitated, making Beau stop at his side. Beau's hand went to the small of his back as if magnetized, and Rory smiled up over his shoulder at him and said, "It would be easier if everyone was wearing their nametags, wouldn't it? They should've color-coded. Everyone in Pulmonary wear... blue?"

Beau smiled gamely at him and said, "Or purple, maybe," and, right on cue, the black woman said in Beau's direction, "Oh, is your first

165

rotation Pulmo? I'm a third-year, I'll be one of your seniors. Cora Benn."

"Oh!" Beau shot Rory the tiniest glance, realizing what Rory had done, before he smiled and shook hands with her. "Beau Jeffries, and this is my husband, Roland."

Cora's eyes widened slightly, and Rory noted the way her hand tightened on Beau's; her heartbeat sped up, her scent strengthening in the way that meant her body temperature had risen abruptly.

So they'd told everyone on the Pulmonary rotation which new intern was the werewolf, then.

"I'm the werewolf," Beau continued, unprompted, and with a bit of humor in his voice, giving her the opening to acknowledge what she obviously knew. "I mean, Roland and I both are, but I'm the only one among the interns, as far as I know."

The other intern froze; her partner turned toward Beau, shouldering slightly between them and looking openly wary.

Cora collected herself first, smiling in a way that didn't look entirely insincere. "Oh, wow! Great to meet you! I think I'm going to be on that overnight shift you have. We don't usually have interns working nights this early, but they didn't want you to lose hours because of the whole—you know." She pivoted toward the other intern and said, "This is Kelly Latham, have you guys met? I know the first couple of days are just kind of a blur."

Beau offered his hand; Kelly stepped around her partner to take it. The partner was still watching Beau distrustfully.

"This is Jay," Kelly said. "My fiancé. We moved from California—"

"I'm actually from Texas," Jay interrupted, in a tone that meant the words might as well have been, *I have a silver bullet with your name on it.*

Kelly winced and shot Beau an apologetic look. Rory leaned in closer to Beau's side and, before Kelly or Beau could actually acknowledge Jay's challenge, said brightly, "Did you go to med school in California, then?"

"Oh, yeah, UCLA," she said quickly, obviously glad for the diversion. "What about you, Beau?"

"Northwestern," Beau said. "Chicago was as big a city as I could handle. I don't know what I would have done in LA for four years."

Jay started to say something, and Kelly grabbed his hand hard, effectively silencing him. They managed to limp through a few more exchanges of small talk without Rory having to jump in, and then Beau had the sense to extricate them before it went further. "Anyway, I should go say hi to Dr. Ross. Good to meet you, Kelly, Cora."

Jay stayed stonily silent while others said their goodbyes, and Rory just smiled and waved before turning away, still tucked under Beau's arm. They'd gone barely three steps before they met the man Beau had first pointed out to Rory—his adviser, the one responsible for deciding whether Beau was following all their rules.

Rory looked up at Beau, and Beau made quick introductions. Dr. Ross offered his hand, and Rory shook it. He smiled, and thanked Dr. Ross for his congratulations on their wedding, and almost managed not to listen for anyone who might come up on them from behind.

By the end of the barbecue, Rory had managed to make sure Beau, seemingly naturally, met everyone he would be working with in his first rotation, whose reactions to meeting a werewolf intern had ranged from politely-suppressed nervousness to politely-suppressed curiosity. None had seemed actually hostile. None of them proclaimed their hunter-state origins. It could have gone a lot worse and Rory wasn't honestly sure it could have gone much better.

Dr. Ross and the members of the program administration they'd met had all seemed friendly and unsurprised by Rory's presence. One or two had asked questions that seemed rather pointed, about whether they would mind being only two instead of having a whole pack around them, but Rory had managed not to bristle at the implication that he couldn't do whatever Beau needed.

Of course, by the time he and Beau got home afterward, too exhausted to do anything but fall onto the nearest couch together, Rory was starting to think that maybe they were on to something.

It wouldn't usually be like this, though, would it? Beau would only have to deal with a few of these people at a time, plus patients, and Rory would usually be left at home twiddling his thumbs, doing laundry, and generally having nothing better to do than look after Beau when he came home.

And on the bright side, all that careful, showy closeness during the barbecue plus their mutual state of total collapse meant that Beau wasn't bothering to try to keep any kind of distance from Rory now.

"Did you actually eat anything?" Beau mumbled after a while.

Rory shook his head. He'd made a show of nibbling at things to excuse his own silence while standing supportively by Beau's side, but he'd been too much on alert to force much of anything down his throat, and he knew Beau had simply abandoned his plate about twenty minutes in. He'd circulated with a cup in his hand after that.

Beau was silent for a few minutes after Rory's reply, and then said, "Pizza?"

Rory closed his eyes and nodded against Beau's shoulder, and was nearly asleep when he felt Beau wriggle his phone out of his pocket and make the order.

It wouldn't always be like this, Rory told himself. It couldn't. They'd be all right. He could take care of Beau. He could earn his place in their home, in Beau's arms. He just had to take a little nap first.

Buying a car was, somehow, actually worse than the barbecue. Rory still wasn't sure, hours later, that his near panic attack over the possibility of a car salesman calling the cops on Beau hadn't been justified, although it had all been smoothed over after Rory's brief flight to the bathroom distracted Beau from his frustration.

Neither of them even made it to a bed that night; they slept tangled together on the family room couch. It was the best Rory had slept since the empty moon, and he knew Beau slept just as soundly. When Beau's phone alarm went off early Monday morning, Beau woke up looking bright-eyed, thrumming with energy.

Rory felt similar, but he kept his eyes half-closed, hoping to invite a lingering touch, a secret kiss.

Beau just sighed and went upstairs, so Rory got up and made breakfast.

~

On Tuesday, Rory got bored.

He had finished *A Canticle for Leibowitz* and finished alphabetizing all of Beau's books. He had picked out the simplest-looking of all of Beau's old textbooks, and read about three pages of Introduction to College Biology before the letters started swimming and he had a splitting headache. He wasn't sure he'd even understood any of it, so that had been for nothing anyway.

The house was clean. There was nothing to do. He'd never watched much TV, and didn't think it would help his vision or his headache any to start now.

By mid-morning he found himself pacing around the living room and then stopped and stared at the front door.

He could go outside. He could just... go. He had keys, and shoes, and a phone. He had a wallet with his ID and cash and cards. He could just walk right out. He could...

He didn't know what he would do. It had been a long time since he didn't have to worry about survival, whether that meant finding food or shelter, or just avoiding making his alpha angry. It felt like something out of science fiction—like being weightless.

He didn't know which way was up, and it was a little nauseating.

After another moment he realized that he couldn't *not* go outside at this point. He wasn't going to let *a lack of obvious things to be scared of* stop him from doing at least that much. Even if it was just going down to the sidewalk, or around the block, he had to do the thing now that he had thought of it. Now that it was possible that he might not.

He glanced down at himself. He was dressed as usual—barefoot, in his hand-me-down jeans and a long-sleeved t-shirt. He hadn't bothered to cover his throat beyond wearing a collared shirt at the barbecue and to the car dealership over the weekend, and no one had given any particular sign of noticing his burns more than his bare head and general scrawniness. Both of his good shirts were hanging in the closet in his room upstairs now; he could put one of them on, or get his old scarf, or his cravat, or...

Rory went into the little downstairs bathroom and looked at himself in the mirror, not letting himself avoid the sight of his reflection. He hadn't looked at himself like this, on purpose, probably since the last time he needed to check how quickly a bruise was healing. He wasn't sure when that had been.

He was startled by the sight of himself.

He looked almost normal. Too thin, maybe, but not skeletal, not obviously sick. His hair was still barely there, but a faint blond fuzz covered his scalp now; he twisted this way and that, searching for bald spots, but couldn't find any obvious ones. He ran his hand over his head and it felt strange—half the silky-softness of new hair growing in, half the firmer velvety stubble where the hair he'd shaved was growing back. But he couldn't find any completely bare places.

Even his scars weren't as hideous as he'd imagined them being. And they were definitely scars now, fully healed. There were two or three places where the shiny bright pink patches rose above the neck of his t-shirt—on either side of the front of his throat, and over his spine—but there wasn't the complete burned ring he had imagined. It wouldn't be obvious that he had been collared, forced to keep his human form, forced to submit to his alpha.

They were just scars.

He touched them with his fingers, then touched a hand to his belly, where the secret internal scars remained. Even Beau couldn't see those; no one who he just walked past outside would have any idea. They might not even know he was a werewolf, or an omega, unless he said so. And if he did meet another werewolf, they would have no power over him. He was married, if not fully bonded to his alpha-husband; he was a person with every right to be wherever he wanted. No one would run him off for loitering, or watch him suspiciously, waiting for him to steal something.

That thought felt like... a lot, though. And Beau had the car, which meant Rory would have to walk anywhere he wanted to go. He didn't need anything, and he didn't think he was going to force himself to hike half a mile down the main road to the nearest strip mall just to prove anything to himself.

He should probably save something for tomorrow, after all. Today, he was just going to go outside. He hadn't even really looked at their own yard yet. Given how well the inside of the house had been scoured clean, Rory was reasonably sure he wouldn't find wolfsbane or poison oak growing in the yard, but he had no idea what there *was* out there.

With that thought, he headed for the front door again. He thought of going and getting his keys, and then decided to just leave the inner door open behind him, and only close the storm door. If he was only going to be in the yard, no one would be able to step onto their property without him hearing.

Of course, it would be easier to be sure of that if he knew exactly where their property began and ended. Rory walked down to the sidewalk through the grass, which was getting tall, noticeably taller than the neighbors'. He'd have to ask Beau about buying a lawnmower unless there was already one stashed in the garage, or they were going to be Those People on their block.

Maybe they already *were* Those People, judging by the lack of neighbors popping by with cookies or casseroles. Or maybe people didn't do that anymore? Or around here?

Or maybe the neighbors knew the house had sold to werewolves, and they were all mail-ordering wolfsbane to plant in their yards and griping about their property values.

Still. They needed to mow the grass. He doubted Beau had ever had to think about that at all, living in an apartment for ten years and out on some rural pack lands in Michigan before that.

That would be something Rory could take care of for him. He might not be up to full strength yet by a long way, but he'd been able to push a mower around the yard in good straight lines by the time he was ten. His dad—

Rory pushed away the thought and looked down at his feet, walking scrupulously along the sidewalk until he reached the perfectly straight line of shorter grass that clearly marked the end of their lot. He glanced toward the next house, making an apologetic face—he could just imagine the neighbor glaring at their house while mowing their lawn exactly up to the property line—and turned the corner, walking up the border of their yard.

There were plants in the beds across the front of the house, which he'd vaguely known, but now he took the time to observe a little more than *green things, how nice to have green things around*. There were a couple of little ornamental trees, one by the corner of the porch and one at the corner of the house, and across the front of the house was a somewhat random assortment of shrubby things and clumps of flowers.

He was probably going to have to find out what they were if he wanted to do anything about them. *Like black-eyed susans but purple* and *green leafy things with whitish edges* wasn't going to get him very far.

For now he stuck to his boundary walking, proceeding down the side of the house, where two big flowering bushes—lilacs, maybe?— stood at either end of an empty planting bed, bare soil sporting only dandelions and a few hopeful little maple sprouts that definitely were going to need pulling before they got any bigger.

The rest of the backyard was a pretty nondescript stretch of green, bordered on two sides by fences and on the third side by a geometrically exact line of freshly-planted small bushes. Rory crouched down beside one, carefully on their side of the line, to try to get a better whiff of it. Wolfsbane didn't grow in shrubs like that, at least, so he was pretty sure it wasn't *that*. Hazel, maybe? Protective, but not hostile. And they hadn't put up a fence.

He glanced toward the neighbor's house, but all the blinds were closed, and he carefully did not focus his hearing to try to detect whether anyone was inside. He would know if they wanted him to know.

In the meantime he stood up and finished his circuit, walking up

172

the property line on that side to the sidewalk, and across their drive-way. He hesitated there, considering whether to have a closer look at the plants or go look in the garage to see if maybe, among all the other things he'd had delivered, Beau had thought to order a lawnmower.

Then he saw a woman on the other side of the street start walking toward him with a covered plate in her hands and a bright smile on her face, and he froze.

She was a werewolf. He could tell from her scent, but there was also the mark of a bonding bite showing above the collar of her t-shirt, utterly unconcealed.

She walked up their driveway, just to where the sidewalk crossed it —the very edge of entering onto their territory. "Hi there, welcome to the neighborhood! I'm Jennifer Niemi, I live just down the street. I kind of got elected as your personal welcome wagon since it seems like you might be related to some cousins of mine?"

The semi-acknowledgement—*I know you're a werewolf and I can tell you know that I'm one*—was so smoothly done it seemed normal, nothing to fear and nothing to calculate. They were standing out in the bright summer sunshine, visible to all their neighbors, and Rory nodded and said, "Yeah, I... think I probably am. We are, my husband and I. I'm Roland, he's Beau. Jeffries."

She smiled wider. "Welcome! I don't know if you guys are looking for a pack—"

Her friendly smile faltered and she stopped short; Rory wasn't exactly sure what his face and body had done at that word, but it felt fairly redundant when he said, "Uh, no. We're not. We both had pretty bad experiences with the packs we came from, so we're pretty happy to be just us. Is that...?"

He waited for her to stop smiling and turn away, to throw the covered plate at his feet, to turn pale and tired.

He realized, right then, that she smelled a little like his mother— not in a way that made him think they actually were related, but she was a female werewolf of that age and had that mother-smell about her. He shifted his weight backward a little, prepared to retreat.

"I'm sorry," she said, and held out the plate, still offering. "I'm sorry that happened to both of you. I know a lot of people who... well, the Revelation was hard on everyone in different ways. I doubt that's any comfort to you, or will change your minds, but I understand. If you ever do need a pack to help out with anything, or just to know where it's safe to run on the full—or if you need to borrow a cup of sugar— we're the fourth house down on the other side, with the green shutters. I put my phone number and email on a post-it on the plate."

Rory finally reached out and accepted the plate from her.

"It's just cookies, nothing special," she said, offering a wry smile. "No big obligation, I promise. Just... do give us a call if you ever need anything, or just want to talk or anything, all right? Or if the other neighbors are getting to you." Jennifer glanced in the direction of the house the brand new hazel bushes belonged to, and Rory wondered if Jennifer was looking forward to her family not being the only werewolves on the block anymore, not having to deal with wary humans alone all the time.

"Thanks," Rory said, looking down at the cookies and back at Jennifer, wondering about the process of her getting "elected" to greet the new werewolf in the neighborhood. "I, uh. I'll try to... be a credit to the family."

Jennifer gave him a wry, understanding smile, werewolf to werewolf. "You already are, I'm sure. Anyway, I'm home with my kids— they just aren't ready to be in school with humans all day yet—so you'll usually find me, and Troy works security at the Clinic, so he might cross paths with your Beau sometime. I'll tell the pack, all right? Not to push you guys."

Rory nodded, feeling stunned by her kindness and easy kinship as he wouldn't have been by fury or coldness. "Thank you. I... thanks, really. I'll... I'll put you in my phone. I'm, um. I'm usually home, too, if you..."

Not that she could need anything from him, when he was new in town and had nothing of his own. He didn't think there was even a bag of sugar in the house.

But Jennifer smiled. "Thanks, Roland. Good to meet you. And, uh, don't be surprised if a few more plates show up, now that I've broken the ice. I mean, not *everyone* will—" Jennifer didn't glance toward the neighbor's house this time, but Rory smiled a little anyway. "But you'll probably get a few. Folks are pretty friendly around here, and they're even more nosy."

Rory glanced around the street again, at every house but the one next door, wondering how many of their human neighbors were covertly watching Jennifer greet him in the street.

Jennifer winked when he looked back at her. "We use Facebook now, too. Everybody doesn't have to be stationed at their windows. Are you on Facebook?"

Rory shook his head, smiling slightly. "I'll, uh. Maybe I'll set it up."

"Good," Jennifer said, and then the front door of the house with the green shutters slammed open and a kid leaned out and yelled, "MAMA! SUMMER *DABBED*—"

"*Five minutes,*" Jennifer muttered, and Rory wondered whether she'd just come over for the chance to get away from her kids, and smiled wider. She gave Rory a last little wave and turned and ran back toward her house, not bothering to hide her werewolf speed.

CHAPTER 19

The house smelled like cooking food when Beau walked in—something rich with cream and chicken, and under that something sweet. His mouth watered, and his exhaustion from another day of information overload and the press of humans lifted slightly.

"Rory?"

"Hey!" Rory called back from the kitchen, and Beau walked inside to find him standing at the counter with his hands on his hips. There were four different plates of cookies in front of him.

"There's casserole and pie in the oven," Rory explained. "They need about ten more minutes, but then we can eat."

"What..."

None of the plates the cookies were on looked familiar, and there was no evidence of Rory doing any cooking visible in the kitchen.

Rory gave him a crooked smile. "The neighbors have found us. Jennifer—four houses down on the other side—is a werewolf, and once she broke the ice..." Rory gestured around the kitchen.

Beau filled in the rest of Rory's day from the obvious results: a day of easy, friendly chats, settling comfortably into the neighborhood, welcomed by everyone, and feeling safe under the guidance of a female werewolf. Everything the opposite of his own day, right down to the contrast of this bounty of homemade food versus those dire boxed lunches. Though he did at least know the other interns headed toward the same rotation, thanks to Rory's subtle but determined direction at the barbecue; tomorrow they would be observing rounds together for the first time.

"I was just thinking you should try these," Rory added. "And I could pack some up for you to take with you each day for the rest of the week? To share with Kelly and Jamie and Doug, or... they can't be giving you enough to eat, I don't think."

Beau walked over to stand next to Rory at the counter, just a little closer than strictly necessary. "You don't think I'll spoil my dinner if I eat cookies first?"

"More for me if you do," Rory said blithely. "And honestly whatever you manage to eat before you fall asleep face-first in it is a win at this point."

Beau didn't dignify that with a response, other than reaching for the nearest chocolate chip cookie.

The cookies helped—he hadn't even realized he needed to eat more than he was getting during the day—and the newness of everything was starting not to be so new. When orientation ended and the actual rotation began, the following week, Beau was simultaneously impatient to begin and terrified of fucking up completely right out of the gate, but everything was scheduled, regimented, and supervised. He let the enormous machine that was the Rochester Clinic Residency move him along hour by hour.

And at the end of every shift, he went home to Rory.

Being around people who were sick and injured and struggling to breathe all day—close enough to catch their scents and hear their distress, even when he wasn't in the room with a patient—made it all the more obvious, every time he came home, how much Rory had recovered. The bitter sickly scent of the suppressants was long gone, and so was the depleted sourness of exhaustion that had lingered around him.

Rory smelled healthy now, even happy, and as the moon waxed, he smelled more and more strongly like *omega* and *mate* and *mine* to Beau. It took more effort every day to refrain from pulling him close, from following him to his bed and climbing right in.

And then Beau was signing out at the end of a shift and Cora said brightly, "Happy full moon! See you Monday!"

Beau blinked at her, saw her starting to look awkward, and hastily smiled back. "Thanks. I, uh, almost forgot. See you Monday."

Cora gave him a quizzical look, but didn't ask how he could possibly forget the impending full moon, letting Beau make his escape.

There wasn't actually any escape, though, because he was driving home to Rory, who would smell even better now than he had twelve hours ago.

Beau still hadn't talked to Rory about how they were going to handle tomorrow night.

Not that they needed much of a plan, really, other than Beau promising to leave Rory alone. He could even offer to spend the full moon night down in the basement bedroom, as far from Rory as he could get in the same house.

His cock throbbed at the thought of it: the pull of the moon, the wildness calling to him. He'd have nothing to do, no distraction from it, and he would be surrounded by the mingled scents of himself and Rory, the memory of Rory's body pressed close to his, Rory's kisses...

Beau was rather more than half-hard, foggy with lust that drove out the day's exhaustion, by the time he pulled into the driveway. He stayed still a moment, looking around to see if any of the neighbors were in sight while he forced his body to calm. He thought he saw a twitch of curtains at the house to the left, but he was probably imagining it.

When he did finally get out of the car and walk to the house, he had just a second of wondering where—and doing what—he might find Rory. Lurid images flashed across his mind in the second of unlocking the door and pushing it open, but they ended as soon as he stepped inside.

Rory was sitting at the kitchen table facing toward the door, the pages of their pre-nup spread in front of him. He smiled a little stiffly as he met Beau's eyes. "Hi, Beau. I know you're probably tired, but we should talk about tomorrow night."

"Oh," Beau said, and like Rory's guess had been a command, all that fizzing energy left him. Tired, yes. He ought to be tired; he was always tired when he came home to Rory. "Uh, okay. Of course. That's a good idea."

"It wasn't mine, really," Rory said, making a face and standing up. No sign that *he* found the thought of tomorrow night unbearably arousing. "But I was talking to Susan and she wanted to know what my—our—plans were, and when I couldn't tell her anything specific she told me we'd better *have* plans, and, well. I'm not gonna cross Susan."

He was walking to the fridge as he spoke; Beau moved closer just to keep him in sight. Rory retrieved a plate of sandwiches and bowl of salad from the fridge, bringing them back to the table.

"Here, we can eat while we talk," Rory said. "I don't want to make you choose which of those you can fit in before you fall asleep, I know better than that."

"I can do two things before I fall asleep," Beau muttered, although for the last week that had only been true if the second one involved sitting on the couch feeling vaguely guilty about not doing more things before he fell asleep.

"Of course you can," Rory said easily. "But why choose? Come on, sit down. Eat."

Beau sat, because there was no alternative, and took a sandwich. Rory put some salad on a plate for him and pushed it closer, and poured him a glass of water. Beau took a sip, mumbled some thanks, and all the time he was only watching Rory's hands, tidying away the papers he'd been studying, taking his own portions of food.

"What, um," Beau dragged his gaze up to Rory's face and forced himself to ask a coherent question. "What kind of plans did you have in mind?"

Rory bit his lip, his shoulders slumping a little. "I guess... whatever you want? Just as long as we both know, right?"

Rory took a bite of his sandwich, and Beau had a feeling that they had reached the end of whatever Rory had been ready for. He'd gotten up a head of steam, pushed himself far enough to literally put this topic on the table, and now...

Well. Maybe now he needed his alpha to take the lead on this.

Beau glanced over at the papers, wondering what Rory had been looking for in them. Susan and Ms. Dawson had both sworn to him that they made sure Rory understood everything in the pre-nup before they went to the clerk's office, but Rory hadn't exactly been at his best then, or in any position to quibble with what Beau was offering.

"I don't expect anything," Beau offered hesitantly. "I told you I would give you your own space. You have room here, where you can be alone and safe."

Rory nodded, but something flashed across his face—a tension Beau might have read as *pain* if he saw it in one of his patients. His scent didn't lighten at the reassurance. His breathing—marvelously healthy and even by the standards of the Pulmonary ward—had a too-steady rhythm, too quiet and shallow. He was controlling it consciously, holding himself in check.

Beau's reassurance wasn't what he'd needed to hear.

"Do you..." Beau tried to control his own breathing, to keep from sounding eager. "Would you rather *not* be alone for the moon, baby? Is that it?"

Rory's whole body jolted at Beau's question, his eyes flashing wide. The pupils flared as he stared for a few frozen seconds, his lips parting softly before he managed to nod.

Beau struggled to hold down his own reaction. He'd just been wanting this, fantasizing about this, but it wasn't as simple as Rory saying he wanted Beau. Rory had probably said a lot of things to other alphas in the last eight years that might have sounded like that, even looked like that, but Beau wasn't going to treat Rory the way they had treated him, even if it was all Rory knew to expect or ask for.

"Tell me what you want," Beau coaxed. "Just to be together somewhere, out running or something, or...?"

Rory licked his lips. "I think I'd like it. Sex. With you. If you would... and you said I won't go into heat yet, I'm not strong enough. It doesn't feel like that anyway, or—do I smell like it, do you think?"

Beau breathed in, shook his head, and then said, "Can I...?"

Rory nodded, and Beau stood and moved around the table to lean over him. Rory leaned back in his chair, shoulders loose, and tilted his head back and to the side, offering his throat. Beau's mouth watered and his cock twitched, but he made himself focus; it was a matter of diagnosis, really, detecting hormonal levels and so on, even if he didn't know what any of it would translate to in clinical terms.

He pressed his nose right to the pulse point and inhaled, and then again behind Rory's ear. His hair was growing, the fuzzy stubble of it brushing against Beau's cheek as he sniffed.

Rory smelled good—*omega, mate, mine, willing, yes, yes*—but that extra something wasn't there, that intoxicating sharp-sour-sweet note that promised a heat coming on. This close to the full moon, it would be there if Rory's body were preparing for a heat tomorrow night.

It took Beau another moment to pull away, to stop breathing in Rory's warm, soft scent and straighten up. He forced himself to return to his own chair before he said, "No. You won't have a heat tomorrow night—certainly not a full heat, and I don't think even a very marked pseudo-heat."

Rory nodded. "But I'll still feel the moon. I'll want to... I won't want to be alone. And you said if we do anything together it's for real, but I have to want it too, or we can't."

None of that sounded exactly like what Beau had wanted to make Rory understand, but none of it was exactly wrong, either.

"And I know you haven't before and maybe you want to wait for someone who—but I was just looking, to be sure that it doesn't change anything, if we do. I can still go at the end of the three years if we have sex, as long as we don't have children, but I—I can't..."

Rory's voice had been getting smaller and smaller as he spoke, and there it dwindled into nothing.

Beau felt choked by the quiet hopelessness in Rory's voice; it was nothing like Rory trying to offer something to please Beau, or trying to fulfill some obligation he felt he had. It was Rory asking for something he thought he wouldn't get. *If you want to wait for someone who...* What? What did Rory think Beau could possibly want to wait for? Beau had never wanted to pressure him, but...

"Rory," he said slowly. "There's no one else I want to wait for. You're my husband. My omega."

Rory looked away, but Beau could see the flush heating his cheeks, could smell his scent's sudden strengthening as the blush raised the temperature of his entire body.

"I didn't—I never wanted you to feel you *had* to do that. I thought, after everything, after the other alphas, the way you were treated," Rory flinched from that, drawing in, and, right, it probably sounded like Beau was judging Rory for not being virginal and untouched. "No, I just—I thought you wouldn't want to. Because you had to, before, and so..."

Rory picked his head up and stared at Beau for a moment, his brow wrinkled. "But you said... I asked you, I know I did. Before I agreed."

Beau frowned back. "I said...?"

"You said, no one else. Only you, and me, and no one else. And I'm yours, all proper and legal and everything."

Beau blinked at Rory, struggling to flatten all his physical reactions as he fully understood what Rory was saying. As far as Rory was concerned, apparently, any sexual abuse short of *whoring him out* was Beau's right as his alpha, and he'd only wanted to be sure that he wouldn't be subjected to being shared against his will.

Well. No fucking wonder he got nervous and jumpy when there were a lot of strange alphas in the house.

"I'm sorry," Rory whispered, and Beau dragged himself out of his own struggle for control to see that Rory had curled himself small in his kitchen chair. "I'm... maybe you didn't realize. How many. How... I'm sorry. I'll—"

"No," Beau said, because the core of this hadn't changed even after that little bombshell. Rory still thought that the issue here was that Beau didn't want him, that maybe no one could want him, because of everything he'd been through. Beau reached for him across the table, settling one hand over Rory's. "No, baby, please, there's nothing to be sorry for. You didn't do anything wrong."

Rory didn't look so much disbelieving as unutterably weary at that. He didn't pull his hand away, but it stayed perfectly motionless under Beau's. "You don't have to lie, Beau. I know what I did. What I am. I know I..."

Words alone couldn't help this; Rory needed something that couldn't be a lie. Beau stood up and moved around to Rory's side, and bent down to breathe in the scent of him again. It had gone sour and cold and ashen now, like he would stop having a scent if he could curl that into himself as well as his arms and legs.

"Baby," Beau repeated softly, and curled his arms around Rory despite the awkward angle. "You're mine. I chose you. I saw you at the refuge and I chose you. And I just wanted you to have choices too, that's all. I didn't want you to feel like you had to do anything for me, I wanted you to be able to choose."

"I did choose," Rory whispered. "I chose you. I said yes. I meant it."

Now was decidedly not the time to try to make Rory understand that that had barely been any choice at all, when his other option was dying alone among strangers. He would come to understand it later, when he was better, when he had more distance from it. But he might never get there if he got stuck on this, on believing that even his own alpha couldn't see past where he had been and what he had done.

"Okay," Beau said softly, remembering the quiet way Rory had chosen him, the acquiescence without fanfare. "Okay. Then I'm yours, baby, and if you don't want to be alone you don't have to be alone. If you want me tomorrow night, I'll be with you."

Rory twisted in his arms to look up at him, his scent warming with hope and, at long last, relief. "Are you sure? You don't—just because *I* want—"

Beau hushed him with a kiss, soft at first and then abruptly turning heated as he pulled Rory against him and Rory's arms went around his neck. He licked hungrily into Rory's mouth, holding Rory tight against him, and Rory responded eagerly, pressing close and kissing back.

It was only the sharp rattling of the plates that made Beau pause and realize that he had pulled Rory out of his chair entirely; they were leaning awkwardly against the table, and Rory had one leg up around Beau's, steadying himself.

Beau was hard, his whole body hot with desire at the feel of his omega in his arms, eager for his kisses. He couldn't help grinding up against Rory a little, and Rory pressed closer, making an encouraging noise—but there was nothing reciprocal in the motion, no sign of him seeking his own pleasure. He wasn't hard, and...

Beau shifted his grip and pressed his nose to Rory's throat, breathing in the scent of him instead of the air between them that mingled their heated scents into one.

There was still no flavor of arousal there, no tang of omega readiness.

"Beau, please, I promise—"

"Shh." Beau kissed him again, softer now, and kept holding him close. "Just means we'll wait until tomorrow night to do more than this, okay? No more than this until you're ready. I'll leave my door open tomorrow night, and you come find me when you want me. Tomorrow, for the moon, I'm all yours."

"Tomorrow," Rory echoed, but he kept his arms clasped around Beau's neck, and kissed him again. "But for now...?"

"For now," Beau hefted Rory up properly into his arms, and Rory's legs wrapped around him automatically. When he was steady, Beau turned away from the kitchen table, aiming for the nearest couch. "We'll do what feels good now, huh?"

Rory was kissing him again before they even got there, and Beau told himself that was enough. He wouldn't tell Rory no now, not when he couldn't hear anything but the rejection. Beau wouldn't leave his omega alone.

Like Rory had said, it wouldn't change anything. Rory would still be free at the end of three years. Beau could have this now, take care of him this way, and it wouldn't change anything at all.

CHAPTER 20

*R*ory went to bed feeling tingly all over, warm to the tips of his fingers and toes and almost too happy to breathe. Beau had held him and kissed him on the couch until they were both dozing off, and there had been no hesitation, no pulling away at all until he had carried Rory to the door of his bedroom.

Even then Beau had lingered for a few last kisses, a low-voiced promise that his door would be open, that he would wait for Rory to come to him.

It had seemed impossible, enchanted. Something out of a movie, something that would never really happen for an omega like him. Rory had lain awake for what felt like hours, feeling the waxing moon even when he couldn't see it, thinking of Beau holding him. He had been able to smell and feel how much Beau wanted, and yet Beau had never pushed him, never asked for more, never seemed to be punishing Rory for not offering more.

Rory had slept easily despite the pull of the moon, and he didn't wake until after the moon was down. He heard Beau downstairs, smelled the scents of breakfast being prepared, and smiled into his pillow. Just like in the beginning, in Chicago, when he was always waking up to Beau fixing him something to eat; clearly Beau had shaken off last night's exhaustion.

Rory dressed and headed downstairs, where Beau greeted him with a grin and a mountain of pancakes—and whipped cream and powdered sugar, already set out. Rory couldn't help grinning back.

As they ate, Beau said, "I'm gonna need something else to do today. A project, or something. I can feel it, I'm gonna go nuts if I try to just sit around all day waiting for," Beau glanced at him, then away, "The moon."

Rory squirmed a little in his seat, butterflies starting up in his stomach, undeterred by the weight of food. "You could..."

He hesitated instinctively. It was Beau, he knew it was Beau, he knew Beau liked him to suggest things, but the words still caught in his throat. Especially when they were waiting for... the moon.

"Rory? If you have an idea, I'd love to know it. You've seen a hell of a lot more of the house than I have since we moved in, you know what needs doing."

Rory bit his lip. The yard wasn't the house, exactly, and Beau certainly saw the front yard, at least, every day when he left for work and came back. If Rory pointed it out, that was pointing out that Beau hadn't noticed, had neglected something.

But Beau had asked, and Beau wouldn't get angry. Rory was almost completely sure that Beau wouldn't get angry.

"The grass," Rory managed to say, his voice coming out small. "It, um. It's..."

Beau looked toward the window, frowning a little, and then stood and walked to the back door and looked out; Rory could see him looking around, comparing their backyard to the others it bordered.

"Oh, wow, we're gonna be knee deep pretty soon," Beau said, turning back to Rory with a smile. "Guess we'd better go buy a lawn-mower first, huh? Or... research first, I guess, I don't know a thing about lawnmowers. I've never even used one."

Rory bit his lip, pushing a triangle of pancakes through a puddle of melting cream. "I..."

He had done research, waiting for himself to work up the courage to mention it to Beau, so that his alpha wouldn't have to worry about that part. But then he'd thought maybe that would be presumptuous, telling his alpha how to spend his money, and then he'd thought maybe he should just buy one himself with the card Beau gave him and have it delivered, so his alpha never had to think about it.

And then he'd done none of those things until now.

"Oh, hey, yeah, you grew up in the burbs, you must've had a lawn, huh?" Beau came back to the table and sat down in a chair beside Rory's instead of around the corner, scooting close. "Hey, baby. If you know what we need, that's good, that means I can go get one and mow some grass instead of having to sit still and do research. And if you don't know what we need, that's okay, we'll figure it out."

"I know," Rory whispered, and he couldn't help sitting taller when Beau grinned at him. Beau darted in and gave him a quick kiss, and Rory grinned into it, feeling incandescent.

Rory made it through the trip to the big box store to buy a lawn-mower—and, once Beau got to chatting with a salesman, also a weed trimmer and some electric hedge-trimming thing just short of a chainsaw that would *probably* be sufficient to take on the lilac bushes. He even managed to demonstrate his mowing technique to Beau, and stood and watched while Beau took over to try it out.

Beau, of course, got the hang of it immediately and mowed the lawn in surgically straight lines, so Rory went inside to make some lunch for them both. Beau ate his sandwiches standing up on the patio, eyeing the nearest lilac bush like he was gearing up for a fight; Rory wouldn't have been surprised if he skipped the hedge-trimmer and attacked it with teeth and claws instead.

Rory took the dishes back inside to wash, and when he was done with that and looked around for something else to keep him busy, it hit him. The feeling of the full moon approaching, the feeling of waiting for his alpha, waiting to be fucked, waiting for who-knew-what...

He tried to tell himself the things he knew. *It's Beau, just Beau, he won't hurt me, he won't even come into my room. He wants me to like it.*

But that just turned into more fear, now. Beau was expecting him to want it, to like it, to be *happy*, and that was more than any other alpha had ever demanded of him. Even when they drugged him out of his mind with heat-inducers and who knew what else, they didn't demand that he like it. Just that he was there, just that they got to use him. Or maybe he did like it, when he was in heat, maybe that was part of what was mercifully washed away after. Maybe he *would* like it tonight, maybe he wouldn't be able to help liking it.

I want to like it, I want to feel good, I want to like it with him, Rory tried to tell himself, but it was like whispering in a thunderstorm. The fear rose up and swamped him until he felt like he was drowning, gasping for air and clutching the edge of the counter.

The back door opened with a bang and Beau was standing there, his hands scratched and bleeding and half-curled into fists. His sweaty body radiated the scent of *alpha alpha alpha,* and his eyebrows were lowered, his eyes dark and intent on Rory.

Rory's knees trembled. He felt himself getting hot, starting to get wet, and he turned and ran up the stairs and into his room.

He didn't stop until he'd locked that door and the bathroom door behind himself. He fumbled his way into the enormous shower and turned it on full blast, not caring whether the water came out scalding or ice cold. He just needed to wash all scent from his nose, all sound from his ears, to be lost in the white noise and the cleansing rush.

He didn't know how long he'd been standing there when he was able to realize that the wild panic was fading out of his mind, leaving him only tense and anxious with the approaching moon, and pleasantly warm and clean under the spray of hot water, although also weighed down by the sopping-wet clothes he hadn't stopped to take off.

The first coherent thought that came to him was, *Beau was worried about me.*

He hadn't been angry. He hadn't rushed into the house because he was bent on having Rory before the moon could even bring him as close to readiness as he was going to get. He hadn't been... anything any other alpha might have been. Beau had heard Rory starting to panic over nothing and had rushed to him, worried about him. His hands had been bleeding from fighting those lilac bushes, not...

Rory saw, for just a second, a flash of the midwife's strong, blood-streaked hands, felt the tearing pain flash through his belly and lower, the midwife's fingers and something else pushing inside him too far. *There. No need to worry about you getting pregnant now, omega.*

Rory had stolen the bottle of suppressants from the midwife's bag while the midwife was settling up with Martin. He hadn't dared to actually take the pills until he got away, but that was where it had started. That was when he had begun to really plan how to leave for good, though it took him more than a year to actually do it.

And he had gotten away. He was with Beau now, and Beau had promised to keep him safe, and Rory had let Beau take that bottle of suppressants away for good. Now he was getting stronger, getting healthy, and now the full moon was coming, only hours away.

And Beau had to be twice as worried about Rory as he'd been to begin with, because when Beau came to check on him, Rory had run away like he thought Beau would hurt him.

Beau wouldn't hurt him. Beau had promised to leave his door open tonight, so Rory could come to him if he wanted, but Beau wouldn't demand it, or punish him if he didn't come. Beau wouldn't do any of the things Martin or the ones before him had ever done.

Rory shut the water off and grabbed a big fluffy towel to wrap around himself. In the quiet, with the water off, he didn't have to open the locked bathroom door to know where Beau was; he could hear Beau's breathing and his heart beating.

He was in the upstairs hall, just outside the door to Rory's bedroom.

The door wasn't anything special, even if Rory had stopped to lock it; Beau was an alpha, and this was his house. He could have kicked the door in if he wanted to. But he had waited, and was still waiting, outside. He must have come upstairs as soon as Rory turned the shower on—but not until then. If Rory had heard Beau following, he didn't know what he would have done, but he definitely wouldn't have missed noticing.

"Beau?" Rory sat down on the plush rug next to the shower, huddling in his plush new towel. "I'm sorry, I didn't..."

"It's okay," Beau said immediately, his low, gentle voice carrying easily. "You didn't do anything wrong, baby. I should have known better than to startle you like that today."

Rory had to hide his face in the towel for a moment, feeling too many things at once—tears sprang to his eyes, and his skin felt too small and tingly all over. The sound of Beau's voice was like a caress everywhere, right on the line between feeling good and feeling too much to be anything but terrifying.

"Are your hands okay?" Rory asked. "Did they heal?"

"My... oh." Beau sounded startled. "I didn't even notice. They're okay, but I should probably wash them before I touch anything. I'll have to make sure I didn't leave handprints anywhere on my way up."

There was no sound of him moving away from Rory's door, though.

"I could help," Rory said, fists clenched tight as he held the towel around himself. "Clean it up, I mean. If you did."

"That would be sweet of you, baby," Beau said. "But it's my mess, I'll take care of it if it needs taking care of. I didn't spend six years as an emergency responder without learning how to clean blood off of everything I own."

"Oh," Rory murmured, leaning his forehead against his knee. "Yeah, of course."

"Baby," Beau said softly, and then nothing for a moment. Rory just sat and listened to his heart beating, the soft sounds of his slow breaths, until Beau said, "Can you tell me what happened?"

Rory took a shaky breath. "I'm not—it wasn't—I'm not scared of *you*. I'm just. Scared. And I forget somehow, that you're not like that. It's not going to be like that. I mean I don't forget, really, I know that, but..."

"Yeah," Beau said quietly. "It's what you're used to, isn't it? It's been like that for a long time. And you said, even before, it was the moons that made you realize you were an omega. So it was the full moons that..."

Rory squeezed his eyes shut and did not cry and did not think about those moons. It just took him a few minutes to be able to say, "Yeah. The... the moon only ever takes things away, it seems like."

Beau made a soft sound, nowhere near a word, that gave Rory the feeling that Beau would be wrapping his arms around him if he could. Rory wrapped his own arms around himself, wanting Beau to hold him so badly that even the wanting was terrifying right now.

"Do you remember the last time it was good?" Beau asked after a while. "Or... any time it was good? When you were little, you and Georgie and your mom?"

Rory's heart did something funny at the way Beau mentioned his family, like they were people he knew, people Rory still had some connection to. It took him a moment to even be able to think of a time when the full moon held no menace, no darkness hidden in that nighttime light.

"We had a rec room, in the basement," Rory said slowly. "Sound-proof, so it was safe. We would play all night down there, chasing each other. Me and Georgie, but mom, too. And da—" Rory's breath caught, but he didn't correct himself. His dad had still been his dad, then. "Dad would get up early and make breakfast for us, and when the moon was down he'd come down or let Spencer come down and open the door and tell us it was time to eat."

"And before?" Beau prompted softly. "When you could feel the moon coming, but it wasn't here yet?"

Rory looked around the bathroom, gauging the light and trying to refine his panicky feeling of the full moon's approach into some sense of how far off it actually was. It was early afternoon now. "We had to go to school. Mom wouldn't risk anyone noticing. I'd listen to Georgie's heartbeat and she'd listen to mine, and it was like a game, who could be calmer. Georgie usually won, but I did okay. After school... chores, usually, or mom would find some excuse to send us upstairs and downstairs over and over, so we could move, but still..."

They'd had to be under control. Hidden. Not obvious, not anything the neighbors might notice.

"Well," Beau said. "We've got a whole yard, and the neighbors already know what we are, so if they see us playing tag all afternoon at least they'll know we're not out in the state park taking down deer with our teeth."

Rory blinked, thinking of it. Beau chasing him around the yard, just for fun, not getting angry at Rory for running away, not cornering him...

Beau said, "You're it!"

Rory stared toward the doors as he heard the sound of Beau's footsteps moving away from the door, slowly at first and then faster.

You're it.

He meant for Rory to chase *him?*

Rory stood up, towels and all, and clambered into the enormous bathtub under the window that looked out into the backyard; he could hear Beau open and close the back door, and then the alpha appeared on the grass below him. He waved and then started trotting backward, slowly. It was the way Rory's mom used to pretend to run away from him and Georgie when they were small, the way he and Georgie had played with Spencer, who could never hope to match their speed.

Rory just stared for a moment, and then looked down at himself. He was wearing Beau's jeans, still. They were sopping wet and clinging coldly and heavily to his legs now. He peeled out of them, which left him in shower-soaked underwear and a t-shirt, a towel wrapped around him from shoulders to waist. He pictured himself running outside just like this, barely clothed and spreading his arms so that the towel flapped behind him like a cape as he ran around the yard.

He nearly choked on it, but a sound made its way out of his throat. It took a few seconds for Rory to recognize it as a laugh. He was standing in a Jacuzzi tub he'd never used, looking out the window at his husband in the backyard, still running in slow motion and watching him with a hopeful look. The full moon was only hours away. And Rory was laughing.

He turned his back on the window and ran to the door, unlocking it before he could lose his nerve. He grabbed a pair of flannel pants that hung on the back of the bedroom door and raced through the house like something was chasing him; he didn't dare stop long enough for his fear to catch up.

$\sim$

He yanked his pants on at the back door—it was a hilarious thought, but he wasn't *actually* going to run around the yard practically naked. Once he was decent he chased Beau around the yard, grinning with the sheer pleasure of using his body, of being able to run and jump. For the first time in a long time the moon's pull didn't run into painful conflict with the weakness of his body, or with his alpha's commands. Beau always kept just out of his reach, so there was never any danger of turning the tables and becoming the one chased.

They'd been at it for long enough that his t-shirt and underwear had dried and his sleep pants were grass-stained halfway to the knees when Rory chased Beau up onto the roof of the garage and came to an abrupt halt at the peak of the roof. Beau was a little way below, crouching on the sloped shingles. Below them, down on the driveway, stood Jennifer and three small werewolf children.

"Hey, guys," Jennifer said, sounding a little longsuffering but not really annoyed. "I told the kids it was a *married folks* thing, but they wanted to know if they could come play tag with you until it's time for us to head out to the park. Totally okay if not, but..."

Beau looked over his shoulder at Rory, and Rory couldn't help looking down at the three kids. The smallest was just a toddler, a boy with messy dark hair and chubby limbs. The older two were both girls, blonde hair already coming loose from their pigtails, bouncing with eagerness to run and play.

He thought of himself and Georgie, and what it would have been like to play on the afternoon of a full moon with their neighbors, in full sight of all the humans. To be what they were, openly and safely.

And then too, it would ward off the fear, the memories, that kept creeping up on him. To be playing chase with children, to hear them laughing, to breathe in their clean baby scents, was the furthest thing from any full moon he'd had in years.

Rory nodded, looking to Beau, who just watched him, letting him choose what to say, and then to Jennifer. "Yeah, of course. Come around back."

All three kids cheered and bolted away from their mother without a look back. Rory jumped down and chased them, and Beau, around and around the yard, up into trees, onto the roof, for what seemed like a golden sunlit eternity. Beau would pick up the smallest when Rory got close and run off with him, which always made him laugh and cheer; sometimes the older girls would jump on Beau and demand that he protect them, as well, and he did so without hesitating.

At some point the number of children in the yard multiplied; human kids had joined in, Rory realized. They were identifiable mostly by the fact that they shrieked a little more than they laughed and required Beau to "rescue" them more often, but they laughed and mixed in just like the werewolf kids. Rory looked around and saw a few parents watching—two women sitting out on a patio in a nearby yard, a father lingering in the side yard.

The lady next door, on the other side of the hazel bushes, was peering out from her back door. Rory, in a giddy rush of fearlessness, waved to her, and one of the Niemi kids saw him do it and stopped to yell, "Hi, Mrs. Lindholm!"

Every other kid in the yard followed suit, yelling and waving, which almost covered Summer's piercing whisper to Rory. "Mama said she's nervous about wolves and kids and strangers so we just gotta be nice to her *even harder*."

Rory wasn't sure whether he wanted to laugh, or cry, but he didn't want to do either with Mrs. Lindholm watching, so he just started running again, careful never to actually quite catch anyone.

~

Eventually the kids had to go home, to dinner, or to run with their pack overnight.

"You're welcome to come with," Jennifer called out, collecting her three. Rory still wasn't sure of their names—the littlest was Oliver, he thought, and one of the girls was Summer but he had no idea which. "Or I can show you on the map the unclaimed areas—everyone's usually pretty chill about unattached wolves taking a run there."

"We're fine," Rory put in, without looking at Beau. "But thanks."

Jennifer winked, smiling knowingly, and said, "Well, anytime. Thanks for keeping the pups busy!"

In a shockingly short time, he was alone with Beau, standing in their driveway with the late-summer sun sinking behind the trees. The nearness of the moon was suddenly all he could feel, a buzz in his blood and all over the surface of his skin. He took a quick breath, almost a gasp, and he could smell Beau, *alpha* and *male*, his body hot with his exercise, his scent all bright and open with happiness.

Rory felt his cock twitch, his hole suddenly wetter than he'd felt it in a long time, and he turned and bolted into the house before he could think or speak.

It wasn't panic this time, or not *only* panic. The feeling that pounded through him was partly that traitorous wanting, too. It felt something like that weakness in him, that hunger, that made him seek out a new alpha every time he got away from an old one, but it was something else too, something basic and physical. He couldn't remember feeling it this simply and purely in a long time, maybe not since he was in his teens, lonely and bored and determined to hate everything about the pack he'd been exiled to.

He had touched himself then, locking himself away and feeling as if he was defying someone, somehow, by enjoying the omega parts of himself. He'd gotten his hands filthy with his own slick, stroked his cock with slippery hands and traced the sensitive edges of his opening, and he'd gotten off over and over and over. He'd scratched the itch, satisfied the desire, and then just kept going, because there was nothing better for him, nothing else he'd rather do.

And then he'd met Sean, and Sean told him that what he could do himself was nothing to what an alpha could do for him, that touching himself was kid stuff. Rory had believed him—and that part had even been true, at first. It was just everything else that was worse.

It was true, maybe, that he could never have done to himself everything an alpha had done to him. Without an alpha—without all those alphas...

But there was no use thinking about that. The moon was coming, and he had an alpha again, but a different one this time. An alpha who spent the hours before the moon playing chase in the sunshine, scooping up werewolf kids and human ones too, so they could all run as fast as an alpha.

"Beau," he murmured under his breath. Not *an alpha*. Beau. His husband, who exhausted himself among humans every day because he wanted to heal them. Who waited outside Rory's door when Rory ran from him and promised to leave his own door open for Rory tonight. Who had never had an omega before, never had anyone at all—only his own hands, like Rory had back before... everything.

He wished he could have been that with Beau. He knew the timing didn't work that way, but he wished that he had run from his pack at the same time Beau was cast out by his, that they had found each other somehow, converged on Chicago at the same moment, and...

Rory laughed a little, though the sound was choked off and almost desperate now. At sixteen, untouched, just a kid, he wouldn't have known what to do with a good boy like Beau had always been. He had scoffed at all the polite and well-mannered boys of his own pack, had barely noticed their attempts to court him or even befriend him. He had had to throw himself into the path of disaster first. A hundred disasters. He had had to be nearly dying before he let a good alpha take care of him.

And now he had Beau. Now he was Beau's, and Beau was his. At least for now. Tonight.

The panic was still there, and the wanting, and the pull of the moon and the fading sunlight. But Rory focused on the sounds of Beau moving around downstairs. He locked the doors, and closed all the windows, and went into the kitchen for something... several somethings... and now he was coming up the stairs.

Rory stood utterly still, barely breathing, and listened while Beau turned the other way at the top of the stairs and went into his own room. He was setting things down, and there was a soft whispery sound—had he folded back the covers on the bed, or just smoothed them out? He hadn't taken his clothes off.

He hadn't closed the door.

Beau. Rory licked his lips and took a few deliberate breaths, and then said it aloud. "Beau?"

He heard Beau go still, and he heard the sudden speeding of Beau's heartbeat. Wanting him, wanting to answer the moon's call, but staying so still. Beau was always so careful with him.

"I'm right here, baby. The door's open whenever you want to come in. But if you—"

Rory shook his head. He was with Beau now, after all this time, after everything he'd done wrong. He had Beau, and he wasn't going to let his incredible good luck go to waste. Rory shoved off his grass-stained pajama pants, yanked open his own door, and hurried down the hall, right across the threshold and into Beau's room without stopping.

Beau was perched on the end of the bed—still dressed, with a few grass stains on his clothes, giving off the sunshine scent of playing in the yard. He was looking up at Rory, his hands between his knees and his dark eyes wide, hopeful, and fixed on Rory's face. Rory was only in his underwear; his hardening dick had to be obvious, the slick he was starting to produce. But Beau just kept looking at his face, waiting.

"I want," Rory said, breathless as if he'd had to run a mile to reach Beau's room. As if he'd had to run for eight years. "I want this. You. Please, Beau."

It was only after he spoke that he felt a sudden surge of energy: the full moon had broken the horizon, calling to them as it called to every werewolf. He saw Beau feel it the same way he did, but Beau didn't jump up from the bed, even now that Rory had come to him, had asked for whatever Beau would give him.

Beau raised his hands, opening them in invitation, and Rory rushed toward him, straddling his lap with his knees on the mattress and his hands on Beau's broad shoulders. He felt a shiver go through Beau; he could feel that alpha power under his fingers, the scent of an alpha's desire filling him with every breath, all multiplied by the full moon shining on them.

But when Beau tugged him down it was only into a kiss, with one of Beau's hands wrapped around the nape of his neck, the other on his hip. Beau's mouth was hot against his, but not rough, not pushing. Coaxing and sweet.

Rory made a helpless, shaking sound as Beau sucked on his lower lip, teased his tongue. Rory's cock was definitely hard now, and he was so hot inside. He was turning open and wet, and he hadn't felt that in so long. The moon sped his racing blood, but it was still only the moon, not a heat coming on. His head was clear; it was just that he wanted this. Wanted Beau. He'd hardly remembered how just wanting could feel, pure and simple and good.

"You can," he tried to say. "I'm ready—"

Beau just kept kissing him, barely holding him in place. Rory wriggled under his hands, but they didn't tighten, didn't push him anywhere. Finally Rory took the initiative and squirmed down to sit directly on Beau's lap. The bulge of his cock pressed up through his jeans and Rory rubbed himself against it, trying to encourage Beau to get on with it.

Beau groaned against his lips and his hips jerked up, pressing him harder against Rory's ass. Rory felt a sharper thrill of fear and hunger, edged with pleasure from that halfway friction. He might not be *ready*, technically, not easy like he would be if he was in heat, but he wanted to do this. He wanted the waiting to be over, and he knew Beau would at least try to make it feel good. Even if it hurt, he wanted it. He wanted to be whole. He wanted his alpha.

"Please," Rory mumbled against his mouth. "Beau, please, just—"

"Okay," Beau murmured, tilting his head back to look up at Rory.

His always-dark eyes looked blacker than ever, but bright under his heavy lids. "Okay, baby. Can I take your clothes off you?"

Rory figured that was built in to the whole thing where he came to Beau's room to have sex with him on the full moon, but he couldn't summon up the words to tease Beau about being so careful. He nodded instead, keeping his eyes on Beau's while Beau's hands settled at his waist, at the hem of his shirt.

"Hands up." Beau's voice was a low rumble that made Rory shiver as he obeyed, letting go of Beau's shoulders and raising his arms above his head. Beau didn't quite touch him as he skimmed the t-shirt up and off, tossing it aside, and then Rory was looking down at his alpha, his hands still lingering in the air above his head.

He was exposed from the tops of his hipbones up, and for a long, suspended moment Beau just looked. Rory knew he couldn't be seeing anything so special—even now that he was mostly recovered and starting to look less starved, he still showed his bones too prominently through his pale flesh, and the livid scars around his throat were far from the only ones he bore.

But maybe the little bit of moonlight leaking in through the windows painted him forgivingly, because Beau didn't seem to see anything at all that he didn't like. He just looked and looked, and then he leaned in and pressed a kiss to Rory's breastbone, right over where his heart was hammering away.

The brush of Beau's lips punched a little sound out of Rory, and he felt his nipples go tight, his cock jumping under the slight cover of his underwear. Beau's hands were at his hips again, so close. Rory was tempted to be greedy, if Beau was going to keep being kind.

"More," he gasped without thinking, without taking time to be afraid.

Beau looked up at him and grinned, his teeth glinting in the moonlight, and then he kissed Rory's chest again, and his mouth brushed over one stiff nipple. Rory gasped sharply at the thrill of pleasure, easy and unlooked for, and Beau took it for encouragement, licking and then sucking.

Rory could feel Beau's cock pressing ever harder against him, but

Beau still made no move to get either of them undressed further, using his mouth every way he could on Rory's chest. He kept teasing until Rory could hardly catch his breath and was squirming constantly all over Beau's lap.

When Rory couldn't bear it anymore he shoved at the top of his own underwear, trying to push them down and gasping out whatever words he could think of, mostly *Beau* and *please* and *more, more*.

Everything swung around suddenly, startling Rory into stillness as he landed on his back on Beau's bed. There was a sharp moment of realization, relief and cold recognition: *Oh, here it is*.

Except Beau was sliding down to kneel on the floor as he flung Rory's underwear away, his hands sliding gently up the insides of Rory's thighs.

"I told you I've never done this," he said, still smiling as Rory's legs parted instinctively. "So, you know, tell me if I'm doing it wrong."

"You still have your pants on," Rory observed blankly, and Beau laughed as he lowered his head to nuzzle at Rory's stiff little cock. Rory's mouth fell open and he felt himself getting wetter, but Beau still didn't touch him there, petting the insides of his thighs and—oh —*licking*—

Rory's head fell back against the bed and he stared up at the ceiling, gasping for breath as Beau's mouth kept moving over him. Every tentative touch was another thrill of impossible pleasure, and over all of it was the mind-blanking reality that Beau was on his knees for *Rory*, using his mouth, his hands, for nothing but this. Not even to open him up, only to pleasure him.

"Good, baby?" Beau asked, his breath still puffing against Rory's cock, and Rory had to pick his head up and look.

Beau's mouth was all pink and wet, just barely out of contact with Rory's cock. Rory whimpered and nodded.

Beau grinned, showing a flash of teeth, and Rory's legs fell open wider automatically.

"You taste so good," Beau said, ducking his head again. "I never want to stop."

Rory made a noise that was nowhere near being an actual word, and Beau's mouth just kept dragging lower, down the underside of his cock, down over his balls, and finally down to where he was hot and wet. Rory's hips tilted up, one heel catching the end of the bed and slipping off; Beau's hand curled around his ankle only to guide his leg over Beau's shoulder. Rory arched up into his mouth and sobbed.

Beau's tongue was just flickering against him, teasing, and Rory felt dizzy and hot and still strangely clear-headed. It was nothing like heat, everything like *wanting*. He couldn't believe he'd ever forgotten what this was like, this basic, animal need.

"Beau, Beau, please, I need—"

He didn't know what he needed, but Beau's tongue pressed more firmly against him, lips sealing over his hole, and Beau wrapped a hand around Rory's cock. Rory tried instinctively to strangle the sound that tore out of his throat, but a stuttering cry escaped him as the pleasure of his alpha's touch tore through him. He lost all track of what Beau was doing. He only knew that it felt good, purely good with no edge of pain or fear, nothing sick or rotten at the center of it. The pleasure of it piled up, more and more, until it couldn't be contained.

Rory's whole body arched as he came, his cock pulsing and his hole grasping hungrily at Beau's tongue. It was something beyond pleasure; he felt as if his whole self opened for a moment, moonlight pouring through him in a blinding wash of brightness.

When he was aware again, after, he picked his head up and looked for Beau. He was right where he had been, kneeling between Rory's wantonly spread thighs, his mouth and chin glistening wet with Rory's slick. The air smelled of sex and pleasure and desperately aroused alpha, and the full moon was shining down on them, bright in every beat of Rory's still-racing heart.

There was a long night ahead of them, and now it was Beau's turn. Rory grinned and crooked one finger, beckoning him closer.

CHAPTER 21

For hours Beau had been telling himself: *Don't hurt him. Don't scare him. Don't lose control.*

He had been afraid, down underneath everything, that the moon, the scent of his omega, and the desires he had spent his entire life controlling, would all combine to drive him out of his mind. The half-feral alpha that humans feared had lurked in the back of his head, an image of what he could become if he let himself go.

He hadn't had much time to worry about it, though, because he'd been busy looking after Rory, keeping him distracted, helping him feel safe. And then Rory had come to him, shy and frightened and determined and wanting all at once, even before the moon's pull reached its full force.

He would have let Beau do anything, that was obvious, but from the first moment he brought Rory pleasure Beau hadn't wanted to do anything else. What could be better than driving out Rory's fear and replacing it with delight? Beau couldn't think of anything to compare with watching Rory, *tasting* him, as he lost all restraint, melting into pure ecstasy from the touch of Beau's tongue and the grip of his hand.

Watching Rory come, all he could think was, *I want this forever. I want to make you feel this every way there is. Only you.*

Then Rory crooked that finger at him, and Beau was abruptly aware of the debauched omega sprawled naked in his bed, and his own cock throbbing with need. It was a wonder he hadn't come already.

He was frozen for a moment, resisting the urge to *pounce*, to take what Rory couldn't really mean to offer.

Rory moved before Beau did, sliding down off the bed so that he was straddling Beau's lap again, just like he had on the bed. Beau could feel the difference in every inch of Rory's body; every movement was liquid-loose, utterly at ease. He kissed Beau slowly, licking at Beau's lips and taking the taste of himself back from Beau's mouth.

His other hand dropped to the fly of Beau's jeans, and Beau groaned into his mouth. "Baby, you—you don't have to—oh, *fuck.*"

Rory had flipped the button open and got the zipper down, and Beau's cock pushed out through the opening, straining against his underwear. The head of it popped out over the waistband at the slightest touch from Rory, and Beau's hands clamped on Rory's slim hips without a thought, wanting, *needing* him.

But he didn't push, didn't move. He held on to his omega, who wanted him, who wasn't afraid. Rory kissed him again and curled his hand around Beau's cock.

"Oh, *oh,*" Beau moaned. Rory's hand started to move, and Beau could hardly breathe for the pleasure of it, the shocking rightness. The air was full of the scent of satisfied omega, the moon was shining down on them and within them, and he had never needed anything as much as he needed Rory's touch. "Please, baby, anything, I —I won't—"

Rory's mouth covered his, and Rory settled lower over him, so close Beau could feel the heat of him. Rory wriggled a little, and then his other hand slid down Beau's cock, drawing it fully out of his pants, and the touch was slippery and hot, the scent of omega rising more strongly between them.

Rory had wet his hand with his own slick.

Beau *pushed*, thrusting up into Rory's grip, tipping Rory back against the bed and kissing him frantically. Rory moaned into his mouth, still stroking as Beau thrust into his hands in hard, uncoordinated motions.

Don't, Beau told himself, *not yet*, but he couldn't hold it back. The pleasure crested, and he was coming in Rory's hands and over his belly. The orgasm rushed through him fast, knotless, a blinding rush to the end.

After a moment he picked his head up. "Sorry, baby," he mumbled, easing away from Rory, who was still pressed back against the edge of the mattress.

Rory blinked up at him and didn't move to a less awkward position; his thighs were still splayed over Beau's. Beau's come was splattered all over his belly, and Rory was half-hard again, or still, and his thighs were wet with slick.

"Tell me," Beau started, and then he couldn't tell what to say. *Tell me what you want* or *tell me that was okay*, though he could smell Rory's satisfaction, still without any tinge of fear or hurt.

"Take your clothes off," Rory said, breathless but without hesitation. "And take me to bed."

Beau had to kiss him again first, claiming that wet pink mouth, his lips already hot with kisses. Rory pushed up his t-shirt and Beau raised his arms, breaking the kiss just long enough to let Rory pull it off him entirely. Beau stood up under him—Rory's thighs tightened around him—and he twisted to fall backward onto the bed, keeping Rory on top.

Rory shook his head but kissed Beau again, shoving his pants down. Beau arched up to help him, scooting up the bed as he wriggled out of his jeans and kicked them off. Rory kept kissing him and rubbing down against him, his sweet little omega cock hardening against Beau's belly, the mingled scents of them filling the heated air. Beau grabbed him by the hips and tugged him up, so he was straddling Beau's chest and Beau could push up on one elbow and taste him again.

Beau mouthed at the head of his cock, tasting the pre-come leaking from it and his own come where it had dripped down. Rory trembled above him, hips twitching a little, and Beau let his lips brush his cock as he said, "You can, baby. Give it to me. I want it. I want you to get what you want. Can you do that for me?"

Rory stared down at him, the green of his eyes looking like the thinnest rim of moon-silver around pools of black. "Beau, you—"

Beau opened his mouth, taking the head of Rory's cock on his tongue, and tugged firmly on Rory's hip, urging him on. Rory moved, a tentative little push, his eyes fixed on Beau's, and then dropping to stare as his cock pushed into Beau's open mouth.

Beau groaned at the taste of him, the feeling of his omega's desire and pleasure heavy on his tongue, and his own cock surged to full hardness again.

Rory whimpered and pushed a little deeper, starting to trust that Beau meant what he'd offered, and Beau sucked hungrily at him, feeling him harden and pulse on Beau's tongue. Rory's cock was proportioned to the rest of him, not much more than a mouthful, and Beau wanted every inch, every drop of his omega. He kept his eyes on Rory's, watching him lose himself in pleasure, forgetting to be shocked that an alpha would do this for him and giving himself up to Beau.

Still, Rory was an omega, and getting his dick wet wasn't the only thing he needed. After a few more thrusts Rory was whining, his movements turning restless.

"Beau," he gasped. "Alpha, I need, I need you—"

Beau released Rory's cock with an obscene wet sound and rubbed his hand up and down Rory's thigh. His own cock was standing up, throbbing with readiness, but that didn't matter, not if it wasn't what Rory wanted. Beau was hungrier for Rory's pleasure than his own, chasing it like he was on the hunt.

"Where, baby? What do you need?"

Rory's fingers went unhesitatingly between his wide-open thighs, touching his opening, where slick was dripping constantly now. Beau's hips rocked instinctively, his cock aching to be there, but he ignored that.

"Need—need you. Please, Beau."

Beau brought his fingers to join Rory's, threading them in so that he could touch right where Rory was touching. Rory was still just touching his opening, not pressing any further, and Beau rocked his finger along the rim where he was so very wet, feeling the way the muscle softened at a touch. Rory moaned and pushed a finger into himself, and Beau's finger followed to be squeezed tight inside.

Rory gasped, folding forward to press his forehead against Beau's, his panting breath puffing against Beau's face. Beau crooked his finger, stroking, searching for the best places to touch, and he felt more wetness gush out past his fingertip and drip down his hand. Rory keened, his cock jerking untouched, but he drew his finger out, and Beau followed suit.

"What do you—" *need*, he meant to say, but that was as far as he got before Rory bent backward and closed his hand unerringly on Beau's cock.

It was Beau's turn to gasp, the sudden touch and what it promised blazing through him.

"Please," Rory said, picking his head up to meet Beau's gaze. "Alpha. Beau. *Please*, I need you. In me. All the way. Let me be yours. *Please*."

Beau couldn't breathe or think, consumed by the need to hold absolutely still against everything the wolf in him wanted—to throw Rory down and take him, to cover his mate's body with his own and mark his claim with his teeth, plant his seed deep, fuck him and knot him and never let him go, never stop giving him what he was asking for right now.

But *that* wasn't what Rory was asking for, and Beau would die before he ever saw the pleading in Rory's eyes and the eagerness in his scent turn to fear and pain.

"Okay," Beau managed to say after a moment, and then he pried his own hands away from Rory with a monumental effort. He reached up and pressed both palms flat to the headboard of the bed while Rory stared, baffled.

"Okay," Beau repeated, pushing up a little into Rory's hand. "I'm all yours, baby. Take what you want. Only what you want, only what feels good. That's all I want."

Rory stared at him for a few seconds, and Beau watched understanding dawn on his face as he realized what Beau was offering him. "You... *alpha*."

"You, omega," Beau agreed, grinning. "If you want it, take it, baby."

"You fucking—" Rory folded down over him, kissing him hard, his hands framing Beau's face while Beau kept his hands pressed hard to the headboard, every muscle in his arms rigid as iron. His good intentions could only do that much; with Rory's mouth open to his he couldn't help pushing inside, tasting and exploring Rory's mouth, claiming him in the one way he dared to let himself.

Rory was whining against his mouth, wriggling above him, and finally Beau pulled away to breathe. Beau's cock was aching, untouched now that Rory was leaning low over him, and he could smell Rory's desire, the slick dripping from him to ease the way.

"Go on, baby," Beau said softly. "Get yourself off, make yourself feel good. Can you do that? Is that what you want?"

Rory nodded sharply, his eyes still wide, but he looked present, cognizant. He wasn't lost to the moon; there was still no hint of a heat, or even the edge of one, in his scent. Rory was still in control. The moon was just lighting him up.

"Tell me what you want," Beau said, as gently as he could manage with his cock achingly hard and his omega kneeling over him, wet and begging for it and keeping them both on this edge. He wouldn't force Rory to say it if he couldn't, but Beau needed to know he was guiding him the way he actually wanted to go.

"You," Rory managed, and then, "your cock. Want you inside me."

"Go on, then, baby," Beau said, rocking his hips, jerking his chin in the direction Rory needed to move. "I'm all yours. Take it as slow as you need to."

"*Beau,*" Rory breathed, but it wasn't a question, or the start of anything. It seemed like all the remark he was going to make—and then he was scooting backward, his eyes still on Beau as he got himself into position, straddling Beau's hips.

His straining cock pressed against Rory's thigh, all soft skin and dripping slick, and Beau groaned helplessly, pressing his whole body back into the bed to keep still. He had offered this to Rory, offered himself. He had to be what Rory needed.

He was concentrating so hard on keeping still that he was taken by surprise when he felt the first hot wet touch on the head of his cock. Beau let out a startled sound and let himself look.

Rory was looking back, watching him with wide eyes, but Beau only met them for an instant before his gaze dropped to his cock between Rory's wide-open thighs. He could see them trembling, saw Rory hesitating, struggling, with his opening just kissing the head of Beau's cock. He was so hot right there, slick leaking from him, and it was making Beau's breath come short, this feeling of being almost inside, knowing that this exquisite touch was only the very beginning.

"Feel so good, baby," Beau couldn't help saying. "So good. I could come just from this. You're so—"

Rory let out a shaky breath and moved, and Beau's words cut off into a helpless sound as his cock pushed inside that tight opening. The pleasure of it was overwhelming, but Beau couldn't stop staring at the sheer fact of their bodies being joined together like this. He was inside his omega now, clasped tight even if it was only a couple of inches, and there were no words for how good it felt, how right.

Only you, he couldn't help thinking, wanting to touch, to kiss, to wrap himself around every inch of Rory while Rory was wrapped so tight around two inches of him.

Then Rory let out another breath and moved again, sinking lower, taking more, and Beau shut his eyes and focused on not coming as his cock was swallowed up in tight heat. The easy, slippery glide of Rory's body down over him made his balls draw up tight, and still he couldn't sense any pain at all—no scent, no sound betrayed it.

Rory wanted this. Wanted him. And Beau had never wanted anything more.

Rory's hands landed on his chest as Rory's body shifted, tightening and easing around Beau's cock, and Beau's eyes opened as Rory leaned low over him again.

His eyes were shining with tears, but his mouth was stretched in a grin.

"Baby," Beau gasped.

"It's good," Rory whispered. "It's so fucking *good*, Beau. I forgot. I forgot it was—it was never—"

Beau had to kiss him, and before he knew it he had one hand cradling the back of Rory's head as he claimed Rory's mouth, kissing deep and hard and fast. His hips starting to twitch up helplessly, rocking by tiny increments, his cock barely sliding back and forth where he was buried in Rory.

Rory responded in every way, meeting the hunger of Beau's kiss, rocking his hips in counterpoint to Beau's. His cock was pressed between them, hard against Beau's belly, and his fingers dug into Beau's shoulders, holding on rather than trying to push away.

"Good?" Beau gasped, pulling back from the kiss. He could feel himself teetering on some brink—not coming, not yet, but his control was fraying, and he had to know. "Baby, it's—it's good? You—"

"Good, fuck, so good," Rory gasped back, moving harder over him. "Come on, Beau, you know it's good, you feel it, you—"

Beau finally took his other hand from the headboard, his hand finding the base of Rory's spine and spreading wide there to guide his movements as he rose and fell on Beau's cock. Rory groaned, nodding, and caught Beau's mouth in a kiss, and Beau let himself get lost in it— in Rory and the moon, in the pleasure and the connection surging between them. Rory's body and his own seemed to make one creature, full of the moon's glow, brimming over with delight and more sensation than one body could contain.

They were a completed circuit, a circle as round and full and perfect as the moon shining on them, give and take, desire and satisfaction. It went on and on and was over too soon, crashing into a shattering climax as they cried out in one voice from two throats.

Thoughts drifted back in to a mind whited out with sensation: Beau was lying on his back, staring out the window, his arms wrapped around Rory and his cock still inside, though he was softening a little now. He hadn't knotted, had come just as fast and hard as the first time, and now Rory was heavy on his chest, smelling satisfied and drowsy.

Beau nuzzled his hair, and Rory made a sleepy noise. He squirmed a little but didn't tense. He was still utterly given up, trusting and sated and half-asleep with his alpha wrapped around and inside him.

"More?" Rory mumbled. "You can..."

"Not right now," Beau murmured. The moon was still calling, but he closed his eyes to it, focusing on something far nearer, and far more compelling. His mate wasn't in heat; nothing pushed them to keep going and going and going. Beau wouldn't quite sleep, but he could rest while Rory did, and wait for him to want more.

～

Sometime past midnight, Beau couldn't keep still anymore. He turned, carefully depositing Rory on the mattress, still drowsing, and got up to stretch and move a little, tidying up their clothes and getting himself a drink and a snack from the supply he'd brought upstairs earlier.

Rory stirred behind him, and Beau was back to the bed without a thought, settling at his omega's side. Rory didn't have a chance to speak before Beau was holding the bottle to his lips. Beau read all he needed to know in Rory's heavy-lidded gaze, the flush on his cheeks and the way his fingers wrapped loosely around Beau's wrist as he drank what Beau offered him.

Beau was hard again just watching the movement of Rory's throat, just being close to him, and when Rory polished off what was left in the bottle, Beau threw it away without looking, curling down to kiss him. Rory's mouth was soft under his, the movement of his tongue and lips still easy and sloppy, without urgency.

Beau pulled his mouth from Rory's and kissed the bridge of his nose and above each eyebrow while Rory squirmed under him, giving up the warm scent of slow-burning desire. "What do you want, baby? Sleep some more? We don't have to—"

Rory shook his head and curled up just far enough to lean into Beau's lap. Beau's breath cut off as Rory's hand curled loosely around the base of his cock, and then there was a light, soft touch, the brush of Rory's lips against the head of his cock.

Beau rested one hand on Rory's shoulder and closed the other into a fist in the sheets, not letting himself push. Rory kept moving with lazy ease, licking and tasting, stroking Beau's cock now and then. There was no rhythm, no hurry, but every touch wound Beau tighter, pleasure thrilling through him, his balls tightening as his pulse pounded in his cock.

"Baby," he gasped finally, the word coming out broken. Rory picked his head up and gave Beau a sly, satisfied smile. It took Beau's breath away, seeing that teasing look, knowing that Rory had been *playing* with him. "Ror—"

That was as far as he got before Rory turned his face down again, taking the head of Beau's cock into his mouth. Beau tightened his grip on Rory's shoulder, then immediately loosened his hold, gasping as that hot, wet tightness worked the most sensitive places on his cock while Rory's hand stroked him in steady motions that got faster and faster as Beau gasped and moaned. "Fuck, fuck, baby, so—so good, oh, *fuck*—"

Rory jerked back as Beau started to come, both of his hands moving on Beau's cock as he spurted over Rory's lips, spattering his face.

Marking him.

It felt so good, so right, that Beau hadn't even caught his breath before it occurred to him that it was what he couldn't have. Not really —not a permanent mark, no matter how hungry he was for it, his teeth wanting to lengthen, itching in his mouth like they hadn't in years. The pale skin of Rory's throat seemed to glow in the moonlight, begging for a permanent mark, a bond.

He shook his head and shifted his grip on Rory's shoulder, tugging him up to perch on Beau's knee as Beau kissed him, tasting himself on Rory's lips and licking away the evidence he'd left on Rory's face. "God, baby, that was—I didn't hurt you? It wasn't too much?"

There was nothing but pleasure and a certain triumph in Rory's scent and the easy motion of his body. He looped his arms around

Beau's neck and tilted his face up for Beau to kiss and lick clean. "I'm good, Beau. I'm fine. Better than fine."

Beau's hand settled on Rory's hip, squeezing gently. "You're sure I didn't..."

Rory shook his head. "It was good, it was so good. If you'd knotted me it might have been a lot, but it was—"

Beau couldn't resist anymore and pushed Rory down to the bed, settling over him. His face was clean, but Beau kept kissing and licking down his throat, over his collarbones, nuzzling and tasting him every inch of the way and not biting, not lingering to make even a temporary mark. Rory giggled and squirmed under him, but he didn't try to push away—and didn't go still like he was bracing himself, either. Beau kept making his way down, kissing over Rory's ribs and the concavity of his belly, down to that sparse patch of dark blond hair and Rory's cock.

He wasn't hard this time, only a little plumped up and flushed, the tip tilted up a little. Beau glanced up and saw Rory biting his lip— nervous, maybe, but not fearful, not resistant. Beau kissed his way down the short length, and Rory's legs fell open wider, a little moan shaking out of him. Beau took Rory into his mouth, then, and while he wasn't hard, he was far from limp. Beau sucked and licked the hot little length and it twitched on his tongue, drawing gasps and cries from Rory.

But he didn't harden, and Beau knew he couldn't finish his omega off this way. He let Rory's cock slip from his mouth and moved lower, closer to the intoxicating scent of Rory's slick mingled with traces of his own come. He licked over Rory's hole, wet and soft, and it opened readily to him, the little ring of muscle barely offering any resistance at all, still ready after the last time.

Beau buried his face there, between Rory's thighs, licking and nuzzling until Rory was crying out loud, his feet on Beau's shoulders and his hips coming right off the bed. Beau slid two fingers inside him, then, and alternated using his mouth on Rory's sensitive rim and his half-hard cock. He worked his fingers against the sensitive spots inside, and Rory's cock began to spurt, weak little dribbles of come pushing out of him even though he wasn't hard. Beau kept it up until Rory seemed to hit a climax, arching up, grinding into Beau's mouth and fingers, and fell limply to the bed, panting.

His eyes were barely open when Beau lay down beside him and gathered him close, but his mouth was stretched in a smile. Beau kissed his open lips and tucked one knee between Rory's thighs, and his hand wandered up and down Rory's back and over the scant curve of his ass until Rory drifted into sleep.

Beau stilled then, only holding him close. No one, not even him, ought to be allowed to disturb his omega when he was so contentedly sleeping, trusting his alpha to protect him.

~

Rory was still dozing when Beau felt himself harden again, his arousal building into something he couldn't ignore, just from the closeness of his mate and the urgency of the moon thrumming in his blood. He tried for a while anyway, or at least tried to hold still while unable to think of anything but how hard he was. He turned bit by bit until he was lying on his back with one arm still around Rory, one leg still tucked between Rory's thighs.

He closed his free hand on his cock and only managed to halfway stifle his groan of relief.

Rory stirred beside him, making a drowsy, inquisitive noise as he scooted closer to Beau. He settled his head on Beau's shoulder, one arm across his chest, and his legs tangled with Beau's. One of Rory's thighs was tantalizingly close to his cock, and Beau gripped himself tight and rubbed his nose against Rory's short hair, making the softest soothing sounds he could to ease Rory back to sleep.

When Rory's breathing was even again, his body limp and warm draped half over his, Beau dared to move his hand again, jerking off achingly slowly.

He'd barely gotten into a rhythm when Rory made another little noise, and his arm over Beau's chest slid down, his hand finding

Beau's and his fingers coaxing Beau's to interlace, curled together around Beau's cock.

Beau couldn't help moaning at the touch, at how much better it felt just to have Rory's fingers on him as well as his own. Then he shut his eyes and held utterly still and said, "Baby? You awake?"

"Mm-hm," Rory muttered, nuzzling into his chest without seeming any more alert.

"Tell me my name, then, baby. Tell me you know where you are."

Rory made a little amused *tsk* that brought Beau's eyes open again, looking down just in time to see Rory's face tilted up, one green eye open just far enough for Rory to peer out through his eyelashes. "Who else would try to let me sleep when he wanted to fuck? Husband. Beau."

"Rory," Beau said helplessly. He had to curl down to kiss him then, tenderly, as if even the press of his lips might leave a bruise. Rory allowed it for a moment and then snuggled down into Beau again, tightening his fingers around Beau's, still on his cock.

Beau moaned at that and moved his own hand, tangled with Rory's, and gave himself up to sensation, pleasure, something quiet this time, gentle, soft as the way the moonlight fell toward morning, when the youngest and smallest of the pack couldn't keep up anymore. The feeling built and built, sweetly slow, but he still found himself gasping at the peak of it, needing that completion as much as any of the ones before.

Rory pressed a kiss over his heart and slipped his hand free of Beau's to stroke him just right. Beau gasped and his hips jerked up, his cock spilling again over both their hands.

Beau lay still for a moment, catching his breath, and it occurred to him suddenly that he had never had a full moon so still, and that he remembered seeing other alphas behave this way during the brightest night of the month. The ones whose mates were pregnant or had recently given birth would stay back from the run, and wouldn't go, either, to one of the isolated cabins set aside for omegas in heat. They would stay at home, near the houses, tending the bonfire and minding the littlest children, and above all, waiting on their mates.

Now and then a couple would go a little way into the woods, or into their homes, an obvious signal that they wished to be ignored. They would come back smelling like... well, like mates who had just enjoyed some private time together. But the moon fell gently on them, knowing that they needed an easier night than racing through the woods or the wildness of heat—as it fell on him and Rory, knowing that they weren't ready for more than this.

Rory made a smug, satisfied noise and raised his hand to his lips and started licking his fingers clean, and all memories of childhood full moons went right out of Beau's head. He caught Rory's hand with his own, sucking two of Rory's fingers into his mouth and tasting himself there.

Rory opened both eyes—still heavy-lidded and seeming only half awake—and took two of Beau's fingers between his lips, cleaning them with his tongue. Beau had to close his own eyes, still sucking at Rory's fingers.

He could hardly blame the moon at all for what he wanted tonight, it seemed. But at least he could be sure that he wouldn't push too far and betray Rory's trust. And Rory didn't seem to mind, when Beau finished cleaning his hand and found Rory's mouth to kiss instead.

"Do you need to sleep more, baby?" Beau murmured between kisses. "Should I let you alone for a while?"

Rory just kissed him and snuggled closer, and that was answer enough for now.

CHAPTER 22

$\mathcal{R}$ory woke up feeling warm and safe and deliciously still tired, thoroughly ready to slip out of bed for a snack and a drink and then climb back in to drowse the day away.

It was the morning after the full moon, and he knew it without any moment of uncertainty, even though he'd never woken up from a moon feeling like this. His mate was curled around him, holding him in strong arms and keeping him warm, and...

Beau was awake already, Rory realized, his own drowsiness melting away. Beau's hand was low on his belly, fingertips rubbing back and forth in a motion that was gentle but not at all idle.

Rory closed his eyes. He didn't want to know what it meant, didn't want to think about *that* when the morning was so quiet and good, but... who knew what Beau was thinking, after last night? Rory couldn't hide from him, not anymore. Not if... not now.

"Can you feel it?" Rory asked quietly.

Beau's lips touched the juncture of his neck and shoulder, and his fingers stilled on Rory's belly.

"Where—where I'm broken," Rory said, forcing the words out. He'd told Beau at the beginning, but they had never spoken of it after that. "Can you tell?"

Beau's breath, when he let it out, was warm and then cool on Rory's skin. That was why Rory shivered.

Beau took his hand away from Rory's belly and found a blanket they somehow hadn't kicked entirely off the bed. He tugged it over both of them. Only when they were covered did he ease away from Rory, gently prodding Rory to turn over and face him.

Rory turned where Beau wanted him, but he couldn't make himself meet Beau's eyes. He could feel his husband's gaze on him, as warm and gentle and steady as Beau's hands.

"It's not something I'm trained in," Beau said softly. "I'm not a midwife, I don't know the things a midwife would know about what's normal or abnormal for an omega. Humans are a little different, and... all the differences would be little things, with this. But... nothing felt really obviously broken. To me."

Rory had to look then, meeting Beau's eyes. His own felt wide, and he didn't know what to think of the caution in Beau's voice, the possibility Beau was implying.

"I don't know," Beau repeated gently. "But you'll need to see a midwife soon anyway. I promised you we'd find one when you were healthy again. By next month, I bet you'll be feeling even better than you are now, so you won't want to put that off."

Rory closed his eyes again. Suppressants. Poison. But on the other hand: no heats. None of that danger, none of the fear, no feeling lost and out of control, at the mercy of his alpha...

No full moon night spent with Beau when he'd be able to do more than fuck once or twice and sleepily lend a hand whenever Beau got worked up again. No chance of finding out whether a heat could be good, if it was with Beau, the way last night had been.

And he would have to see a midwife. Beau wouldn't just get the suppressants for him without Rory having to actually see the midwife; Beau wouldn't think that was safe. It *wouldn't* be safe, probably. So Rory would have to tell a midwife how and why he'd been broken, let them examine him, maybe even let them stick things inside him and pass their judgment.

He was shaking, and Beau's arms had tightened around him. Beau was pressing kisses to the top of his head, murmuring to him in between. "Shh, baby, it's okay, I've got you. You're safe, you're safe, I won't let anyone hurt you ever again."

"It was," Rory was gulping for air, clinging to Beau and trying not to remember being folded ass-up over the edge of the bathtub, hard hands pinning him down and other hands pushing inside him. "It was a midwife. Who did it. Broke me. Not fixed, *broke*. Whatever they did, they—they knew what they were doing. They said I can't, I won't—"

He smelled anger and tried to go limp. It would hurt less if he could just relax, and there was no way he could fight—but he was lying on his back on the mattress. Beau wasn't holding him in place, but propped over him protectively, pressing soft kisses to his cheeks and forehead.

Rory was crying. He didn't know how long he'd been crying.

"That's... Rory, I'm so sorry. That was... that's against everything a medical professional should do, to—to do something like that against your will."

"He said," Rory gulped back a sob, trying to get the words out. "Martin. Called it. Fixing me, but I *wasn't broken*, they *broke* me. He was my alpha, he said it was for him to decide. But we weren't bonded, we weren't married, he had no right. I tried to tell the midwife, I *tried*, but he wouldn't—and she wouldn't—and she said it was best anyway, said I shouldn't be getting pregnant just to—to—"

Rory sobbed again, remembering the midwife's flat, stern look, and Martin gloating, and the collar already fastened around his neck, preventing him from shifting. If he could shift, morning and night from the full to the empty moon like he'd been taught, then he wouldn't have had to worry about getting pregnant. But he'd started slipping into his wolf shape for days at a time, trying to avoid his heats, trying to avoid Martin's *parties* and his *friends* and their hands and their cocks.

Martin had found it amusing until Rory fought back against the heat-inducing drugs with claws and teeth, and then he had decided to solve the problem. Permanently. A collar, and then the midwife, so Rory wouldn't escape from heats by getting pregnant. Ever.

Rory remembered, too, with the moon so freshly on the wane, the first midwife he'd ever met, back when he was thirteen. The one who'd come to their house in Waukesha, come into his bedroom and told him to *relax*, told Rory he just had to *check*. Rory had tried to be good and quiet, like his parents wanted, but he hadn't been able to help himself, and it hadn't made any difference.

The midwife confirmed that Rory was an omega, and he'd taken Rory away. Rory had never seen his brother or sister ever again, his father suddenly wasn't his, and it all started with that midwife telling him to spread his legs and be quiet.

He wasn't just crying, Rory realized. He was screaming now, wailing into Beau's shoulder. Beau was barely touching him, just letting him hold on, but Rory couldn't stop.

"Don't," Rory sobbed. "Don't send me away, please, please, don't make me leave, don't make me go to the midwife—"

Please keep me. Please let me be good enough to keep.

Beau's arms went around him then, holding him and rocking him like a child, and he remembered that dream he'd had, coming out of the suppressants, of begging to go home. Begging for his suppressants, and being held and murmured to, just like this.

"I've got you, baby, I won't let you go. I won't send you anywhere. I'll stay with you, I won't let anyone hurt you. I won't let anyone do anything you don't want, not ever again. I promise, Rory. I promise."

"Not yet," Rory begged into Beau's shoulder, the words a garbled mess. "Not yet, don't make me go yet."

"Not yet," Beau echoed softly. "Not yet, baby, and not alone. I promise."

Beau put food to his lips and Rory ate. Beau put water to his lips and he drank. Beau carried him all the way to the shower—not the enormous one off Rory's room, but the one off the hall, across from Beau's room—and began to wash him clean, and Rory had to accept that he was awake. Life was going on, and *not yet* was coming sooner with every breath he took.

Beau was running a soapy washcloth over his belly, scrubbing a little to get him clean, and Rory said, "Do I have to?"

Beau stilled and looked at him. "I won't force you to do anything, baby, but I don't think any remotely trustworthy midwife is going to dispense suppressants for you without at least seeing you in person. And I think, considering what that other midwife did, it might be good to have someone check you over physically. When you're ready."

Rory looked down at himself, as if there would be some visible sign, but there never had been. Beau's hand, washcloth and all, slipped lower. Beau had touched him before, probing, and Beau had said that he couldn't feel any brokenness inside Rory. As if he thought that maybe Rory *wasn't*...

"Do you think... but I never. I never—I was collared for almost two years, I couldn't shift to make sure I didn't catch, and I never got pregnant. Not once, not even a hint of..."

Beau's lips parted, and Rory couldn't help blurting out, "And it's not like I didn't get fucked enough."

Beau flinched a little, but his voice was steady and calm as he said, "I know, baby. I know. But... it's hard to do anything really permanent to a werewolf that isn't really, really obvious."

He glanced up, meeting Rory's eyes in silent question. *Was it something obvious?*

Rory shook his head slowly. That had been the worst part of it, in a way, the fact that—apart from feeling shattered by what the midwife and Martin told him, and Martin going on and on about what a good thing it was that Rory was *fixed*, it almost could have been nothing at all. It had only hurt that night, and a little the day after.

But it wasn't nothing. It was everything.

Beau looked down. "Maybe there's something midwives know that I don't. I'm sure there are a *lot* of things midwives know that I don't. But maybe it's something broken that could be... healed."

Not *fixed*. He was glad Beau hadn't used that word, even to mean the right thing.

Rory pressed his fingers to his own belly, trying to imagine it. If it wasn't forever, if there was a cure...

If there was a cure, Beau would get it for him. If there was a cure, Rory could have children who could grow up safe and loved and never be sent away. He could be a proper mate to... someone.

To Beau? Could Rory be good enough then? Could he really stay, not just for three years but forever?

He wanted that, and it was clear to him as he stood there looking at Beau's hand and the washcloth, the water still falling warm all around them, that there wasn't much he wouldn't do for the chance.

"Okay," Rory said, barely louder than the water falling, but he saw Beau hear him. Beau gave him a cautious smile and went back to washing him. Rory closed his eyes and let him.

"I could contact the packs around here," Beau said quietly, reaching around to clean Rory's back. "The neighbors were... which pack?"

"Niemi," Rory said, leaning into Beau. "You don't have to do that. I'll talk to Jennifer, and see when... when we can see the midwife."

Beau's arm tightened around him, but he said only, "My schedule's on the fridge. Just let me know when, okay?"

Rory nodded against his chest and went right on letting Beau get him clean. He was saving his own strength for something much, much harder.

~

Beau didn't say anything else about it that day and night, though they slept through most of it anyway, recovering from the moon. Beau didn't suggest that Rory return to his own room that night, and Rory didn't suggest changing the sheets. They curled together in the welter of their shared scents, exchanging a few sleepy kisses before falling into sleep together.

The next day, after Beau had gone off to work, Rory waited until mid-morning—until the flurry of getting children fed and clothed and settled into their morning activities would be mostly over—and then he called Jennifer.

He could have walked across the street, theoretically, but this way no one could see him curling around the pillow that bore Beau's scent most strongly.

"Roland!" Jennifer said as soon as she picked up. "Hi, how's it going? How did the moon treat you?"

Rory took a careful breath. The background noise on her end was nothing much—none of the children was too nearby, or doing anything loud.

"You said your pack..." Rory started, and then hesitated.

Jennifer was quiet, waiting for him.

"I need to see a midwife," Rory said finally, and as the words came out of his mouth he realized how it might sound, with how Jennifer had looked at him and Beau before the full moon.

But she heard the way he said it more than the words.

"I'll give them a call as soon as I'm off the phone with you," Jennifer said evenly, without a hint of congratulations or sympathy. "You probably won't want to go out to the pack lands to see them, but I'll bet they could come pay a visit—you could come over to chat with them here, or I could bring them over to your house and introduce you?"

"I," Rory closed his eyes. "If you could bring them here. When my husband is home. After... seven, say? Any night this week."

There was a little silence, and then Jennifer said, "Roland, you—if you want to see a midwife without—"

Rory laughed a little wildly, and pressed a hand to his mouth to cut himself off. "No. Thank you. But no. Beau is not the problem here, believe me. I couldn't do this without him. I don't want to."

"Okay," Jennifer said, a little less cautiously. "Okay, I'll... see what we can do, and I'll let you know as soon as I can."

"Thanks," Rory said, and didn't think to add anything else before he ended the call.

After that, it was all he could do to send Susan a few texts—and a selfie featuring him curled up in the obvious disarray of Beau's bed—to assure her that the full moon night had gone really well for him. She sent back encouragement and some obliquely obscene emojis, and Rory burrowed into the pillow to take a nap until the next time his phone buzzed with a notification.

A text from Jennifer: *7:30 tonight okay? I'll bring Casey over.*

He sent back a thumbs up, and then texted Beau. *7:30 tonight.*

He didn't get a response right away—of course he didn't, Beau would be in the middle of rounds or something. He got up and got dressed, tidied up the bed but still didn't change the sheets, and was curled up on the couch with a book when his phone finally buzzed again. *I'll be there, baby.*

He smiled then, feeling stupidly warm all over. He resisted the urge to take a screenshot of the text, and tucked his phone down under his hip before he returned to his book.

Beau got home barely after six, and the first thing he did was to take Rory in his arms and hold him tight. Rory clung to him for the space of several breaths, but finally remembered to say, "There's... dinner?"

"Okay," Beau said, and went right on holding him for another minute before kissing the top of his head and walking hand-in-hand with him to the kitchen.

They hardly spoke while eating, or while doing the dishes afterward, and when they curled up on the couch in the living room—within sight of the front door—neither of them even pretended to be doing anything but waiting. Rory hid his face against Beau and breathed in his alpha's scent. Safe. He was safe. This midwife wouldn't be like that other one; this one belonged to a proper pack.

And he had Beau at his side, and Beau was nothing like Martin.

He heard the footsteps as soon as they started to approach up the driveway, and still jerked, startled, when the knock came on the door.

Beau squeezed him tight and kissed the top of his head. "You want me to answer the door?"

Rory knew exactly what Jennifer would think of *that*. He shook his head and detached himself from Beau, forcing himself over to the door. Two heartbeats were audible on the other side. Two were-wolves. Jennifer, and the midwife.

Rory opened the door and was startled to see that the midwife was a male omega who was probably close to his own age, and not much taller. He was wearing jeans and a t-shirt that showed his bare throat with no sign of a mating-bite. He had battered but clean sneakers on his feet, and had a mop of curly dark hair and startlingly bright blue eyes.

"Roland," Jennifer said, and glancing over his shoulder added, "Beau, this is Casey Niemi, who I told you about."

"Hi," Rory managed, tangled up in fear and not-fear and mostly landing on confusion.

"Thank you both for coming," Beau added. "Please, come in."

Jennifer gave Rory a searching look, and Rory tilted his head and nodded slightly. *I'm okay.*

"I actually need to get back to the kids," Jennifer said, taking a half-step back. "See you later, Case?"

Casey had been studying Rory with a slowly deepening frown, but his focus shifted to his packmate at the sound of his name, and he nodded quickly. "Yeah. Thanks, Jen."

"No trouble," Jennifer said, and turned decisively away.

Rory took a step back to let Casey in and, not accidentally, plastered himself against Beau. Beau's arm went around him as Casey stepped inside and pulled the door shut behind him, and some buried fragment of manners spurred Rory to say, "Can I get you something to drink, Casey?"

"Glass of water would be nice," Casey said agreeably, giving no sign that he thought it was strange to be still standing barely inside the house.

Rory nodded and Beau turned slightly, so that he would be between Casey and Rory if Rory turned away. Rory took off for the kitchen, listening intently as Beau invited Casey over to the kitchen table. He poured three glasses of water and Beau came to take them to the table, leaving Rory to grab a plate of cookies to bring along.

Beau set two glasses at seats side-by-side, across from the chair Casey had taken. Casey was smiling slightly now, his gaze going back and forth between them.

When they were both seated across from him, Rory's hand held firmly in Beau's, Casey said, "So... welcome to Minnesota. I hear neither of you is in the market for a real place in the pack, but you did need someone with my expertise? I know I look young for it, but I promise you I'm properly trained. I started early."

Rory nodded, and Beau nodded along at his side.

Casey took a sip of water, still studying them thoughtfully for a moment before his gaze settled on Rory; suddenly it was as if Beau had become invisible to him, his focus was so perfectly undivided.

"You know this isn't normally how we work—midwives, I mean. This is usually held to be omegas' business, not for alphas to get into the middle of."

Beau tensed a little at his side, swallowing something like what Rory said for them both. "Well, if that was how all midwives worked I wouldn't need to see you."

Casey's eyes widened slightly, and he sat back from the table, setting both hands on its edge. "Ah. I see. I am sorry, then, for whatever experience you've had with midwives before now. Would you like to tell me about it?"

Rory had been wondering, as much as he'd been able to think about this at all, how he was going to explain his whole history. But the way Casey asked it made it almost simple.

"A midwife did something to me," Rory said. "I don't know what exactly. It was about two years ago, something my alpha—my *ex-alpha*, not Beau—asked her to do. She made it so that I couldn't get pregnant. Ever."

A spasm of rage went through Casey like a wave through water.

Rory could see it, smell it, hear it, just for a second, and then Casey closed his eyes, tightened his grip on the table's edge for a moment. And just like that wave crashing on a beach, when Casey opened his very blue eyes again, it was gone.

"I'm so very, very sorry," Casey said softly. "You haven't seen another midwife since then?"

Rory shook his head, then shrugged. "I was at a refuge for omegas in Chicago for a while. There was a midwife there, but I didn't tell them about what happened, just asked for a salve for—" Rory touched his throat. Casey's lips tightened, then relaxed, his calm returning faster this time. "I didn't... I didn't want anyone to know. What was wrong with me. That I was broken."

Beau's hand tightened on his.

"Before that," Rory said, the words suddenly on his tongue though he hadn't meant to speak of it. It was something about the way Casey just listened, just absorbed things, the way Beau stayed quiet beside him.

"When I—when I was thirteen. I didn't know that I was an omega. No one knew, I—my father was human, we lived human, but then I started having these fevers on the moons, and my mom called a midwife from her pack to visit us, and he—the midwife said he had to check inside, to see if I was an omega. Said it should've been done when I was a baby, but now they had to, and I, I didn't want him to touch me, but they made me. My mom and dad both had to hold me down, and then... I had to go away after that. And my dad wasn't really my dad, I guess."

Casey's eyes closed halfway through that tumble of half-coherent words, but he stayed still and calm. Beau didn't speak either, keeping the same grip on Rory's hand until he stumbled to a halt.

"Wow," Casey said softly after a moment. "Okay. So, honest to God, I think being a midwife is one of the most important things any omega can do, and I love every minute of my work, and I personally would not blame you if you just came at any midwife you met with teeth and claws. You have gotten the worst end of everything I've ever heard of a midwife doing, and I'm so honored to have the chance to work with you to help you with anything I can, going forward."

Rory took a slow breath and nodded.

"You told Jennifer that you needed to see a midwife," Casey added, his attention flicking sideways to Beau for just a second before settling entirely on Rory again. "And, I mean, we get that a lot right after the moon, but... I'm guessing that your reasons are a little different from the usual."

Rory looked down for the first time. This was the simplest thing, the thing he'd always been absolutely clear on, and he couldn't quite get the words out. He looked over and met Beau's eyes. *Please.*

Beau just looked back at him. Rory thought that Beau would probably tell him that he had to do the talking himself, prod him through it, and he didn't know if he could do it except that he knew that Beau could make him.

But then Beau gave a tiny nod and focused on Casey, and Rory breathed a sigh of relief and rested his head on Beau's shoulder.

"When we met, Roland had been on suppressants for several months continuously. He hadn't, obviously, been under a midwife's supervision and was guessing at the dose and how to take it, and he had become very sick—close to liver failure, I think—as a result. I persuaded him to stop taking the suppressants until his health improved, but... given the way things went under the moon, it seems possible that next month he could be looking at having a heat, at least pseudo-heat, if he doesn't go back on some kind of suppressants, and I promised him that he wouldn't have to do that if it was possible to avoid it."

Rory opened his eyes while Beau was speaking, turning his head enough to watch Casey as he listened to Beau. His eyes were still on Rory until Beau stopped, and then Casey looked over at the alpha again. "You're a doctor?"

Beau inclined his head slightly. "I completed my MD. I've just begun my residency at the Rochester Clinic. I can't claim any kind of expertise that's useful to Roland's case."

"You know more about suppressants than the average alpha," Casey pointed out.

Beau tilted his head in acknowledgment. "I grew up in a pack where the midwives were tolerant of my curiosity, and one of my classmates from med school is interested in researching omega medicine."

Casey frowned slightly. "An omega in medical school?"

"No," Beau said, a faintly apologetic tone entering his voice. "He's an alpha."

Casey's expression went very controlled, and then he rubbed one hand over his eyes, barely breathing the words, "Moon save us from alphas who think they know best."

Beau took a breath, and Casey picked his head up and lowered his hand to give Beau an extremely unimpressed look.

Beau shook his head slightly. "I just... I may be getting ahead of myself. I know I don't know anything about this. And," Beau looked over at Rory, "My impression is that the main reason Rory wanted to see you was just to request suppressants. But I think there's a question about what happened with that midwife two years ago, exactly."

Casey frowned, focusing on Rory again.

"I just wanted to ask you," Beau went on. "Because I have some idea how it might be for a human, but... if you were approached by an alpha who wanted an omega who he wasn't even properly bonded with to be... sterilized, if you had the impression that this wasn't something the omega in question wanted, but also that the omega in question wasn't ready to walk away from that alpha, and it wouldn't be safe for them to get pregnant... what would you have done?"

Casey's face tensed into a frown as Beau spoke. He looked over at Rory again, his gaze sinking down toward Rory's midsection, as if he could see right through the table, right to the place inside where Rory was broken.

"Roland," he said slowly. "What the midwife did... did it leave any scars? Was there a lot of blood, or a feeling like silver inside you?"

Rory shook his head, bringing his other hand over to cling to Beau's. It had *hurt* almost beyond bearing at the time it happened, but he'd been tense, unable to stop resisting the force of the midwife's hands. The blood hadn't been more than any minor accident's worth, and silver... it had been something between a nuisance and a torment around his throat, but that was nothing to the agony it would have been if it had touched him inside.

"What are you saying? You think it wasn't...?"

Casey glanced at Beau and then back to Rory. "Obviously it's had the effect that it's had. If they didn't do that much damage, but those were the effects... have you shifted at all since then? Even once?"

Rory bit his lip and shook his head, throat tight with the memory of that choking sensation, trying to shift while collared in silver. The burns on his skin had been the least of it. When the collar was gone, even before he'd felt as sick as he was when Beau found him, he'd never been able to bring himself to try.

"I've never heard of it being done," Casey said, shooting another glance at Beau, who tilted his head, "not for a werewolf, at least. But I think it could be that the midwife didn't damage anything inside you, or... take anything away. I think they might have put something inside you that stayed in place—an IUD, a device that sits in your womb and prevents you from conceiving."

"A..." Rory looked at Beau, who smiled slightly, giving him a hesitantly hopeful look. "You mean, then, someone could take it back out? And then..."

Casey bit his lip and glanced over at Beau again.

"Humans use them," Beau explained. "They're designed to have a string attached, so they can be pulled out pretty easily. If the midwife wanted to be sure that no one would know it was there, not you and not your alpha, the strings might not be where they're supposed to be, which would make it harder, but... yeah, the whole idea is that it can be taken out, no harm done."

Rory looked at Casey again. "But how... how could I know? How do you know it wasn't... something else?"

Casey shrugged. "I don't, really. But I don't know of anything that midwives normally do to prevent pregnancy that would work how you describe it, either. I've heard stories of... things that you definitely would have known about, if that was what the midwife did. If it was something relatively quick, that maybe hurt or bled at the moment it happened, but not too badly or for too long after..."

"My belly hurt, I was sore, but..." Rory shook his head. "I always... I always thought it was strange, that something so quick could do something so permanent. I even thought maybe it wasn't really what the midwife said, but... but then I never shifted or did anything else to prevent it, and never got pregnant."

Casey nodded. "If you shifted... if there's something there that we could remove, I think you would feel it as your shape changed around it. That would be a way to check. Otherwise, I *might* be able to feel it from the outside, but that would probably hurt, and might not work well if you were tensed up really tight, which you would have every reason to be just having me in the room, let alone touching you. And if I couldn't be sure that way... you could try to get a human doctor to do a scan, but that's awful—"

Beau grimaced, nodding agreement, and Rory thought of the sound-feel of a microwave running and winced.

"Or we'd just have to... go in and look for it," Casey finished, with a grimace of his own. "Which, obviously you don't want me, uh, just poking around inside when we have no idea whether there's even anything there. So unless you're in a hurry to try for a pregnancy, I'd say, try shifting and see what you feel, and we can go from there."

Rory nodded, unable to really take in the possibilities. But Casey said *try for a pregnancy* as if it were a perfectly possible thing, as if... as if he thought Rory really could...

"What about suppressants?" Beau asked, jolting Rory back to reality. "Would it be safe for him to take them, next moon?"

Casey sat back a little, studying Rory some more. "I could mix something up, I think. Just a few days' worth, to take right before the full—not too harsh, just enough to take the edge off and help keep you calm. I wouldn't want to stress your system too much, especially if you're not back to having full heats anyway. Would that be okay?"

Beau gave him a worried look, and Rory thought about it—another full moon, like this one but *more*, but still not that mindless lost blur of the heats he'd had before. If he got too scared, if it was too much, he wouldn't have to go near Beau. But if he wanted to...

"Okay," Rory echoed.

Beau still looked worried, but he squeezed Rory's hands and nodded firmly. "Whatever you want."

As if it were that easy. As if Rory had any idea what he wanted, except to have Beau's hands holding his, and Beau at his side.

CHAPTER 23

*B*eau should have been working—he couldn't get behind on charts *already*—but he spent the rest of the evening staying close to Rory. It was a heady feeling, helping him to feel safe, and to feel the faint thread of hope that brightened his scent and kept him turning wide, wondering eyes on Beau from time to time all night, even after they'd bedded down together.

Sometime after midnight, Beau jerked out of a light doze to Rory saying, "What if I can't?"

"Won't make any difference to me, baby," Beau murmured, sleepily aware that that probably wasn't the point but not awake enough to think twice before saying it.

Rory huffed and nestled closer, shaking his head. "Can't shift, I mean. It's been so long and I... I don't know if I can even feel my wolf anymore. It's like there's part of me still hiding, even when I know it's safe. I'm safe."

Beau drew him closer. "Then we'll just have to be patient with the part that's scared, that's all. There's no rush. You're safe, and you're going to keep on being safe. Sooner or later every part of you will know that."

Rory nodded against his shoulder, and Beau added, drifting into sleep himself, "Everybody says it's a terrible idea to have a baby during first year anyway."

~

During the first moment of the day when he might have been able to start catching up on his charting—barring emergencies, intakes, or inscrutable maybe-hazing-maybe-genuine-good-advice from the senior residents—Beau had a meeting with his adviser instead. He wasn't surprised, except maybe about the fact that he'd been allowed a day to just come back and do his job before his adviser was checking up on him after the full moon.

Maybe Dr. Ross had needed an extra day to check with all the local packs and find out whether they had anything to report on him.

Beau caught himself wondering whether Jennifer—or Casey— would have said anything that got back around to Dr. Ross, and then he pushed the whole question aside. He'd spent the full moon with Rory, which was exactly what he should have done; he hadn't put one toe—or tooth—out of line, on-duty or off. He had nothing to worry about.

He was glad Dr. Ross couldn't hear how fast his heart was beating, all the same.

"So, how was the full moon?" Dr. Ross was smiling genially, as inscrutable as ever.

Beau absolutely did not blush. "It was, ah... I was grateful to have the night off, sir, definitely."

Dr. Ross *winked*. "I'm sure you were, I'm sure you were. And seems like you came back yesterday without losing a step, so that scheduling worked out fine."

Beau nodded and didn't argue, or point out that making up the hours over the empty moon might *not* work out fine. He would handle it. Somehow. Maybe it wouldn't be that bad.

"And moving on to when you *have* been here," Dr. Ross went on. "So far, no complaints from patients about being treated by a werewolf, so that's good news!"

Beau blinked. "I... haven't been introducing myself as one. I'm not obligated to disclose that outside of—"

Dr. Ross flapped his hand, obviously aware of the circumstances under which Beau would be required to disclose his lycanthropy to a patient. "No, exactly. That's what we want right now, is to establish a solid track record of you being a resident just like any other resident, doing good work without particularly rocking the boat. It's important that you behave with absolute professionalism right now—without even any *appearance* of unprofessional behavior, right? We need to establish your reputation as beyond reproach."

Beau nodded, hearing the message loud and clear. *Keep your head down. Don't be noticed, don't give yourself away. Don't give anyone any reason to look at you and think "werewolf" instead of "doctor."* He could do that. He'd spent years doing that.

"Yes, sir. I understand."

Dr. Ross nodded. "Now, on the other hand, we don't want to neglect your particular abilities, so I want to hear your observations on some of the patients you've seen since starting your rotation."

Beau felt a panicky flash of *oh no I didn't study for this test*, but then Dr. Ross called up a chart, and Beau recognized it and could easily recall his scent-impression of the patient. Describing it to a human was harder, but Dr. Ross was patient, and asked good questions.

It was such a relief to be able to discuss the things he noticed, which he normally had to try to ignore or forget, that he barely even minded that he didn't have time to eat lunch before he had to rush back to the ward for an intake.

In the afternoon he had a shift at Rochester's affiliated walk-in clinic, which gave him a chance to see local patients with a range of fairly ordinary complaints instead of the mostly severe and often rare or complex cases which were admitted to the renowned hospital. It was a relief to be able to treat and fix things, to see patients who, underneath a cut needing stitches or a sinus infection calling for antibiotics, were basically healthy. Parents bringing in children or family members accompanying a patient might be a bit stressed and anxious about having to make a trip to the clinic, but it was nothing to the grinding long-term weariness and grief of some of the people close to patients he saw on his regular rotation.

At the walk-in clinic, Beau was the first point of contact for patients; he was making his own diagnoses, even if it was just spotting a cold or the flu, a break versus a sprain, how deep a cut went and whether it would close on its own or needed stitches. He made extra notes of his observations and found that he was almost looking forward to discussing them with Dr. Ross at their next meeting.

He was jotting down notes on the way a cleanly clotting wound felt and smelled when Cora walked up. All of the Pulmonary residents had the same shift at the clinic, so half the medical staff was familiar faces. Cora was his favorite of the senior residents, and seemed more at ease with him than any of the others, but her expression was serious now.

"Hey," she said, "you're between patients?"

Beau nodded, instantly on alert. Cora's heart was beating quickly, and there was a strained quality in her voice. "You need me for something?"

"I want you to come with me to take a look at a patient," Cora said. "Just to observe, and then we'll discuss afterward, all right?"

Beau nodded, glancing at the unusually thick file in her hand. A patient with a long and complicated history here in the walk-in clinic, then. "Yeah, of course."

Cora nodded firmly. "Let me do the talking. You're officially shadowing me, okay?"

Beau nodded again, and mimed zipping his lips for good measure.

Cora turned on her heel and led him through the maze of exam rooms to one with a pink indicator flag beside the closed door, indicating a female pediatric patient inside, not contagious or acutely injured.

Cora knocked briefly and opened the door almost immediately, putting on a sympathetic-friendly smile. "Amy, Mr. Vaughn, hi there.

This is Dr. Jeffries, he's a junior resident. He's shadowing me at the clinic today to learn how things work. He's just going to observe, if that's okay?"

Amy was sick in a way that Beau couldn't put a finger on. She was slim and small and he guessed that she was older than she looked, maybe ten or eleven but still nowhere near coming into puberty. Her hair was in two blonde braids, her skin paler than any of the kids who had come to run around their backyard on the full moon. She wore glasses with glittery purple frames which didn't quite conceal the dark circles under her eyes.

She smelled... maybe tired, maybe anxious, maybe in some kind of persistent pain? Maybe just sick. Her heart seemed to be beating harder than it should, when she was just sitting on the exam table fully clothed. The bones showed prominently in her wrists, but her clothes were clean and well-fitting, and her shoes were new.

"Fine with me," Mr. Vaughn said briskly. "Okay with you, kiddo?"

Amy looked up from staring at her hands and gave a stiff shrug of her shoulders, nodded, and looked down again.

Mr. Vaughn, who had fair coloring and sandy hair similar to his daughter's, looked to be around forty, with a stocky build. He wore jeans and work boots, but his hands were soft, the gold ring on his wedding finger without scuffs. He smelled and sounded somewhere between most of the parents he'd seen today and the ones he saw with admitted patients. He was tired, a little impatient, perhaps anxious but not grief-stricken. He seemed physically healthy; his daughter's health hadn't begun to take a toll on his own.

"Answer the doctor, Amy," Mr. Vaughn said sternly.

Beau darted a look at Cora, but her expression was calm, slightly expectant.

"Okay," Amy said, a faint, hoarse whisper that obviously cost her an effort. She flicked a quick glance up at Cora after she spoke.

Cora smiled. "Thanks, Amy. You want your lollipop now, or a drink of water?"

Amy shook her head, and then made a few quick, stiff signs, some of the handful of basic ones Beau knew. *No, thank you.*

"Not a good day for talking, huh?" Cora said. "Is it okay if your dad tells me what brings you in today, or would you like to write it down for me?"

Amy looked over her shoulder—her father hadn't positioned himself that he could easily see her signing, or so that she could see him—and there was a faint sound of her not-quite vocalizing. From the motion of her jaw, he would guess she mouthed, *Daddy?*

Her father sighed, his expression turning tired and fond. "Yeah—it's all written down anyway, it's just the usual." He tugged a small battered notebook out and stepped forward, brandishing it at Cora. "She needs a tube. Unless you think you can actually figure out what's wrong with her this time."

Amy ducked her head at that, her whole small body curling in slightly. Her heartbeat ticked up a little faster, and her already sickly scent turned a little more sour-sharp.

Cora took the notebook, and tilted it in Beau's direction as she flipped through it. It was a food log, recording painfully tiny amounts of food consumed, supplemented to a greater or lesser degree by protein shakes. The log was punctuated every two or three days by a notation about a tube feeding. The handwriting looked to be all the same, a quick, masculine style. Mr. Vaughn's, if Beau had to guess. Not Amy's own, and no other parent's, either, despite the ring Mr. Vaughn wore.

Cora studied the most recent entries, which even indicated how much water Amy had had to drink. Other than that, and half a protein shake, she hadn't had anything at all in twenty-four hours.

"Not a good day for eating, either, huh," Cora said sympathetically. "Any reason it's extra tough yesterday and today?"

Amy touched her belly and mouthed almost soundlessly, "Hurts."

Cora nodded, clearly not surprised or enlightened by that answer. "Okay. Do you mind if Dr. Jeffries helps me check you over before we go get the tube kit?"

Amy's gaze darted to Beau, lingering a little longer than the first time, and Beau put on his gentlest nonthreatening smile. Amy looked

240

back at Cora and nodded, raising her hand to show her thumb and forefinger in a circle, the rest of her fingers raised. *Okay.*

"Okay," Cora agreed. "Dr. Jeffries, do a throat exam first, then check abdomen for tenderness or swelling and listen for gut sounds."

Beau nodded obediently and washed his hands before retrieving a tongue depressor. Cora stayed at his side as he stepped up in front of Amy, crouching a bit so that Amy wouldn't have to tilt her chin straight up and Cora, who only came up past his shoulder by virtue of the elaborate arrangement of braids on top of her head, could still see something.

"Make an *ah* for me?" Beau said. "It's okay if it's silent."

Amy obediently opened her mouth wide and flexed her tongue to let him check her throat—there was some redness and irritation, but no blood, no sores, nothing obvious. Her breath was, unfortunately, minty, so all he could really tell was that she wasn't into ketosis yet— but clearly the tube feedings were protecting her from severe malnu- trition.

He did an external check as well, pressing his fingers gently under her jaw and down her throat, but she showed no sign of pain, and there was nothing unusual to feel.

"Okay," Beau said. "Lie back and I'll check your belly, all right? I'll be as gentle as I can, but raise your hand if it hurts."

Amy glanced his way again, nodding once before she fixed her eyes on the ceiling. Beau began the slow, careful survey of her abdomen. He could feel how little subcutaneous fat she had, the shape of every organ and bone obvious under his fingers, but for all that, he couldn't find any abnormalities apart from the muscle tension that came with pain or the anticipation of it. She winced a few times, when he pressed against seemingly random points on her belly, but if there was something going amiss somewhere in her gut, he couldn't tell what it was by touch.

"Everything feels okay," Beau said. "Looks like you've got some sore spots, though, so let me take a listen."

He got out the stethoscope, and not only for show. It was a useful way to focus his hearing in a particular spot. There weren't any sounds of active digestion, but he wouldn't expect them after a fast as long as hers; there weren't any indications of dead spots or blockages, either.

He glanced at Cora, and she nodded slightly and then said, to Amy and Mr. Vaughn, "Okay, we're just going to go get the kit, we'll be back in a few minutes. Amy, try to drink a little water?"

Mr. Vaughn had already retrieved a purple water bottle, adorned with various stickers and hand-drawn designs in marker. He nodded to Cora's instructions, tired and resigned.

Beau let himself out and started toward the nurses' station with Cora on his heels. There was a feeding kit already waiting behind the counter with the printed labels bearing Amy's name, but Cora pulled him into the office and shut the door.

"Okay, so," Cora said. "Could you tell anything?"

Beau shook his head. "Not beyond the obvious. She's malnourished and stressed."

"Yeah, but," Cora blew out a breath. "Look, this has been going on since *my* first year. We've never been able to pin down anything organic—the kid's had so many scopes and scans she should glow in the dark, and she's been on literally every elimination diet known to man—her dad had her on FODMAP for like three months, and that makes exactly one person who I would actually believe has ever genuinely followed that thing. Nothing helps, nothing works."

"So... what, anorexia?" She seemed young for it, but... "How old is she, anyway?"

"Twelve," Cora said tightly. "Thirteen in December. She doesn't fit any of the actual psychological factors for anorexia—she's not proud of being skinny, she doesn't resist or try to throw up the tube feedings, although she complains that they make her stomach hurt, which —so does literally everything, apparently, but she's a kid, so *what does that mean?*"

"It... means her stomach hurts, probably," Beau suggested, but it was obvious that that wasn't an answer. They'd obviously ruled out any detectable cause of the pain.

"The leading theory is Munchausen's by Proxy," Cora said, folding her arms and not even deigning to be annoyed by Beau's useless answer. "So that's what I'm asking you. Did you sense anything, notice anything, that would make you think her dad is doing this to her? Causing this?"

Beau struggled to think of what that would even *be*. He hadn't been bullying or controlling in the way that might signal straightforward abusiveness—he'd let Amy speak for herself even when that meant signing, and she hadn't cowered from him. He thought of her ease in turning toward him, that unheard *Daddy* when she asked him to speak for her.

Munchausen's by Proxy would be different from the ordinary kind of cruelty; the victim themselves might not even recognize it as abuse, especially a child. But Mr. Vaughn hadn't moved to draw attention to himself over Amy's ailment; he'd expressed a little weary frustration with not knowing what was wrong with her, but he hadn't fawned over Amy, hadn't even stayed close at her side.

Beau shook his head slowly. "You know we're not psychic, right? I might be able to tell more easily if she's afraid or in pain, but that's usually visible anyway, if you look for it. Why are we blaming her dad? Just because we can't figure out what's wrong?"

"She's had a couple of... remissions," Cora said, waggling the thick file at him. "Which also argues against anorexia—times when she was able to eat without pain, or with less, and did so, and rebounded to a fairly healthy weight, even grew pretty normally. Both of them coincided with, and continued for a time after, she was sick in a normally identifiable way. Pneumonia last fall, that remission lasted about two months. Nasty case of strep this spring, that got her about a month."

Implying, Beau supposed, that when her father was occupied with her being sick for real, he didn't... do whatever they were supposed to suspect him of doing to keep his child from eating.

Beau shook his head slowly. "That's weird, but... maybe it's something else? I still don't see it being him."

Cora blew out a breath. "Me either. And if somebody calls CPS on him from here, or starts pressuring him to get into some kind of therapy, or get Amy into some kind of therapy—which she's in, actually, it just doesn't seem to make any difference—I don't know what he's going to do. Buy NG tube kits off the internet and quit taking her to doctors at all, probably, but that means no one ever gets a shot at figuring out what's actually going on."

"Ah," Beau said, considering again the thickness of Amy's file and the fact that they were a walk-in clinic. "Her previous doctor...?"

"Her previous *five* doctors," Cora corrected. "In the first *year*. He moved them here for her, for the clinic, but he's never been able to get her admitted. They lived in Iowa before she got sick—her mom died a few years before that, and she's all he's got. I think he's about at his wit's end, and I can't blame him. Not gonna lie, I was kind of hoping for magical werewolf insight, but... how's your intubation technique?"

"Well, I'm guessing Amy's an old pro," Beau said, thinking again of her hoarse voice, the faint irritation in her throat. "And... yeah, I have steady hands."

"Okay. Let's get this done." Cora opened the office door and led him back out of the nurses' station, scooping up the feeding tube kit and paperwork as they went.

Amy *was* an old pro at getting the tube down her throat, taking tiny sips of water to help it along while Beau carefully fed it in. Her dad checked the label of the feeding solution pack, snapping a photo of it with his phone before he let Cora attach it to the other end of the tube.

Once the tube was in place and the nutrient mix was running down it, Cora said, "Amy, honey, do you mind if your dad and I step outside and talk? Dr. Jeffries will stay here with you."

Amy glanced up at Beau, then nodded to Cora. Her dad squeezed her hand before he followed Cora out, and Beau drew up a stool, adjusting the height so he could sit eye-to-eye with her. He could *feel* Amy coiling tighter, every muscle in her body tensing. She wasn't in pain yet, but she was waiting for it.

"Amy," Beau said quietly. "Are your hands cold? Your hands look cold."

She shrugged a little, and he held his own hands out, hovering to

244

either side of her tiny ones, which were clinging to each other in a white-knuckle grip.

"Can I warm your hands?"

Amy hesitated, then nodded slightly, uncurling her hands.

Beau closed his hands around hers and began chafing them gently. They did feel cold, even more than humans usually did; as thin as she was, she probably felt cold most of the time.

"You're doing just fine," Beau said softly. "I know you're waiting for the part where this starts making your stomach hurt."

Amy looked up and actually met his eyes, and he saw that hers were hazel, a mix of brown and green.

It flashed through his mind—*if Rory and I ever*—and he quashed the thought to focus on his patient. "But it helps it hurt a little less if you can keep from being afraid, so I just want you to focus on your hands, not your stomach, okay? It's all right if you find yourself noticing how your stomach feels, but every time you do, I want you to just bring your attention back to your hands. Feel how warm my hands are around your hands?"

Amy nodded, fixing her gaze on her hands again.

Beau nudged her thumbs from side to side with his; she resisted for a second, then moved easily.

"That's it, just feel how easily your thumbs move back and forth. Nice and warm, nice and easy, not hurting at all. Nice and loose. Can you make your neck nice and loose just like your thumbs?"

Amy tilted her head from side to side in time with the slow movement of her thumbs.

"Good, good, that's right. Just keep noticing how your hands feel, Amy. You're doing great, that's good. Nice and warm, nice and easy."

He kept talking soft and steady, moving her fingers one at a time, squeezing the tip of each in turn. He coached her to relax her shoulders, her back, her arms and legs, until she was just barely sitting upright, barely even awake. Her eyes were heavy-lidded, and he couldn't help noticing again that her eyes looked like a mingling of his and Rory's. If they had a child, she might have eyes like that, and if...

It occurred to him, as he kept talking, that he had learned this from his father, teaching him to keep calm in day before a full moon. His dad would hold Beau's hands between his just like this and talk to him, guiding him into that quiet place in his mind where even the moon couldn't reach. He hadn't thought of that in years.

He glanced up and found that the bag was nearly empty, and then he realized that Cora and Mr. Vaughn were both standing just inside the door, watching.

There were tears in Mr. Vaughn's eyes.

"Okay, Amy, we're all done," Beau said softly, focusing on her again. "We just have to get rid of the tube and you're all set for today."

Amy blinked, returning to herself; she looked down past her hands to her belly, then up at the bag, and then at her father, and finally, wonderingly, at Beau.

He smiled. "See? It helps if you can just think about something else. I bet your dad could help you do that sometimes, too. It just takes some practice."

Of course, removing the tube broke the meditative spell, and Beau could feel her tensing, curling into herself, while he was still stuffing everything into the biohazard bin. But her father gathered her close, hugging her and murmuring things that Beau carefully did not hear.

He excused himself, letting Cora finish up the appointment—Amy had been her patient anyway, not Beau's, and sure enough as soon as he stepped into the hall a nurse said, "*There* you are. Exam six," and shoved a chart into his hands.

Beau focused firmly on the next patient, and the next, and never did write down any observations about Amy. She hadn't been his patient anyway; Dr. Ross wouldn't quiz him about her. Officially Beau hadn't been there at all.

～

When he got home, Beau found Rory stretched out on the couch, just shoving his phone into his pocket as Beau opened the door. He got up, smiling, and opened his arms, and Beau hurried to him, pulling Rory into his arms and breathing in the healthy, unhurt, well-fed scent of his husband.

"You look worn out," Rory murmured, then sniffed ostentatiously at his shoulder and added, "Clinic today, huh?"

It was on his schedule; Rory hadn't needed to pick up the scent of more strangers than usual to guess that. Beau felt warmed by the solicitousness anyway and squeezed Rory tighter. "Yeah. It was good, mostly. Just... a lot."

Rory nodded into his shoulder. "Come on, let's eat and you can tell me about the good parts. Or the not-good, whichever you feel like talking about."

Beau tipped Rory's chin up to look down into his eyes—green, pure and bright as dew shining on spring leaves. Not bloodshot anymore, he couldn't help noting, nor yellowed. He shook off the automatic diagnostic checks and bent his head to kiss Rory softly.

Rory's arms went around his neck, yielding readily to the kiss and returning it sweetly until Beau straightened up. Rory looked up at him, dazed and distracted, and Beau pressed a last quick kiss to his parted lips and then took his hand and tugged him toward the kitchen. "Dinner?"

"Dinner," Rory agreed.

Beau watched him as he moved around the kitchen, taking a dish from the oven and another from the refrigerator. He was still slim, but his collarbones weren't so sharp under his shirt, and the knobs of his wrists didn't stand out so far anymore. He was getting better—he *was* better.

Rory turned and found Beau watching and smiled. "Like what you see?"

Beau grinned. "Very much, baby. Like to see you eating even more, though."

Rory rolled his eyes, still smiling fondly, and joined him at the table. "So, how was it today? Only mostly good?"

"There was a case—a little girl..." Beau wanted nothing more than to tell Rory about her, but he didn't know how to, even as much as he could without violating confidentiality, without bringing up the specter of Rory's own recently fragile health. And there was no ready cure for Amy, so it was a sad, unfinished kind of story.

Plus, Beau didn't know if he could keep himself from saying what he'd thought, about the idea of children who were his and Rory's and how much he'd like to teach them to calm themselves when the moon called louder than they could bear.

Rory hadn't married him to have children, or even to stay. Beau couldn't put that on him, couldn't spread the sadness of a discouraging case. Not when Rory was smiling and content.

"It was... complicated," Beau said, shaking his head and looking down to cut himself a bite of chicken. "We did our best for her, that's all. But I also stitched up five different people and worked on figuring out how to describe—you know the smell of blood clotting? And you can tell how long it'll take to heal?"

Rory nodded, and Beau went off into explaining that, and the better parts of his meeting with Dr. Ross, and left the rest aside, too. No need for Rory to be worrying about whether Beau would mess up and reveal himself and draw a patient complaint. He wouldn't, that was all. If he lost his residency he would have to let Rory go, too, to find someone who... had any stable job prospects at all, for one thing.

He wasn't going to lose his residency. He wasn't going to do anything to drive Rory away sooner than Rory chose to go.

Rory listened, and made him rephrase things a few times to explain them better, which helped him think about what he actually perceived. He made a few mental notes of the best phrases to use to explain his observations, and finally said, "What about you, baby? How was your day? Nice and relaxing?"

Rory's lips twitched in a half-smile. "Yeah. Kind of boring, honestly, now that I can get through a whole day without napping for half of it. I mean, not that there isn't plenty for me to keep busy with," Rory added hastily. "I'm not complaining! I just... it's just different, that's all. Figuring out what to do with myself when I'm not..." Rory waved a hand vaguely.

"Well, I'm sure you'll figure out what you're interested in," Beau said, knowing it was a useless platitude but not knowing what to say without pushing Rory toward something that might not be what he wanted at all. "If you need books or anything, don't hesitate to use your card, okay? Or if you want to go out—do you have the There-Wolf app, for rideshares and stuff? I think it operates here."

They both got their phones out, and finished eating while getting the apps set up and connected to Beau's credit card. Checking for available rides showed that Rory should be able to get around easily using the service; there were plenty of wolf-identifying and wolf-friendly drivers in the Rochester area.

"There," Beau said, sitting back. "Should've done that weeks ago, but at least now you won't be stuck inside all the time, huh? You can explore around, see if there's anywhere we should go on my days off. I don't think there's a Penzeys, but maybe there's some other kind of spice store we could check out."

Rory gave him a startled look, as if he hadn't thought Beau would remember that story, and then smiled down at his phone. "Thanks, Beau. This is... thanks. You're sure you won't... you don't mind where I go?"

"Anywhere you want, baby," Beau said firmly. "I'm not going to be using it to check up on you, I promise. If you want to make your own separate account and use your card number..."

Rory shook his head. "It's fine, I know you won't. It's just... new."

He smiled over at Beau again, and Beau leaned in and kissed him softly until he had to stop before he started pressing for more. This wasn't the full moon, and Rory wouldn't be interested now.

Beau thought ahead as they cleared the table and did the dishes together. Rory *had* shown a clear preference for sharing his bed, ever since the full moon, and Beau could feel his own desire stirring. One more makeout session and he wouldn't be fit company at all. Maybe Rory wouldn't mind, the same as he hadn't minded curling close to Beau and lending a hand toward the end of the full moon night, but... maybe it would be better not to let the issue come up at all.

It would be good for other reasons, too, he thought. And it had been too long. And Rory might benefit from the example; his wolf would naturally respond to Beau's.

After they'd both dried their hands, Beau hesitated by the sink. "Baby, would you mind if..."

Rory looked up at him a little shy and startled, and Beau realized that the desire he was trying to head off had leaked into his scent a little. Beau shook his head, and promptly muddled his message by leaning in to press a quick kiss to the corner of Rory's mouth.

"Actually I was thinking... I don't think it's been as long for me as for you, but I barely remember the last time I shifted, either. I thought I might try that tonight, just to relax a little, and maybe it would help you get a feel for it again?"

"Oh," Rory said, his expression flickering through a blankness Beau couldn't read and then into curiosity. "I'd like that, I think. Maybe... upstairs? That way if you shed everywhere I can just change the sheets."

"Sure," Beau agreed, except that he never wanted Rory to change the sheets, wanted them to smell like the full moon forever. But Rory probably didn't need to sleep in a bed full of the scent of sex when he wasn't interested in it, and the more the moon waned the less he'd like that. "Yeah, of course. Probably could stand to anyway, huh?"

Rory shrugged and looked away, and Beau realized that had maybe sounded like a criticism, like he'd expected Rory to wash the sheets promptly after the full moon. Before he could think of how to say it better, Rory turned away, saying, "I'll just change for bed, then, and you can... change too."

"Ror," Beau said, reaching for him. Rory melted easily into his arms, letting Beau take a last moment to hold him while he could. It was silly—he didn't have to shift, and he could shift back whenever he wanted to—but he was still aware of going away from Rory in a certain sense, and he never wanted to do that.

Finally Rory gave a little push against his chest. "Go on, Beau. Go shift."

Beau went. He stripped without closing the bedroom door, forcing himself to focus not on the sounds of Rory taking his clothes off down the hall, but on his own body, the way that its current form was only half his nature. The wolf waited under his skin, inside his bones, in every cell, and Beau only had to call it out.

It took a moment to find it, to make every part of himself believe that, yes, he really could be a wolf now, when he spent so much time determined to hide that part of himself. But then he found the change waiting in himself, and in the blink of an eye he shifted.

CHAPTER 24

*R*ory heard the sound of Beau's shift into wolf form. He froze for a moment, standing by the dresser in the ridiculously spacious bedroom where he sincerely hoped to never sleep again. The urge to shift along with his alpha raced down his spine, awakening the wolf inside him. It wasn't a bad feeling, exactly, but every bit of him, wolf and man, felt the danger of something new and strange, and wanted to hide.

Then there was a soft padding of enormous feet, and a low *whuff* from just outside the bedroom door. Beau was there, waiting for him. He was still Beau, in any shape, and Rory was suddenly overwhelmed with curiosity to see his alpha's other form. Rory hurried to the door and opened it to find Beau standing there.

He had exactly the kind of fur Rory would have expected—a uniform coffee-dark color, not quite black, thick and soft-looking and standing out in all directions. Rory wondered if Beau kept his hair so short, in his human shape, because it did the same thing if he let it grow any longer.

His head was as high as Rory's hip, and he looked like he'd hardly lost any of his muscle or weight in shifting, but his tail gave a slow, cautious wag. He was looking up at Rory with bright eyes, his ears eagerly pricked forward.

Rory couldn't help smiling. "Hey, Beau, there you are. Ready to curl up in bed?"

Beau stepped forward and gently, delicately, caught the drawstring of Rory's sleep pants between his teeth, then tugged on it.

"Well, yeah, obviously I'm coming with," Rory agreed.

It was easier, somehow, to talk to Beau like this. He was still him, the same person and the same intelligence behind his eyes, and he still understood what Rory was saying to him, but the exact words never mattered quite as much to a wolf as the feeling of them. Rory didn't have to worry so much about saying things just right.

"Let me just grab my phone," Rory added, gesturing over his shoulder.

Beau let go of the drawstring and sat down in the hallway, still watching him with the same expression of patient, happy anticipation. Still not setting foot in the room that belonged to Rory alone.

Rory forced himself to turn away, just long enough to grab his phone where he'd set in on the dresser while he was changing. He tucked it into the pocket of his pajama pants before taking the drawstring in hand and offering it to Beau.

Beau took it delicately from his fingers and then backed down the hallway, tugging him along step by careful step while Rory struggled against the giggles that threatened at the sight of a full-grown alpha wolf leading his omega, literally on a string, to his bed.

Once they were through the door Beau let go in favor of nudging Rory from behind, herding him onto the bed. If Beau had any complaints about Rory's housekeeping and the messiness of the bed, he didn't seem concerned with them now. And, Rory noted, he'd dropped his own clothes where they fell before he shifted. Rory would have picked them up, but Beau didn't give him a chance.

Well, fine then. Rory would worry later about whether Beau expected him to have changed the sheets before now. It was just that it smelled so good, felt so *right*, to go to sleep in his alpha's arms, surrounded by the scents of the two of them from the recently-passed full moon night. And it wasn't like he'd been in heat; the sheets weren't *that* dirty. Not really.

Beau jumped up after him. Not content simply to have Rory sitting on the bed, he pushed and prodded until Rory was curled up comfortably with every pillow on the bed tucked behind him and a blanket over him. Rory did give in to the giggles halfway through that process, but Beau just lolled his tongue out in a wolfish grin and then kept up his efforts. When he was finally satisfied, he lay down against Rory's back, his tail curled around a pillow and his head resting on Rory's thigh, and let out a long sigh of contentment.

Rory smiled and sighed a little too, setting his hand on Beau's back. His fingers sank into the dense, soft fur, and he let them rest there, not quite petting and not quite holding on. He could feel the solidity of Beau under his hand, the beat of the great wolf's heart under fur and muscle and bone.

With his other hand, Rory pulled his phone out of his pocket.

Beau's ears tipped in that direction, just briefly, but when Rory just set the phone down on the mattress where he could see and reach it easily, Beau seemed to pay no more mind. Beau's eyes were half-lidded, the beat of his heart and the rise and fall of his breathing both slow and calm. Relaxing, like he'd said he needed to.

Because he'd had a complicated case today, one he hadn't even tried to explain to Rory. He'd been patient with Rory's questions when he did talk about something, even seemed pleased to explain, but the other thing, the thing that Rory could see actually bothered him... he hadn't even tried. He obviously thought that that would be too far beyond Rory to even explain what had been hard about it.

Rory navigated with a few taps to the saved shopping cart he'd been looking at on and off yesterday. It contained a few books to help him prepare for the high school equivalency test, plus one called *Medical Terminology Workbook*.

With one decisive tap, he hit *Buy Now*, and was informed that the books would arrive in a couple of days.

He knew he could never possibly catch up to Beau, or learn enough to truly understand everything Beau did. But he could start.

He could try, and once he'd gotten somewhere with it he could let Beau see him trying. The gap between them wouldn't be quite so far, then, and Beau would see that Rory *could* learn things, so it wouldn't be a waste to tell him, or impossible to explain.

Rory was pretty sure that he could learn things.

Well, he'd have plenty of time alone to try. With access to rides, he could even go get tutoring, maybe, if he got stuck on something. He was sure Beau wouldn't mind him going to classes. He'd just hate to have to tell Beau he was failing those classes, or taking something embarrassingly basic.

So, books. He would start there, and when the time was right, when he'd learned enough to be proud of, then he could show Beau. Then Beau would know that he wasn't useless, helpless, just lying around all day doing nothing while Beau was working himself to exhaustion.

And if what Casey had said was right, then maybe... maybe he would be good enough. He'd done all right with Beau's classmates and instructors at the barbecue, after all. It had been easy there, of course, to conceal his own background. He might not manage it so well in other circumstances. But Rory hadn't fucked it all up yet, so maybe. Maybe there was hope. Maybe, at the end of three years, he'd be able to prove to Beau that they should just stay together.

Maybe...

He'd heard what Beau said, just before falling asleep the other night. *Everybody says it's a terrible idea to have a baby during first year.*

Did that mean that during second or third year he might consider it? Or... might not be upset if it happened, anyway? Rory wouldn't want to *trick* Beau into having a baby with him, but... if Beau wanted that, if Rory was well enough, maybe... maybe it would just happen, somehow, and then Rory could stay. Maybe if he could give Beau a baby, a family, then he'd be good enough for Beau to want to keep him.

Maybe Beau could even love him, a little.

He didn't have to; Rory wouldn't mind if he didn't, not when he was so kind, and wanted Rory to be only his own. Rory could figure out how to make Beau happy, to keep him close. He could make a real bond with him, make a family, and then...

Beau snuffled and stood up, moving to lie along Rory's front, his head heavy on Rory's chest. Rory pressed the button to lock his phone and shoved it under a pillow, closing his arms around the furry warmth of Beau instead.

Enough thinking about maybe. He had Beau here now, and he shouldn't waste the chance to enjoy this.

Rory got up when Beau did in the morning, fixed breakfast for him when he was in the shower, and pulled him back at the front door for a lingering kiss. Beau looked back a half dozen times as he walked to the car, backed it down the driveway, and started down the street, and Rory was watching every time, tallying each look and hoping.

For a moment it felt strange, and he wasn't sure why. He'd spent an awful lot of the last several years hoping—and then he realized that he was hoping that something *would* happen, instead of hoping that what he knew was coming *wouldn't*.

Rory finally turned away from the door. Sitting around hoping might feel different this time, but he didn't think it would actually *work* any better than it ever had before.

He went upstairs first, stripping the sheets from Beau's bed before he let himself hesitate over it. He dumped them on the floor and found a fresh set of sheets, then made the bed picture-perfect, fluffing every pillow and smoothing the covers just so. He gathered up Beau's dirty clothes while he was at it; it was only when he had the sheets and laundry all bundled up together in his arms that he faltered, breathing in the scent they bore.

It wasn't just Beau's scent, though that was the best part of it. It was *them*, together. *Mates*, even if they weren't properly, truly bonded. Even if he couldn't point to a mark on his body that Beau had left, staking a claim, it smelled real enough. When he breathed it in he remembered the moon, and how Beau had been sweet and patient with him even then, had given as much pleasure as Rory could bear before he took his own.

Rory couldn't bear the thought of dumping *that* into the washer, drowning it in soapy water until it might never have been there at all. After a moment of hesitation, he took the dirty laundry into his own empty room, which bore only his own lonely scent. The bed in here was made neatly, though with no particular care, but Rory stripped it, tugging all the perfectly clean sheets free and dumping them on the floor.

He shook out the sheets from Beau's bed to get the worst of the wolf hair off them, though there wasn't much, and made up the bed with the well-used sheets. He smoothed them neatly and made the bed up again so that the difference wouldn't be obvious from the door.

That was as far as Beau ever came, anyway, and the covers would keep the scent in. It would only matter if Rory had to sleep in this bed again for some reason—and then he wouldn't feel so alone here.

He went to get his own clothes to wash with Beau's. He shook out the jeans he'd left puddled in the Jacuzzi tub on the afternoon of the full moon—they hadn't dried fully and had developed an ominously musty scent. As he scrutinized them, his eye caught on the little designs stitched into the inside of the waistband—the charms and well-wishes from someone in Beau's old pack.

If he'd stayed in the pack and married some nice young alpha, that kind of thing would have been Rory's job, making or altering and washing clothes for his family, and stitching in the charms. Someone had done that for him, for the three years he lived in the pack, and Rory had persistently picked the well-wishes right back out every time he found them. He hadn't wanted to accept anything from the pack, certainly not their blessings.

He'd never regretted it until right now, because it meant he didn't have the least idea how to do this for Beau. A proper omega would know how, and then Beau would have well-wishes in his clothes, to carry with him secretly among all those humans.

Rory studied the stitching in his own jeans. These had been intended for Beau after all; if Rory could just duplicate them, maybe...?

But maybe that would be like a child copying what he thought were written words and producing total gibberish. Beau might not know the difference, but Rory would. If Beau had just wanted copies of his old pack-charms sewn into his clothes, he could have done it himself anytime in the last ten years. What Rory wanted to give him was something real, something meaningful, not a child's awkward copying.

It wasn't something he could order a book about, though. He'd need...

Well. He'd need an omega who had properly learned their pack's lore.

And as it happened, he had Casey's number already programmed into his phone.

He dumped the jeans onto the pile of laundry to be washed, and carried it all downstairs while he thought that over.

Casey had known that Rory and Beau didn't want to join the Niemi pack—Jennifer had obviously gotten that across. But Rory had already asked for the midwife's help with suppressants, and advice about the rest of his situation. To ask this, as well... he would be indebting himself. Allying himself, even more than he already had.

But he had accepted food from Jennifer, and he and Beau had played with Jennifer's children on the day of the full moon. They were... friendly neighbors of the pack, if nothing else, already. One more connection wouldn't make such a big difference.

And then too... Rory had run away from his pack once, but he knew now what could become of an omega alone; he'd hated the pack for not being his family, but they hadn't mistreated him the way Beau's pack had done to him. The refuge had become Rory's pack in a way, and he would surely have died without them. Without the refuge protecting him and pushing him to look to his future and getting him signed up with the match agency, Beau would never have found him and saved him.

It wouldn't be such a bad thing to have a pack in their corner. And even if they weren't really a part of the pack, managing relationships among packs was always the work of omegas. If he and Beau were a pack of two, then their connection with the Niemi pack was a matter for omegas to mediate. Rory and Casey, for instance.

Rory just had to call and ask. Casey hadn't told him that his number was only for emergencies, or midwife things, and he'd particularly given it only to Rory, and not to Beau. That had to mean that it wouldn't be wrong just to ask.

He got the laundry started and then went to sit on the old bed in the basement bedroom, with its familiar shared scents, and pulled up the contacts on his phone. He had four, now: Beau and Susan, Jennifer and Casey.

He could call Jennifer first, and ask if she thought Casey would mind; she might well even know herself how to stitch the charms into her children and husband's clothes. Susan might know, too. She was an omega, after all, and a grandmother. But she and the refuge were the pack he had left behind to marry Beau and come here; the Niemi pack was the pack he needed to make new connections with now.

Rory tapped out a text message to Casey. *Can I ask you something? An omega question, not a midwife question.*

Casey responded almost instantly: *Sure!* A few seconds later, while Rory was still staring at that first answer, he added, *You can call if you want, or keep texting if that works better for you.*

Rory considered trying to explain what he was asking about, one little thumb-typed message at a time, and then pressed the button to call.

Casey answered almost before the phone had completed a single ring. "Hi there! Great to hear from you, Roland, how's it going?"

The enthusiasm, and the speed, of his response startled Rory into silence. For the first time it struck him that this wasn't only a decision he'd made to ask for help; Jennifer, and Casey, and maybe the entire Niemi pack had decided to be there to be asked, even though he and Beau had said they didn't want a pack.

"Hi," Rory said belatedly. "I, um. This is probably a silly question. It wasn't an emergency or anything, I was just wondering..."

Casey gave him a few seconds after he trailed off, then said, "Well, that's all right. It's nice to talk about something that's not an emergency sometimes; when you're a midwife people start to think that's all you *can* talk about. I'm glad you thought of me when you had a question, Roland."

Rory flushed a little at the warmth in Casey's voice, the kindness, and the knowledge that he was still only asking Casey to share some expertise. But if Rory was ever going to be a person other people could call on, he had to learn this stuff somehow, and that meant asking.

"I was wondering about the things the omegas and aunties stitch into everyone's clothes, in the pack. If your pack does that. Mine did, but I never paid any attention, because I... well. I didn't want to be the kind of omega they wanted me to be, I guess. Beau still has some clothes from before he left his pack, and they have the stitching in them, and... I know enough to know it means *something*, but I don't really know... what, or how, or... anything."

"Oh," Casey said. "Yeah, I know what you mean, the Niemis do those too. One of our older midwives told me once that they're partly just laundry marks, to keep everyone's clothes straight. Everyone has one that's particular to them, usually at the back of the collar or waist. So that mark on Beau's clothes would mark them as his."

Rory reached to the small of his own back, hooking his fingers into the waistband of the clean pair of Beau's jeans he was wearing. He could feel that design he'd seen before under his fingers, overlapping shapes in yellow and red. Marking Beau's possession: the jeans, and maybe also Rory himself.

Had Beau thought of that when he gave these to Rory to wear? It was there anyway, in giving him clothes that had belonged to Beau and carried his scent, but these, particularly, bore the special mark from Beau's pack.

"And then there are others that really are well-wishes, though I think all of it carries the intention that goes into it, you know? But the charms are simpler designs, usually, I think. I don't know if they're the same in every pack. We do a fang or a claw somewhere on the right

261

side—the shoulder or inside the sleeve, or at the hip—for strength, and a circle or an empty moon for protection. Children, especially, always have circles stitched in their clothes, all over the right sides. Every omega and mother in the pack might add her own to a new baby's clothes."

Rory tugged the right hip of the jeans away from his skin, already knowing what design was hidden there. "What about a star?"

"Ah," Casey said. "That's... guidance, I think, is the usual intention. On the left, it's to guide someone home."

Rory's fingers tightened on the jeans. "On the right it means they're going away?"

It made sense: whoever made these jeans for Beau had known that he would leave them. It was kind of them, to have made the clothes and to have added this small wish for his safety. But now Rory was wearing them, and he had to wonder if Beau had known he was passing *that* wish on to Rory, too, wishing him well when he went away.

It didn't matter, Rory told himself. It didn't mean he *had* to go away, just because he'd been wearing that charm against his skin for days. It only meant someone somewhere had willed that he should be safe if he did.

"Well," Rory said, recognizing that Casey was waiting for him to say more. "I guess I need to buy some needles and thread, then, don't I?"

Casey gave a small sound, not quite a laugh, but as warm and encouraging as one. "That would probably be a good start, yeah. Have you ever done embroidery before?"

"Uh," Rory said, trying to remember. "Well, how hard could it be?"

Casey laughed for real that time.

CHAPTER 25

*B*eau texted Rory to let him know he would be late and then stayed camped out in the residents' office until he was absolutely, completely caught up with everything, distractedly drinking coffee to quiet the growling of his stomach. He arrived home late, exhausted and so hungry he felt almost sick with it, and the first scent he caught was Rory's blood.

Adrenaline flashed through him like lightning, and he was yelling Rory's name, running further inside, at the same time he registered the sound of Rory's heart beating steadily—faster now—and Rory came into view, darting toward him from the family room.

Beau reached for him, anxiously patting him, looking for a wound, for...

Rory held up his fingers, reddened here and there in pinpricks, and Beau finally grasped that for all he'd scented blood, it was only a trace. Rory had pricked his fingers, that was all.

"I was, um, trying a sewing thing," Rory said, when Beau finally managed to focus on him speaking rather than the roar of panic in his own ears. "Takes some practice, that's all. And thimbles are no joke, I guess. I'll get some thimbles tomorrow."

Beau let out a gusty breath and kissed each of Rory's fingertips before he tugged Rory closer, crushing him in a hug. "Sorry, sorry, I just—we had a patient with this bleed today, and it took forever to find where he was bleeding from but I could smell that he was bleeding all the time, and... Sorry. Sorry, baby, I just..."

Rory's arms tightened around him. "It's okay, Beau. You didn't do anything wrong, just startled both of us. It's all right. You've had a long day, huh? Come on, let's eat something."

Beau pulled back again, raising one hand to cradle Rory's cheek, tracing the contour of it with a thumb. "You didn't wait for me, did you? You need to eat."

Rory shook his head fondly, like Beau was being ridiculous and overprotective. "I snacked. I like eating with you. Come on, it's just soup, it's keeping warm. I don't know how you noticed two drops of blood over that."

"Priorities," Beau murmured, but he let Rory steer him to a chair at the kitchen table. There was already bread and cheese set out, bowls and spoons and napkins and a pitcher of water. Rory went to the stove to get the pot of soup, and the rich, warm scent of it finally struck Beau's nose, reawakening the hunger he'd forgotten in his frantic rush to see that Rory was safe. He barely managed to make himself serve a bowl for Rory first before ladling his own full; Rory poured water for each of them while he did that, their hands passing between each other across the table until they were both ready to eat.

Beau dug in then, eating quickly and steadily; he was only aware of Rory as a reassuring quiet presence at the table, eating and drinking at a more leisurely pace. His foot gently brushed Beau's under the table, and Beau captured Rory's ankle between his without thinking or looking up.

Rory made a little amused noise but didn't object, or do anything else to distract Beau from eating his fill.

He was scraping his third bowlful of soup clean when the exhaustion he'd been fending off all day settled over him. He sat at the table, dazed, thinking of all the steps of cleaning up the kitchen, until Rory came around the table and tugged at his shoulders.

"Go to bed," Rory said softly. "You're asleep sitting up. Go on, I can handle this."

"You cooked," Beau murmured. "You..."

"I've been home all day, not saving people's lives," Rory said patiently, still tugging at Beau's shoulders. "Go, go to bed."

"I..." Beau couldn't say it, couldn't ask it. But he didn't want to leave this warm, bright space with Rory in it. He didn't want to sleep alone, or even pretend to try.

"All right," Rory said, softer. "Just—put your head down, then, honey."

Rory's hand pressed between Beau's shoulder blades, and he found that the space in front of him was miraculously already clear, so he could fold his arms to pillow his head on the table. Rory's hand brushed over the back of his head to the nape of his neck and then was gone, but Beau was too drowsy to protest the loss. He half-listened to the sounds of Rory clearing away the dishes from the table, washing them and tidying up the kitchen, but mostly he was drifting in a half-dream of going to bed with Rory, pressing him down into the sheets and...

He snapped awake at a touch and looked up at Rory, who was looking down at him with dark eyes. His gaze dropped from Beau's face to his lap, and Beau opened his mouth to apologize for being half-hard, for wanting too much.

Rory bent down to kiss him, stopping the words.

Beau groaned into the kiss and pushed back from the table, pulling Rory down into his lap, and Rory came easily. His whole body felt pliant and his arms went around Beau's neck, his mouth opening readily for Beau's kiss. Beau just held him and kissed him, trying not to push further—but he was still wearing scrub pants, which offered no camouflage or restraint as his cock hardened, pressing up against Rory as it did. Beau managed not to grind up against him, but Rory didn't pull away, just kept kissing him and holding him—smelling so warm and good and sweet and *his*—as Beau drove himself wild just on that.

Rory took his hands from around Beau's neck, leaning back from the kiss, and Beau froze, panting. Rory was smiling, though, with his kiss-reddened lips.

"Just thought you could use a hand," Rory said, rearranging himself on Beau's lap so he could slide one hand under the waistband of Beau's scrubs.

Beau's breath caught, and he chased Rory's hand with his own. "Baby, you don't—"

"Shh," Rory breathed, almost into his mouth, as Rory's fingers curled around Beau's cock. "Shh. Maybe it's just a dream, then, huh? Maybe you listened to your husband and went to bed, and now you're dreaming about him."

Beau opened his eyes and met Rory's and saw nothing but happiness and fondness, and he didn't have the strength to argue.

"Maybe so," Beau sighed, leaning in for another kiss as Rory stroked him. "That would've been very sensible of me, wouldn't it? Listening to my husband?"

"Mm-hm," Rory agreed, smiling into an easy kiss, stroking Beau steadily while Beau's hand rested on his chest, feeling the quickening beat of his heart.

It really was like a dream, drowsy and well-fed in the brightly-lit kitchen, Rory all warm and willing in his lap, drawing pleasure from him with every flick of his wrist and brush of his lips. Beau surrendered to it, riding the swells of pleasure higher and higher, until he couldn't kiss Rory because his breath was coming short, his body winding tight. He gasped softly as he spilled into Rory's hand, pressing his face against Rory's throat because it was too much to see as well as feel and smell this happening.

He stayed still after, until he was too conscious of the way Rory's fingers still curled around his cock, the way Rory's other arm curled around his shoulders, holding Beau close. Rory's cheek rested against the top of his head, and he could feel Rory's slow, steady breathing, and the way Rory's heartbeat didn't quite slow down to match.

"So," Beau said finally. "If I were to listen to my very wise husband now, what would he tell me to do now?"

Rory's breath caught a little, and Beau tipped his head back to meet Rory's eyes, to see the way he bit his lip.

"I suppose I ought to be in bed," Beau murmured. "And so should he, hm?"

Rory nodded, his arm tightening around Beau's shoulders. He let go of Beau's cock just to press his sticky-wet hand flat against Beau's belly, not holding on, but... making his mark, maybe.

Beau had to kiss him again while he adjusted his grip, and when he stood up Rory let out a startled little laugh but wrapped his legs firmly around Beau's waist at the same time.

"I've got you, baby," Beau murmured, walking surefootedly to the stairs while stealing little kisses. "Won't let you go until you tell me you want me to, I promise you that."

"Your bed," Rory demanded between kisses as Beau climbed the stairs. "Don't want to sleep alone."

Beau couldn't say anything to that, but he kissed Rory again and carried him into the bedroom they'd shared the last few nights, to the bed...

The bed they'd shared, though you could hardly tell from the scent of it, let alone the sight. The sheets had been washed clean, the covers showing no hint that anyone had ever kicked them to the floor while occupied with something much more important.

"I, um," Rory said. "I cleaned, but..."

"Kind of wish you hadn't?" Beau murmured, kissing him again before he could answer.

"Seems so lonely now," Rory agreed, when Beau released his mouth. "Guess we'll have to do something about that."

"I guess we will," Beau agreed, leaning to tug the covers out of the way before he dropped Rory into his bed.

Before Beau could hesitate, or ask Rory what he wanted, or reassure him, Rory was peeling out of his clothes—just a t-shirt and pajama pants.

"You too," he insisted, wriggling out of his pants, and Beau couldn't do anything but obey, stripping before he sat down on the bed and bent to give Rory a long, lingering kiss. Rory's arms came up around his neck, encouraging him to stay, but Beau pulled back enough to meet his eyes.

"Tell me, baby," Beau said softly. "Whatever you want, but I'm not going to guess what that is."

Rory bit his lip again, turning shy now. He wasn't hard, wasn't wet, wasn't turned on the way he had been on the full moon, but it was still obvious that he wanted this.

"I can lie beside you and kiss you and nothing else," Beau offered softly. "I can touch you anywhere you want. I don't think more than that's a good idea tonight."

Rory nodded. "I... I want to kiss. And touch. I... I want to feel. I think I can, if you..."

Rory's voice was faltering already. If Beau left him dangling any longer or tried to drag more words out of him, he would insist he was fine and just wanted to go to sleep.

"Okay," Beau said, stretching out slowly on the mattress and watching the way Rory's eyes went dark, his lips parting hungrily. "So we'll kiss, and touch, and I'll do my best to make you feel good. Tell me if I get off-track, okay, baby?"

Rory nodded quickly, reaching for him, and Beau leaned in, half-covering Rory's body with his, planting his knee between Rory's. He kissed Rory's parted lips, claiming his mouth in languid movements as he got used to the feeling of Rory's naked body under his. Rory squirmed under him with no particular direction, just searching for sensation.

"Let me, baby," Beau murmured, propping himself fully over Rory to kiss and nuzzle down his throat, down his chest, where a flush was rising on his skin, warm against Beau's lips. Rory didn't go still until Beau's lips brushed his nipple, and then his breathing hitched, his whole body stiffening for a moment.

"Found you," Beau said, glancing up to see Rory—still biting his lip but smiling, too, his eyes gone that little bit darker at the first hint of pleasure. Beau had to kiss him again, darting up for a quick brush of lips, and then he lowered his head over Rory's chest, teasing here and there, coaxing little gasps and movements from him with lips and fingers and tongue. After a time those movements took on rhythm, direction, and Rory tugged him up again.

Beau kissed him slowly, still coaxing, but he ran a hand down Rory's body, between his eagerly parted thighs, to find the evidence that he was starting to feel this the way he wanted to. He whined at the brush of Beau's fingers over his opening, which was barely damp, far from being ready to admit anything inside, but enough to show that Rory's body was beginning to cooperate.

"Can I use my mouth somewhere else?" Beau murmured, breaking off the kiss as he rubbed the heel of his hand against the base of Rory's cock, his fingertips just brushing his rim. "Would that feel good?"

Rory exhaled and nodded, even giving him a little push. Beau grinned and moved down the bed.

He took Rory's hips in his hands, steadying him, and then began to mouth at Rory's cock—soft and small, but obviously still sensitive. He trailed his mouth lower, nuzzling and licking his way to Rory's hole, and Rory's legs spread wider, whining in his throat, before Beau's tongue pressed against him.

None of it was as easy, or obvious, or *fast* as it had been during the moon, but Rory still tasted better than anything Beau had ever had before. Beau still couldn't imagine wanting anything more than he wanted the noises Rory made as the pleasure started to swell in him, the way his scent turned warm and open and eager as Beau pleasured him. It built and built until Rory's little gasps turned to moans and then cries, his hips moving constantly as he pushed into Beau's mouth, onto his fingers.

Beau felt half-hypnotized. Not even the moon could reach him here, every sense buried in his omega. It felt like he might keep going forever, pushing Rory onward through these slow stages of pleasure, and then all at once Rory tensed under him, going rigid as his cock spurted and his hole pulsed tighter around Beau's fingertips. He nearly howled as the climax was wrenched from him, and Beau couldn't stop tasting and touching him until he went limp again, shuddering a little.

Beau rested one hand on Rory's thigh, and his cheek on the opposite thigh, just looking up Rory's body to his flushed face.

After a moment Rory looked down and said, "What're you doing down there? Your legs are hanging off."

Beau grinned and kissed the top of Rory's thigh, then moved back up the bed to pull Rory into his arms and kiss him. Rory licked tentatively at his mouth, his tongue dipping between Beau's lips as he tasted himself on Beau's tongue. Beau had to pull away a little, reminding his body that he'd already had his turn and he had to wake up in a depressingly small number of hours.

Rory squirmed in his grip, settling himself comfortably in Beau's arms, but all the time he was looking at Beau with such fondness, such drowsy ease, that Beau could hardly think. His pulse beat with nothing but alpha satisfaction at the sight of his omega, well-pleased and ready to sleep in his arms.

Rory's eyes drifted shut, and on the very edge of sleep, Beau thought, *No one but him. No one but me for him. Always.*

I love him.

Beau's eyes flashed open. It wasn't that the thought was so surprising—he'd cared for Rory from the beginning—but it came with an utter certainty.

He could make Rory love him; Rory probably already nearly did, or thought he did. Beau was undoubtedly the best alpha Rory had ever had—but what the hell did that mean, given the alphas Rory had had?

What did it matter, though? If Rory was happy, and Beau was happy, what did it matter if it was only because Rory didn't know any better, and had never had a chance at anything else?

Beau felt a little sick at that greedy turn of his thoughts. It did matter. It had to matter. He couldn't—he must not—try to lure Rory into something permanent, not as things stood now. Not when he was the only person Rory had in the world, with nothing to compare him to and no one else to turn to.

But maybe... if he could find a way to give Rory other options before their three years were up, if Rory *did* have other people to depend on, so his choice wasn't between staying with Beau and being all alone in the world again, then maybe it would be all right. Maybe Beau could find some way to make it all right, and still keep him. Still love him, and earn Rory's love in return.

For now, Beau just held him close and slept.

～

The next day, when he finally managed to take something resembling a lunch break in something resembling privacy—at two-thirty in the afternoon—he did some Googling on his phone.

Georgia Lea Wisconsin werewolf

The first result was a Facebook profile, and Beau tapped on it, expecting to have to guess about whether he'd found the right Georgia Lea. But she had green eyes he'd seen just that morning, blinking up at him from his pillow, and honey blonde hair.

Right under her photo it said *Intro*, and under that were just a couple lines of text. The second one said, *Forever missing my brother Rory. Please come home.* And then there was a URL.

Beau clicked it and found himself at a website that seemed to be devoted to missing omegas—the page loaded slowly and awkwardly on his phone, but in another moment he was looking at a green-eyed, round-cheeked kid on the cusp of puberty, side-by-side with an image that might have been Rory today, plus another forty pounds and two inches of hair, too smooth at the edges and betraying its artificially generated origin.

There was some basic information about Rory below that, and an email address to send information to: *bringroryhome@gmail.com*

Beau hesitated—maybe he should ask Rory first, leave this to him —but then he thought of what it would feel like to have Rory out in the world somewhere, to know nothing but that he was alone and in danger, that he might not even be alive. Georgia Lea had been waiting eight years to know where her brother was.

Beau tapped on the link.

I don't know whether Rory is ready to come home, or even ready to be in touch with you, but I want you to know that he is safe and well.

The words were inadequate, but Beau could do better than that; he pulled up the photos on his phone. He'd taken one this morning, telling Rory he needed something nice to look at during the day. Well, he'd taken five, but at least one of them was Rory's-sister-appropriate: a shot of Rory smiling sunnily, swathed in a hoodie of Beau's that hid some of his thinness and the scars on his neck, which Beau almost didn't notice anymore.

He attached the photo, hit send, and turned off his phone before he headed back to work.

CHAPTER 26

"*H*ey, there you are," Casey said, popping out of a little blue car liberally coated with dust a moment after Rory had gotten out of the ThereWolf car that brought him to the sewing store.

Casey was grinning, looking so pleased that Rory utterly forgot the words he'd been rehearsing in the car. He had meant to apologize to Casey for intruding on his time and thank him for agreeing to meet Rory and help him pick out supplies for his sewing project. Now Rory only managed to grin back and say, "Hi."

Casey bumped shoulders with him companionably—they were close to the same height, so it even worked—and they headed into the store together.

"I'm glad you asked me to meet you," Casey said, looking around the fluorescent-lit store full of humans and a nose-itching scent of potpourri. "I, uh..." Casey looked over at him and then quickly away again, striking out confidently into the store as he said, "I don't really get to hang out with other omegas much when I'm not, you know. Delivering their babies."

Casey was his own age—maybe a little old to be unmated, for an omega living traditionally with the pack. There was no hint of an alpha's scent about him, no sign in his voice that he was longing to be delivering his own baby.

Rory pushed away his own tentative hopes and said, "Other than the refuge, I haven't really been around a lot of other omegas either. Not for a long time."

Casey smiled at him and added, "Plus, you're—I mean, of course you're a friend and neighbor of the pack, but you haven't been around for the last twenty years. You don't look at me like I'm, you know. Still six years old and tragically orphaned."

Rory heard the *please don't ask about it, please don't listen to what anyone else says about it,* behind those lightly-spoken words. Casey didn't look at him like he was only what he'd suffered, either, and Rory could certainly return the favor.

He hooked his arm through Casey's, feeling bold and safe with another omega, even if he did happen to be a midwife. Casey knew about him and seemed to understand, and was here to help.

"Okay," Rory said. "So where do you think we find thimbles?"

When they were done shopping and there was still most of the afternoon left before Beau would be home, Casey offered to bring Rory back to the Niemi pack lands. That way he could meet some of the other omega midwives and get their opinions on his little sewing project.

Rory had a feeling that sewing wasn't the only thing he'd be hearing the Niemi midwives' opinions on, if they were anything like the omega midwives he remembered from his mother's pack. He'd hated it at the time, all the pointed noticing that only pack elders could get away with, the advice they offered at the least excuse.

He was kind of looking forward to it now.

Casey slowed and turned off the paved road onto a dirt one, narrow enough that the trees met over their heads. They hadn't gone far before Casey said, "We're on the pack lands, now."

Rory thought he might have known even if Casey hadn't

announced it, from the way Casey sank a little into his seat, his grip on the wheel easing. The road itself changed, too, smoothing out. Clearly the pack maintained its lands well.

Rory stared at the dash of Casey's car as memories flooded back of all the chores that went into maintaining the pack's property when he lived there. Alphas and betas had handled things like caring for the roads and paths, clearing snow in the winter and mowing grass in the summer, mending fences and painting buildings. Rory's chores had run more to pulling weeds in the gardens and hoop houses, mending clothes and cleaning indoors. It had rankled, all of it, being suddenly effectively one of the girls, even if everyone still called him a boy.

He remembered his dad's voice—in the brief slice of time before he wasn't Rory's dad anymore—hissing in an angry whisper as loud as a shout to a werewolf kid listening to his parents when he should have been sleeping. *What does that even mean, omega? Is he a boy or a girl or what?*

Rory hadn't known either, then, except that he wasn't what he thought he was, what he was supposed to be to belong in his family and stay at school.

"Hey," Casey said softly, looking over at him, and Rory realized he'd closed his hands into fists in his lap.

Rory took a breath, forcing himself to relax. He was just visiting; he would go home in an hour or two, to his house. To Beau, who definitely hadn't minded about the sheets or expected him to be anything but what he was. Who had taken one picture after another of Rory as he was getting ready to leave this morning, because he wanted them to look at while he was at work.

Rory summoned up a smile for Casey, and said, "Sorry. I haven't been around a whole pack in a long time."

Casey nodded. "Well, I promise it won't be the *whole* pack. They wouldn't all fit in the Midwives' House, for one thing."

Rory nodded, and made himself look around, absorbing all the differences that told him this *wasn't* his mother's pack's land. The road skirted a lake instead of crossing over a rocky creek, and then Casey took a turn that led them in a downhill curve, and he saw the first buildings belonging to the pack—a few small cottages and a long, low garage. Casey kept going, taking another turn that brought them to a two-story house made of stone, with a wide covered porch across the front of the building.

There was no one on the porch just now, but he could see baskets left beside a couple of the worn wooden chairs, a small pink blanket left hanging over the railing. The door and windows all stood open, awaiting them along with any afternoon breezes on this late-summer day.

Casey didn't dawdle about getting out of the car, so Rory didn't either. This was a new place, he told himself, nothing like anywhere he'd been before, and if he was about to be surrounded by midwives...

Casey's hand slipped into Rory's and he squeezed before he started towing Rory up the steps of the porch. Rory held on tight. He knew Casey; he knew Casey wouldn't hurt him. Casey had said it was wrong, what those other midwives did to him. He wasn't even here to ask them about any of that stuff; he was just here for help with learning to embroider properly.

It was, he thought, stepping over the threshold a half-step behind Casey, probably stupid to think that he was really only here for embroidery advice. But...

"Oh, there you boys are—goodness, you didn't say he was so skinny! Let me just go get some cake."

Rory barely glimpsed the omega—just an impression of short-cropped white hair and motherly curves—before she was turning back toward the kitchen.

Casey smiled and rolled his eyes at Rory and led him inside, to a room where couches and chairs were arranged facing a fireplace. There was already a pitcher of lemonade, a pitcher of iced tea, and plate of cookies on a coffee table, and Casey towed him in that direction.

"Sit where you want, I'll pour," Casey said, finally letting go of Rory's hand. "Tea or lemonade?"

Rory swallowed and sat down on a couch that gave up a pack-family scent of long use, clutching his little bag of sewing things in his lap. "Um. Lemonade?"

"Sure," Casey said, pouring, and by the time he perched beside Rory and handed him the glass, the white-haired omega had returned, bearing an iced cake and a stack of plates and cutlery.

"Oh," Rory murmured, glancing from the cake to the cookies, his stomach already in such a knot that he wasn't sure he could make it accept lemonade. "I, um, I don't..."

"No, no, it's just there so you can remember how to be hungry once you've relaxed," the omega said, setting the cake and plates down. Rory's eyes went to the mark of a mating-bite on her throat, silvery-pale with age and looking like a decoration on her softly wrinkled skin.

"I'm Auntie June, dear, and you must be Roland. Casey's told us all about you and your Beau, and he said you're trying to teach yourself a bit of good old-fashioned omega home-craft."

Rory took refuge in a sip of lemonade and nodded.

Auntie June kept looking at him expectantly; it was obvious she knew what he wanted to learn, and equally obvious that she was waiting for him to say something about it. He glanced over at Casey just in time to see Casey cram half a cookie into his mouth, smiling brightly and unhelpfully.

"I, um," Rory frowned down at the little bag in his lap—all new things, all brought fresh at once, not like the hand-me-down history of a house like this, the long continuity of the pack. It seemed ridiculous to tell this Auntie that he wanted to make his own pack traditions, just for him and Beau, as if that was something you could just invent and have it mean anything at all.

But that was why he'd come here, after all, because he knew he needed to borrow a little from the Niemi pack to make it real. He just had to *say* something.

"I just want to do something for Beau," Rory said, still staring down at the bag in his lap. "He's so good to me, and he works so hard, out among humans all the time. He's a doctor—a resident, I mean, but he's going to be a doctor, because he wants so much to help people.

But I can see how hard it is, and he's only just starting. He's got three years of this, and I can't help him with the really hard parts. Anything I can do to make it better, easier for him, I want to. I just don't know how."

"Well, you know the important part," Auntie June said, briskly comforting. "Which is to come to the pack when you're in a fix."

Rory bit his lip. "We're not, I mean..." He hesitated, trying to answer correctly, without offending Auntie June and, by extension, the Niemi pack, and also not promise something he shouldn't, or put Beau into an awkward position with them.

"Neither of us parted from our packs on good terms. For me, I don't really blame them for not stopping me from being a dumb kid, but Beau's pack..." Rory shook his head. "The way they treated him, I know he doesn't want another one, and I don't blame him. He's got me, and we look out for each other. You've all been very kind, but..."

"Well, you're the first friend Casey's ever brought home for us to meet," Auntie June said, throwing a significant look past Rory to the younger midwife.

Rory remembered what Casey had said, about being orphaned and people always looking at him that way, and hurried to draw Auntie June's attention back to himself. "Casey's doing me a favor, really, so thank you."

"It's no trouble," Auntie June said. Her gaze did return to Rory then, and after a quick up-and-down look she put two cookies on a plate which she passed to Rory with such firm authority that he didn't think of refusing or hesitating to take a bite. "Your alpha must be the one at the Rochester Clinic?"

Rory went very still. Casey and Jennifer both knew where Beau worked, but the way she said *the one* sounded like she knew more about it than that.

Auntie June huffed. "Chew your food, child. The Niemi Alpha and a few of us other elders met with some folks from Rochester last winter. They wanted to know what a werewolf would need, how to make it possible for him to succeed there. They came here, you know, onto the pack lands—humans begging a favor, though they did beg it of every pack hereabouts, so as not to make any commitments in advance for your Beau. I suppose if he wouldn't join a pack, at least making sure he found a mate wasn't a bad compromise, and it was pretty obvious they didn't want to let him go if there was going to be any hope at all of him making it through the training."

Rory looked down again at the bag in his lap. They'd known all along, then, that Beau had only married him because he had to.

"But I've never seen an alpha who could be made to take a mate when he was set against it," she added. "Not without making things a misery for their mate and everyone around them, so I guess that's going all right."

Rory did look up at that, startled. It was on the tip of his tongue to explain that Beau had only promised him these three years, had only agreed because he had to and it was temporary, but... Beau *was* happy with him, Rory thought. And Rory *meant* to make it permanent if he could.

Auntie June wouldn't be at all pleased to hear that it had begun as a sort of sham—the absence of a mating-bite on his throat was probably bad enough already. If he told her they had never intended their marriage to be forever, it might get back around to the people at the Rochester Clinic who had come and talked to the pack in the first place, and Rory couldn't be responsible for messing that up for Beau.

He smiled cautiously instead. "He's always been good to me. I was pretty sick when we met, and he took care of me. He still does, as much as he can with all the work he's got to do."

Auntie June nodded approvingly. "Anyone can see that on you, dear. But sometimes it gets a bit much, doesn't it? Being treated like glass? You'll never break him of it entirely—that kind of alpha will always want to take care of his omega—but it won't do to be forever kept safe on a shelf, either."

She reached out and patted his knee firmly. "You'll just have to show him what kind of strong an omega can be—and more than any other kind of wolf, the omega's strength is the pack. He can be as stubborn as he likes about thinking every pack will be the same, and you can just look after things for him until he gets his head on straight."

Rory nodded hesitantly, smiling a little more easily. Auntie June talked like he was the same kind of omega as her—his alpha's mate, as good as a member of the pack even if he didn't really join. Not some useless, helpless, broken person, but someone who could take care of his alpha like a proper mate would.

"That's what I want to do," Rory said.

Auntie June nodded firmly. "We'll help you along, then. These alphas—the more stubborn they are about going it alone and being the great protectors, the more they need a sensible mate to manage them, I swear. The best thing is to make sure they never notice they're being managed. That's easier when you've got a pack to help you with it."

"There is something to be said," Casey put in, startling Rory a little as he finally broke his silence. "For open, honest communication between partners. I mean," Casey smiled wryly. "So I've heard, anyway."

Auntie June gave a judicious nod. "If only because making them actually talk sensibly is a better punishment than just about anything else you can do to an alpha like that, yes. But there is *also* something to be said for the ancient omega art of paying attention and doing what needs doing without making a production of it. So, my dear—you wanted to learn to stitch a well-wish?"

"Yes," Rory said, feeling a distinct sense that he had passed some test and would now be rewarded. "For the scrubs and coats Beau wears at work, at least."

Auntie June nodded. "Well, let's see what you've got to start with."

Rory opened the bag and started pulling out sewing supplies, dumping things into his own lap and onto the coffee table, slipping a thimble onto his finger. Auntie June scooted toward him, picking up the embroidery hoop and cloth and showing him how to combine those two objects into something he could work with, rattling off further advice about how to make this work with actual clothes that might have seams or buttons in the way.

She pulled out some things from a basket he hadn't even noticed—including a big sheet of cloth with dozens of designs embroidered in neat rows. "These are the individual marks we use," she explained. "Someone's got to keep track of them—now you don't have to use our system, obviously, but it's a way to see what you might want to do for your alpha's mark, and your own."

Rory somehow hadn't thought of that—making marks on his own clothes, as well as Beau's. But if they were a pack of two, that meant he was a part too, and he had to take care of himself as well as Beau, or else the whole thing fell apart.

"I, um, I thought for Beau..." Rory pulled out his phone to show her some pictures he'd taken of the designs from Beau's jeans. "Something similar to his old mark, but not quite the same..."

"Oh, goodness, that must be a Michigan pack," Auntie June said, squinting at the stitching. "What's his name now? Jeffries? Beau, that must be from the deVries pack, somewhere in John Beaumont's line...."

Rory held very still, saying nothing. Beau hadn't told him his old pack's name, only his own. He didn't want to be giving away secrets that Beau hadn't even entrusted to him, let alone anyone else.

Auntie June patted his hand. "Neither here nor there, dear, not if he's not one of them anymore. Quite all right. So, what about something like..." She sorted through the designs on the cloth, pointing out different elements and colors.

Rory got absorbed in it, listening to her mingled explanations of stitch techniques and pack relationships. It wasn't long before he found himself clumsily drawing a design on his practice cloth and taking a threaded needle from her hand to try his first stitches.

"Not bad, not bad," Auntie June said, as he traced the first line. "You'll get quicker at it as you go, but you've got the idea. Keep right along, I'll be back in a moment."

Rory nodded and kept his head ducked over his design; when Auntie June walked away he realized that Casey had left sometime while he was consulting with her, leaving Rory entirely alone in the room. But he could hear the other omegas somewhere else in the

Midwives' House, and not too far away the hum of activity that meant the rest of the pack was going along with their lives elsewhere.

When someone came back in Rory didn't even look up until she sat down beside him; it wasn't Auntie June but another white-haired omega, thinner and even older.

"I'm Granny Tyne, dear, don't you mind me," she said. "Just keep on breathing. Oh, that looks nice, you're doing wonderfully."

Rory kept breathing and kept stitching and only let his eyes close for a second when he felt her hand on the small of his back. She didn't do anything else right away, and he let himself relax into the touch, still breathing, listening for Casey and Auntie June and the rest. She couldn't hurt him. She wouldn't. He knew that.

Her other hand touched his belly and slid down slightly, probing. He waited for pain, for pressure and force, the strength he knew was hidden in a midwife's hands. But after a moment she just said, "Ah, copper. Well, that's a trick Casey wouldn't have seen. We haven't had to resort to that in ages around here."

Rory managed, barely, not to stab himself in the finger as he twisted to face the midwife, and she drew her hands away from him and sat back. "What—you're sure?"

She smiled and raised her hands, thin and knobby with age. "I have a bit of a touch for metal. Like a dowsing rod. And yes, I'm quite sure. Copper in your belly—that last midwife you saw slipped you a coil to keep anything else from taking root there. It's saved many an omega arguing with their alpha about whether they need another little one in the family, and it's surer than anything you can do without leaving a mark. As I said, we haven't had to do one around these parts in a while, so it's no surprise Casey didn't feel sure of what you were describing."

Rory's heart was racing, and he forced his gaze back down to the little design taking shape under his hands. He could do this. He could be everything Beau would need.

It took a moment for him to realize he was smiling, and when he did it burst out into a laugh that didn't let up until he ran out of breath. By that time Granny Tyne had cut each of them a thick slice of cake, and Rory found he could eat it without any trouble at all.

~

Rory drifted around the house in a haze after Casey dropped him off, picking things up and putting them down again. *Not broken, not forever.*

He should tell Beau—he had to tell Beau—but how could he, without giving away everything he wanted, and how close he'd gotten to the pack as well? It was too soon for any of that, and he wouldn't want Beau to think that the pack meant something sinister by making friends of them.

But how could he *keep* from telling about today? He wasn't broken! There was nothing really wrong with him, he was just *on birth control*, even if he hadn't known it. He could have children someday, *Beau's* children. He could fill this house with round-cheeked babies with big dark eyes, stitch circles of protection into their clothes, take them to play with their neighbors in the pack so they wouldn't be strangers. So they would always have another home as well as this one.

Before he left, Auntie June had brought out a baby blanket from her basket, already adorned with more than a dozen circles stitched in different colors, clearly each by a different pair of hands.

"You should add one," she said. "We like to gather as many well-wishes as we can before a new baby is born into the pack. You may not be one of us, but you can still add your touch, and your charm, if you're willing. No doubt you'll have a well-wish to offer this child that none of us within the pack would think of."

She had told him that that was the true heart of these well-wishes —not only the right design or a well-practiced technique, but the wish that they represented, the reason that the person doing the stitching had picked up the needle in the first place. She had set up the blanket on a hoop for him and badgered him into choosing a color, then coached him through threading the correct needle. Before he knew it he was bent over the little blanket, soft as anything he'd ever touched before, thinking, *Always know where your home is. Always know you can go home. Always know your home is yours.*

It was what he would wish his own children; it was what he couldn't quite believe would ever be true for him. But someday—if Beau would make a real bond with him, if he and Beau had children— then he might be able to be sure that regardless of anything else, he would always have a home with Beau.

He couldn't ask yet, but someday, a day he could almost see from here, he might be healed enough, might be good enough, to offer himself to Beau like that. For real. Forever.

He heard the car pulled into the driveway and froze where he was sitting. He hadn't made any dinner. He'd been too scattered. It was a good thing he *didn't* mean to ask Beau today, because he wasn't making any kind of good showing of himself. But he had time; he had three years, if it took him that long to be ready, though he felt sure he wouldn't have to wait that long.

Beau wasn't coming inside. Rory walked to the front door and leaned against it, listening to Beau's heart beating—still in the drive-way, still muffled inside the car. Just sitting in there, not coming in. What was he waiting for? What was he doing?

Rory knew he should open the door—look out the window— should just *calm down*—and then he heard the car door open and Beau stepping out. Rory pushed off from the door then and opened it, and watched Beau come up onto the porch.

He stepped right into Rory's arms. Rory clung to him and breathed him in, nuzzling at Beau's chest and seeking out his familiar body-scent under all the hospital-smells and stranger-smells clinging to him.

Beau held him just as tight, and Rory was barely aware of Beau maneuvering them away from the door until he heard it close. Beau kept moving, guiding them to the couch, and Rory sank onto it with him gratefully. They sat together without speaking, holding on and breathing each other in, until their breathing and heartbeats had settled into the same rhythm, their bodies melting comfortably against each other.

He was just trying to think of what to say, if there was anything he could say at all, when Beau beat him to it.

"I did something today that I probably should have discussed with you first," Beau said.

Rory stiffened at that, because as soon as Beau said it, he thought that *he* really ought to have talked to Beau first about what *he* did today, and here he was not planning to tell him at all.

"It's good, or at least, I think it's a good thing. And if it's not good, or you're just not ready, then it can just be nothing, if that's what you want. You don't have to do anything with this. But I did a search today, for your sister."

Rory jerked upright and stared at Beau, feeling like he'd been struck by lightning; it was so far from anything he'd been thinking of, and yet how could he have gone a single day without thinking of it? How had he not even been thinking of Georgie, when he was imagining a future for himself, building a family and a home of his own?

Beau looked worried, but his grip on Rory didn't let up. "When I found her, I knew right away it was her, because practically the first thing on her profile says how much she misses her brother Rory and wishes he would come home. And when I saw that... I didn't really think, baby, I'm sorry. I just couldn't leave her another day not knowing if you were all right. Because if I hadn't seen you in years and I didn't know you were safe, it would be eating me up inside, every minute. Every second, every breath I took and didn't know whether you were still breathing."

Rory pressed himself hard against Beau, hiding his face against Beau's shoulder. "Did you—"

Beau tightened one arm around him, but let go with the other—to pull his phone out, Rory realized after a second. He clung tighter, pressing his face harder against Beau's shoulder.

"The first reply came back in less than a minute," Beau said quietly. "And it's good, baby. She was so glad to hear that you're okay. I sent her a picture from this morning, so she would know for sure, and she was so happy to see you."

"What," Rory said, "Which—" But he thought he knew which one

Beau would have sent. Not Rory still in bed, or brushing his teeth, or eating breakfast. The one where he had burrowed into Beau's hoodie, giving Beau a silly smile; that was what Georgie would have seen. And she had written back.

"That one where you're all bundled up," Beau confirmed. "I didn't tell her anything about where we are, or even anything about me, just that you're safe and you might not be ready to talk to her. But that was enough, baby. She was so glad to know that. If that's all it can be, then I won't push you for anything more or contact her again, I promise you."

Rory kept still, barely breathing as he tried to get his head around the news. Beau had found Georgie. Georgie knew he was alive, but nothing else, none of what he would eventually have to tell her if he saw her again. If she was going to be his sister again.

But she had missed him. After all these years she had still put something up on the internet that mentioned him by name and said she wanted him to come home.

Rory turned his head so he could see Beau's hand holding his phone, though Beau hadn't turned the screen toward him yet. It was there if he wanted to reach for it. He wasn't sure he could yet, but it was there.

And so was something else. "You said that was the *first* reply?"

Beau squeezed him tighter. "Yeah, baby. The second one was just a little while ago—while I was driving home. That's why I was sitting in the car, I wanted to see what it was. She... she sent a video. And it's not just her in it. Do you want to watch that?"

Rory let out a sob and clapped his hand to his mouth, and Beau's other arm came back around him, the phone disappearing behind Rory's back.

"I know it's a lot, baby," Beau murmured. "You don't have to do this right now, it's okay. It's okay if you're not ready."

"But it's," Rory couldn't make his breathing steady. "It's—they —Georgie?"

"Yeah, baby," Beau murmured. "Georgie made the video for you, and she wants you to see it. I think it's a good thing too."

"I didn't make any dinner," Rory said helplessly. "I'm not—"

Beau's arms around him shifted. "I'll order some pizza," Beau said, his cheek against the top of Rory's head. "And then we'll both be free the rest of the night to watch this or whatever, okay?"

Rory pressed his face against Beau's chest, listening to a familiar cadence of thumb taps, until Beau said, "Do you want to just listen, Ror? Would that be easier?"

"Can you," Rory said, barely making a sound. "Just... start it, and..."

"Yeah," Beau said. "Yeah, okay, here we go."

Rory stopped breathing at the sound of a woman's voice, strange and familiar all at once. "Okay, Spence, Mom, Dad—"

Rory couldn't not look, and the video was right there on the phone cradled in Beau's hand: his baby brother grown into a lanky teenager, and his parents—*both of his parents*—sitting side by side by side at a familiar table.

"I want to show you something that I got today which is probably pretty self-explanatory, but—here you go."

A photo—Rory just recognized himself in the oddly angled view—slid across the table to them. His mother clapped a hand to her mouth, and his father's—her husband's—arm went around her. It was Spencer who yelped out, "Rory? Is that *Rory*? Oh my God, it is!"

"Where," his dad said, looking past the camera and then into it for a moment, and then to his wife. "Is he... is he okay?"

"I don't know," Georgia said. "I got his message today—no real name attached, and they said Rory might not be ready to be in touch yet, but they wanted us to know he's okay. So I thought we should let him know how glad we are to know that."

"So glad!" Spencer said immediately, focusing on the camera with a fierce expression. "Rory, it was complete bullshit that you had to go away, and no matter what happened since then, it's not your fault! We love you, that's all that matters."

His mother said nothing, her hand still pressed to her mouth. She raised her other hand to the photo on the table, and then finally, finally looked up at the camera, her eyes shiny with tears.

"Rory," she whispered, behind her hand. "My Roland—sweetheart —please—"

The tears spilled down her cheeks, and Spencer leaned in to hug her.

His father cleared his throat, and Rory's fists clenched tighter in Beau's shirt.

"I'm sorry," he said on the screen. "Son, I'm so sorry. Spencer's right. We love you, Rory, and nothing else matters."

Rory pressed his face to Beau's chest and sobbed out loud, and Beau's arms came tight around him again. Beau rocked him, kissing the top of his head and murmuring words Rory couldn't take in.

CHAPTER 27

$\mathcal{R}$ory sat up and ate pizza when it arrived, leaning against Beau but not needing to be fed by hand. Afterward he asked to watch the video again.

Tears streamed down his face through the whole thing. This time he made it to the end, the moment when the camera turned and the woman who could have been Rory's healthier twin smiled tearfully into it. "You know I love you, Ror. I miss you. Anytime you're ready, I'm here, little brother."

He sniffled, wiping his own tears away, and then reached out to navigate back to the email that had come before the video, the one Georgia had sent back within a minute of Beau's first message.

WHOEVER THIS IS PLEASE TELL HIM I LOVE HIM
  RORY I LOVE YOU
  PLEASE COME HOME I MISS YOU ROR I LOVE YOU
  CALL ANY TIME DAY OR NIGHT I'M HERE I LOVE YOU

Georgia's phone number and home address followed.

"Can I," Rory sniffed again. "Can you send me this?"

"Of course," Beau said, and forwarded it right then to the email address they'd set up for Rory not long after moving in. "There, all yours. I'll delete it if you want."

"No, it's." Rory pulled out his own phone just to look at the notification of the email received and shove it back into his pocket. He curled into Beau, hiding his face again, and shivered in his arms. He wasn't crying, but he was far from calm.

Beau held him and bit back the questions he wanted to ask, which all boiled down to *please tell me I did the right thing for you,* or *please tell me I didn't hurt you more than I helped.* It wasn't fair to ask that of Rory when he'd obviously barely absorbed what the messages meant; even if Rory reassured him, there was no knowing yet whether it was as good a thing as Beau hoped it was.

When Rory's shivers died down into an exhausted limpness, Beau murmured, "Can I do anything, baby? Do you need anything now?"

Rory took a deep deliberate breath, and said, "It's just... it's so much, I can't... do you think you... could you shift again? I think if you did, then I could, and I... I think I need to."

A wolf's mind was simpler, with less room for the kinds of questions and complications that were no doubt running through Rory's mind right now. It was the natural way to take a break from too-human worries, and it hadn't been available to Rory for so long. If Beau could give his wolf back to him as well as his family...

"Of course," Beau said. "You want to head upstairs first? Or right here?"

"Upstairs," Rory said, still clinging to him, and Beau rubbed his back and waited for him to make the first move. It wasn't long before he did, and then Rory insisted on tidying up the pizza and turning off the lights before they went upstairs. Beau trailed after him, checking the windows and doors.

Eventually they made it to Beau's room, and Beau had a chance to brush away tears and kiss Rory's face. Rory kissed his mouth, pushing up into it with a startling intensity. When he pulled back, Beau thought that he could have pushed this another way, gotten Rory's mind off it by other means, but Rory gave him a little shove and Beau stepped back and stripped, preparing himself to shift.

He looked over his shoulder and found Rory already naked, kneeling on the floor, watching him. Waiting for his alpha to lead.

"Here we go, baby," Beau said, and then he closed his eyes and drew the wolf out of hiding.

It was easier this time, having done it so recently and knowing that Rory needed this from him. He sensed it when Rory followed him, changing shape nearly at the same time.

Rory let out a little startled yelp of pain as he shifted, and Beau hurried to him, only to realize that Rory was curled in a ball, nosing at his belly.

The IUD. Casey had said he would probably feel it if he shifted, and clearly he had. Beau pressed his muzzle in next to Rory's, nosing gently at the spot. Rory uncurled slightly, licking Beau's muzzle, and Beau took a step back and looked at his omega in this new form.

He was thin, of course, though his fur hid it a little better in this shape. He looked like he was barely grown out of puppyhood, all long limbs and slightly awkward lines covered in light-colored fur. Beau nosed at his ribs and up to his throat, where he could feel scars lurking under the fur. Rory rolled easily onto his back, offering himself to his alpha without reservation.

Beau stood up over him and nosed past his throat, gently closing his teeth on Rory's scruff to tug him up off the floor. Rory came with him readily, jumping up onto the bed, and in a moment they were curled together, just as they should be.

In the days that followed, Beau heard or saw Rory watch the video and reread the email at least a dozen times, and he was sure that was only a fraction of the times Rory actually spent poring over those messages. His reactions, when Beau was there to witness them, were never easy to gauge. Sometimes it was mostly delight, sometimes anger, sometimes grief or guilt, but the emotions were always mixed with each other, and as far as Beau could tell, none of it had yet advanced to the point of sending Georgia any response.

Since Rory hadn't asked him not to, or expressed any unhappiness toward Beau for sending the original message, he did take the liberty of replying briefly to Georgia.

Thank you for the messages. I've passed them to Rory and I think he's still deciding how he feels and what steps he's ready to take. Beyond that I won't speak for him.

Georgia's reply in return was even briefer—a restrained *Thank you so much*—and that was where it was left, hanging in the air, by the time Beau cycled around to another Tuesday afternoon at the walk-in clinic.

They were shorthanded, for reasons Beau didn't really have time to find out, so he had little time to make his own extra notes on the patients he saw. He struggled to focus on them the same as he would any other time, not to make the patients themselves feel rushed, to keep from overlooking any signs that might be important.

By late afternoon, the frantic pace was already taking its toll -and his mind was starting to turn toward home, and Rory, and the hope of spending some time curled up together on the couch, or in bed, before he passed out from exhaustion. That was when a nurse walked up to him with a familiar thick file and said, "Amy Vaughn?"

Beau looked around and realized that he hadn't seen Cora all afternoon, though he could have sworn she was on rounds that morning. Had she gone home sick? Had to stay on Pulmonary because someone else was out?

There was no time to wonder about that. He reached out for the file. "Did Mr. Vaughn ask for me?"

"For Dr. Benn first, then you," the nurse confirmed. "We don't usually allow requests, but he agreed to wait behind the patients we'd already assigned to you, and... you know."

Beau nodded. He could see Mr. Vaughn trying to be careful about which doctors saw Amy, given the theories that he must know about. Cora must have told him, if he hadn't already seen it for himself, that Beau could be relied upon to be sympathetic.

He took the file down to the exam room where Mr. Vaughn and Amy were already waiting, knocked and let himself in. He greeted them just like Cora had the week before, and noted that they both looked much the same, except that they both lit up a little at the sight of him—whether because they'd had to wait so long, or because Amy had had a relatively painless feeding session last week, he couldn't guess.

He went through the same procedure Cora had followed the week before, asking the necessary questions even though he already knew the answers. He dutifully studied the record of Amy's eating when Mr. Vaughn handed it to him.

"Seems like eating's been getting harder and harder for you lately," he said to Amy, trying not to wince visibly at what the notes told him. She was barely eating solid foods at all, this week; there was a tube feeding noted every other day.

Amy nodded, her shoulders hunching a bit.

"Last doctor already told her she might have to get a g-tube if this keeps up," Mr. Vaughn put in. "I don't like the idea—and if it's anything like tube feeding it'll still hurt but with added chances of infection—but it's starting to seem like there's really nobody who can give us a better option."

Beau gave a slightly apologetic smile to Mr. Vaughn and then to Amy, and he kept his eyes on her as he said, "I really wish I could, Amy. In the meantime, let's check your belly and see what we can do for today, shall we?"

Amy flicked a glance up at him and nodded, and Beau got on with the physical check, silently hoping that any identifiable, treatable problem would show up. He took his time, attending to every sensation he could gather, but there was still nothing he could make sense of as a cause of Amy's pain. Nothing to suggest any possible cure, or a treatment that wouldn't make everything worse.

"Okay," he finally said, and a glance at the clock showed that he had already spent more time than he could spare. "I'll go get the feeding kit."

The feeding kit was waiting at the nurse's station, but when Beau tried to pick it up, one of the nurses—Allie—stopped him. "Just put in the order, then we've got another patient waiting for you. Linda's going to do the feeding."

"I—" Beau started to protest, and stopped short at the expression of *I do not have time for this* on Allie's face. She would try to argue with him in deferential words and tones, because she was a nurse and he was a doctor, but she had worked in this clinic every day for years, and he was a brand new medical resident who dropped in one afternoon a week. He could throw a fit and insist on doing what he wanted to do, or he could shut his mouth, listen to the nurse, and see the next patient.

Allie knew he was a werewolf, even if none of the patients did. What might only get any other resident a scolding for being too possessive of their patient would look different if he did it; depending on how Allie spun it, it could look *very* different. She might not even mean it maliciously. She might genuinely think it was a Bad Sign that she had to report, if he insisted on treating Amy rather than letting a nurse handle it.

And they were short-staffed; there were people waiting, people who had been triaged and needed to see doctors, people who he might really be able to help. He could keep Amy calm, help her fend off her pain for a moment, but there wasn't anything he could really do for her in the long run. He had no better option to offer her.

It might be easier, after all, not to have to go back into that room and spend another twenty minutes he couldn't spare facing the fact that there was nothing more he could do. And he was already so awfully tired.

It all flashed through his mind in a second, in the moment he watched Allie brace herself to try to argue with him without seeming to argue.

"Yeah, of course," Beau said, looking for the chart. "Uh, the code for the feeding kit—"

"Here," she said, relieved, passing him a post-it that told him how to enter it properly. "And then you've got a ten-month-old with diarrhea in Exam 4."

"Wonderful, thank you," Beau said absently, and Allie actually smiled a little as she took the chart from him.

～

The ten-month-old's case was relatively straightforward, though his attempt to make mental notes veered off into unhelpful meditation on human squeamishness about certain smells and the information those smells might convey. He took a moment before going in to see his next patient to drag his thoughts back on track, standing outside the exam room door and ostentatiously studying the chart in his hand.

A door down the hall opened, and Beau registered a particular familiar scent—*tears pain sickness*—and kept his expression carefully neutral, his head ducked at exactly the same angle, as Mr. Vaughn stepped out, his footfalls weighted. He was carrying Amy, whose heart was beating fast, her breathing muffled but ragged.

Focus, Beau told himself. *Focus. Not your business now.* He didn't let himself hear what Mr. Vaughn was saying to his daughter—but when they were just about to step through the door to the waiting room, he said something Beau couldn't help hearing.

"Maybe we'll find a werewolf to bite you."

Beau didn't raise his head, but he couldn't resist a glance down the hall—and that was enough to show him that Mr. Vaughn was looking directly at him.

It could have been a coincidence. He was maneuvering to open the door and fit through it without banging any part of Amy's body on the doorframe; maybe that was why he turned that way. But there was something about the steadiness of his heartbeat as he spoke, the directness of his gaze, that made Beau certain it was not.

He closed his eyes and did not let himself wonder what it meant. He could not. He *did not have time for this*. He opened his eyes and read the chart and *focused*.

After that there was an endless stream of patients, and Beau couldn't think of anything but being present and focused on each one in turn. He wound up seeing patients an hour past the clinic's closing time, just to get through all the patients who had checked in before they closed the doors, and then there was another hour of making sure all the charts were in order before he signed off.

He was the last resident to leave, and his steps dragged as he walked outside the clinic into the long shadows of a late summer evening. He headed down a sidewalk that would take him halfway across the pleasantly spacious green spaces of the Rochester Clinic's campus to where he'd parked that morning. The buildings connected, so he could have walked indoors nearly the whole way, but it was a relief to be in open, clean air and the relative quiet outside, where every sound wasn't echoing off glass and tile.

He was thinking of Rory, of the home-scent of their house, and hoping that they could just spend the rest of the night wrapped around each other. There was a vague, worried ache in his stomach, and he traced it to the waning moon; the empty moon would arrive at the end of this week, and he still had no idea how he or Rory would deal with the fact that he had to spend it here, away from home and his mate.

There were other people walking along the paths under the trees, though they seemed empty in comparison to the hallways indoors. Beau didn't pay any of them any mind until one stepped out in front of him.

"Dr. Jeffries."

It was Mr. Vaughn. He seemed only half himself, because Amy wasn't anywhere within earshot, but of course it was him. After the first instant of confusion Beau wasn't even surprised; it was almost a relief. Whatever the man was about to say to him, at least Beau wouldn't be left wondering if he'd imagined it, if he was making up things to worry about out of sheer paranoia.

"Mr. Vaughn," Beau said, keeping out of arm's reach, his hands carefully open at his sides. "Good evening. I'm surprised to see you still here."

Mr. Vaughn, who was half-shadowed by the nearest tree, dusk falling deeper in this particular spot, huffed something like a laugh. "Well. Not like I gotta get my kid home and feed her dinner, right?"

Beau looked away, casting his gaze out over the other paths, the nearby buildings. Where *was* Amy? He couldn't sense her anywhere around them.

"Mr. Vaughn," Beau said carefully, recalling everything he could of the instructions for speaking with unhappy patients. *Don't apologize or admit any wrongdoing without a Rochester Clinic lawyer present* was the one that came most readily to mind. "I know your visit to the clinic didn't go quite the way you would have liked, but as I said this afternoon, I can't offer you anything beyond what we did today. Everyone at the clinic is doing their best for your daughter."

Vaughn shook his head. "No, hey, I get it," he said, in a weary, dismissive tone that was surely camouflage for something else, though Beau had no idea what. "Amy was just disappointed because—we've been trying that thing you did, the relaxation stuff. Guided meditation? We've tried it before once or twice, but this week we've really been working on it, and I just don't think I have the knack."

It was reasonable, almost, except that the man had been *lying in wait for him*, and he still hadn't made himself clear about the part of this that really mattered.

"You, uh," Vaughn rocked on his heels, ducked his head so that his face was entirely in shadow. "You seemed to have a real gift for it. You were like magic with her last week."

Beau gritted his teeth for a moment, fighting down the sick, exposed feeling that came with knowing that a human knew what he was and was being coy and deniable about it. He wasn't supposed to have to feel like that anymore; he'd been open for years. People knew or didn't know, but they couldn't usually dangle what they knew over his head.

He didn't have to let this human, either.

"Mr. Vaughn, to be absolutely clear," Beau said, his voice cool and flat and calm though his heart was beating much too fast. "I am a werewolf. While I don't preemptively disclose that fact to every patient I treat, it is not a secret."

Mr. Vaughn straightened up, raising his hands in a gesture of harmlessness, or maybe warding him off. "Hey, none of my business, right? I know it's rude to just go around guessing or... or accusing somebody. I had a hunch, but I honestly don't give a shit. I just know you helped my kid, and I know you've got no reason to, but I was wondering if you'd help her again, just for a minute. Just let me see what you do that's different, that's all, I swear."

It sounded like a lie—or at least, it sounded like something being said by someone who was stressed while saying it.

It would be safer to say no, to refuse to have any contact with a patient outside the clinic, to walk away.

It would be *correct*, anyway. It would be the thing that supported an *appearance of professionalism*, a *reputation beyond reproach*, which Dr. Ross had already told him he needed.

On the other hand, he'd just disclosed that he was a werewolf, when he'd been told to keep from being noticed as one by patients. If Vaughn complained about him... Beau could get in trouble, or the walk-in clinic could refuse to treat Amy anymore, given that half the staff already thought the problem wasn't medical at all.

More to the point, Vaughn had already waited for hours to catch Beau alone. If Beau said no and walked away, was Vaughn going to leave it at that? No human was going to physically overpower Beau or hurt him in any way that would keep him down for long—not without silver or wolfsbane in hand, and Beau didn't sense either of those on him.

But anything Beau did to stop him would turn into *werewolf attacking human*, and even if it didn't become a physical altercation, Vaughn could make enough of a nuisance of himself to drag in clinic security and turn this into an Incident that would drag on for hours—while Amy was alone somewhere in pain, wondering where her father had disappeared to? While Rory waited at home for Beau to return?

Beau could run away, he supposed—Vaughn wouldn't be able to catch him if he really used the speed he could command—but then what? Go home to Rory and spend the whole night thinking about how he'd run away from a child in pain because he was scared he'd get in trouble for talking to a patient after hours?

It was nothing, really. Just talking to a sick kid.

"I can't offer any medical advice or treatment," Beau said firmly. "I'm only a resident—I'm not licensed, and I'm not under proper supervision right now—and I'm acting in my own personal, private capacity, not as an employee of the Rochester Clinic. Do you understand? I can talk to you and Amy about relaxation techniques, but that's all."

Vaughn was nodding eagerly, the scent of relief wafting off of him, his weary expression breaking into a smile. "Yeah, yeah, of course. I mean, you're the last doctor I'd want to complain about, right? You don't think I'm crazy, or that Amy is. You're doing us a huge favor, doc, believe me. I know that."

Beau nodded, and gestured for Vaughn to lead the way. They headed off in a new direction, away from the walk-in clinic but not any nearer to where Beau had parked. They'd been walking for some time before it occurred to Beau that perhaps it would have been polite to make conversation. He usually remembered to make some kind of innocuous small talk with patients—it could be useful diagnostically in several ways, as well as being polite and normal—but this situation was so outside of any routine that he had defaulted to silence.

Vaughn wasn't speaking either. Well, it had probably been a long day for him too.

Eventually they came to a parking lot, distantly attached to one of the hospital buildings, and Beau's half-conscious scanning latched on to the sound of Amy Vaughn's heart beating in a truck parked on the edge of the lot, well-shaded by the trees that grew along that side. The windows were half-open, and she was curled up in the front seat, staring intently at a phone in her hands that was emitting little boops and beeps as she tapped away with her thumbs.

He felt a little silly for imagining her huddled there shaking with pain and fear all alone, but the closer he got, the more of her scent he could pick up. She might be distracting herself, but her face was set in tense lines that didn't belong on a child's face. He hadn't been entirely wrong. He hadn't come here for nothing.

She looked up when they were nearly within arm's reach, and her face lit up a little just as it had in the clinic that afternoon. This time, though, she immediately flushed and looked down.

Vaughn opened the passenger door, but gestured Beau to move into the open space beside her.

"Hi, Amy," Beau said. "Your dad said you could use a little more practice at relaxing like I helped you last week, so I thought we could give it another try. I—" *Don't apologize, don't admit wrongdoing.* "I thought I would be able to this afternoon, but we had a lot of patients to see."

Amy shook her head, glanced at her dad and then looked at Beau. "It's okay, I get it." Her voice was the same papery whisper as always, but Beau could hear her easily enough. She made a little face and added, "Sorry about my dad."

Beau smiled at that evidence of a normal kid's embarrassment. "It's fine. He just wants you to feel better, and so do I. Want to give me your hands again?"

She was still holding the phone in her lap, but she quickly set it aside and offered her hands to Beau, her heartbeat jumping a little as his hands closed around hers. They were still cold, though the heat of the day had barely faded.

"Okay," Beau said. "Here we go. Feel how warm my hands are around yours..."

He kept talking, focusing only on Amy, ignoring Vaughn's presence at his side, ignoring everything but helping lull her down into a state of peace. She went easily. The worst of her pain from the tube feeding must have faded by now, and with the rare feeling of a full belly, her whole body wanted nothing but to drowse, once she was able to slip sideways from the pain. Curled in the familiar seat of her father's truck instead of sitting on a chilly exam table, she dozed off within ten minutes. Beau kept talking for a few minutes more, letting her settle into a deeper sleep, before he let go.

"That's all," Beau said, turning to Vaughn again with a shrug. "Like I said, it's just a matter of practice."

Vaughn exhaled a shaky breath, like a man close to tears. "Well. Like I said, you've got a knack. Thanks, doc."

"Not here as a doctor," Beau reminded him. "Just... just as a person who cares."

Vaughn nodded, and shook Beau's hand before he stepped in to fasten Amy's seatbelt. Beau slipped away while he was occupied with his daughter, and was out of a human's earshot before he turned around again.

CHAPTER 28

"*Y*ou wouldn't let a stranger in if somebody showed up at the door when I'm not home, would you?"

Rory tensed under Beau's arm, suddenly fully awake when he'd been drifting to the edge of sleep. Beau had sounded wide awake, and the words set off echoes of memory. *Who was here? Who was that you were talking to? Who are you looking at? I can smell him on you—*

"Hey, hey, it's okay," Beau murmured, nuzzling at Rory's neck. "Sorry, don't worry about it, it's nothing. I didn't mean to scare you."

Rory snapped back into the present. Beau hadn't said he wasn't angry. He said he didn't want Rory to be *scared*.

"What kind of stranger are you thinking of?" Rory asked, trying to guess what Beau was thinking of.

Beau shook his head. "It's nothing, I'm just thinking too much. I had to disclose to a patient yesterday. That I'm a werewolf. And, I don't know, it's probably just the empty moon coming, making me worry about humans knowing, that's all."

Rory turned under Beau's arm, throwing his own arm and leg over Beau and thinking of the empty moons he'd stitched, in carefully matched thread so no one would notice them, into the shoulders of

Beau's scrubs and white coats. He'd been slipping them to the bottom of the pile when he finished them. Beau hadn't worn one with a well-wish yet. Tomorrow, though. Tomorrow he'd have the tiny protection of those cotton threads and everything in Rory's heart.

"I won't let any strange humans in the house when you're not home," Rory promised firmly. "If anybody comes around looking for you, asking for you, I'll tell them to call the clinic, and I'll call Jennifer, okay? She can see our front porch from her door."

Beau exhaled, smiling a little and nodding. "Thanks for humoring me, baby."

Rory smiled cautiously back. Maybe this was a good time; Beau had sort of brought it up, even. And in a few days they wouldn't be able to avoid it anymore. "Speaking of the empty moon..."

Beau winced and pressed his forehead to Rory's, so their eyes couldn't meet. "I'm so sorry. I don't see any way of getting out of that shift. I hate the thought of you here alone, but if I was going to ask them to reschedule I should've done it before now, and... I just don't want to rock the boat. They gave me time off for the full moon, and they obviously thought that was enough of an accommodation."

Rory bit his lip. "Have you... told them? About what the empty moon is like?"

Beau's hands tightened on him, and he shook his head a little. "I can't ask for too much too soon. I have to show them I can get through my first rotation, at least."

Rory thought about pointing out that people from the Rochester Clinic had gone around the local packs, begging help from them to learn how to keep a werewolf in the residency program—but that would mean explaining to Beau how he knew that. And however it had looked to the packs, who had no particular stake in things aside from the Niemi pack being well-disposed toward Casey's new friend and Jennifer's neighbor, that might not be how it looked to Beau, who was the one who had to prove himself. He would know best what he could push for.

"Okay," Rory said. "I, um. I had an idea about how to make it not so bad, but I think it might be better if I don't tell you about it before-hand. Is that okay?"

Beau clutched him tight, kissing down the side of Rory's face. Beau smelled miserable and possessive, and Rory clung right back, his alpha's feelings seeping into him. If he couldn't pull off his plan, if it went wrong and he ruined everything...

"Whatever you need, baby," Beau murmured. "You do what you need to do. All I want is for you to be safe and feel safe. If you need anything from me, if you need to... you can tell me if you're going to go somewhere, I won't stop you. I wouldn't."

Rory clung tighter. He didn't think the somewhere he planned on going was quite what Beau was thinking, given the resigned unhappiness in his voice.

"You, um," Beau said. "I noticed you... or I haven't noticed, I guess, but... you seem to be watching that video from your family less?"

Rory tucked his face against Beau's shoulder, putting together Beau's train of thought from the empty moon to that. Beau thought Rory would go all the way to *Waukesha?* To spend the empty moon with people he hadn't seen in ten years, and leave his mate hundreds of miles away alone?

Beau rubbed his back gently. "I don't want to bug you about it. It's your business. But whatever you want, baby, whatever you need."

"I haven't," Rory said, tilting his head just enough to speak. "I... I know I need to say something to Georgie. I just... there's so much to explain, or keep secret, and then it's not just Georgie, it's my mom and dad and... Spence was seven when I went away and now he's this... *guy.* And my—my dad...?"

Beau squeezed him. "It's a lot, yeah. If you're not ready, that's up to you."

Rory held on right back, thankful that he didn't have to try to put it into words any better than that. "I'm not going to Wisconsin for the empty moon, Beau. I *would* tell you if I was thinking of something like that."

Beau let out a breath. A little of the misery seemed to lift, but he didn't ask anything about Rory's plan, and he didn't seem much happier.

"Hush," Rory murmured, squirming against him, trying to adjust their frantic mutual grip to a comfy cuddle. "We're both here now, and not a stranger in sight. Don't borrow trouble, alpha."

"Ah," Beau relaxed his grip and nuzzled against Rory's hair. "There's my wise husband again. Quite right."

Someday, Rory thought, someday Beau would say that without teasing. But for tonight at least Rory could help him sleep.

CHAPTER 29

*B*eau's shift started well before the sun was actually down. He'd spent the whole day curled up in the basement bedroom with Rory, dozing when he could stop worrying about the coming night long enough to close his eyes. Rory had fixed enough food to keep them all day without having to go even as far as the kitchen, and packed more for Beau to take to work with him.

"It's gonna be fine, honey," Rory told him over and over. "We're gonna be fine. Safe and sound, both of us. Safe and sound."

Rory's fingers had crept again and again to the bit of embroidery at the shoulder of Beau's shirt—a well-wish for safety that now adorned all his scrubs and white coats. He'd felt absurdly warmed by it, and then guilty when he realized that this was what Rory had been pricking his fingers for. Beau had never even thought to wonder what he'd been sewing, or why.

"You didn't have to," he'd said, hating the thought of Rory feeling like he had to be some perfect traditional omega to please him.

But Rory had kissed him and said, "I know. I wanted to. I know it's not any real help, but I wish I could help you. So take the wish with you, at least."

Beau had had to kiss him back for that. "Of course it helps, baby. Thank you."

And it did help a little, knowing that he was carrying something from Rory when he had to leave and drive in for his shift. He'd tucked Rory into the basement bed before he left; he knew Rory wouldn't stay there, that he had some plan to make this bearable somehow. Beau still wanted to be able to think of him like that, in the safest, most hidden den in their house, in the bed that still smelled of both of them without any trace of sex, only shared closeness.

Beau didn't let himself wonder what the plan was. He hadn't asked. He didn't want to know for sure that Rory would be safe with someone else—that someone else would be protecting his omega while he was elsewhere, alone among humans, some of whom knew exactly what he was.

It was stupid to worry about, logically. The people who knew were the doctors and nurses he'd already been working with for weeks on this rotation; Cora was the senior resident for this shift, and she'd never been anything but friendly. Their patients were mostly asleep, and they weren't expecting any new admits tonight. Nothing was going to happen.

Nothing except that there would be no moon in the night sky, and Beau would spend the whole night far from home, among near-strangers, not knowing where his mate really was. Not knowing whether Rory was truly safe.

Beau knew within about half an hour of starting his shift that he couldn't do this again. He would have to talk to Dr. Ross, to *someone*, to get his next schedule changed. It took all his focus to be sure that he was being reasonably polite to his colleagues, that he wouldn't fly off the handle or endanger a patient. At least, at the start of the shift, he was sure to have things to focus on, handling all the details of the handoff from the earlier shift. As the night stretched on...

He couldn't think about that. He could only think about handling what was in front of him, which was mostly the outgoing doctors and a stack of charts. That lasted until an hour after his shift began, when he was starting to run out of things to keep absolutely busy every second and he could feel sunset approaching in every cell of his body.

That was when a security guard knocked on the open door of the office where they were doing handoff.

"Sorry to interrupt," the guard said.

Beau realized instantly that he was a werewolf, and that he smelled and looked vaguely familiar. The name tag on his uniform said T. NIEMI. "Dr. Jeffries is needed up in the security office on the fifth floor. Won't take long."

The other doctors looked baffled—Cora looked concerned—but Beau was starting to feel a wildly unreasonable hope, the first possibility of relief. He stood. "Yes, of course. Sorry, I'll..."

"Go, go," Cora waved him off. "We're pretty much done here anyway. I hope everything's okay."

Beau nodded and turned away, following Niemi to the stairwell door, which was just across from the office.

Rory was standing on the first landing, wearing a hoodie of Beau's over his pajamas and grinning hugely. Beau took the stairs in what felt like a single bound and wrapped Rory up in his arms, clinging to him like he'd drown if he let go.

"Told you," Rory whispered. "Told you I had a plan. Safe and sound."

Beau had to look around then, remembering that they weren't alone. Niemi was standing a few steps below, watching them with an expression of fond amusement.

"We've got your back, cousin," he said when Beau met his eyes. "I don't think we've met properly—I'm Troy, Jen's husband. We live down the street."

Beau took a breath, and it felt like the first he'd gotten without effort in hours. "We played with your kids, before the full."

Troy nodded, smiling a little. "Jen was glad as hell for a couple hours without having to corral them, so our turn to do a favor, huh? More than half the security guards here at Rochester are wolves. It means we can't all be home every time we want to be, but we *can* work things around so we can function—everybody working security tonight in this building is Niemi pack or connected somehow. Makes it easier to think of it as protecting our own territory, you know? So you've got wolves watching out for you tonight—including keeping this very friendly trespasser detained in the fifth floor security office until someone can take charge of him and drive him home."

Beau blinked, looking down at Rory and then back to Troy. "Is that... you can...?"

Troy shrugged. "Security's job is to keep unauthorized persons out of secured areas. Roland here is obviously not authorized, but since he's not causing any actual problems we have some discretion about how to handle him. Isn't worth calling the cops, and we don't just kick people out with no way to get home, it just leads to them loitering on the grounds. So, yeah, shift leader can write it up to sound perfectly reasonable, nothing to do with you. But you should be able to hear him from down on the fourth floor, and if you want to come up and say hi when you've got a break, security office is right across from the stairwell door."

Beau looked down at Rory, feeling like he'd just stepped into a dream. Rory was still beaming, radiating a scent of excited pride.

"I thought it was better if you didn't know in advance," Rory explained. "In case we couldn't pull it off all the way, and so if anyone asked you could say you didn't know anything about it beforehand."

Beau tightened his grip again, tucking his face down into the neck of the hoodie, where his lips could brush Rory's throat. "Baby, you—I can't believe this. You're amazing. I never—I couldn't even imagine how—"

Rory squeezed him tight. "Just gotta trust your husband, honey. Safe and sound, just like I said."

"Safe and sound," Beau agreed, although something caught his ear just then—a phone ringing out, heralding some emergency or a late admit to the ward. "I gotta—"

"I know." Rory pulled away slightly, and Beau forced himself to let go. "I'll be listening for you, and you listen for me when you can. But we'll both be safe, and not too far. Under the same roof and everything."

Beau nodded, straightening his slightly rumpled white coat, brushing his fingers over the embroidery on the shoulder. He wanted to say something more—he wanted to say *I love you*—but he couldn't. Not yet, not when they weren't even alone and he couldn't linger. He just looked, taking in the sight of Rory standing there, strong and smart and unafraid, and then he turned away, hurrying back down the stairs. Back to work.

But all the time he could hear Rory's heart beating, not too far away.

It still wasn't easy—nothing would have been easy that wasn't being denned up at home with Rory—but it was survivable. Beau managed to focus when he had to focus, with the beating of Rory's heart there to steady him like a metronome. And when there was time to breathe, time when he would otherwise have been spiraling into panic, he could murmur Rory's name, and Rory would start reading aloud.

It sounded like he'd found the glossary of a medical textbook, and Beau hoped that he had something more interesting to occupy him when he wasn't giving Beau his voice to fixate on.

Towards morning he was yawning as he read, and Beau glanced around to be sure he was reasonably alone and whispered, "Go to sleep, baby, it's all right. I can listen to you sleeping."

"M'here," Rory mumbled. "Learning about," another yawn escaped him, "the vascular system."

Beau grinned. "I already know enough about the vascular system for both of us, Ror. Go to sleep."

Rory's heartbeat skipped a little at that, but Cora was walking toward him and he could hear a patient's heartbeat going haywire, so he wasn't sure it was Rory he had heard at all.

Handoff, inevitably, took forever, but the sun was still low in the sky when Beau was finally free to go upstairs to the fifth-floor security office again. Rory had met him in the stairwell twice overnight, but Beau made it all the way into the office this time before he found him. His husband was sleeping in a corner, curled up in a nest made with a blanket and pillow from their basement bedroom.

"Here to take charge of our stray intruder, Dr. Jeffries?"

Beau looked up, startled. He hadn't even noticed the security guard manning the office—not Troy, but another werewolf. This one's nametag said A. FRASER, and Beau vaguely recalled that Fraser was the name of one of the local packs.

"Yeah," Beau said. "Thanks for, uh, keeping him secured."

Fraser nodded, making a gesture as if tipping an invisible hat and smiling slightly. "All in a day's work, cousin."

Then he stepped out the door, ostentatiously turning his back. Beau knelt beside Rory, curling one arm around the blanket-padded shape of him and nuzzling at his cheek to breathe in the home-smell of his sleeping omega.

"Mmm," Rory wiggled a little, his heartbeat rising as he woke. "Morning, honey."

"Morning, baby," Beau murmured back. "Ready to go home?"

Rory's eyes flashed open, his body going stiff as he realized where he was, or possibly only where he wasn't. Beau tightened his grip. "Shh, safe and sound, remember, wise husband? But I'm done now, we can go home and den up for the day. How does that sound?"

Rory sagged into Beau's grip and nodded against his shoulder. "Good." He started squirming to free himself of the blanket. "I brought a bag, so no one will see..."

Beau glanced over and spotted an old duffle bag he'd rarely used. He pulled it over and Rory stuffed the pillow in. Something fell out of the folds of the blanket, hitting the floor with a sharp sound. Rory flinched, grabbing after it too late, and Beau picked it up.

Medical Terminology Workbook. It looked new, but he could smell the sharp ink of the notes he glimpsed in the margins, and it bore the scent of Rory and their house.

Rory was staring fixedly into the duffle, frozen in the act of jamming his pillow inside. A red flush was rising on his face, a scent of something like shame, and Beau thought of that sleepy protest, his own casual dismissal.

"It's good to learn new things, baby," he murmured, tucking the book gently into a pocket of the duffle before he leaned in to kiss Rory's hot cheek. "Let me know if I can help explain anything, okay?"

Rory gave him a quick sideways look, and then his gaze went past Beau to the door—where Fraser was still standing, politely not-seeing and not-hearing. Rory nodded quickly and then reached for the blanket, and Beau helped him stuff it into the bag and said nothing else about it.

~

The drive home was a gray blur of exhaustion, surreal in the morning light; halfway home he was stopped at a light and looked over at Rory, who was watching him with an expression of concern.

"Do you know how to drive, Ror?"

Rory shook his head and glanced away to the light, which had turned green.

Beau forced his attention back to driving, and it was another couple of minutes before he managed to say, "I should teach you sometime. Or. You should learn, anyway. If you want to."

"It might be good," Rory said quietly. "But not much farther now and we'll be home."

Beau nodded and focused on driving. He knew that his werewolf reflexes would kick in if anything unexpected happened, but it was better to keep things boring, especially when he had Rory in the car.

He nearly dozed off in the driveway, and was vaguely aware of Rory herding him inside, helping him undress, and pushing him into bed. He was back in their bed, down in the basement, belatedly denned up again. Rory returned the pillow and blanket he'd brought with him to the bed and crawled in beside Beau, letting himself be gathered close. Beau would have been content to pass out immediately, but Rory insisted on feeding him some of the snacks leftover from the day before. Beau didn't open his eyes, but he did as his husband told him, chewing and swallowing in a daze, and eventually he was allowed to sleep.

He woke up a few more times, but Rory was always there—asleep in his arms, or sitting up in the bed, but always there. Beau opened his eyes once and found that his head was pillowed on Rory's thigh, Rory's hand resting on his hair while his other hand held a pen, tapping softly on the pages of his workbook.

Beau wanted to say something—the right thing, encouraging and not patronizing—but he fell asleep under Rory's absent caress before he thought of what it was.

～

He took a new picture of Rory in the morning—wearing Beau's hoodie again, or still, sitting at the kitchen table with a glass of orange juice and a different study book than he'd had the night before. He'd set the book down and shot Beau a shy look, and Beau just smiled and raised his phone.

Beau leaned down for a kiss, afterward, and Beau caught his shirt, stopping him from straightening up right away.

"Will you... I'll do everything I can to help, but this was so hard on you," Rory said, his leaf-green gaze steady, his forehead creased with worry. "Will you ask about next month, or the month after, at least? Please?"

Beau closed his eyes and kissed him again. "Of course, baby. I have to listen to my husband, don't I?"

"Technically you don't *have* to," Rory murmured. "But you definitely *should*."

He blushed as soon as he said it, biting his lip. Beau kissed his pink cheek before he turned away.

～

As with the full moon, he was given a day's grace before he met with

Dr. Ross again, the meeting crammed in just before his clinic hours. He apologetically explained the timing, and Dr. Ross waved dismissively at the lunch Rory had packed for Beau.

"Yeah, eat, of course. Never miss a chance to eat or sleep, these next three years."

Beau nodded obediently, opening up a Tupperware container and digging in.

"I suppose it does make it difficult to have you tell me how things are going if your mouth is full, but we'll make do," Dr. Ross went on. "Still no complaints from any patients—"

Beau kept chewing, kept his heartbeat and his expression absolutely steady.

"And none from your supervisor either, so that's full speed ahead. We can go over some of your observations, but first—you're three quarters of the way through your first rotation, you're probably starting to get a feel for things, or at least you'll think you are. Do *you* have any complaints?"

Beau stopped chewing and froze completely.

Dr. Ross laughed, waving a hand. "Yes, yes, of course. You have plenty of complaints. Do you have any issues you would like to raise with your friendly old adviser, in the most diplomatic language you can think of? Any doubts, concerns?"

Beau swallowed laboriously and named the most benign thing he'd been worrying about, in spare moments when he wasn't worrying about everything else. "I, uh. I haven't gotten much extra studying done. I went to the two lectures I was scheduled for, but—"

Dr. Ross was waving a hand again. "First month, you're still burning in. You'll figure out where you can make time, once you're a little more in the rhythm of it, and by third year we'll be giving you more time for focused study for boards. You'll get there. Don't *not* worry about it, but however far down your list it is right now—that's where it belongs."

Beau nodded and took another bite of food to give himself time to work up to saying what he needed to say. It was obvious that Dr. Ross wasn't finished prodding him on this topic, but he didn't want to just blurt out his scheduling demands—and now it was less than a week until he would be starting his new rotation, so those schedules must already be complete. Actually, his next schedule might well be in an email somewhere that he had marked as read and then ignored, too worried about the empty moon to think of anything else.

"How's the husband holding up?" Dr. Ross asked while Beau was chewing. "He seemed like kind of a people person. Have you had a big fight yet about him being bored while you're gone or feeling neglected because you're not up for much when you're home?"

Beau stopped chewing for a second again, trying to picture having an actual fight with Rory. The thought made him feel sick, the food Rory had made turning to paste in his mouth.

"Whoa, okay, newlyweds, I'm guessing that's either very yes or very no?"

Beau swallowed with effort. "No, he's... he understands. He's been very supportive. He's worried about how hard it is on me."

"Ah," Dr. Ross said. "So it's been hard on you."

Beau looked away, took a careful breath. He could just say it. Not complaining, not asking for anything different, just... say it. Dr. Ross was his adviser, and Beau was supposed to be getting advice and support from him. He couldn't do that without showing where he needed advice and support, even if it felt like showing his throat, his belly. Like giving someone an alpha's power over him, inviting the punishment that must inevitably follow.

"The, uh," Beau took a careful breath and looked down at the food in his hands. Rory had asked him to ask. Rory was right. "The night shift, this weekend, it fell on the... the new moon, humans call it."

He didn't look up; he caught the slight change in Dr. Ross's heartbeat, his scent, heard him shift back slightly in his seat. Curious, interested. "Werewolves have another name for it?"

Beau nodded. It wasn't a real secret that he was betraying. He wasn't putting other werewolves in danger. Troy who lived down the street with Jennifer and their children, Fraser who had stood aside while he woke Rory up, Casey... none of them would be hurt by his just saying the word. No one would hurt them, and Beau wouldn't be helping anyone who wanted to.

"Empty," he said, barely above a whisper. "It's... the opposite of the full."

It was a stupid thing to say. Obviously that was why one was called full, the other empty.

"The opposite," Dr. Ross repeated, his tone thoughtful. "Hm. The pack representatives we spoke to mentioned that on the full moon, werewolves feel... powerful, energized. Not necessarily dangerous to anyone, although hunting is a traditional activity, but... if the empty moon is the opposite of that, I suppose... that is probably something that's usually very... private?"

Beau stared down at his food, forcing himself to nod, though the movement might have been too slight for a human to register as one. "It's usually... we usually stay at home on that night. So it was a bit difficult, being here instead."

"Just a bit difficult, which is why you're choking on your words trying to talk about it," Dr. Ross said, very dryly.

Beau kept his head bowed, and his hands right where they were, holding his lunch. "Yes, sir."

"Hm," Dr. Ross said. "Well, your schedule for your next rotation is already set, of course—"

Beau *really* had to look through his email when he got a chance.

"But I will see what I can do about that situation. It will sound... *a bit* better from me than from you, I think."

It wasn't hard to hear the emphasis and know just what Dr. Ross meant by *a bit*. Beau swallowed hard and nodded. "I'd... hate to start my next rotation on the wrong foot with everyone there."

Dr. Ross nodded. "Definitely not. Your next supervisor was... skeptical of the premise, shall we say. But if you run into any genuinely unfair treatment, I want you to bring it to me. We brought you here to train you up into a Rochester doctor, not to chase you out. Clear?"

Beau nodded.

"I think you mentioned a specific interest in oncology in some of your application materials—you think you'll be able to put your senses to good work there?"

Beau nodded again, pushing back the old memories of a little girl and a strange sickly smell he couldn't name. He'd encountered it plenty of times since, and he had finally come to a place where everyone whose sickness he smelled would be getting the very best possible treatment.

"I think I have an idea of how to detect cancer, generally," he said. "Obviously the only way to calibrate that is to come into contact with a lot of patients, where I can test my observations against the diagnoses."

Dr. Ross nodded. "Eminently reasonable. I suggest you mention exactly none of that to your supervisor and attendings, just so we're clear, but I'll want to be hearing your observations as you go along— speaking of which, what have you sniffed this week?"

Beau smiled a little and opened his notebook to refresh his memory.

∿

His clinic hours flew by, constantly busy but not as madly rushed as the week before. It wasn't until after they'd closed the doors that he encountered Cora and thought to ask, "Did you see Amy today?"

She looked startled and then shook her head. "You didn't?"

Beau shook his head. It was on the tip of his tongue to ask her whether she'd said something to Vaughn when she took him out of the room, if that was how he knew what Beau was, but... what did that matter? He knew, one way or another.

"Maybe she..." Cora turned away. "Hey, Allie? Was Amy Vaughn in today?"

Allie made a worried face and shook her head. "Haven't seen her since..." She glanced at Beau, and Beau knew what she hadn't said.

"Maybe she's been feeling better," he ventured, but he remembered what Vaughn had said, the way he'd referred to other doctors starting to press them to move on to another solution. *We'll find a werewolf to bite you.* And then he had been waiting.

"Maybe," Allie said, with another brief grimace, before she hurried away toward the last occupied exam room.

Cora shot him a worried look—worried about Amy? Worried about what she said? It hardly mattered now.

Beau wished her a good night and looked around for his last patient.

~

The walk-in clinic's supervising physician pulled him aside when he got out of his last appointment; everyone else seemed to have left already. "You were asking about Amy Vaughn."

Beau kept his expression neutral. "Ma'am."

"Look, obviously she's a regular and we treat whatever acute cases are presenting when they come in here, but we're not her primary care provider, okay?" The harried doctor shook her head. "You can't go getting emotionally involved, or—or *possessive* of patients."

Possessive sounded like *territorial* when she put that particular emphasis on it, and he knew better than to protest that Cora had been worried too. The supervisor had probably heard about it from Allie, and Allie had been the one who put her foot down about him not doing Amy's intubation last week; so much for trying to be meek enough to stay off everyone's radar. Beau getting *possessive* of a patient, getting *emotionally involved*, meant something. It would not be seen as strictly professional, *beyond reproach*.

He swallowed all his objections, all of his concerns about what alternative care Amy Vaughn might be getting, and accepted the warning, hoping this wasn't going to go further, and be reported to Dr. Ross as well. "Yes, ma'am. I understand. Won't happen again."

~

It really wasn't a surprise this time; Beau had every sense attuned and sure enough, Vaughn was waiting for him under the same tree. Beau stopped on the sidewalk and stood there watching him, waiting to see how this was going to shake out.

"Don't look at me like that," Vaughn said. "What's the point of bringing her here if you can't do anything for her that I can't do at home? What's the fucking point?"

"I suppose that's up to you," Beau said. "You know your daughter. I think you're doing your best to take care of her."

Vaughn raised one hand, tilting it from side to side. "There's always more you can do, isn't there? Might not be easy, or nice, but..."

Beau kept his hands at his sides and did not clench his teeth.

"There aren't a lot of doctors like you," Vaughn said. "I think people would be interested to know, don't you? Even the ones who know you're a werewolf would probably be pretty interested to hear about you hanging out in a parking lot with my kid after-hours."

Beau closed his eyes. He felt like he was falling, like he was just waiting to hit the ground. "What do you want?"

"Come by our place. Not as a doctor, right? Just as a person who cares, like you said. She's not even your patient if she's not coming to the clinic. You just come by and you talk to her. No harm done."

"I can't heal her," Beau said, keeping his voice steady. "The meditation—in time she might use it to manage her own pain, but it will never cure her. She needs medical care for that."

"Come and talk," Vaughn repeated, holding out a card to Beau with a scribbled address. "Tomorrow, what time can you come?"

He could say no. He could say go to hell. But it wasn't going to end any better than it would have last week; a werewolf's strength and indestructibility would be useless against the kind of pressure this human could bring to bear. He already had at least enough to get Beau into serious trouble, and he wouldn't even have to lie to make it sound much worse than what Beau had actually done. Beau was going into a rotation where he really, really had to keep his head down. If this all blew up while he was on rotation with an unsympathetic supervisor...

Beau took the card and glanced at the address. It was only a mile or so from Rochester's campus; there were probably all kinds of staff who worked here living in that same apartment complex.

"Early," Beau said. "Get it over with before my shift. Seven-thirty."

"Hey, now, don't talk about Amy like that, she's a good kid. None of this is her fault."

Beau ducked his head and did not bare his teeth. He did not growl. He did not present any menacing aspect to a human which might make that human call the cops, or hospital security, on a dangerous werewolf.

"Seven-thirty," Beau repeated, and walked past Vaughn without another word, and without looking back.

∾

Beau slipped out of bed early, pressing Rory back down to the mattress when he stirred. "Early meeting, baby, gotta run. I'll see you tonight. Go back to sleep."

He packed his scrubs and white coat to change into later, running his fingers briefly over Rory's embroidered well-wishes. He'd put these clothes on later, after... whatever he was about to get himself into the middle of. He could shower at the hospital and change there, so he wouldn't carry the residue of it with him all day.

He pulled into the parking lot of Vaughn's apartment building at 7:26, and Vaughn was waiting for him just outside the door to the apartment, smoking a cigarette, which would render his scent mostly unreadable. Beau wondered if he knew that, or if he was just nervous. It couldn't be a regular habit; Beau would have smelled it on him before.

Vaughn gestured Beau ahead of him into the apartment when Beau reached him, dropping his cigarette and crushing it out underfoot before he followed. Beau automatically checked for Amy's heartbeat as he crossed the threshold. The shower was running, and what sound he could catch told him Amy was probably there.

"So let's cut the bullshit," Vaughn said, shutting and locking the door behind him. "I've got you by the balls now, you've come to my house and we both know you're officially outside the lines, so if you don't want me calling Rochester on you, you're going to heal my kid."

Beau turned to stare at him as it dawned on him what Vaughn meant. Maybe it should have been obvious. The man had said it, straight out, a week ago. "You're insane. I can't heal her."

"You're a werewolf. This shit doesn't happen to werewolves," Vaughn insisted doggedly. "You bite her, she's good."

Beau pinched the bridge of his nose, half-hiding his face, muffling his sense of smell to mostly his own skin. He regulated his heartbeat and breathing and tried to think of the words that would reach someone who had already gone this far.

"If that actually worked in the way you're saying, the Rochester Clinic would be empty," Beau tried after a moment, dropping his hand and meeting Vaughn's eyes. He didn't *look* crazed, but Beau should have known better than to trust that appearance. "If it worked, people would do it all the time. There are three hundred million people in this country; thousands of people die every day of serious illnesses. You are not the first person to think of this. It *doesn't work.*"

"Are you telling me people don't turn into fucking werewolves when they get bitten?" Vaughn's certainty wasn't wavering.

Beau took a breath. "Werewolves don't bite people who won't survive the change. Tell me—who's Amy's closest werewolf blood relative?"

Vaughn's teeth clenched. "If she had one, I'd be asking them."

"If she has no wolf blood at all, then her body is not primed for the change," Beau said grimly, resisting the urge to try to explain the cell biology involved, Lycan bodies and cell wall elasticity and all.

"It will not take. She's already weakened. A bite could kill her— have you ever seen an infected bite wound? She would suffer even more pain than she's already in, and then she would die."

Vaughn's eyes were narrowed. "You've seen that happen?"

Beau hesitated, and that was all Vaughn's insane fixation needed.

"You haven't," Vaughn insisted. "You've never seen it. You don't know. That means there's a *chance.*"

"*Dad.*" Beau whipped around to see Amy, hair hidden under a towel, a soft, thick robe covering the bit of her body visible as she peeked around the open bathroom door. Her expression was defiant, but Beau could taste the edge of fear under it. "I don't *want to*."

Vaughn sighed and went to her, and Beau tried not to be too obvious about eyeing the door now that Vaughn wasn't between him and it.

"I know, princess," Vaughn said softly, tugging Amy into a half hug. "But you don't want to die, or hurt all the time, either, right? We talked about this."

Amy looked down, then snuck a sideways glance at Beau.

"I won't bite you if you don't want it," he said firmly. "It definitely won't work if you resist it, if it's forced."

Not to mention that a forced bite was the shortest route to a werewolf getting himself killed as a demonstrated danger to humans; his life would be forfeit forever if he forced a bite on Amy and anyone found out. Even with proper consent it would lose him any chance of practicing medicine—as it should, because *Amy would die.*

"Then I guess you better find some other way to help her," Vaughn said, undeterred. "Or you better convince her to want it. You're the best shot I've got for her, and I'm not letting you walk away now."

Beau closed his eyes, wondering how far it would go, what Vaughn would dare. He already had enough to destroy Beau's career, and likely enough to claim Beau had threatened him or Amy in some way to justify killing him, but that wouldn't get him what he wanted.

And Beau was pretty sure that there was no way Vaughn could know that Rory existed, or where to find him. So it was only Beau's career, only everything he'd worked toward for a decade, that Vaughn could threaten—that and Amy's wellbeing.

"Okay, Amy," Beau said, opening his eyes and focusing on her. "I'm guessing your dad has all the stuff for doing tube feedings at home now?"

She nodded.

"Let's get you fed, then," Beau said. "That's the best I can do today."

Tomorrow... he'd figure out what to do about tomorrow when it got here. For now he could just about handle today.

CHAPTER 30

*B*eau was worse at lying than any other alpha Rory had ever known, which was comforting in a way.

Rory had never been with an alpha who was really good at it, or bothered to be good at it to an omega, at least. They depended on the fact that the lies they told were the kind an omega wanted to believe. *It'll never happen again. I love you. Of course I'll take care of you. You're special.*

Beau didn't tell him those lies, for the most part, and the things he did say still felt like truth. It still felt like truth when Beau came home to him every evening, when Beau held him close and slept beside him.

But now Beau was waking up an hour earlier than he had before, slipping away without showering or changing into the scrubs and white coats that Rory had so carefully stitched his clumsy well-wishes into. He let Rory fix him breakfast, but he didn't linger over it or take pictures of Rory to look at while he was gone.

He had put up the schedule for his new rotation on the fridge. It still showed that he would be working through the empty moon, and there was a clumsily crammed-in notation showing that he had a *study group* at 7:30 every weekday morning.

It wasn't even a convincing lie. Beau didn't actually try to sell Rory on it; he never spoke of it. He just left early every morning, smelling of guilt and anxiety, and came home every night with a bag that held the change of clothes he'd been wearing that morning, which smelled of some humans Rory had never met, and sickness and pain. Rory didn't say anything about it, just did the laundry, wiping that scent away as quickly as he could.

There was no hint of sex on Beau's dirty clothes, but Rory doubted Beau would have gotten around to that yet. He had taken his time with Rory, after all—and he still had Rory at home to get that from if he wanted it.

But Rory wasn't sick and helpless anymore, and Beau had found someone else who needed his care. So far it was guiltily stolen hours before his clinic shifts, but...

Rory put his face in his hands, trying to push the thoughts away. Beau was a doctor, or would be. Even if Rory succeeded in convincing Beau to keep him, Rory would always be sharing him with sick humans in need. This was nothing, not really. Beau's scrubs smelled like sick people, too, and obviously Beau didn't lie about spending most of every day with them.

Except that Beau was lying about whatever he was doing each morning before he went to the hospital, and every time Rory thought of asking him what was going on, his throat closed up in fear of what the answer might be. Yet more transparent lies? *That's none of your business?*

He knew Beau wouldn't hit him, or send him away, not just for asking, but those were the easiest scenes to imagine, and they swirled around and around his mind, leaving everything they touched tarnished and cold. He couldn't look forward to Beau coming home, because he would bring that bundle of laundry that smelled like strangers, and he still wouldn't tell Rory the truth.

Beau would smile, and say everything was fine, and *that* lie was also obvious. His scrubs and white coat reeked of fear-sweat, and Beau came home with shaking hands, too tired to eat. Looking at him each evening, Rory felt like the worst kind of bitch for resenting whatever lies Beau told. At those times, Rory wanted only to feed

Beau and cuddle him and comfort him for whatever it was that was wearing him out.

Only a few days into the new rotation, Rory dared to bring up that part of it. They were already in bed, the lights out, and Beau was holding him tight, his nose against the fluff of Rory's hair, still not grown quite long enough to lie down under its own weight.

"This one's hard, isn't it?" Rory said quietly. "This rotation."

"It's just that it's new," Beau said, holding Rory a little tighter. "And my hours are longer now. I'll get used to it, baby, I promise."

My hours are longer now. But Rory ignored that part, focusing on the part that Beau didn't have any reason to feel guilty about or hide from him. "It must remind you of being sixteen, smelling cancer all the time. People who are sick the way your friend's sister was. That must be hard."

Beau stiffened slightly, and then seemed to force himself to loosen his grip on Rory. "I... I hadn't thought of it that way. But... yes, I suppose that... that is a factor."

See, Rory wanted to scream, *I can help! I understand things!*

He wanted to make a joke about being the wise husband, but he couldn't offer any actual advice to help Beau with what he remembered. He tried to regulate his breathing instead, to make his body pliant, receptive, inviting Beau to talk to him for once, and after a moment it worked.

"I guess it's also..." Beau laughed a little, a hollow, unhappy sound. "A lot of the patients I see are receiving chemotherapy. And chemotherapy is basically poison, dosed and administered so that it hopefully kills the cancer without killing any healthy organs. But they all smell *that* kind of sick, too. A lot of them lose their hair, and have trouble eating."

Rory's heart started beating faster for no good reason, and he reached up to touch his own regrowing hair. "So they remind you of me, too."

"I think so, yeah," Beau said, in a thoughtful tone as if this was also only just occurring to him. "It makes it harder to be as detached as I need to be. But at least I can come home to you every night, baby. You don't know how much it helps me to come home and just breathe you in, and see you, healthy and... and happy."

That last word wasn't quite a question, but Beau's uncertainty was loud as a siren even if his voice was soft.

Rory nuzzled at Beau's chest, not wanting to tell the lies he'd gotten good at telling. Omegas always had to know how to lie, but he didn't want to do that with Beau. He didn't want to make Beau like other alphas, even in his own head.

"I'm okay," he said quietly. "Just miss you, and... I can't help being worried when you are, that's all. But if this is how I can help, I'll work on being as happy as I can for you."

"I'd rather you were happy for *you*," Beau murmured, brushing his lips over Rory's temple. "It's all right not to be, if you're not. I don't want you to pretend to be happy if..."

Rory had mostly had in mind that he should watch something funny on TV, or turn on music and dance, before Beau came home, so that his scent would be suffused with happiness and healthy energy. Pretending, of the kind Beau meant, never worked well, or for long.

Of course, if Beau's hours away from the house got any longer, it wouldn't be much of a challenge to keep it up when Beau was home.

"I'm fine," Rory assured him, pushing that thought away. "I keep myself busy."

"Are you..." Beau sighed a little, loosening his grip and tugging Rory's chin up with two fingers so that their eyes met. "I like thinking of you safe here when I'm not home, but I don't want you to be cooped up, or lonely."

Rory smiled easily at that. "I'm not, I promise. I've been making friends with Jen down the street—I'm going to watch Oliver for a few hours tomorrow—and Casey..."

Rory stopped there, abruptly realizing something.

"That's good," Beau murmured, his thumb brushing softly over Rory's chin. "I'm glad you're making friends, baby."

Rory shook his head slightly—not that he wasn't making friends, or didn't think Beau was pleased, but that wasn't why he'd hesitated. "Beau... Casey's making suppressants for me, for the moon. Is that—

do you want me not to take them? Will I smell sick to you again if I do?"

Beau tensed for a second, then shook his head, relaxing with what looked like an effort. "I don't think... if Casey gives them to you, if you're only taking them for a little while and you follow his directions... it shouldn't make you that kind of sick, I don't think. If it does, then something's wrong."

Rory nodded slowly, but he was remembering the way Beau had reacted to catching the scent of just a few drops of his blood on the air.

"If you don't want me to," he started, but he couldn't finish the sentence. It probably wouldn't be a real heat anyway, but he wanted to be able to spend the moon with Beau. He wanted to be something good for Beau to come home to.

If he smelled sick, Beau wouldn't want to leave him. Beau would remember that Rory needed him too.

"No, baby," Beau murmured. "You do what you need to do. I'll handle it. I don't think it'll make you sick, anyway. Not... not anything like you were."

"Okay," Rory murmured, and he snuggled close to Beau again, trying not to feel the guilty roil of his stomach, and the too-familiar feeling that every choice was wrong.

Oliver was adorable and entertaining and exhausting all at once. Rory had collected him from Jen's house along with a backpack full of toys, books, diapers, clothes, and snacks.

"Uh... you said two hours, right?"

Jen laughed. "Yeah, if it's longer than that you'll just have to improvise, because believe me, that's all I packed for."

Rory looked down at Oliver, who was looking up at him a little dubiously, but when Rory offered his hand, Oliver took it, and toddled back down the street at his side. They were inside with the door firmly locked behind them before Rory heard Jennifer's car go down the street with Jennifer and the girls inside, off to some errand that would be easier without Oliver underfoot.

The next two hours passed in a blur as Rory followed Oliver around the house while the toddler explored. Rory read every one of the books in the backpack—two of them five times in a row each—played with blocks and puzzles, and administered a diaper change, a snack, and a direly-needed change of clothes.

Jen laughed when she came to pick Oliver up. "I won't ask you how soon you plan on making one of your own, then."

"Oh," Rory said, running one hand over Oliver's silky hair while he was snuggling into his mother's shoulder. "I don't know, it was..."

Jen grinned. "Maybe next time I'll ask you to watch him while Beau's home, and you can see how *that* goes."

Rory bit his lip, trying to think of when Beau would be home and what it might be like to watch Beau reading or playing with Oliver, coaxing him to eat his snack.

"Anyway, I better get back to the girls before they set something on fire," Jen said. "Thanks again, Rory!"

"No problem," Rory assured her.

The house was awfully quiet and empty once she and Oliver were gone. He tidied away all the signs of an inquisitive and energetic toddler's presence, and then curled up on the couch. His thoughts chased each other in circles, as endless and unhelpful as Oliver himself.

A baby—a baby who was his and Beau's—babies were helpless, after all. And Rory would need his alpha's attention and care if he were pregnant. And then Beau would never, ever let him go.

But that didn't mean Beau would trust him, or tell him what was going on, who he was secretly seeing. It didn't mean Rory would be good for Beau the way he wanted to be.

It didn't mean Beau would love him.

This wasn't over yet, not by a long shot, but right now Rory could see how he might fail at winning his place with Beau, at making something with Beau that he would *want* to seal with a bond, with children. And if it came to walking away...

This time he needed to have somewhere to walk away to. Not just the refuge, and not a pack where a single omega would be a problem to be solved by marrying him off to the nearest alpha. *Especially* not if he found he had to leave before Beau's residency was over, so that taking shelter with the Niemi pack would mean being so near to Beau afterward.

Rory picked up his phone and thumbed to the contacts screen, which had a new entry now, illustrated with a carefully-selected screencap from the video that he had watched so many times he could play it in his head any time he closed his eyes.

Georgie.

The thought of trying to actually talk to her on the phone was enough to make his mouth dry and his throat go tight, but he had to start somewhere. She'd been waiting for days—for *years.*

He tapped on the text icon and spelled out his message. *Hi, this is Rory. I miss you too.*

Rory barely had time to wonder whether it would take a while before she saw his message—it had been nearly a week, after all, so she probably wasn't expecting him to reply right now—when he saw the dots that meant she was typing.

Rory! I'm so sorry if those emails were kind of crazy. I've missed you so much.

Rory smiled down at his phone. *It was a nice kind of crazy, Jor. I've watched that video about a hundred times.*

Georgie sent back a little red heart, which made Rory's eyes prickle, and then, *Hey, would you mind sending me a selfie?*

Rory snorted softly. *Proof of life?*

I mean. Yeah. It's kind of hard to believe after all this time?

Yeah, I get it, Rory replied, and didn't bother to explain to her that she wasn't even the first person to want pictures of him to be sure he was okay. He nestled down into the couch and carefully angled his phone as he took the picture. It made his chin look even sharper than it was in real life—and made him look like the rest of him was being swallowed by the couch—but it hid his silver scars and he was smiling, so he figured Georgie would be satisfied.

He sent it before he could think too much about it, and a moment later he got back a picture of Georgie, smiling with teary eyes.

She had her hair up and a suit on, obviously at work somewhere.

Should I let you get back to work?

I can spare a few minutes for my brother, Georgie assured him.

Rory bit his lip, wondering what to say. He didn't want to talk about Beau right now, and everything in his life radiated from there, in one way or another.

Speaking of brothers, Rory tapped out. *Tell me about Spence? He was so little when I went away.*

He saw the typing dots appear and disappear a few times before a message came through.

Spence is the one who never gave up on you. He gave dad hell after you disappeared, for driving you away. Not loving you enough. I'd never seen dad cry before that. He was different after that, Ror. Too little too late, maybe, but if you give him a second chance he won't blow it.

Rory blinked back tears of his own, trying to imagine it. Spencer would still only have been ten or eleven when Rory took off, just a little kid taking on his own dad for the sake of a brother he hadn't seen in years by then.

Spence is this crazy little internet activist for werewolf rights and omega rights. Mom and Dad managed to keep him mostly quiet until he was fifteen or so, but now he has a YouTube channel and is involved in all these demonstrations and protests and things.

I worry about him. He's human, but... that means he's breakable, too. And people treat him like a wolf in a lot of ways, or worse than one.

Rory's throat went tight at the thought of how he'd shaped his baby brother's whole life, without even knowing it. It seemed pretty obvious that Spencer's passion had started with Rory's disappearance, and who knew where it would end? If Spencer got hurt because of the stand he was taking, because of Rory, how could Rory ever look their parents in the eyes again? How could he ever go home?

Tell him to be careful, Rory tapped out, knowing it would be at least as useless as warnings would have been for him, but feeling helpless to do anything else.

He is, Georgie said quickly. *I don't mean for you to feel like you have to worry about him. He's okay, he's just... a lot, sometimes.*

There was a little pause where Rory knew he should ask, and he wondered if Georgie was thinking it, and then a text came through: just a phone number, nothing else.

Rory saved it with Spencer's name and sent back, *Thanks, Jor. Love you.*

Love you, Ror. Take care of yourself.

Rory didn't know how to answer that, so he told himself that was enough getting-in-touch for one day.

CHAPTER 31

*B*eau had a meeting with his adviser on the last day before the full moon. It wasn't when they usually met, but Beau was so close to crawling out of his skin, between the waxing moon and a week on the Oncology ward plus early morning visits to Amy Vaughn, that he didn't even wonder about it. He was too busy being glad for the respite, sitting in a small room with just one familiar, healthy human.

Dr. Ross frowned at him as he took his seat. "You're looking a bit more ragged than I'd like to see this early in the year. I guess werewolf stamina isn't everything, eh?"

Beau swallowed his annoyance at the way humans just *remarked* on things like that, all uninvited. Dr. Ross, as his adviser, had the right; Dr. Pavlyuchenko had done the same sometimes, though he had been a little more wolfishly circumspect about it, except when it was really bad.

Beau looked down at himself, wondering if there was something obvious he'd missed that made Dr. Ross feel it necessary to say something. His scrubs and coat were still as neat as could be expected in the middle of the day. He pressed his hand to his thigh to keep from running his fingers over the stitching of Rory's well-wishes; the touch to his own shoulder was already becoming a habit, reassuring himself a hundred times a day that his husband was thinking of him, and would be there for him at the end of the day.

At the end of *this* day... But Beau didn't let himself think of that, pasting on a polite smile for Dr. Ross. "Oncology has been a little more... intense than I quite expected, sir. I'm sure I'll adjust."

"To your patients? I'm sure," Dr. Ross said, frowning down at some papers. "Whether your supervisor and attendings will adjust to you seems to be an open question."

Beau gritted his teeth and said nothing. There was nothing he *could* say. They hadn't *done* anything, particularly, giving him impossible assignments or making him redo charts beyond reason or outing him to patients. Not quite.

They just watched him all the time, smelling of wariness or anger or fear or *interest*, and made comments that he ought not let himself overhear but couldn't help hearing anyway. There was a tone they used when they spoke about him; they might as well have shouted his name every time they whispered about him.

He had been vaguely aware that Rochester had put their best foot forward with him, early on, and the humans he met at his interview and most of his first rotation must have been to some degree chosen because they were sympathetic to him. He hadn't realized how many of the other kind there would be, or how soon he would find himself thrown in among them.

"It's new for everyone," Beau said neutrally. "I obviously have to learn to work well with humans who aren't enthusiastic about working with a werewolf."

Dr. Ross nodded slowly. "If it's more than that... if it crosses a line... I do want you to come to me. Immediately."

Beau nodded obediently. If things got truly bad, it would be for his adviser to handle. He did know that. But he also knew very well that he couldn't go crying to his adviser because no one on this rotation *liked* him.

"Well, enough dwelling on that, then," Dr. Ross said. "Any other questions, before I start prodding you about what cancer smells like?"

Beau's hands closed into fists, and he felt suddenly almost frantic not to rehearse those memories, his stomach giving a queasy turn. He searched his mind for any way to put off the inevitable, and latched on to the one thing he must not speak of to anyone: Amy Vaughn, and how he was ever to help her, or convince her father that he *couldn't* help her.

He'd been sneaking in research where he could, trying to track down any cases or studies that matched her symptoms, any rational treatment he could offer. There wasn't much time for it, especially since he didn't want anyone to see him researching something so obviously not related to his present rotation, but there was one thing he hadn't even tried to research. He didn't dare leave that trail, and anyway he was sure there was nothing to find.

He was nearly sure.

But he could ask Dr. Ross, couldn't he? If he didn't say why, if...

"I did have a... hypothetical question," Beau said carefully, looking up to gauge Dr. Ross's reaction. "Just... a research curiosity, nothing to do with the rotation."

Dr. Ross sat back a little, making an interested face and giving him plenty of room to go on.

"Being a werewolf," Beau said hesitantly. "I know that the research on werewolf biology is still in its infancy, obviously. But the other day I heard a patient's family member say—jokingly—that if the treatment didn't work, they'd have to find a werewolf."

Dr. Ross's expression turned cold and he sat upright. Beau dug his fingernails into his palms and kept his voice steady.

"I just wondered whether any kind of study had been done, because—I'm sure that's not an answer, but I only have... anecdotes. Impressions, tradition. Not data."

Dr. Ross shook his head sharply. "What *exactly* did you say to the patient's family member who suggested that?"

Beau swallowed back his useless arguments against Vaughn, focusing on that comparatively innocent moment in the clinic as he told the exact truth. "It wasn't said to me—I shouldn't have been able to hear, if I was human. So I didn't say anything. I just wondered... I thought I, of all people, ought to be able to—"

"You never," Dr. Ross said grimly. "You, *of all people*, never, *ever* engage with that question while you are in the employ of the Rochester Clinic, whether you are on duty or off. You do not touch it with a ten-foot pole. *Ever*. Especially not while you're on *this* rotation, for God's sake. They're all *waiting* for you to suggest biting terminal patients."

Beau nodded frantically. "No, sir, I—I know, of course. Of course. It's not medicine, it's not—I would never."

Dr. Ross blew out a breath and nodded. "If anyone *ever* asks that of you—you say that's a question you can't answer, you find an attending, and you call me. Immediately, that *minute*. Clear?"

Beau nodded, wide-eyed, and wished that he'd had that option with Vaughn, that he wasn't already so far down the path of questionable conduct that he could never tell anyone. He doubted Dr. Ross would have been able to convince Vaughn that the bite wouldn't save Amy, either, but... no use wishing. At least he knew that bridge was burned.

Dr. Ross sat back slightly, his expression easing a fraction. "There were a couple of papers circulated about the effects of a werewolf bite, I think—never made it into any of the journals, obviously, because it was the first year or two of the Revelation and no one was ready to be first to put their money down on it all being real. These concerned anatomical changes—the, ah, omega—aspect, is it? not gender?—so that made it doubly unappealing to the establishment. And it was some independent scholar, too. I don't know why they never came back around after it was all in the open, come to think fo it. What was the name... Vine? Vanek?"

"Vinick?" Beau blurted out, thinking of Adam's touchiness about all things omega, Adam saying, *there are XY humans who become omegas when bitten.*

Adam's last name was Vinick, but he would have been a child during the Revelation; he wasn't much older than Rory, for all that his seriousness had always matched or exceeded Beau's.

For all his passion about the treatment of omegas, he never talked about his mother.

Dr. Ross frowned at him. "That... sounds right. Am I telling you things you already know? Did you track down those papers already?"

Beau shook his head. "It's the name of a classmate from med school. Maybe he was inspired by a family member."

"Mm," Dr. Ross said, skeptically. "Well, those papers were never peer-reviewed or validated in any way, so I wouldn't cite them even if you do find them. And speaking of our commitment to proper empiricism—let's talk about your patients, shall we?"

Beau told himself that is wasn't a punishment, just his job, and opened his notebook.

~

The waxing moon, one night away from being full, was nearly up by the time Beau got home, finally free of his rotation for a merciful couple of days. Rory had been somewhere in sight when Beau walked through the front door every day this week, but today he was sitting on the front porch, basking in the last of the early-evening sunlight.

Beau just sat and looked for a moment, letting his whole body begin to calm down at the sight of his omega, safe and sound, with freckles coming out on his nose and his hair standing out in an adorable puff around his head. After a moment Rory opened his eyes and looked back, smiling in a warm, careless way that Beau didn't think he'd ever quite seen before, and it occurred to him to wonder about those suppressants that Rory had gotten from Casey.

The little glass bottle had been sitting on the bedside table last night, and Rory had said only that he hadn't felt the need to take them yet. Before Beau could ask if that was okay, if they would even work if Rory didn't take all of them, Rory had kissed him, a little shy but very clear on what he wanted.

Beau had been thoroughly distracted, and then asleep.

He wondered if Rory had felt the need to take them today—or

hadn't felt the need to. His heart was beating fast now for an entirely different reason, and Beau got out of the car.

There *was* something different in Rory's scent; he knew that as soon as he took a breath in the open air. But it didn't have the sickly tang of the old suppressants, or any other medication. It was almost like...

Rory got to his feet, still smiling as Beau approached.

"Hi, baby," Beau said, reaching for him while he stood one step lower, so he could tuck his face into Rory's throat and breathe him in. He hadn't covered his scars, and Beau brushed his lips over the nearest one, noticing the tender pink skin surrounding it as it healed. "How're you?"

"Mm, I'm good," Rory said, folding his arms easily around Beau's shoulders and nuzzling at his hair. "I took one of those pills Casey gave me and I think I know the secret ingredient."

Beau jerked back at that, and Rory giggled. His pupils were a little wider than they should be, with the sun still lighting the sky, but not utterly blown. He wasn't exactly *stoned*, but...

"Sweet wolfsbane," Rory confirmed. "Just a little, I guess. Not enough to be mind-altering, he said. It'll just keep me calm, and help the moon shine lightly on me. It's nice. You want one? You've had a rough day."

Somehow, with Rory's fingers gently skritching through the hair at the base of his skull, it sounded nothing at all like Dr. Ross telling him he looked ragged. Beau tipped his head back into the touch, offering his throat to his husband, and for a second he actually considered it. He'd metabolize it entirely in the next forty-eight hours, so even if he got randomly drug-tested...

The idea was too alluring, though. It was probably better not to go down that road. To say nothing of what would happen if it inspired him to be as talkative as Rory was right now. There were altogether too many things he had to remember not to say; he'd assumed the moon would keep them much too busy to talk at all.

"What if I want you to help me get calm some other way?" Beau asked, his voice coming out low and rumbling.

"Ohh, yeah, I had an idea about that," Rory said agreeably, turning half away and catching Beau's hand to tug him along. "Come on, let's go inside and get started."

"Started?" Beau followed willingly as Rory led him straight upstairs. He wondered if he should take it back, tell Rory he didn't have to help him relax in quite this way, but he wanted it too, and he was never going to tell Rory *not* to take the lead.

Rory led him to the right at the top of the stairs, though, toward the master bedroom. Beau hesitated on the threshold, enough to make Rory turn back, still holding on firmly to Beau's hand.

"Are you sure you want," Beau started, but that was as far as he got.

Rory flashed a toothy grin and hauled on his arm, making Beau stumble inside. Beau laughed, startled, and let his momentum carry him right into Rory, wrapping his other arm around him and hauling him in for a kiss, breathless and awkward because they were both laughing now.

"Come on, almost there," Rory said, wriggling in Beau's hold.

Beau's eyes went automatically to the pristine bed, which looked as if no one had ever slept there, but Rory tugged him in the opposite direction, and Beau realized he could smell something—herbs and salt and food on the steamy-warm air.

"You had an *idea*, huh," Beau said, following Rory into the enormous master bathroom, where slightly clouded water was giving up pleasantly scented steam. Beside it on the broad ledge, a platter of sandwiches and veggies, all of them cut up small for easy one-handed eating, and a pitcher of lemonade with fruit floating in it waited beside two glasses already half full of ice. "This looks like more than an idea."

"I had an idea several hours ago," Rory said, flashing another smile and peeling out of his t-shirt. "And then I had a plan, and now I'm going to have a nice relaxing bath with my husband to help him unwind from work and get ready for the moon, if my alpha permits?"

"Your alpha," Beau reeled Rory in for one more kiss before he started shedding his own clothes, "is married to a genius. I would never dare contradict his extraordinarily clever husband."

Rory rolled his eyes, still smiling, and climbed into the tub, sliding into the scented water. He seemed to disappear from more than just sight, with the water covering his scent, and Beau hurried to join him, barely noticing the silky warmth of the water as he reached for Rory through it.

Rory laughed but allowed Beau to pull him close, reclining against Beau's chest while Beau leaned against the side of the tub. There was a conveniently—cleverly—placed towel that he could lean his head against, and another to wipe his hand on so that he could pick up a perfect, jewel-bright slice of pepper and hold it to Rory's lips.

Rory chewed obediently, nudging at Beau's hand until he reached for a sandwich-quarter and took a bite himself.

"I was going to do that part," Rory said when he'd swallowed. "Feed you, pour you something nice to drink, maybe wash your hair or just rub your shoulders..."

"That sounds very good," Beau said, nuzzling at Rory's hair. He ought to get his own cut soon; it was starting to grow out enough to curl. "But we can get to that later. I think right now I'd find it very relaxing to hold you and feed you dinner, if that doesn't ruin your excellent plan."

"Mm, I can allow it," Rory agreed, allowing his toes to pop up from the surface of the water and wiggling them as he tipped his head back against Beau's shoulder. "I want some of that lemonade before the ice melts, though."

It took a little maneuvering, but Beau poured a glass they could both drink from in turns, and refilled it as necessary as he fed Rory and himself a solid half of the bountiful food. All the time he had Rory's body nestled against his, skin to skin with nothing but the water to cover them, silky with salt and with some fresh herbal scent that drove away all the hospital smells that had been lingering in his nose. There was nothing in the air now but himself and Rory as they moved against each other with a lazy, slow-motion sensuality.

When neither of them wanted more to eat or drink, they just floated for a while. The water had cooled slightly, but it wasn't unpleasant. Beau moved one hand up and down Rory's thigh under the water, feeling the firm, wiry muscle under the skin, beginning to be padded by a little fat. At this rate he wouldn't have to worry about Rory blowing away or freezing in a Minnesota winter, even in his human shape.

Rory made a low, pleased noise at the touch, and then twisted around, moving to kneel astride Beau's lap. He was taller this way, looking down while Beau kept his head resting on the folded towel, his throat fully exposed. For a few seconds Rory just looked down, his green eyes full of warmth that sank even deeper into Beau than the heat of the water.

"My turn," Rory declared softly. "Gonna make you feel so nice and calm you won't even know what to do with yourself."

Beau's cock stirred under the water, and he thought that he was probably going to be able to think of one or two things to do no matter what Rory had planned. "What if I wasn't done with my turn yet?"

Rory smiled and shook his head. "Your turn is tomorrow night. I have a feeling you'll be taking care of me all night long, alpha."

It wasn't going to be a heat, but Rory was a lot stronger and healthier than he'd been four weeks earlier. Beau's cock gave a definite twitch at the thought of that, and Rory's smile widened like he'd felt it. Like he wanted it, like he was looking forward to it.

"Yeah," Rory said, and bent his head to press kisses to Beau's throat. "Like that. So right now it's my turn."

"Understood," Beau said hoarsely, and closed his eyes, letting Rory have his way.

CHAPTER 32

*E*verything seemed beautifully clear in the early light on the morning before the full moon. Lying in bed, watching Beau sleep, Rory felt like he had begun again, like the sun was rising on his entire life.

He hadn't realized how much fear he still carried around with him until Casey's pill quieted all the whirring calculations in his head. He hadn't wondered whether Beau would dislike the surprise, whether he ought to do anything differently, whether he was doing enough to win a place in Beau's life. He'd been able to let everything go and simply enjoy a night with his alpha; between that and the moon above, so near to full, he'd had no trouble taking pleasure in every touch they exchanged.

That moon had set now, and Rory could feel that the effects of the pill had worn off. He could feel the background noise in his mind, but it was so much easier to push it aside now that he had had a night without it. It was much easier to remember that Beau had never been anyone he had to fear. Last night, when Rory felt free to do whatever he liked, Beau had responded with nothing but enjoyment.

And tonight would be the full moon—another night like last night, but more. He wouldn't go into heat; with this newfound clarity he could sense that without second-guessing. But the moon would pull at him, pull him and Beau together. He could take another of the pills Casey had given him, to assure that the pull wouldn't be too strong, wouldn't affect his mind too much, but maybe...

Beau stirred beside him, stretching with low groan that seemed to touch every part of Rory at once, and he twisted toward his alpha to start the morning with a kiss.

~

They spent the day much the same as they had the day before the last full moon, except that they already owned a lawnmower—and Rory had been using it to keep the lawn under control when Beau wasn't home—so they wound up pulling weeds and fighting the lilacs and making elaborate, and maybe slightly moon-wild, plans about how to replant the flower beds.

Every time Rory offered his own opinion or corrected Beau about anything, he noticed the little frisson of fear creeping back in. He could still push it aside, but it took more and more effort as the day went on, until he felt an actual rush of relief when he noticed the Niemi kids standing at the end of the driveway looking hopeful. Kids meant he was safe, meant that Beau wouldn't—but no, Beau wouldn't hurt him even if no one was around. He knew that.

He did know that.

Beau had noticed the kids too, of course, and was smiling. "You want to play tag again?"

Summer and Amber nodded eagerly. Oliver tried to break his sisters' grips on his hands and run over to Rory, but the girls managed to hang on.

"Do you need a break, Ror?" Beau asked. "Need to get ready or anything?"

Rory shook his head firmly. "I'm fine. I can play."

Beau studied him for a moment, then said. "Okay. If you need a minute, you know I won't mind if you go on inside. One of the kids can take a turn chasing."

"I know," Rory said, trying not to let it come out either annoyed or pleading.

Beau nodded, turning his attention back to the kids. "Okay! Better hurry or Roland's going to catch us!"

He darted away as he said it, dashing toward the kids and scooping up Oliver. Rory shook off everything else and ran after them.

Playing tag helped, but not as much as it had before the last full moon; the pull of the moon felt stronger, and the fear was harder to keep at bay. Every time he found himself trying to push it aside, he was aware of doing it, and aware that he shouldn't have to.

It didn't help that he felt a lot closer to going into heat than he had before. Every time he caught a too-direct whiff of Beau's scent, or Beau's t-shirt rode up as he scooped up a kid and ran, or he found himself staring at Beau's thighs... he felt himself getting wet, felt that pull of desire, and it only heightened everything. It was what he was supposed to feel, what he *wanted* to feel, but it was all tangled up in the old, ingrained fear. All the layers of self-conscious second-guessing tied him up in knots.

There was still an hour before sunset when the sight of Beau laughing, tossing Oliver in the air, made his dick go hard, and Rory just froze right there in the middle of the backyard. Slick was trickling down the inside of his thigh and he *wanted* and he had to hold absolutely still or he was going to run away. He just had to stop being scared, he knew that, but he couldn't seem to get a grip on his own (slippery, *slick*) thoughts.

Beau looked right at him, and the laughter vanished, his eyes going dark. Rory felt paralyzed, like he was collared. Defenseless.

Beau looked away, smiling again, as if nothing had happened. "Hey, kids, that's enough for today. Time to head home."

There was a general outcry from the kids, but Beau herded them all out of the yard, leaving Rory still standing there. Still frozen, and still burning with not-quite-heat.

He should go inside. He should go somewhere, do *something*, instead of just standing here staring at nothing. But he was still just standing there when Beau reappeared, bending a little to look Rory in the eye without Rory having to look up.

"Baby," he said softly, "do you know why it is that you don't want to take another one of those pills tonight? Was last night not what you wanted?"

Beau's voice was mostly level, but Rory heard the question just beneath the one he asked. *Did I hurt you? Is it me you're scared of this time?*

Rory shook his head. "I just..."

He closed his eyes, feeling stupid in both the ordinary way and the way where it was hard to think with Beau and the full moon both so close. "It had worn off, this morning. And I still wasn't scared. And I just wanted to keep... not being scared. Without..."

"Ah," Beau said, the single syllable warm with understanding. Rory felt the shift of his weight, his arms rising a little. He stepped into the half-offered hug before Beau could hesitate, pressing his face against Beau's chest and clinging.

Rory *wasn't* scared of him. He wasn't. Even if he thought he was sometimes, even if his body got confused sometimes.

Beau's arms came around him lightly, not pinning him in place, and Beau pressed a kiss to the crown of his head. "You had a lot of practice being scared, Ror, and for a long time it was important that you didn't forget. That was how you protected yourself for years. No surprise if you need more than one night's practice at not being scared, is it?"

He wanted to argue that he'd already had more than one night's practice, but Beau had a point. Susan had told him, way back at the beginning, that it took time. That it could take years.

"We'll get there," Beau said softly. "We just have to keep practicing. But for tonight, if a pill makes it easier to not be scared, and that's how you want to feel, maybe..."

He didn't push, didn't even say it. Rory thought if the moon wasn't coming, Beau would be willing to just stand there with him for hours until he made up his mind. But the moon was coming, and Rory's heart was beating faster the closer it got, and he just kept breathing in the smell of Beau, *alpha*, all sweaty-warm and good and...

Rory nodded as he pushed away and ran inside without looking back at Beau. He didn't stop until he reached the little bottle on the bedside table, and he didn't let himself hesitate before he tipped out one of the two remaining into his palm and knocked it back. He dropped the bottle back where it had been and started pulling his clothes off. He wasn't going to hesitate; he wasn't going to waste one moment. He wasn't going to be scared. He *chose* not to be scared.

Rory flung himself down on the rumpled bed, clutching the sheets against the impulse to cover himself. His heart was racing and he couldn't even tell what he felt, except that he was wet, and half-hard, and the sun was sinking toward the horizon, the moon closer to rising every moment.

Beau stopped in the doorway and stared at him, startled for a second before he smiled, his gaze softening and heating as it roamed over Rory's defiantly bared body. "All right, then, baby."

Rory pushed up on his elbows. "Come here, I want—let me—"

Beau stripped out of his t-shirt as he stepped inside, dropping his shorts at the next step. His underwear didn't do much to restrain his cock, bulging out hard and huge under them. Rory's mouth watered, his ass dripped slick, and he was up on his knees, reaching for Beau, when he felt something inside him just... let go.

He stopped, startled by the feeling. It took him a moment to recognize the sensation of his fear, and resistance to fear, all coming undone and washing away as his rushing blood carried Casey's formulation to every cell of his body.

"Oh," Rory said, looking up at Beau, and he grinned as he took in the sight of his alpha with this new perspective. No fear at all now, nothing to hold him back from wanting. From *having* everything he wanted. "Oh, yeah. That's all right."

Beau was grinning back at him. "Looks like it is, baby. But why don't we just..."

Beau sat down on the bed, still wearing his underwear, which was only in the way now. He caught Rory's hands when Rory reached to tug them down.

"Hang on," Beau said, pulling on his hands until Rory scrambled into his lap. "Let's just—"

Beau wanted to go slow, of course. Beau wanted to be careful with him.

Rory could feel words on his tongue with no fear to hold them back, and he lunged to kiss Beau before they escaped. *I love you, I love you, how can I ever possibly deserve you?*

That was a problem for another time. For now, he was kissing Beau, and Beau was making hot little pleased noises against his lips and running his hands so lightly over Rory's bare skin that he wanted to shiver, or scream.

He kept kissing his alpha, instead, and teased him right back, running his hands in similar sweeps over all the bare skin Beau offered him. But he understood once he started why Beau couldn't stop; it was addictive to just touch, to be allowed and invited, to take the time just for this. He pushed and tugged until Beau was laughing into their kiss and sprawled back on the bed, and then Rory could sprawl right over him, touching everywhere, with only that thin and increasingly damp layer of cloth between the thick hardness of Beau's cock and Rory's belly.

They would get to that; they could take their time. For now they were kissing and touching and waiting.

The full moon rose like a soap bubble bursting, ending that delicious not-quite-yet time. Rory could feel its light fall upon him, suffusing his body with *want*. Not heat, but closer to it than he'd been in a long time, and it felt so strange that he froze for a moment, waiting for...

Waiting for the fear, or the loss of himself. But neither came. There was just the flush over every inch of his tingling skin, the slick rush between his legs, and Beau, watching him with lust-dark eyes and holding every bit as still as Rory was.

"Yes," Rory gasped, grabbing for him, and then no one was holding still at all. They were kissing frantically, and Rory hooked his fingers into the band of Beau's underwear and more or less tore them off. Beau's hands were on his ass, then his thighs, spreading him open. Rory didn't know if he was saying or only thinking *yes, yes, yes,* but it was obvious that Beau understood either way.

Two thick fingers pressed into him, gliding easily, and Beau groaned, or Rory did, as Beau stroked him. He was already sloppy-wet and so hot inside that Beau's fingers felt cool—or maybe that was just the relief of having some part of his alpha inside him at last.

Rory got his own hand on Beau's cock, but he got distracted from his intention to get it inside him by the noise Beau made at his touch, and the way Beau's fingers curled roughly inside him in response. Rory couldn't help crying out, and he had to keep touching, stroking, drawing more sounds from Beau. They both just kept going, pleasuring each other in an endless cycle and prolonging the anticipation, delicious and maddening all at once.

"I need," Rory gasped, when he realized how close he was to coming, just from this, and how much more he wanted. "Beau, I need —you have to—"

Beau growled and kissed him, and Rory forgot that he needed anything but this, lost in his alpha's mouth claiming his.

Then Beau moved, breaking Rory's grip and taking his fingers away so that Rory keened at the emptiness. But Beau's hands clamped down on Rory's hips, holding him close and guiding him into place, until the head of Beau's cock was brushing against him, almost where he needed it. Rory gasped at the feeling and let Beau's hands move him then, lowering himself onto Beau's cock.

Rory could feel how slick he was inside. He needed to be filled, stretched open to make a space in himself for Beau, for the two of them to be joined. He knew, dimly, that he might not be quite ready, but he didn't care, and he wasn't afraid. He sank down, taking what he needed, what Beau was finally ready to give him.

His breath went out with a harsh sound as Beau's cock entered him. The stretch was shocking, a little painful, but it was what he needed. Rory wriggled his hips, getting the angle right, and then sank lower, taking Beau deeper into himself. The only sound was the wet glide of flesh on flesh; he wasn't breathing and he didn't think Beau was either, holding himself utterly still to let Rory take what he needed.

Rory leaned into his chest, gasping, when Beau was fully seated inside him. Beau's hands changed their grip, one settling between his shoulder blades, the other on the nape of Rory's neck, gently tipping his head back. Beau's lips came down on his, feather-light, and Rory groaned, nodding in answer to some barely-asked question.

Beau's hips surged up under him, driving Beau's cock somehow deeper.

Rory howled, digging his nails into Beau's shoulders to cling to him through the impossible rush of pleasure-pain. Beau's arms tightened around him, and Beau pressed fervent kisses over his throat until Rory fell quiet.

"Do you," Beau gasped. "Baby, I'll—"

Rory shook his head, wrapping his legs around Beau's hips and keening at the way it shifted the Beau's cock inside him. "Don't. Don't stop. I want it. Everything. Give it to me, give me—"

Beau groaned and kissed him again, on the mouth this time, so that Rory's words were lost in the thrust of his tongue. Beau moved again, but this time he rolled Rory over, pressing him into the bed. Rory loosened the grip of his legs a little, so that Beau could move in him, just rocking at first and then pulling back enough for real thrusts. The first ones still made him gasp with the edge of pain, but his body adjusted faster than he had remembered was possible. Soon it was only bliss, having his alpha driving into him again and again, faster and harder every time.

Rory let his head fall back and lost himself in sensation, the pull of the moon and the way his alpha was answering, driving into him with the unstoppable power of the tides, crashing against and into Rory's body. The need and the satisfaction and the pleasure that built between the two, stoking higher and higher until Rory was on the edge of coming and then was jerked back from the edge.

It hurt again, suddenly, between one surge and the next. Rory gasped, grabbing at Beau's shoulders, and Beau froze again. His dark eyes were moon-bright, dazed with pleasure, but he stopped dead as soon as Rory grabbed hold of him, and held himself still, frozen.

Rory twitched under him, arching up onto Beau's cock, and this time that twinge of pain made sense to him. This time he understood. It wasn't that he had somehow become less accustomed to the thickness of Beau's cock. It was that Beau's cock was thickening at the base, the knot swelling.

Beau closed his eyes, resting his forehead against Rory's, sweaty skin to sweaty skin. "I don't have to, baby. I won't. I won't hurt you."

Rory shook his head and pushed up, locking his ankles across each other as he drove himself to the root on Beau's cock. It hurt a little, but he could feel Beau's pulse in the throbbing of the growing knot, and his own heart was pounding out the same rhythm.

"I said everything," Rory whispered, nearly choking on the words he wouldn't let himself say as he struggled for the ones that would make Beau understand. "I want you. I want. *Everything.*"

Beau took a ragged breath and then nodded. He straightened up on his knees, his hands closing on Rory's hips, and Rory felt a thrill of something that wasn't fear but maybe should have been. This was an alpha, ready to claim his omega under the full moon, to take absolutely everything offered to him and make it his.

"Yes," Rory gasped, raising both arms above his head to close his hands in the pillow, bracing himself a little against what was coming —but not protecting himself from it.

"Baby," Beau said. "Baby, you—"

And then he moved, his hips driving in, his cock forcing its way in again, and in and in as he set a relentless pace. Rory tipped his head back, baring his throat, but he could still feel Beau's hot, dark gaze as surely as he could feel the silver light of the moon though he couldn't see it here, under a roof.

Each thrust forced the swelling knot into him and then drew it back to push in again, stretching him over and over. It would have been everything he craved, if he were in heat, if his body were truly ready for this, but as it was his body was slow to catch up, the pleasure lagging behind the pain, and still he wanted it, wanted Beau, wanted to be choosing this, clear-headed and sure.

"Rory," Beau said, nearly a growl, and Rory had to look, and once he saw his mate's eyes he couldn't look away. Beau was gazing at him like there was nothing else in the world, no one else, like there was no one else under the moon but them and it shone for them alone.

Rory gasped in a rough breath and moaned it back out, pain dissolving at last into perfect pleasure as Beau sank into him one more time.

The next movement of Rory's hips was only a sharp little rocking, the knot inside him sliding just to his rim and stopping there. They were joined now. Locked. He was so full, so thoroughly claimed, and Beau was still looking at him like that, like he never wanted to see anything else.

"Oh." The sound shook out of Beau, and he curled down over Rory again, gathering him close. "Oh, moon, I didn't—oh, oh Ror—"

Beau was trembling a little, and his words were dazed, loud in the sudden stillness. Rory was almost there with him, *almost*.

"Touch me," he breathed, forcing his hands to release the pillow he was clutching so he could wind his arms around Beau's neck. "Touch me, just—just—"

Beau's hand slid between them, curling gingerly around Rory's dick, and Rory moaned and thrust up into the touch, clenching around Beau's knot inside him as he did. Beau gasped, and Rory did it again, the pleasure mingling with the strange quiet certainty and the thrill of holding his power over his alpha, owning as much as he was owned.

Beau stroked him one more time, his thumb rubbing over the head of Rory's cock, and Rory came, spurting over Beau's fingers and clenching again and again around his knot until Beau was moaning helplessly against his neck. The pleasure seemed to go on and on, which Beau's knot pressing against the sweet spot inside him, keeping him hard, keeping him coming long after he should have been done.

Beau was coming too, or had started to, and would keep on coming in those slow waves that would last nearly as long as the knot.

He clung to Rory, making helpless little sounds, even after Rory could think straight again, and Rory couldn't look away from him.

He didn't know how many alphas he'd been tied to like this, but he knew he'd never felt like this with any of them. Rory tipped his head back, looking up into Beau's face, his glassy eyes and parted lips. He was helpless right now, overwhelmed, and Rory remembered abruptly that it was *Beau's* first time being tied like this. The sweet feeling of power given and taken and doubled back surged into a tenderness that almost hurt.

"Oh, honey," Rory whispered. "Kiss me?"

Beau did, clumsily, his hands moving restlessly. It was like he was searching for some way to pull Rory closer, even though they were already joined as deeply as they possibly could be.

Rory brought his own hands down to catch Beau's, lacing their fingers together, and Beau picked his head up as he squeezed Rory's hands. Their eyes met, and Rory couldn't breathe at the sight of Beau's face, naked and open to him. For a moment he felt as if it weren't Beau inside him but him pushing into Beau; his alpha wasn't just naked with him but somehow vulnerable, needing something that only Rory could give him.

There could be no lies here, no evasions. This was truth. This was them. There were no words, so there was nothing to hold back, nothing to hide. There was only them, joined into one creature under the moon, an ecstasy beyond pleasure, beyond their bodies, a silver-tinged perfection.

It seemed to last forever, or just the space between two racing heartbeats, Rory could never have said. His eyes filled with tears, blurring his sight of Beau, and he gasped for breath, and then Beau was peppering his face with kisses, his hips rocking minutely deeper into Rory, driving him toward a dizzy crest of pleasure. He squeezed his eyes shut and chased it, and didn't think.

CHAPTER 33

$\mathcal{B}$eau had never been more reluctant to get out of bed than he was on the second day after the full moon. He and Rory had spent a night and day and night in bed together, barely setting foot outside the bedroom. There had been a few hurried trips to the kitchen for food, and another long lingering bath in the afternoon, but otherwise they had stayed in bed together under the moon and the sun, dozing and waking to make love again and again.

They hadn't been tied again, after that first time, but it hardly felt necessary. They couldn't be closer than this.

They hadn't talked much; that hadn't felt necessary either. But something had changed, Beau knew. He couldn't deny that he wanted Rory to stay forever, and he knew that Rory wanted that too. Beau might have to work to make that a good choice, but he would have a lifetime to make sure Rory never regretted it.

First, though, he had to get up and go to work. Rory made a small protesting noise, but after Beau quieted him with a kiss he lay still, watching as Beau pulled clothes on and got his scrubs and coat together. He'd never been so aware of Rory watching, and he wondered if this was the day Rory would finally ask him where he was really going. He didn't know what he would say if Rory did.

When he looked back to the bed, Rory was entirely hidden under the covers, his heartbeat already slowing back toward sleep.

Beau couldn't help smiling. He turned away, telling himself it was better this way. He could do what he had to do without lying to Rory, or upsetting him.

He was going to have to find a way to fix this, but he had already known that. The situation couldn't stay this way forever; Amy was going to get sicker, or else... But he couldn't think of any alternative, and he still couldn't think of a solution.

His circling thoughts stepped short when he stepped out of the house and realized that the faint steady sound at the edge of his hearing was a steady downpour. He dimly recalled hearing thunder at some point in the wee hours, but he had only held Rory closer and huddled under the covers. The world outside their bed had been far away and unimportant.

He couldn't avoid it now; the temperature had dropped sharply since he was last outdoors, the end of summer having arrived overnight. The steady rain muffled the range of his senses, leaving him with nothing to smell or hear but the rain beyond his most immediate surroundings. It would make him drive more slowly, feeling half-blind, which meant he had absolutely no time to spare, but he still hesitated.

He didn't want to have Rory's scent washed off of him. He didn't want to step into the rain and instantly lose the sound of Rory's contentedly sleeping heartbeat.

Beau shook his head, gritting his teeth. It was just rain. Rory would still be here when Beau came home, and in the meantime, Beau had responsibilities. He wouldn't have much to offer his omega if he couldn't walk outside and do his job.

Beau stepped into the rain.

Thanks to the steadily driving rain—and his own rushed preoccupation—Beau didn't realize the Vaughns' apartment was empty until he'd knocked twice and thought to lean against the door, listening intently.

The unexpected silence sent his thoughts racing. He tugged out his phone, checking for any message from Vaughn, any reason they'd be gone. If Amy had already gotten worse in his absence—but that would be good, if she was finally in a hospital, except...

Beau whirled before the outstretched hand could touch him. He found himself face to face with Vaughn, rain-soaked and wild-eyed, and Beau knew that nothing good had happened here.

"I can't find her," Vaughn gasped, sounding nearly as frantic as he looked. "You—you have to—do you need something with her scent? You have to find her, I don't know where she went."

Beau felt his habits kicking in automatically, facing the upset parent of a child in danger. He regulated his breathing and heartbeat and set his thoughts firmly in the direction of triage checklists. He hadn't done this particular one before, but he assembled the beginnings of one in the moment it took him to understand: Amy was missing, and Vaughn had already been searching for some time but couldn't find her.

"Let's start at the beginning," Beau said evenly. "Let's go inside."

Vaughn bounced on his heels, his face twisting, his hands rising; Beau braced himself, but there was no attack, just a rush of words. "She's sick, she's—it's so cold, she didn't even take an umbrella, she just—"

"She's a smart kid," Beau said gently. "She's not just standing around in the rain. Let's go inside and figure out how to find her."

Vaughn hesitated another moment, then nodded, gesturing at the door. "Go on, it's not locked. I didn't want her stuck outside if she came back. Did she—"

Beau was barely inside before Vaughn rushed past him, hurriedly looking around for any sign of Amy's presence, but Beau's senses hadn't deceived him. There was no one else in the apartment. Wherever Amy had gone, she hadn't returned.

Now that they were indoors, out of the rain, Beau pulled his phone out. His contacts list wasn't long, and more than half of it consisted of numbers to various offices at Rochester.

Vaughn turned on him as he tapped one. "What are you—who—"

An automated message played, one Beau had never expected to hear. He didn't let himself think about that, or about what might follow. Amy was missing; he had to help Vaughn find her, or nothing else was going to matter.

"This is Beau Jeffries, first year resident, Oncology," Beau recited blandly. "I'm sorry for the late notice, but I have a family emergency and won't make my shift today." He hung up, not allowing himself to attempt further explanations or apologies. He turned his phone off and pocketed it again.

"If you don't find her," Vaughn said, his voice shaking, but not enough to conceal the threat.

"I'm going to help you," Beau said, not bothering to let Vaughn finish, or to think about what was going to happen to him if Amy was hurt, if—

No. None of that mattered. Amy mattered. Amy was missing.

"When did you notice she was gone?" Beau asked. "Could she have just gone to a neighbor's, or a store, or—"

Vaughn was shaking his head hard, reaching into an inner pocket of his jacket to pull out a phone. The hard plastic case didn't hold scent well, but Beau recognized it; Amy usually had it somewhere near at hand while he was helping her meditate. It was the same phone she'd been playing with the first time Vaughn brought him to her outside the clinic, when he left her in the car. She hadn't been really alone then—her father had been only a phone call away.

Beau took the phone when Vaughn held it out and tapped on the screen. The lock screen wasn't the family picture Beau vaguely remembered seeing there—a younger Amy, with both her parents— but a photo of a handwritten note.

You need a break from me and I need a break from everything. Don't worry, I'll be in touch. Love, Amy

Beau took a breath, feeling halfway reassured. She hadn't said *goodbye*; she promised to be in touch. It could have been worse.

"Okay," Beau said. "So she decided to run away. When?"

"She was gone when I went to wake her this morning. I woke up when I heard the thunder, but I didn't check on her—she sleeps with her door shut now, she's, you know, growing up, doesn't want her dad barging into her room all the time. It was just thunder, I didn't—"

"You didn't have any reason to think otherwise," Beau agreed. And Vaughn might only have heard the thunder; Amy could have left without him hearing her earlier or later than that. "When did she go to bed? When did you last see her?"

"A little after nine. I, uh—" Vaughn grimaced, running a hand through his hair. "I had a couple drinks, went to bed about midnight. I don't—she couldn't have gone out before I went to bed. She couldn't, I was right here—" Vaughn waved a hand at the couch, from which he would have had a view of the kitchen and the door out of the apartment. "She *couldn't*. I was—I was *right there*."

Which meant she probably could have, Beau concluded. And she probably could have made a hell of a lot of noise leaving after Vaughn was out, because it had probably been more than two drinks.

"Okay," Beau said, not bothering to argue. "That's a pretty broad window. You said she didn't take an umbrella, what did she take?"

Vaughn was nodding briskly. "Backpack, a jacket, her sneakers, jeans, some notebooks, her little laptop, the book she's reading."

"Money?" Beau prompted. "Anything that would help her get around? She doesn't have ID or credit cards, obviously..."

"She... I know she had some cash, I don't know how much," Vaughn said, his shoulders sagging. "From... birthdays and stuff, she would hoard it, she was always, you know, saving up for something. And... she has an ID, but it's got her damn birthday on it, nobody's gonna take a 12-year-old anywhere."

Beau raised his eyebrows. "Credit card?"

"She—yeah, I got her one with her own name on it, my account, just for stuff online. I already have it set so I get a notification when she uses it," Vaughn dug out his own phone and tapped at the screen, already shaking his head. "Nothing."

"Okay," Beau said. "So... obviously she had a plan, she packed her things, she wrote a note and put it on her phone for you to find. So where would she go? She still could have just walked to a neighbor's apartment."

Vaughn was shaking his head already. "She doesn't... we don't know any of the neighbors, really. I homeschool her, she doesn't have friends. There are some games she plays online with other kids, but I watch what she says in those chats, she's not—she wouldn't. There's no one."

Beau did not point out that that was just asking for a kid on the cusp of her teens to run away. Not when everything he knew about runaways involved loading them into ambulances. They were going to find her.

"Family?" Beau offered. "Back in Iowa, or somewhere else?"

Vaughn was shaking his head again. "We don't... we're not in touch, really. We were never that close, and after her mom died—no. She's all I've got, I'm all she's got. We just—everything's been on hold except getting her better, when she's better we can..."

Vaughn trailed off again, looking around in directionless agitation.

"Okay," Beau said, not thinking about how many reasons Amy had to run as far and fast as she could without thought for the consequences. He had to stay calm. He had to work his way down the checklist, even if he was inventing it as he went. "Where have you looked already?"

An hour later they'd searched the complex and all the obvious nearby hiding places, including canvassing the nearest neighbors. No one had seen Amy, and Beau had caught no fresh trace of her scent—unsurprising, as the rain was only now tapering off from a downpour to a steady, chilly drizzle.

They'd returned to the apartment and surveyed it more carefully; Beau stood in the doorway of Amy's bedroom, watching Vaughn paw through her dresser and dirty laundry, trying to determine exactly what was missing.

"Vaughn," Beau said after a moment. "You have to call the police. You have to—"

Vaughn straightened up sharply. "The fuck I do. What do you think's going to happen then? Even if they can find her, they'd take her—everybody I've taken her to already thinks that what's wrong with her is me hurting her or her being crazy, you think this won't convince them? They'll put her in foster care, or some group home, and then what'd happen to her? Nobody's going to take care of her right. I'm all she's got, and they would *take her.*"

Beau didn't allow the words *maybe they should* to rise to his tongue or show on his face; he knew that Vaughn wasn't deliberately hurting Amy, but the way their lives had curled in around her illness wasn't helping her either. That was an argument for another time, though.

Beau swallowed with an effort. It wasn't like *he* wanted to get mixed up with the police on this either; it would make a big public mess of everything, but Amy's safety mattered more than any of that. "They can do more to find her. Get her picture and description out. They have manpower, they—"

"No," Vaughn said. "No. I've got *you.* And you are going to find her. You know her scent—" Vaughn threw a t-shirt from the dirty laundry hamper at Beau and he caught it automatically. He tried to hold it away from himself, feeling somehow incriminated just having the little pink scrap of fabric in his hand. The air in here was saturated with Amy's scent; the t-shirt didn't make any difference.

"I can't do anything special," Beau said. "I know you think I can, but it's been pouring rain for hours. There's nothing to smell, there's no trail to follow. I can't just find her because you want me to."

"Because *I want you to?*" The humming frantic energy that had been ebbing and flowing in Vaughn throughout their search burst forth all at once; he lunged at Beau, shoving him two-handed. Beau fell back a step, into the hallway, and Vaughn followed, staying right in his face. "You think I *want this?* This is my little girl, this is all I've got. If she doesn't come home safe then I've got fucking nothing to lose and I will *destroy you.*"

Beau gritted his teeth and breathed and did not push back, did not argue. Vaughn was understandably upset. "The police—"

"*NO FUCKING POLICE,*" Vaughn shouted into his face. "Do you fucking hear me? *You* are going to find her! You've been fucking useless so far, but *you are going to find her,* or I will go to *your* fucking house and I'll make sure that little bitch of yours—"

Beau didn't think, didn't even feel himself get angry; his hands were suddenly on Vaughn's shoulders, holding him at arm's length, his fangs itching to lengthen.

"You think I didn't know?" Vaughn taunted, almost laughing, wild. "He must be one of those werewolf guys who can get knocked up, right? That what you were busy doing over the full moon? Making yourself a little fucking wolf puppy with him? How are you gonna feel when—"

Beau forced himself to open his hands, pushing out as he did. Vaughn stumbled backward into Amy's room and fell to the floor among her scattered clothes. Beau closed his hands into fists and forced himself to breathe, struggling against the shockingly strong urge to *kill anyone who threatened his omega.*

"You fucking find her," Vaughn gasped, oblivious to the danger he was in. "You do what the fuck you want to me—you kill me, I've already got the information, you'll never cover it up. I will fucking burn your life to the ground if that's what it takes, but I need my daughter back. *Find her.*"

Beau just kept standing still, putting every ounce of his will into not killing the man who had just threatened Rory, threatened their hypothetical child. He knew where Rory lived; Rory would never be safe while Vaughn was in the world.

Rory wasn't safe. Rory didn't even know he was in danger.

Beau turned on his heel, and Vaughn shouted after him. "Go! Fucking find her! *FIND HER!*"

Beau slammed the apartment door behind him and ran for his car, barely noticing the rain at all.

~

Beau came to a sharp halt as soon as he opened the front door, the frantic shout dying in his throat. He could hear Rory's heartbeat again, and it was just exactly like it had been when Beau left: slow and calm. Sleeping. Rory must still be in bed.

Beau pulled the door shut and locked it behind him, taking a few deep breaths. The scent of home was all around him now, Rory and himself and this safe place. He could take a moment and think; there was no danger here yet. Vaughn wouldn't do anything drastic right away.

But there was still Amy to think of; she might have a plan, but she was still just a kid, sick and in pain and small for her age. Regardless of all of Vaughn's threats, Beau did need to find her and make sure she was all right.

The threats... Beau couldn't think about that. He had to keep Rory safe, and he had to find Amy. Everything else, he would deal with after that.

Beau let himself move, once that was clear in his mind. He took slow, measured steps up the stairs and into the bedroom, and he stood for a long moment just looking at Rory sleeping there, so trustingly, so certain that he was safe in this place Beau had made for him.

Then Beau turned away, trying to remember where he'd last seen the backpack with Rory's things in it from when they moved.

CHAPTER 34

*R*ory woke up to find Beau sitting on the edge of the bed, wearing jeans and a t-shirt, though the light from outside the windows had brightened enough that it had to be hours since he'd woken up to Beau getting dressed. Beau was looking down at him with an expression Rory couldn't read, very intent and very still.

For a moment everything hung suspended, strange but not alarming. Rory half wondered if he was dreaming. "Beau? What... why are you..."

Beau looked away, his jaw flexing as he gritted his teeth, and Rory was abruptly very sure that this was real. Beau wasn't wearing the same clothes he'd been wearing when he left—his hair was still damp, but the clothes were dry, and there was rain pattering steadily against the windows. Beau's heartbeat was too fast, and his scent was all tension and misery.

Something had gone very, very wrong.

Rory sat up, and only then saw what was on the floor at Beau's feet: the backpack Rory had used to carry his scant few possessions when they moved in here.

Rory's ears filled with the roar of his own blood rushing, and understanding slammed into him with a force that stole the air from his lungs.

Beau was done with him. Beau was sending him away.

"Baby," Beau said, sounding far away, and how dare he call Rory that *now*, when Rory was still in his bed, when the sheets still smelled of the full moon they'd spent together, and yet he was going to send Rory away.

Beau was still talking, but Rory couldn't hear, couldn't make sense of any of it. None of this made sense, but that didn't matter.

The worst had happened, and now Rory had to figure out how he was going to survive. He leaned over and snatched the bag, then scrambled to the far side of the bed with it, dropping to the floor to dig through it. His wallet and phone were there, along with a few changes of clothes; Beau probably thought he was being nice about this. He wasn't being as cruel as possible, at least.

Rory looked over before he dared to straighten up. Beau was still sitting on the far edge of the bed, his hands spread. "Rory, I just—I just need you to be safe. It's just for now. Please, don't—"

Rory shook his head and bolted for the door, running to his own room and slamming the door behind him. It was raining; it had probably gotten colder. He needed proper clothes, his sturdiest shoes. He needed to get out of here. He wasn't going to listen to the lies, the explanations, the promises that would string him along, make him hope that there was some way of coming back from this. He could see where this ended, and there was no point dragging it out.

He was in the act of yanking on Beau's hoodie—the warmest garment he had ready access to—when he realized that it was Beau's, and maybe he shouldn't take it. But there was nothing else, and if Beau was going to send him away in the rain, Rory would take whatever he wanted with him. He wanted this.

He slung his backpack on, braced himself, and opened the bedroom door, only to freeze at the last sight he'd expected.

Beau was sitting in the doorway of his bedroom, hastily wiping his eyes with the back of his hand.

Just that. Not sobbing noisily, not making a sound. Not lying in Rory's path.

For a moment Rory wavered. Maybe—maybe it wasn't so bad. Maybe he'd overreacted, maybe there was some other explanation. Maybe...

He took a step forward, his eyes locked on Beau, waiting for Beau to say anything, to offer some explanation. To ask him to stay.

Beau looked up at him, his gaze tracing him from head to foot, and he said, "I'm sorry, Rory, I just..."

Rory took another step forward, his knees going wobbly. He was screaming inside, telling himself not to fall for this, not to be fooled again, but it was Beau, and Beau had never hurt him. Beau had promised he could stay. There had to be some explanation, and if Beau would tell him, it would all make sense and he could stay, and they could figure this out together.

"Just—be safe, baby," Beau said, dropping his gaze. "Go somewhere safe, okay? Don't just—"

Rory took off running and didn't slow down until he'd reached the main road at the end of their street. He didn't look back at all.

He felt something like calm by the time he'd walked far enough to start seeing businesses along the road, instead of just trees and endlessly branching subdivisions. The long-ingrained calculations started up automatically: he couldn't go into a drugstore or a party store, because they'd suspect him of stealing and insist on searching his bag. A fast food restaurant would leave him alone as long as he bought something for a dollar, but they wouldn't let him loiter for more than half an hour or so. Some kind of diner would be best, but only if he was clean enough not to be noticed too much.

Rory actually stopped walking when he realized what he was thinking, and looked down at himself. He was wet from the rain, but the clothes he'd put on were clean; he'd had a bath sometime in the last twenty-four hours, and if he didn't smell perfectly spic-and-span it was from sex, not the ground-in grime of living rough. People didn't mind that so much, and humans often barely noticed it.

Then too, he had money in his wallet, ID, even a credit card. He could go anywhere, order anything. He could even call a car to pick him up and drive him somewhere.

He rubbed his face with a rain-damp palm and started walking again, looking out for a restaurant; the one part of his thought process that hadn't been totally habit was the hunger gnawing in his belly. He'd slept through breakfast, and he wasn't accustomed to going hungry anymore.

The rain had let up enough that he caught a whiff of fried food and biscuits just before he spotted the sign, one in a strip-mall row: *Grandma's Kitchen*. His mind flashed to the midwives' house, but he pushed that possibility aside and hurried his stride across the parking lot to the refuge before him.

He breathed a sigh of relief as soon as he stepped through the door, out of the rain and into the warm, fragrant confines of a café. There were only a few people scattered around the tables; a middle-aged waitress glanced up and smiled at him, waving toward the vacant tables. "Sit anywhere, hon, I'll be right with you."

A certain tension melted out of his shoulders, and Rory hesitated only to wipe his feet on the mat and brush off as much rainwater as he could before he settled himself into an unoccupied booth, facing the door and as far from the other customers as he could get. He eyed the stack of single-serving packets of jelly, automatically considering how many he could take without the waitress getting angry, and then shook his head and stared out the window instead.

He made himself listen for the waitress's approach, so he wouldn't be startled, and tried not to think of anything else. He looked up just when she came into view, smiling as she set a menu down. She was human—he was pretty sure everyone in the room was human—and older than him, though he was never good at guessing how much. Her hair was dyed blonde, her makeup bright, and her smile was friendly and seemed more or less genuine. "Anything to drink? Something warm, maybe? You look like you were caught in it pretty good, there."

"Yeah, uh," Rory glanced down at the menu, and reminded himself again that he had money, he could afford to drink whatever he wanted. "Hot tea, with lemon?"

"Sure thing, I'll get that right out," she said, smiling a little wider. Rory opened the menu and breathed in the smell of cooking things. He forced himself to focus on narrowing down what he wanted from *everything* to something he could order without being particularly memorable. Luckily it seemed to the be the kind of place that encouraged generous portions, so there was a breakfast combo that sounded like nearly enough food. He promised himself that he could order dessert if it wasn't, and by the time the waitress returned, he had his order all set in his mind.

She set down the little metal teapot—not silver, he would feel it at this range—with steam wafting up out of it, then an empty cup with a teabag on it and two lemon slices on the saucer, and a plastic bear full of honey. "There you go, that'll warm you right up. Ready to order, hon?"

Rory nodded and gave his order, and she nodded, looking pleased by his appetite, and bustled away again. Rory squirted honey right over the teabag and then poured in the hot water, focusing on every motion of his hands, but it didn't take long before there was nothing left to distract himself with. He curled his hands around the ceramic cup, breathing in the steam, and closed his eyes.

Beau had sent him away. Beau had packed a bag for him while he was still sleeping. Beau hadn't told him why, hadn't explained anything, hadn't told him not to leave in such a rush. Only to be safe. *I just need you to be safe*, he'd said. *Go somewhere safe.*

Rory took a deep, steadying breath, thinking of Beau with tears on his face, still not explaining himself, just sitting there on the floor. Not blocking his path.

Beau had wanted him to leave. Beau had wanted him to leave as soon as possible. Because Beau didn't think Rory was safe in their house.

Beau was at home, at their house, at... Rory looked around and spotted a clock, counting back to try to guess what time it had been when Beau woke him, and how long before then Beau must have gotten home to change clothes and pack Rory's bag. Nine o'clock, maybe half an hour after he should have gone on-shift at the clinic?

He hadn't ever gotten as far as the clinic. Rory knew it with a bone-deep certainty as soon as the thought occurred to him. This wasn't anything that had happened at the clinic—no one at Rochester would hurt Rory, even if something had gone wrong there.

This was about the thing Beau had been lying about for weeks now. The secret patient, the *study group*. Something had gone wrong, badly wrong, and Beau hadn't gone to his shift today, which meant he was going to be in trouble at Rochester—and that whatever had gone wrong was so bad that getting in trouble with Rochester wasn't even Beau's main concern. He was worried about Rory; he was absolutely sure that Rory was in actual danger, so serious and certain that Beau didn't care what trouble he got into.

He had married Rory for this, to get through his residency, and now he was putting it on the line for Rory.

The tea had steeped. Rory opened his eyes and confirmed what his nose told him. He went through the motions of removing the tea bag and adding lemon and still more honey, but this time he couldn't stop his thoughts whirring on as he did.

Rory wasn't the reason Beau was in trouble right now. Beau's secret patient was the reason. Whatever Beau had been doing... it couldn't only be secret from Rory; it had to be secret from Rochester, too, so Beau faced being in more trouble than just a missed shift, probably. But he hadn't told Rory, hadn't considered that his *clever husband* might have some help to offer.

Well, of course he hadn't. *Clever husband* was only for jokes, for silly trivial omega things. Sure, Rory had made a way for Beau to be able to work through the empty moon when Beau had only been able to think of toughing it out without any plan at all, but there was no way Rory could possibly help with anything else, or make his own decision about how to handle a dangerous situation. Of course Rory had *no idea* how to protect himself. Of course he needed an alpha to make those decisions for him.

Hot tea slopped over onto his finger, and Rory raised his hand to his mouth to lick it away and realized that he was *angry*.

He couldn't remember the last time he'd felt this way—not lashing out, not wild, just angry. The heat of it warmed him from the inside, and it felt good. He was right. He was right, and Beau was wrong, and Rory was *angry about it*.

He sipped his tea, going over and over it in his mind, how utterly wrong and foolish and careless Beau had been to send him away like that without a word of explanation, without even considering that Rory could help. He *could* help, probably, if Beau had just told him what was wrong.

The waitress brought his food, and the smile Rory turned on her felt just a shade too fierce. She just raised her eyebrows and said, "Everything look all right, hon?"

Rory glanced down at the plates, barely remembering what he'd ordered, and managed to marshal his expression to something more polite before he looked at her again. "Yes, thanks."

"Good," she said. "Feed that fire in your belly, huh?"

She walked away without saying anything more, and Rory plunged into eating his breakfast as he wondered what, exactly, he was supposed to *do* with being angry. He sort of wanted to go yell at Beau about it, but he knew that wouldn't work. He wouldn't be able to, not with his alpha right in front of him, and if he did...

He thought for a second about Beau still sitting in the bedroom doorway, letting Rory shout at him.

No. No. That wasn't helping. He wanted to stay angry, because he was right, and Beau was wrong, and...

He slowed his eating, staring down at the plate as he thought that through. Beau had sent him away. Beau had kept secrets from him and sent him away and still not told him what was going on, hadn't let him help or even explained to him what he needed to be safe *from*. That wasn't fair. It wasn't right.

And Rory didn't have to accept it. Rory didn't have to ever go back. He didn't have to listen, if Beau came around later trying to apologize. If Beau had fucked up as badly as Rory suspected he had, there might not even be any reason for them to stay married. He could leave, and never go back, and it was all up to him.

The food he'd already eaten felt like stones in his stomach, and suddenly nothing in front of him looked appetizing at all.

He didn't want that. He didn't want to leave. He didn't want everything to be over.

But it might have already happened, whether he wanted it to or not. If Beau lost his place in the residency, then that would be that. And if he hadn't, if this all just blew over in a day or two and Beau begged him to forget it and come back home... Rory might have to tell him no. Because it wasn't fair, what Beau had done. It wasn't right. And if Rory let it go, then there would be something else, next week or a few months from now, or further down the line, and it would be worse, and the time after that would be worse still, and the longer he let it go, the harder it would be to leave.

He had only just remembered how to be angry. He couldn't go back and forget again. If things went bad with Beau... he wouldn't survive it. He wouldn't escape. Beau was kind enough to keep him hanging on for years, and by then...

Rory felt the sting of tears and tried to blink them back, forcing himself to eat. He was going to have to pay for the food no matter what; he shouldn't waste it.

He made himself push the thought of Beau aside. He couldn't know yet what was going to happen. He had to think of what to do now, today. He had to go somewhere. Somewhere safe, somewhere he would be able to think straight about all of this and make up his mind about what to do.

He thought again of the midwives' house. They would welcome him, he knew. Certainly he couldn't be safer anywhere else. They might even understand if he explained about being angry, about why he couldn't go back to Beau. But he would have to explain everything, and he would maybe have to argue, because they might tell him it was just a matter of managing his alpha properly.

And Beau would be able to find him there, and they would certainly want Beau to come and talk to him, and if he did, Rory wouldn't say no. Not with Beau's scent in his nose, Beau's arms open for Rory to step into.

He could go farther, though. He could go to Georgie. She had told him to come anytime, and she didn't know anything about Beau at all. He wouldn't have to explain anything. It would seem obvious to her that he might need to come and stay with her. She would take his side; she would want him to stay with her, at home.

It was overdue, anyway. She was his sister, and he hadn't seen her since he was thirteen; his chest ached with it suddenly, homesickness rearing up when he thought it had all worn away. He wanted to hug Georgie. He wanted to see how tall Spencer had grown. He wanted to sit in his mother's kitchen, he wanted to curl up in his father's armchair with a battered paperback.

Rory thought of *I, Robot*, then. He'd hidden it so carefully in the basement bedroom and hardly thought of it again. There had been so much else to think of; it hadn't even crossed his mind when he was running from the house, though it had been the first thing he grabbed so many other times.

Rory looked over at the backpack. It had been down in the basement bedroom, and Beau had packed it for him. But Beau hadn't known about *I, Robot*, hidden on the side of the mattress. He wouldn't have packed it. Would he? How could he?

With shaking hands, Rory opened the backpack and reached inside, looking more carefully than that first, panicked glance. His phone and wallet were still right at the top; there were clothes rolled into neat bundles underneath, including his two good shirts—his wedding shirt—and the khakis he'd worn with it. The bottle from Casey with one pill left was tucked in among the clothes, safely cushioned by them And the cravat he'd worn on his wedding day was wrapped around a familiar rectangular shape, tucked behind the rest.

Beau had found his book and packed it for him. There was nothing at all that he ever needed to go back to that house for. Nothing to keep him here.

Rory pulled his phone out and unlocked it, blinking away tears as he ordered a ride to pick him up and take him to the bus station.

~

He noticed the smell first, as soon as he stepped inside; it slapped him in the face. It was the smell of Beau's secrets, the smell of laundry Rory did in a hurry to get rid of that scent: a particular human's sickness and pain.

Rory looked for the source automatically, and spotted the young girl in purple glasses backed into a corner of the vestibule between the outer and inner doors of the bus station. A woman leaned over her, more concerned than threatening, but the girl clearly wanted to escape.

"Honey, I just really think you need to let me call someone," the woman was saying. "I can't just buy a ticket for you and—"

Runaway, Rory realized. Beau's patient, a child, had gone missing, which was why Beau was currently losing his mind. Whoever she ran away from must have blamed Beau somehow, and maybe threatened to hurt someone Beau cared about. Rory could solve Beau's entire problem right now, if he chose to, by calling him and telling him the girl was here.

But would that solve the girl's problem? She wanted to run away; she had to have her reasons, and Rory was the last person who would ever tell a runaway that they had to go back home.

On the other hand, running away hadn't actually worked out that well for Rory, most of the times he tried it. And while the girl had obviously made one successful escape, she was clearly about to be nabbed by this woman, or the authorities this woman would summon, and then she would most likely be dumped right back into whatever home she had run from.

"Hey, there you are," Rory said, without thinking further. "I'm sorry I'm late, Dr. Jeffries had a million instructions for me, but didn't he tell you I'd get your ticket for you?"

The girl's eyes widened with recognition at *Dr. Jeffries*. Rory didn't think she was entirely glad about it, but she ducked away from the woman and darted to Rory's side, slipping her hand into his without hesitation.

"Thanks for being concerned," Rory said, smiling at the woman and squeezing the girl's hand. "But we're okay now."

The woman frowned, looking back and forth between them worriedly, and Rory turned toward the inner doors. The girl came with him, sticking to his side like she was glued there, and Rory led her to the quietest corner of the waiting room.

"Okay," he said, sitting down beside her. The woman came back in, shot them another worried glance, and then turned her attention to a trio of kids—so the girl had picked a woman with kids to help her. Safe bet; smart kid. "So, let's get our stories straight. I'm your Uncle Rory—Dr. Jeffries' husband. You've known him for a little while, right? He's been paying house calls? And you are..."

"Amy," she whispered, squinting at him. "Are you a werewolf? Did he bite you?"

Rory's eyes widened, and he felt a little sick at the thought of what she might have run away from. "I am. I was born this way, nobody bit me. Did you think he was going to bite *you*?"

Amy shrugged, and the motion made it obvious how thin and sharp her shoulders were under the muffling of her clothes. "He didn't want to. He said I would die, and he said he wouldn't if I didn't want him to, and I *don't*. But my dad was trying to think of ways to make him. He was going to tell the people at Rochester stuff about him, or..." She bit her lip. "I think maybe he knew about you. I was trying to go back to Iowa, to my grandma, but..."

Rory nodded slowly. How long was it going to take Amy's father to think of checking the bus station for his runaway? Rory glanced at the listing of buses—none were leaving for at least another half hour, and the soonest ones weren't headed toward Iowa. The mother with her kids glanced at them again, still looking worried, and Rory made up his mind.

"I think," Rory said, pulling out his phone, "we need to get to somewhere safe right now—you and me both. Okay? Will you come with me somewhere where your dad can't do anything he's going to regret?"

Amy nodded sharply, once, and Rory pressed the red button on the ThereWolf app: *Emergency Pickup.*

The car that had dropped him off pulled up again in front of the doors barely two minutes later, and Rory led Amy outside, walking, but not breaking stride until they were in the car with the doors locked.

"Niemi pack lands," Rory said to the driver. "Hurry."

CHAPTER 35

*B*eau stayed on the floor after he heard the door slam behind Rory, listening to his heartbeat for as long as he could hear it.

He needed to get up, to keep going. He needed to find Amy, to solve all of this somehow. He had only done the first of all the necessary things; he had warned Rory, and gotten him out of harm's way. Vaughn was still at the apartment, in case Amy returned home. He wouldn't go looking for Rory, for revenge, not yet. And Rory...

Oh, God, Rory had been so scared. So hurt. Everything Beau had wanted to prevent by rushing home, he had done. Him, not Vaughn. He had hurt Rory, in a way that Rory might never forgive.

Rory probably *should* never forgive him; what would be left for them after this? It would be better if Rory just stayed gone, stayed safe and far away from him.

But no matter what happened between him and Rory, Beau had to find Amy before something happened to her. He pushed himself up, forcing his feelings back down under the surface. He couldn't afford to be thinking about Rory, or himself. He had to focus on the real emergency: a missing child, sick and in pain and probably scared by now. Whatever she had planned, she was only twelve years old, and it wasn't likely that she could pull it off without bringing some kind of trouble down on herself.

Beau turned his phone on once he was back in the car, ruthlessly clearing every notification—and there were a dozen calls and texts and emails, mostly from Dr. Ross. He had nothing from Vaughn. Nothing from the police. Amy was still missing, and it was up to him to find her.

He had to be logical. Amy had had a plan; if he wanted to find her he had to try to recreate that plan and follow her through it. She had only said *a break*. There was no knowing how long she intended to be gone. Could she have gone just to the mall, or a library or the children's museum? It still begged the question of how she planned to get to wherever she was going.

Beau parked at the apartment complex, out of the direct line of sight of Vaughn's apartment, and looked around again, searching for some sign of where Amy would have gone. It was less than a mile from here to the Rochester Clinic, but he was certain Amy wouldn't have gone there—and if she had, Vaughn would have heard by now.

Beau walked out to the street and looked both ways, and then groaned when he spotted the obvious: a green bus shelter, only three blocks down the road. If Amy had caught a city bus—paid her fare with cash, maybe boarded in an early-morning crowd of commuters or close enough behind an adult to look like they were together—no one would have noticed her. She could have gone anywhere from here.

But... it hadn't been raining inside the buses. There might be a scent trail he could find; if he knew what bus she'd boarded, what route she'd taken, he could have at least an idea of where she'd gone. He strode quickly to the bus shelter. Two people were already there, huddling out of the rain, and Beau took the opposite corner and closed his eyes, breathing deeply, searching for any trace of Amy's scent. He thought he caught a trace of it, but he knew it could just as easily be wishful thinking; there was nothing in the bus shelter that would hold scent well, and if Amy had been here at all it had been hours ago.

He pulled out his phone and checked the bus routes; only two stopped here, though it wasn't obvious how many buses served those routes. If the one Amy had been on had gone off-shift... Beau shook his head. He had to believe he could find her, because the only alternative was to give up and call the police, and that would bring everything crashing down.

But for Amy's sake... if they didn't find her by nightfall, he would have to, no matter what Vaughn said, no matter what it would cost him. He stepped out of the bus shelter so he could pace, watching for the approach of the bus; the other two people waiting were watching him, he knew. He wasn't doing an especially good job of appearing human and calm and non-threatening right now.

It was a good thing he wasn't at work.

If he ever went back, if he wasn't expelled from the program—but no, he couldn't think of that. Only Amy. A bus was approaching, and Beau strode up to the curb, so that he could board first and check for her scent before more people got on the bus and muddied it further. He belatedly checked his pockets for cash and hurriedly found enough to cover the fare, only to lose endless seconds making the machine accept it. The other two riders were huffing impatiently behind him all the while.

All the while he was taking deep, deliberate breaths, not only keeping himself calm but scenting the air for any hint of Amy's presence. When he finally was allowed to board, he walked slowly down the aisle, searching on every breath, with every step—scanning the faces of the passengers, in case Amy had simply stayed on the bus and was riding in circles—but there was no sign of her at all. He took up a position by the rear doors and exited at the next stop, then ran back to the first bus shelter and prepared to do it again.

And again.

And again.

After the fifth bus yielded no clues, he stayed aboard; he had run out of cash to pay fares, so he needed to get to somewhere he could get more or buy a bus pass. The bus was mostly empty, so he dropped into an empty seat and stared out the window, trying to slow his racing heart, to still the thoughts that insisted frantically that every second he spent on this bus was putting him further from finding Amy.

There had to be a way, but... Beau closed his eyes, struggling to guess what Amy's plan had been. Where would she have gone? *Who* would she have gone to? Vaughn had insisted there was no one, no friends, no family. Beau himself was the only other person who saw her every day, and she didn't talk to him. He had no idea what she might be thinking.

Beau found himself thinking of Rory, which he had been managing not to, as long as he was in motion. Where was Rory right now? Rory had left on foot—not unlike Amy, though he was stronger, being both a werewolf and an adult, and he was well-accustomed to looking after himself. Still, Rory had to go somewhere, the same as Amy did; where would Rory go?

Rory had options, at least. Rory wasn't alone in the world, cut off. Rory could go to his sister, or to the Niemi pack, or even back to the refuge in Chicago. People loved Rory; anyone he went to would look out for him.

There was the thread of a thought there about Amy, but Beau found himself wondering—where would he go himself, if he were going to run away from his life here? He might be about to have nothing, no residency, no future in medicine, no husband. What would *he* do? For so long he had thought of nothing but his plan to become a doctor. He had focused on that and followed every step to get here, and if he had fucked it up now... where would he go? What would he do?

Who would *he* turn to?

Not to his family, for certain. He had made exactly one foolish attempt to get back in touch, sending his parents an announcement of his graduation from college, making sure the heavy card stock of the professionally-printed notice carried his scent before he sealed it up in the envelope.

It had come back to him a week later, returned to sender.

He couldn't go back to them. Where could he go? Who would help him find his way?

He didn't need help, he told himself. He didn't need anyone.

But the thought was desolate, and he knew it was a lie. He couldn't bear the thought of going home to that house where Rory wasn't, and he didn't know what he would do next at all. He didn't know what to do about Vaughn. He didn't know how to find Amy.

He couldn't do this alone. He pulled out his phone and scrolled through the contacts. Rory's number was at the top. Susan, who had only ever spoken to him to be sure of Rory's safety. Vaughn, who was as alone as Beau was, and had made his daughter just as isolated—and look where that had gotten him. Adam, who would probably never speak to him again once he admitted he'd ruined things with Rory. And then a dozen numbers for people at Rochester, none of whom would want anything to do with him when they found out how badly he'd fucked up everything.

There was only one of them he wanted to speak to, only one of them he wanted to reach for. He hardly dared—he didn't deserve a second chance, he didn't deserve Rory's *help*—but he didn't know what to do. He had no one else to ask, and Rory... Rory knew how to connect with people, how to understand them. He might have some idea of where Amy had gone. He might be able to ask the Niemi pack to help Beau find her.

He might be willing to speak to Beau, and even if he couldn't do anything else, Beau was ready to beg just for that.

He tapped Rory's name and pressed the phone to his ear.

"I'm sorry, baby," he blurted out, as soon as the line picked up. "I'm so, so sorry, I did all of this wrong, I need—"

He heard someone take a breath on the other end, and his own breath stopped in his throat. That wasn't Rory.

"Rory doesn't want to talk to you right now," Casey said, and Beau gritted his teeth and didn't make a sound, torn between misery and relief that Rory was safe, and not unreachably far away.

"But he said to tell you that you should bring Amy's dad to the pack lands, if you want to get things sorted out."

"Amy," Beau whispered, his whole mind gone blank with shock. Rory hadn't known her name. "How..."

"Omegas get stuff done," Casey said, sounding more grim than smug. "And once in a while we allow alphas to be a part of that process, if they're willing to follow simple directions."

Casey hung up, and Beau bolted for the doors of the bus.

~

Vaughn had still left the apartment door unlocked; Beau was able to push through almost without hesitating, and Vaughn, sitting at the kitchen table, didn't move except the widening of his eyes. His phone and a bottle of whiskey were on the table in front of him, but it didn't seem like he'd gotten as far as doing anything with either of them.

"I know where Amy is. She's safe," Beau said sharply. "Come on."

"What," Vaughn said. "How—did you speak to her, how do you—"

"*Come on,*" Beau snapped impatiently. He knew, dimly, that he should be calmer now, more able to control himself, now that there was no danger and no urgency, but...

But he knew where Rory was, and Rory didn't want to speak to him, and he had to fix *that*, somehow. *That* desperation was like a wolf in his chest, trying to claw its way out.

"Where is she, what—how do I know—"

Beau grabbed Vaughn's arm, beyond caring what Vaughn might accuse him of when this was all over. "My *husband* found her, in fact, so you can compose your apology and thanks to him while we're going to meet them."

That struck Vaughn silent, and he didn't resist as Beau towed him out the door, only letting him stop long enough to lock it behind them before he was herding Vaughn to his car.

Beau's bag for his clinic shift, with the scrubs and white coat Rory had stitched with well-wishes, was still on the front seat. Beau felt an instant's petty, furious temptation to make Vaughn sit in the back seat, but he didn't want the man that far out of his sight. He swung the bag out of the way and Vaughn dropped into the passenger seat where only Rory had sat before now, getting his frantic, uncertain fear-and-anger-and-exhaustion scent all over everything.

Beau turned up the fan, hoping to keep the human's scent from collecting too much in the small space of the car as they drove.

They were halfway there when Vaughn said, in a small voice, as uncertain as Beau had ever heard him, "Your... husband...?"

"I sent him away so that you wouldn't find him," Beau said, trying not to actually remember the hammering of Rory's heart, his face chalk-white and his green eyes wide with barely-controlled terror and betrayal. "He and Amy must have been thinking alike, and he took her to the Niemi pack. You wanted a werewolf to solve your problems for you, didn't you? Well, you got an entire pack."

Vaughn stiffened at that. "If any of them hurt her—"

"We don't hurt children," Beau snarled, and Vaughn was silent for the rest of the drive. The directions on his phone led them from county roads to a dirt road, and a few miles on Beau crested a low hill and took in the sight of the welcome awaiting them. Vaughn, beside him, stiffened, fists clenching.

"Be *quiet*," Beau muttered, riding the brake as they eased down the slope toward the place where a trio of werewolves awaited them, standing in the road to block their path.

At first he saw only that none of them were Rory; it took another few seconds to recognize Casey. The man and woman who flanked him both had a distinctly alpha look about them, standing tall and square-shouldered while Casey was slouching, looking away. Refusing to be seen to take any of this seriously, let alone be intimidated.

Beau gritted his teeth and breathed, and brought the car to a gentle stop several yards short of them.

"Stay," Beau muttered, and turned the car off, keeping the keys in his hand as he stepped out of the car.

"Ah, you came," Casey said, glancing at Beau and then away again. "Give your keys to Tom, he'll put your car where it belongs. You and Mr. Vaughn can come with us."

No alternative was offered. This was the way this was going to work, and he was to be grateful for it, or else. Beau took a deep breath, inhaling the almost-familiar scent of the pack lands, not unlike the place where he had grown up. That wasn't the most calming comparison right now, but he didn't dwell on it, tossing his keys to the male alpha before he bent down to speak to Vaughn. "Come on. Don't argue, just come along."

Vaughn looked out through the windshield, and Beau thought with something almost like satisfaction that Vaughn was beginning to realize that being human was not *always* an advantage. But he nodded and got out of the car, circling around behind it to stand just behind Beau's shoulder. Beau headed toward Casey and the female alpha, who Casey hadn't introduced; the look she gave him was wary, but not hostile.

Casey led them off into the trees bordering the road, setting a brisk pace. The ground was wet underfoot, but the trees offered some shelter from the persistent drizzling rain, so it could have been worse. Beau kept taking in deep breaths, learning the slightly different scents of this place—different soil turning to mud underfoot, a different mix of trees, unfamiliar werewolves' scents reaching him in little whiffs here and there. He hadn't gone back in time; this was a different pack. Things would be different.

At least, he thought with bleak humor, if they wanted to punish him for betraying them all to humans this time, they couldn't cast him out of a pack he didn't belong to.

But Rory... Rory was almost a part of the pack, wasn't he? Far more than Beau was. If the pack decided he shouldn't have another chance to hurt Rory...

Beau didn't let himself think of that, keeping his eyes on the ground underfoot.

The female alpha stepped up to walk at his side. Vaughn was crashing along noisily a little ahead of them, following practically on Casey's heels, and Casey didn't deign to look back at anyone.

"I'm Callie," she said. "Closest thing Casey's got to a sister. The Alpha here is my father."

Beau glanced over at her and gave a little nod. He would have been her peer once, grandson of his own pack's Alpha with his father likely to follow; they might have met on exchange and been friends. "Beau."

She nodded, and then tilted her head in Casey's direction and rolled her eyes a little. *Omegas, right?*

Beau shook his head and returned his gaze to the ground. Rory might have reacted strongly, but Beau couldn't say he had been wrong, and he couldn't take Casey's obvious disapproval lightly.

"I was wrong," Beau said quietly, pitched for her ears and not Vaughn's. "I should have... I didn't..."

He couldn't put it into words, couldn't even begin to explain, when he didn't know where Casey was leading them to, or what would come next.

"Ah, well." Callie put her hand on his shoulder. "You get used to it. Omegas are never happier than when they're setting us right."

Casey looked back sharply at that and said, "We'd be happier if we didn't have to, Cal, I swear."

Callie smiled serenely. "You'd find something. You're just bored by easy targets."

Casey shot Beau a look and then turned his head forward again, and Beau wasn't exactly sure how he constituted an *easy target* for being set right, unless it was going to be as simple as sending him away again. But Callie had to know something of the situation, and her hand was still firm on his shoulder.

The trees finally thinned, bringing them to a clearing—and the road that they clearly could have driven down, since Beau's car was already parked there—where a big stone house stood. A man stood on the porch, arms folded over his chest, and Beau didn't have to catch his scent—or his family resemblance to Callie—to know that this was not just an alpha, but *the* Alpha of the Niemi pack.

Casey made to brush past him, and the man reached out and caught his arm, reeling him in for a brief touch before he let go. Vaughn had fallen back to Beau's side, and Callie, still with her hand on Beau's shoulder, brought them up to the porch.

"Alpha," she said formally, though with an undertone that made

Beau think she was a little amused by the show of ceremony. "Here's our stray cousin, Beau Jeffries, and Amy's father."

"Sir," Beau said, offering a hand, wondering whether he ought to be offering his throat instead.

Alpha Niemi shook it firmly, without making any effort to crush Beau's hand in his grip, though Beau didn't particularly doubt that he could; he might be twenty years Beau's senior, but a werewolf's long life meant that he was entirely in his prime.

Vaughn offered his hand as well, without speaking, and the Alpha took it with a decidedly stern look. "I hear you've been making life difficult for our cousin here, and none too easy for your little girl, either."

"I..." Vaughn said, and then fell silent, dropping his gaze.

"Mm," the alpha said, releasing his hand. "Not the worst defense I've heard. Go on inside and let the midwives tell you how things are going to be. Beau, I'll need you back out here once I've had a chance to speak with Dr. Ross."

Beau couldn't help showing his surprise, from his dropped jaw to his racing heart. "You—"

"We're not going to let this ruin things for you, and for whoever might come after you," the alpha said firmly. "Letting you fail would be nearly as bad for all of us as letting a human get the idea that he can push a wolf around. Ross is your advisor, isn't he? That's what Rory told us."

Beau nodded, and could only think that he should have told Rory everything from the beginning; he would have had it all in hand weeks ago. Rory would have taken it to the pack, or at least to Jennifer or Casey, and they would have taken it to the pack. Beau had cut himself off from the people who could actually help, in his determination to solve his problems alone.

"Well," the alpha said, stopping Beau from worrying that bone further, "We thought we'd best start with him—he's one of the ones who came out to speak with us over the winter. He'll know how to get this settled, and make sure you know what to do in the future if you run into this kind of problem with another human."

Vaughn looked like he'd have his tail between his legs if he had one, but he also kept darting glances toward the door the alpha had waved them to. Amy was in there, after all. And so was Rory.

Beau nodded to the alpha and managed to say, "Thank you, sir," before he stepped past him, herding Vaughn into the house.

He caught Rory and Amy's scents at once, heard their heartbeats thumping away among the others in the house. He propelled Vaughn at once toward the kitchen, and Vaughn darted away from him as soon as they reached the doorway, running toward Amy with a glad cry that couldn't possibly be feigned.

Beau only barely registered it; he couldn't look away from Rory, who was standing at the kitchen sink, washing dishes without looking around. Beau remembered, suddenly, his first real sight of Rory, sitting on a bench and dressed too warmly for a June day, in the courtyard of the refuge. Beau had knelt then because it was the proper thing to do, because he didn't want to frighten him.

Now he honestly wasn't sure if his legs were steady enough to carry him across the room. Rory had to know he was here, but he didn't look, and didn't look, and—

"Come over here and listen, Beau," a white-haired woman said briskly, and the command set him in motion, carrying him until he was sitting at the kitchen table, across from Amy. Vaughn knelt beside his daughter, leaning against her chair, his chest heaving as he struggled to catch his breath like he'd just run a marathon.

Beau didn't feel like he could breathe at all, yet.

"I'm Auntie June," the midwife explained. "And Amy has consented to be adopted into the Niemi pack—just as she is, human—with me as her personal sponsor. Granny Tyne and Casey are already doing some research into her situation, which certainly is a puzzle, but in the meantime—it is perfectly legal for a pack midwife, or an apprentice under a midwife's supervision, to deliver appropriate traditional care to a member of the pack, whether human or werewolf."

Beau glanced from her to Amy and then to Rory, who still wasn't looking, before he finally met Auntie June's eyes. "Is that what I've been doing, then?"

She nodded, looking pleased not to have to spell it out further. "You're studying the traditional methods of healing under my supervision, to see the ways they can complement your medical training; you didn't tell your advisor because you were worried this would seem at odds with modern medical practice. Naturally, going forward, we'll try not to have crises that cause you to miss your rotation shifts for your pack studies, but this once I imagine it can all be sorted out. And as for Amy's father..."

Vaughn picked his head up, looking anxious again after his enormous relief. He looked back and forth frantically from Amy to Auntie June. "You can't—I mean—please, please don't take her from me, she's all I have."

"Well, that's the trouble, isn't it," Auntie June said, shaking her head. "How's a little girl to shoulder all that? She has the pack now—and you might, too, if you can make yourself useful, or at least not so troublemaking as you've been. You could start by apologizing to my apprentice here for trying to force him into doing stupid things that wouldn't have helped anyone."

Vaughn looked at Amy first, and then over his shoulder in Rory's direction, before he settled on Beau. "I... I'm sorry. I didn't—I'm sorry. And... and thank you. For... all of this."

Auntie June jabbed Beau very neatly in the shin with her toe, and he said, "I understand. I did want to help."

Auntie June nodded. "Amy?"

Amy had been sitting quietly, her head bowed, but now she looked up, and looked back and forth between her father and Beau. In a whisper she said, "I'm going to stay here for a while. With Auntie June and Uncle Rory."

The soft-spoken words caught Beau in the pit of the stomach, but this time he managed not to react too obviously, and no one was looking at him, anyway. Vaughn was struggling not to cry, nodding and trying to look understanding.

"We can put you up somewhere close by, make sure you don't get any more ridiculous ideas," Auntie June said, pushing back from the table and standing up. "Come on, both of you, let's see what Granny Tyne thinks, and then Casey'll take you both to pack some things."

A moment later they were gone, leaving Beau at the kitchen table. Rory—*Uncle Rory*, apparently—was at the sink, his hands still under the water but unmoving.

Beau took a deep breath and stood up. Walking across the kitchen felt like walking across ice; he had to consider every movement, but he kept his eyes on his goal. He picked up a towel when he was nearly to Rory and extended his other hand over the drying rack, where the freshly washed dishes were arranged. "May I help?"

Rory kept his head down, just like Amy, but he gave the tiniest little nod. When Beau picked up a cup to dry, Rory pulled the stopper out and then stood there watching the sink drain until Beau had finished and looked around. "Where..."

Rory cleared his throat and tilted his head. "Second cupboard."

It wasn't the most encouraging thing Rory could have said, but Beau didn't suppose he'd earned much encouragement. He put the cup away neatly and returned, picking up another while Rory rinsed his hands and the sink.

"I'm sorry," Beau said, quietly. The sound might almost be lost under the spraying water, if Rory wasn't listening for it, didn't want to hear it. "I should have told you what was going on—I wish I had."

"So your *clever husband* could fix it for you?" There was an ugly emphasis on the words, and Beau's hands clenched, almost too hard, on towel and cup.

"Yes, partly," Beau said quietly. "Rory... I did need you, for things like this. I do. Not that that's your problem, if you don't want it to be, but... I was wrong, I was foolish, I needed your help and I should have trusted you enough to ask for it. I'm so sorry. And thank you."

"She needed help," Rory said, still not looking at him. "I know what it's like to be on your own like that."

Beau winced, and went to put the cup away, then returned to dry a plate. Rory's hands were resting on the edge of the sink now, and he had raised his head enough to look out the window.

"If you don't want me here," Beau said quietly, "I'll tell them I can't do this. Ask one of the other packs for help, or—"

Rory's hands had gone white-knuckled.

"Say the first part again," Rory said. "Don't—just say the first part again."

"I'm sorry," Beau repeated. "I was wrong, I should have trusted you, I should have told you what was going on. Even if you couldn't help, I should have told you what was going on. I shouldn't have kept it from you."

"You were wrong," Rory repeated, his voice just above a whisper, his eyes closed. "You... you're saying that."

Beau set the plate and towel down very gently on the counter, and finally let his legs give out the way they'd been wanting to, folding down to kneel at Rory's side.

"I'm telling you," Beau said, not letting himself sway forward to rest his forehead against Rory's hip. "It was on me. I fucked up. This was my fault, I'm the one in the wrong, and if—if that's it, if you can't forgive me and come home—"

Rory's fingers brushed his cheek, smelling sharply of soap and the metal of the sink. Beau closed his eyes and took a deep breath, and Rory's hand moved to rest on the top of his head.

"I don't..." Rory said slowly. "I don't believe you. I can't. I don't think it's because of you, it's just... What you're saying, I... I'm still waiting for the other shoe to drop, you know? I don't want to always be waiting for you to hurt me."

Beau clenched his eyes shut tighter and held his breath so he wouldn't make a sound. Rory's hand was still on his head, and Rory's voice had sounded thoughtful, like there was something here not yet decided.

"I can't tell you yet," Rory said finally. "I'm going to stay here a little while, with Amy. It sounds like Auntie June means for you to visit whenever you have time, so if you can wait for an answer, then..."

Beau covered his face with both hands and hauled in a breath, feeling the first dawning of hope. "I'll wait, Rory. I'll wait, I'll—"

"Finish what you started, then," Rory said, lifting his hand from Beau's head to tug gently at his shoulder. "Get those dishes put away."

Beau stood up and grabbed the plate and towel, and Rory stood beside him in silence, looking out the window while Beau dried the dishes and put them away.

CHAPTER 36

*R*ory didn't know how he stayed on his feet, how he kept showing an appearance of calm. It was a relief beyond telling when Callie stuck her head in the door and said, "Beau, Alpha wants you now."

Before Rory could even take a breath, she added, "You too, Rory, if you're willing."

Rory's hands clenched on the sink, and Beau turned and walked away without echoing Callie's request by the tiniest gesture.

Rory wanted nothing but to go fall down on one of the guest beds upstairs, to hide from all of this and maybe be petted and consoled by one of the old midwives. He couldn't keep *doing* this, all calmly and quietly, as if there were no real danger here, as if nothing at all was at stake.

But Beau's career was on the line, among other things. If Rory didn't go out onto the porch and listen to the discussion, he wouldn't know what was happening unless someone deigned to tell him. If he didn't want to be kept ignorant of things, he could hardly refuse to listen when he was invited, could he?

He forced himself to let go of the sink and walked out to the front porch, grabbing Beau's hoodie from the hook by the door and pulling it on like armor. Beau shot him a searching, hopeful glance as he stepped outside, but Rory didn't meet his eyes. He didn't have an answer, or not one that he could trust.

Yes yes yes, take me home, kept bubbling up inside him, but he'd been stupid before. He knew how that ended.

Alpha Niemi was there, along with Callie, and Granny Tyne, and Troy Niemi in his security guard's uniform, and Dr. Ross, looking only mildly out of place and uncomfortable among all these were-wolves. He was the only human present.

Beau had taken a seat near Dr. Ross but not right beside him, and Alpha and Callie and Granny Tyne were arrayed in various comfort-able seats. Troy leaned against the wall a little behind them. Rory went to perch on the porch railing near the stairs, outside of the circle they made but able to see everyone. The rain had gotten heavier again, a steady fall just past the edge of the porch roof.

"I've been hearing some interesting reports of what you've been up to for the last several weeks," Dr. Ross said. "But I thought you might care to explain in your own words, Beau?"

Beau's shoulders hunched a little, but he nodded.

"I want to say first that I realize now that my mistake was in thinking I could, and had to, handle this alone, instead of turning to any of you—" Beau looked up and met each person's eyes in turn. When he turned his head to look toward Rory, the gaze felt like a touch, like Beau kneeling at his feet again, and Rory had to look away first.

"I'm sorry," Beau went on, looking at the others, "That it took me so long to realize that. And I thank you, all of you, for helping me anyway. I know it's not only for my sake—I know if this had gone worse it would have made trouble for other werewolves too—but I thank you."

He let out a breath and began again in a different tone, words he obviously hadn't thought through as carefully. "So, uh, what happened began in the walk-in clinic."

He found his momentum again as he set out the sequence of events, in quiet steady words that Rory thought must be how he would make a report to another doctor, describing the history of a patient's case. He told about Amy Vaughn's visits to the walk-in clinic, her history, how he had been able to help her the first time he saw her, and how her father had pressured him into more help outside the clinic, and demanded the bite.

"Ah," Dr. Ross said. "Yes. You did ask me, didn't you? I ought to have pressed a bit more on that."

Beau winced, ducking his head, looking like nothing so much as a small boy being scolded. Rory wondered how much he felt like one, or like that teenaged boy he'd been, who only wanted to help a human child, and was punished for it. Auntie June had already worked out what pack Beau had come from; would they know the story from the other side, the pack Alpha's grandson who had been cast out?

Rory was tempted to blurt it out, or to make Beau tell it, but that wasn't the way to do this. Rory and Beau were on their way to being part of this pack, or at least firmly attached to it, with Beau made Auntie June's apprentice and Rory staying over indefinitely. Rory could hint at what had happened with Beau's pack, to Casey or one of the Aunties, and the story would find its way around to those who needed to know it, quietly but certainly. That was how packs worked.

Rory was startled out of his thoughts when Beau's story drew to its end and Dr. Ross turned his attention immediately on Rory. "Does that match what you observed of his behavior?"

Rory nodded, piecing it together as he spoke, though he was sure Beau had been telling only the truth this time. "He was leaving early— he wouldn't wear his scrubs or white coat when he went to see her. He was drawing a line, I think. He saw Amy on his own, it wasn't formal medical care, not clinic business. The scent of their home was always on the clothes he was wearing when he left, never on his scrubs. That's how I recognized her when I met her—from doing the laundry and catching her scent on Beau's clothes. If he'd worn his scrubs, it would have gotten mixed up with all the hospital scents and I wouldn't have known her from anyone."

Dr. Ross nodded slowly, then looked over at Beau. "I did try to tell you, didn't I, that we wanted you to succeed? That you could tell me if you ran into trouble?"

Beau didn't look up, just shrugged slightly and nodded.

"I said a lot of things, eh? Well," Dr. Ross said on a sigh. "Chalk this up to trust-building, then, shall we? And we'll work on procedures for similar incidents in the future."

"Us too," Troy added. "You need security backup, we'll make sure you know how to get someone who understands the situation, doc. All the wolves on security have training on this stuff, how to handle humans without threatening them, what the legal standards are. Somebody should've had you come to one of those sessions."

Beau did look up then, nodding cautiously first at Troy, and then at Dr. Ross. "That's... it?"

"Well, your residency is supposed to be a learning experience, isn't it?" Dr. Ross clapped Beau on the shoulder. "I have a feeling you've learned something, and we've learned something as well. Since we should be able to satisfy all the forms regarding the legalities, I believe that's the end of it. You will have to make up your missed shift, of course."

Beau's gaze darted up to meet Rory's, then, but he looked away before Rory could read anything there.

Rory went to bed that night wearing Beau's hoodie—not because the Midwives' House was cold, but because it was so strange to be sleeping alone, in a place that bore no scent of Beau at all. He didn't sleep much as it was, and the more miserably tired he got the more he told himself not to listen to that feeling.

He would get over this; he would learn to sleep alone again. He would learn not to need Beau, not to love him, if he had to. He would survive.

He left the hoodie tucked under a pillow when he made the bed in the morning, so his own scent wouldn't entirely replace Beau's before the next night. He had no illusions that it would be much easier than the last, not so soon.

Auntie June and another of the midwives he hadn't met before, Auntie Helen, gave him dubious looks at breakfast the next morning.

"I'd send you straight back to bed," Auntie June said, "but it wouldn't do you a bit of good, would it?"

Rory shrugged and shook his head. He wouldn't sleep in daylight any more easily than he had at night; now he would lie there and wonder how Beau was managing his first shift back at the clinic, instead of lying there wondering which bed Beau had slept in, and whether he was sleeping easily, surrounded by Rory's scent, while Rory lay awake and longed for him.

"Well, let's keep you busy, then," Auntie Helen said. "I bet I can find someone in this pack who's gotten as little sleep as you, and for better reason."

One of the pack's omegas had given birth for the first time during the full moon just past, to twins. Jonas was at least ten years older than Rory, and his mate, Max, was nearer to Alpha Niemi's age. Even with werewolves' strength, they were being run ragged by the two-day-old twins. Max, especially, was pulled in three directions as he tried to coddle Jonas and look after the babies all at once.

Rory was content to be subsumed into the bustle of helping, especially after Auntie Helen had prescribed a shared nap for Jonas and Max and shooed them to bed for a few hours. Rory changed diapers and ferried the babies to Jonas when they needed to be fed, then took them away again to rock to sleep. The day passed in a blur of tiny urgent tasks, one after another after another, until he went to answer the door, hurrying before the knocking could wake anyone, and found Beau standing there.

It took Rory a moment to realize that Auntie June was with him, and when Rory's eyes finally settled on her she snorted and brushed past Rory into the house. "All asleep, then? Good. You go on and have dinner—my apprentice, here, has promised to make sure you don't fall asleep on the way."

"Oh," Rory said blankly, and stepped out of the house into the end-of-summer twilight. "I... hi."

"Hi," Beau said, smiling a little.

He looked about like Rory felt—like he hadn't slept and had been on his feet all day, running here and there. He was still wearing his scrubs, though he'd shrugged on a flannel shirt overtop. He poked his elbow out, offering his arm like the most old-fashioned of gentlemen. Rory laughed a little, helplessly, and tucked his hand into the crook of Beau's arm.

A tiny thrill ran through him, despite his exhaustion. How long had it been since he'd touched Beau at all?

Beau let out an audible breath, as though some pain had been relieved by that touch. He led Rory off the porch and down the path, heading back toward the Midwives' House.

They should talk, Rory knew. There were things they ought to say. He should have something to tell Beau about the answer Beau was still waiting for, but his mind was a gray fog. He hadn't thought about Beau at all today, too busy and too tired—or he had thought of Beau a hundred times, a hundred little pangs of grief or thrills of hope at the thought of being like Jonas and Max someday, of having their own babies—but that hadn't been thinking, really. That was just feeling.

Rory wasn't going to make this choice just by feeling.

Before he had managed to think of anything to say, they were back at the Midwives' House, and it occurred to him that Beau hadn't said anything either.

Beau released his arm at the doorway, and Rory hesitated. "Have you eaten? I'm sure there's enough. And you're an apprentice here, after all. That must include meals."

Beau still hesitated, and Rory tugged gently at his sleeve as he pushed the door open and stepped inside. "Come on. Eat."

Dinner passed in the same quiet haze—some of the other midwives were still eating, talking over this and that. Rory answered a few questions about the twins, and Beau said something about Amy's case, but though they spent the whole meal sitting side by side, shoulders brushing, they didn't speak to each other. This wasn't the time, or the place.

Once he'd eaten, Rory felt ready to doze off right there. It took a heroic effort to stand and carry his plate to the sink, where Casey took it from him and waved him off.

"Go and sleep, cousin. You've got another shift with the twins tomorrow—and you, cousin," Casey added firmly, and Rory realized that Beau was right behind him, "you have a full day tomorrow too."

They both shuffled out of the kitchen, and Beau walked Rory up to the guest room where he was spending the night. There were two bags waiting outside the door—reusable shopping bags that smelled of home—no, of *Beau's house*. There were more clothes, and his toiletries, and his workbooks and sewing supplies and the paperback he'd left on the couch with a hank of thread for a bookmark.

Rory's eyes filled with tears. Was Beau so determined to make sure that he never needed to come back at all?

"I thought," Beau said, touching his shoulder gingerly. "You didn't come to the house today to get anything. I thought you would've, when you knew I wouldn't be there. And I thought... you shouldn't fall behind on the stuff you're working on, just because I fucked up and you don't want to be there. That's all."

Rory looked up at him, blinking tears away, and he saw the ache in his own chest reflected on Beau's face. For a moment he wanted to say *yes, yes, I'll come home, anything not to feel like this.*

Beau gave him a sad little smile and wiped a tear from Rory's cheek. "This way you can take your time," he said quietly. "Think things through. Only..."

He dropped his hand and dropped his gaze. "Could I... I didn't sleep last night. I don't know if I can, anymore, without being under the same roof with you. I know that's—"

Rory shook his head and got a firm grip on Beau's shirt—the scrub shirt he was still wearing, though normally he hated carrying the scent of the hospital with him. The one that had Rory's embroidered well-wishes on the shoulder, where they would press against Beau's skin. "I can't either. Come in."

Beau didn't argue, letting Rory tow him inside the little room. Rory set aside the bags Beau had packed for him, only pausing to shut and lock the door before he started peeling out of his clothes.

Beau still hesitated, eyeing the door. "You know that everyone in the house will—"

"They all want me to stay with you anyway," Rory said, hanging his clothes on the hooks behind the door. "They're not going to complain, unless—"

Rory stopped short, his face going hot. *Unless we're noisy and keep them up.*

But *that* wasn't going to happen; Rory didn't know if he or Beau would be asleep first, but neither of them was in a frisky sort of mood right now.

"It's just to sleep," he muttered.

Beau nodded and shrugged out of his flannel shirt, moving to hang it by Rory's clothes, before he stripped out of his scrubs.

Rory left his underwear on, and Beau did too, a silent agreement. This far, and no further. Rory climbed into the bed, which was barely the size of the one in their basement, and gave up the well-scrubbed lingering scents of plenty of other wolves, maybe generations of them.

Beau shut off the light and then crawled in beside him. There wasn't room in the bed not to touch, especially since Beau needed to be lying at a diagonal to keep his feet from hanging off the end. Rory cuddled close to him.

"Just to sleep," he mumbled one more time, and Beau made a vague affirmative noise, and then Rory knew nothing more.

He woke in the darkness, in Beau's arms, and knew that Beau was awake too. He felt a little clearer—he'd slept a few hours already, he thought, but dawn was still a way off.

"I'm sorry," Beau whispered. "I... I miss you so much. I never wanted you to leave forever. I didn't want to let you go at all, I hated the thought of our time ending."

"You don't have to miss me right now," Rory said quietly. It wasn't *yes* or *forever*, but he couldn't just spit either of those out like this. Not yet. "Go back to sleep."

Beau sighed but snuggled back down into the pillow, tightening his grip on Rory only a little. Rory lay his arms over Beau's, holding on right back.

This was all right, he thought, drifting back toward sleep. This was safe. They weren't really alone, safely chaperoned. Even now he could hear some quiet middle-of-the-night bustling downstairs; someone would know at once if—if—

Oh, Rory thought. *Oh. That's how to be sure.*

He was asleep again before he could put it into words.

It was halfway through the morning before his middle-of-the-night realization returned to him, and Rory turned it over and over in the hours that followed.

"It's not really Beau that I'm scared of," Rory said, trying out the logic of it. "It's—it's just *how things go*. Because he was thoughtless, or didn't listen to me, or didn't think I could help, and every other time, that's been the first little sign of things going downhill. But Beau— Beau wants to try. Beau's not a bad guy. And I'm better. I can see what's not right. I can tell him what I need, or at least I can make him see it. I think. If I try."

Skyler, the younger twin by fourteen minutes, blinked up at Rory with slate blue eyes and continued sucking his thumb.

Rory nodded. "And whether I try or not—it's different now, because it's not just me. There's the pack, there's my family. Susan. There are people I could talk to, who would see it even if I tried to hide it. It's not only up to me to keep things right. It's not even only up to me and Beau. If we're part of something, then... then it can work. Because there are so many others around who can help us get it right if we start to go wrong. And I... I really want us to get it right."

Skyler's eyes drifted shut, then flashed open again.

"I know, I know," Rory said, smiling down at him. "Very interesting. But you should go to sleep. You can hear more about it when you're older."

~

Beau turned up again that evening, and neither of them were so exhausted this time around; the memory of the night before seemed to hover between them, warm and calm. After dinner they walked out to sit on a fallen tree by the edge of one of the little lakes that were scattered through the pack lands, the soft lapping of waves making it easy to ignore the sounds of dozens of other werewolves within earshot.

"You said, the other night," Rory started. "You said I needed time to practice not being scared."

"Is that—" Beau cut himself off, and Rory looked over and watched him formulate an idea and maybe an objection to that idea, and then Beau focused on him, smiled crookedly, and shut his mouth. He opened one hand in Rory's direction, silently giving way and waiting for him to finish his thought.

Rory nodded. Right. Beau *did* want to listen, even if he forgot to; he would try.

"I feel safe here, like this," Rory said, looking out at the lake. "With the pack all around, with other people who know us and know..." Rory gestured vaguely. "What could happen. How things could go wrong. I miss you and I want to..."

To come home. To stay forever. To say "I love you" and not even think about the power it gives you to know that. To love you.

"I miss you too," Beau said, when Rory had been quiet for a while, struggling through all the things he still didn't feel safe enough to say. "And I always want you to feel safe. To *be* safe. So if this is what you need, then of course. Should I... should I not come back so much?"

Rory shook his head hard. "I still don't think I can sleep without you. I don't want to, honestly. I just... I just need to practice a little."

"Practice as much as you need to," Beau said softly, brushing his fingers lightly over the back of Rory's hand. "I'll be here as often as you'll let me. I don't want to be anywhere else."

They sat for a while like that, Beau's fingers just barely resting over Rory's hand, though they both knew that they would be pressed skin to skin as soon as they went to bed.

It felt... nice. Like being a kid again, before any of the bad things happened. Like starting over.

Rory smiled, stifling a laugh, and Beau leaned forward to peek at his face. "What?"

Rory shook his head, but said, "I was just thinking... I was never really a teenager like this, but..."

Beau's hand closed fully on his and Beau smiled too. "Yeah. We might be doing it all backwards, but—dating seems like a good idea, doesn't it?"

Rory just looked at him, his heart aching already with love for him, with wonder that Beau could exist.

"Come on," Beau said, standing up and tugging Rory by the hand. "Let's find some stones to skip, are you any good at that?"

Rory grinned, dropping Beau's hand and darting ahead of him along the shore. "Just watch me!"

CHAPTER 37

*B*eau felt like he was floating through his days; like he'd been wearing an x-ray apron for weeks and it had been lifted away. Like... like he'd been taking poison that was supposed to be medicine, and finally stopped.

He was meeting daily with Dr. Ross, little check-ins of ten or twenty minutes, and at least once during each one, his adviser looked him steadily in the eyes and said, "Remember, I'm here to help you get through this."

It should have been unnecessary, embarrassing, meaningless, but it wasn't. It was... something real. Something safe, like Rory had said.

Rory. Beau couldn't help smiling whenever he thought of him, which had drawn baffled and amused looks from his fellow residents and the rest of the staff on his Oncology rotation. One of the nurses, on his second day back after the whole bewildering un-disaster of the day after the full moon, said, "You must've had a *really* nice family emergency, huh?"

Beau broke into a grin over the chart he was reviewing. For a moment he thought *don't, don't, rein it in, hide, be normal,* but... what did he have to be afraid of? Wasn't it better to tell, to share something? He tried to think of how Rory would say it.

"I, uh," Beau shook his head, unable to help his grin even though it was all wrong for the words he had to say. "It was awful, that day. My husband... I thought he might have left me for good. But he's letting me try. We're... sort of dating, now? It's... it's good."

April shook her head, but she smiled, too, the warmest expression she'd shown him since he started on this rotation. "Good, I guess? You better have some good dates planned."

Beau bit his lip and looked over at her. "I'm, uh... I'm not great at that. Got any advice?"

By the end of the day, every nurse on the ward had offered him a foolproof suggestion for an excellent date—named a half-dozen movies and the best gifts to bring, foods he should cook or restaurants he should take Rory to—and the other first years were watching him with a sort of admiring jealousy.

After handoff, Tom demanded, "How'd you make friends with *every nurse* all of a sudden?"

It was the least sneering thing Tom had said to him in the last three weeks, and Beau felt almost physically off-balance—especially when he realized that it didn't matter that much. He wasn't crushingly afraid of what would happen if Tom hated him enough to find out his secrets and use them against him; Tom was just another resident, like him, struggling the way all of them were struggling.

Beau shrugged, smiling a little. "I told them I messed things up with my husband and need to make it up to him. I guess they're problem-solvers."

Tom blinked. "You have a husband?"

"Hopefully," Beau said, still smiling as he packed up his things. "I'm working on it."

With all the advice he'd gotten echoing in his ears, Beau stopped at a nursery on his way to the pack lands that evening. He'd done a load of laundry that morning when he stopped at the house before work, and packed a bag to get him through the rest of the week, so he could go straight from the nursery to see Rory.

When he got there, Rory was waiting on the porch for him, and when Beau held out the paper sack, he looked as confused-but-happy as everyone else who'd seen Beau today. Admittedly Beau was giving him more to be confused about than just a change in mood.

"Tulip bulbs," Beau explained. "I thought I should bring you flowers, but then I thought... maybe you'd like some flowers to plant, instead of just to look at for a few days. There's a catalogue, too, if you—"

That was as far as he got before Rory half-tackled him, the bag of bulbs between them. It was worth not being able to breathe for Rory's excited kisses, and by the time he could speak again, Beau didn't feel obligated to say the stuff he'd been practicing on the drive, about how Rory could plant them anywhere he wanted, and Beau just wanted his future to be beautiful.

Instead, he said, "They don't need to go into the ground until the leaves fall, so... no rush."

Rory leaned against him, taking the bulbs and cradling them in one arm like a baby. "That's... I've never... *Beau*."

"Yeah," Beau said softly, pressing a kiss to Rory's hair. He didn't know exactly what the ends of those broken starts of sentences would have been, but then again he understood perfectly. "Yeah, me either. So we can try together, right?"

Rory nodded against his shoulder and kissed him again, and it tasted like something new. Something just beginning.

Beau checked his phone a few days later—he and Rory had been texting, just little thoughts and comments and the occasional picture of their days—and discovered he had a message from Adam.

Please call me when you have a moment.

He had a little time—he'd managed to escape as far as the roof of the hospital building with his lunch, and he had to have at least ten minutes before anyone summoned him back—so he took a few hasty bites and then called. If Adam was asking, it had to be important.

"Beau," Adam said when he picked up. "Hello."

Beau was tempted to check that he'd called the right person, but it wasn't really as if he could have misdialed anyone else who would have greeted him by name. And yet—Adam had *said hello.*

"Hello?" Beau replied tentatively.

"How, uh, how are things? With you?" Adam said, sounding tense and awkward as he bit out these polite phrases in his usual clipped and hurried style.

"Fine," Beau said hesitantly, still waiting for Adam to take charge of the conversation. But he thought of how all the nurses kept an eye out for him now, how much it helped to share things.

Anyway, Adam wouldn't ask for no reason, so Beau elaborated. "Things are good, actually, although I—we—had a rough patch a little while ago. I ran into some difficulties with a patient, and... well, it almost ruined things between me and Rory, but we're working on it now. How are you?"

"Yes," Adam said, then seemed to realize that wasn't a correct answer. "I mean, fine. Research, you know. I'm glad that things are going well with you and Rory. I, ah, I'd been wondering, actually, about that genetic question you asked me."

"Oh," Beau sat back a little, wondering if he could sneak in another nibble of his lunch without it being really obnoxious on the phone. "About Rory's dad? I don't think he really cares anymore, except maybe for curiosity—he got back in touch with his family and they're good now. Last night he introduced me to his sister and his little brother on Skype."

It had been an important step, a really big one, and Beau thought it had gone well. Georgia and Spencer had both been visibly suspicious of everything about him, and Rory had been obviously torn between defending Beau and just delighting in the protectiveness of his siblings.

"Ah," Adam said. "I see." He didn't sound like he saw at all; he sounded a little lost, honestly. "I... I don't suppose, then... just for curiosity..."

Beau squinted at the horizon as he finally realized why Adam had called him. "Are you—do you need research subjects? Is that what this is?"

Adam huffed out a frustrated breath. "I'm sorry, never mind, I'll—"

"No, no," Beau said quickly. "I mean—I guess it must be hard, getting omegas to, uh, to talk to you, or give samples or anything."

There was a little silence, and then in a very small but very grim tone, Adam said, "It's been a disaster so far. I'm being pressured to choose another topic of inquiry."

Beau blew out a breath. Adam, he knew, felt just as passionately about omega health as Beau did about helping humans. He thought of that paper Dr. Ross had mentioned, the one written by someone who shared Adam's last name—someone intimately familiar with how a bitten human transformed into an omega werewolf. Someone who had never had a chance to publish for real, once the Revelation had truly set in. Someone who Adam never talked about.

Now, he thought, was not the time to ask.

"I'll talk to Rory," Beau offered. "I don't think he'd mind. And his little brother—the human one—he's all about wolf rights, and omega rights, so if he understood that it's about helping omegas, I bet he'd give a sample, too. And Rory's staying with the midwives of one of the local packs right now, so—"

"You know midwives?" Adam sounded like Beau had casually mentioned that he had the cure to cancer packed in his lunchbox. "You're and alpha and—omega midwives? They—they speak to you?"

"Yeah, I'm sort of apprenticing with them, technically," Beau said. His apprenticeship so far had mostly consisted of doing chores around the house when he visited Rory, plus a few intense literature review sessions with Granny Tyne—she was determined to figure out what was really going on with Amy, and she had a few promising leads already.

"Apprenticing." Adam sounded like... Beau had honestly never heard him sound anything like it. He wished he could see it; he thought he'd like to hang out with an Adam who could sound like that, instead of mostly angry all the time. "They—they let you—they—"

"I could... ask around for you?" Beau said, reminding himself not to promise anything even as he thought that maybe he *could* see Adam again, have a second chance to build a real friendship with his not-really-pack-brother, the one they'd never managed in med school. "I mean, you'd probably have to come here and meet them to get anywhere with it, but I think they'd listen, at least. And we have a guest room, even if the pack doesn't invite you to stay, or if you didn't want to."

Adam didn't say anything for a few minutes, but Beau could hear him struggling not to hyperventilate. Beau took a few bites of his lunch, and then his phone beeped with an incoming message. He didn't have to look to know what it would be.

"Sorry, my break's over, I've gotta get back to the ward—send me the details about what you need from Rory and his family, and what you want me to ask the midwives about, okay? And I mean it, you should come visit sometime, even if the midwives don't invite you right away."

"I will," Adam said, still sounding a little lost, or maybe newly found. "I—Beau. Thank you."

"No problem," Beau said, packing up the rest of his lunch. "Everybody needs people, right? And we're friends. Kind of pack."

Adam was silent for a second, like that was a surprise to him; maybe it was. Beau didn't think he would have said it, not easily, before a week ago. He wasn't sure that it was completely true even now, but they had to start somewhere, didn't they?

"Yes," Adam said. "I—yes. Thank you."

Beau told Rory about Adam's request that night when they were curled up in bed, as much alone as they ever were on the pack lands. They'd spent the after-dinner hours playing wolf-shaped hide-and-seek-wrestle-tag with Casey and Callie and a few others, so it was the first chance they'd had to talk in words, and Beau hadn't quite thought it out. He had to backtrack to explain when and why he'd asked Adam about it in the first place.

"Sorry, I should have told you about it before. I just—"

Rory touched his fingers to Beau's lips, hushing him gently. "No, it's—that's past, now. You're telling me now. And," he yawned, "I think you're right. Spence would probably be interested. Have to get mom and dad to sign off on it, though—he's only seventeen. But Adam wants samples from them too, so—we'll ask and see what they say."

Beau nodded. "And... do you think the midwives would speak to him?"

Rory nodded, curling in closer, and Beau's eyes closed automatically at the comfortable weight of Rory against his chest. "Depends on what he wants, probably, but... if he's a friend of yours, they'll listen, at least. Not Casey, he can get kind of weird about alphas, but the Aunties and Granny Tyne will hear you out, and they're in charge anyway."

Beau nodded, tightening his grip around Rory, enjoying the simple comfort of their bodies pressing close. They hadn't gone beyond stealing a few kisses here and there, and the absence of privacy wasn't the only reason now—the moon was waning, and would be empty in another few days. Omegas were never very interested in sex around the empty moon, and Rory was naturally less interested than most. That was fine; Beau would wait as long as Rory needed to.

"Oh," Beau murmured, remembering. "Dr. Ross told me today, they've definitely cleared my schedule for the empty moon from now on. I thought... d'you think the midwives will mind me being around here the day before and after?"

Rory snuggled closer, tightening his grip. "Mm-mm. They know who you belong to."

Beau smiled at the thought—he did belong to Rory, and everyone here knew it. Including Rory. He was Rory's, and as long as that was true he didn't care where they slept or what they called it. Rory loved him.

"Always," Beau mumbled, drifting toward sleep, certain that this was going to be the best empty moon of his life. "Love you too, baby."

~

One of Rory's texts that afternoon said, *Could you go by the house after work? I need you to pick up some things.*

Beau wondered briefly what things Rory needed and why he couldn't get a ride out during the day to pick them up, since he wasn't doing entire days with the little twins anymore, but he only texted back a quick thumbs up before he was back to work. He kept reminding himself all day that he needed to go to the house after work, for Rory. It wasn't until he was driving down the street that he realized he'd never asked Rory what it was he needed. He could call when he got out of the car, though, or...

Or he could just ask. Or maybe he didn't have to ask at all.

Rory was sitting on the front porch, waiting for him.

Beau pulled into the driveway with his blood pounding in his ears like thunder. He made himself look down at the gear shift to be sure he put the car in park, at his seatbelt to be sure he would unlatch it and not just tear it away in impatience or sheer inattention. He pulled out his keys and shoved them into his pocket.

By the time he actually got out of the car, Rory was standing up, teetering on the top step like he was considering coming to meet Beau, more than he already had just by being here. Beau closed the distance, possibly in a single leap to judge by the delighted look of startlement on Rory's face, and then he had Rory in his arms, lifting him clear off the ground.

"Tell me this is what I was supposed to pick up," Beau managed to say, with his omega in his arms, his mate's legs wrapped around his waist, his Rory's heart beating so close to his.

Rory's answer was a kiss, arms twining around his neck, and Beau didn't think any further, holding tight to his mate, all but devouring him. He wouldn't—couldn't—have stopped, but Rory pulled back suddenly and Beau froze. He only realized when Rory started to laugh that Mrs. Lindholm had just slammed her front door in a very pointed fashion; she must have seen their whole reunion.

"Sorry about that, Mrs. Lindholm!" Rory called out, cheerful and tactless as one of the Niemi kids. More softly, he added, "Inside, alpha."

Beau did exactly as his very clever husband instructed.

He would have taken Rory straight upstairs, but there were things blocking his path, lined up along the third step: Rory's backpack, and the bags Beau had brought to him, and a laundry bag that must contain all the bits and pieces of Beau's clothing that had migrated into the Midwives' House in the last week and a half.

"Could you pick those up for me, too?" Rory asked, keeping both legs and one arm firmly wrapped around Beau.

Beau growled a little and kissed him again. He let go of Rory with one hand to scoop everything up in an unwieldy mass, hauling it all upstairs with them while Rory laughed and peppered his face with pecking kisses.

"Where," Beau said at the top of the stairs, and Rory said, "Your room. Our room."

Beau dropped all of Rory's things just inside the door—he liked the sound of *our room*, though he thought vaguely that if they were going to share it really ought to be the room that had the magnificent bathtub—and carried Rory to the bed.

It was still unmade, the covers disarranged in exactly the way they'd been after Rory scrambled out of the bed and away from him, the morning after the full moon. Beau hesitated, and Rory looked over his shoulder at the bed, and then up at Beau again, smiling softly. "Well, come on. This time we'll do better."

Beau had to kiss him one more time, and then he laid Rory down. Rory didn't hesitate, scrambling across the bed to curl up in the same spot where he'd been when Beau last saw him here. When he was in danger, and Beau couldn't think of anything but the need to get him away.

But Rory was safe now. They were safe now. Vaughn and Amy had been folded firmly into the care of the pack—and so had Beau and Rory.

Rory nestled into the pillow, feigning sleep, and Beau realized what Rory had meant. He went over to the side of the bed and sat down again, as he had that morning; this time he couldn't bring himself to hesitate for even a second, reaching out immediately to rest his hand on Rory's side. Rory took a deep breath under Beau's hand, and then opened his eyes in a facsimile of a sleepy blink.

"Beau?"

Beau snorted and leaned in to kiss him again, half-convinced he would taste morning breath. "Hey, baby."

Rory reached up, curling an arm around his neck, and said, "Come back to bed, Beau. Come here."

"I'm—I should—" He hadn't showered yet; he was still wearing the day's scrubs. He hadn't wanted to forget to do what Rory needed.

"Uh-uh," Rory said, keeping his grip firm. "Just you, just how you are."

Beau obeyed, only kicking his shoes off before he curled down over Rory, wrapping himself around his mate and breathing in the scent of him in their bed again. "You're really—you're really home? You—"

"Really," Rory assured him. "D'you remember what you told me last night?"

"About... Adam?" Beau racked his brain, trying to think of how that would... oh. He picked his head up to look into Rory's eyes properly. "About... oh, Ror. Did you think I *didn't* love you?"

Rory shook his head, "It's not like I was waiting for you to say the magic word, I just—I'd been so careful for so long not to say it to you too soon. Even before, for weeks at least. I didn't trust myself to have picked the right person this time, to say that to. And last night I realized... I don't know, maybe I'm always going to be a little scared, maybe... maybe I'm always going to be practicing. But I love you, and—"

Beau had to kiss him, and Rory seemed to welcome the interruption; he relaxed in Beau's arms, his breath coming easier.

"I love you," Beau repeated softly. "I do love you, and—and I want so much to do this right. To be worthy of you."

Rory looked up at him, shaking his head a little. "Worthy of *me*," he repeated, barely whispering. "I'm just—"

"Brave," Beau said softly. "So brave, to ever try again. And strong. And kind, and smart in ways I will never be able to learn if I go to school another hundred years, and—everything to me, Rory. You're everything. You're my home. My heart."

Rory laughed a little, sounding near tears, and whispered, "Well, you're not so bad yourself."

Beau grinned, love and pride and everything else swelling his heart so that he didn't think he could make a sound, even to laugh. After a moment he finally managed, "Well, I'm trying."

Rory brushed a thumb over his lower lip, then higher. Over his teeth. He shifted a little on the bed, tilting his head at the same time. Showing his throat. "Beau—if you really—if we're—"

Beau squeezed his eyes shut and ducked his head, brushing his lips against Rory's throat. He was asking for a bite—for a mate bond, sealed by a bite.

There was more to it than just the biting, the same as a bite wouldn't automatically make someone a werewolf if they weren't ready for the change. Beau felt an instant's scrambling panic; he hadn't prepared for this, he wasn't ready, he didn't know how to make a bite translate into a true bond, and then he felt a certainty, deep within.

His wolf knew, which meant he knew. He didn't know *how* he knew, or how it worked, or what exactly would happen, but he knew that if he gave Rory what he was asking for, they would have a true bond between them. They would be mates. Rory would be his, and he would be Rory's. For good.

He wanted to ask if Rory was sure, wanted to second-guess and hesitate, but Rory's hands were in his hair and Rory's throat was bared to his teeth. He could feel the beating of Rory's heart, and he knew that Rory was sure, too. Scared, maybe, just like he was, but sure of this much. Whatever was ahead, they could choose to figure it out together.

Beau brushed a last soft kiss across Rory's dwindling scars, found the place, and sunk in his teeth. Rory's blood welled in his mouth, and Rory only gripped him tighter as the bond unfurled between them, bright and hot and new, and they both knew that this was exactly what they had needed.

EPILOGUE

SIX (AND A HALF) MONTHS LATER

*R*ory had been a little afraid—or hopeful—that he wouldn't manage to keep the secret long enough to have to actually tell it, but Beau was being run ragged by his latest rotation. Half the time when he came home from a shift, he might not have noticed Rory naked and painted blue if Rory didn't actually stand between him and the shower or the bed.

Rory wasn't sure whether tonight would be like that. Beau would want to leave everything in good order before his break, but the prospect of an entire week off, after eight months with only the moons and the occasional thirty-six-hour weekend, might give him a second wind.

Well, if Beau only wanted to come home and go to sleep, that was fine; they could talk in the morning.

Still, Rory wrapped the little box and set it in the middle of the kitchen table. If Beau noticed it, that would be that. If not, he'd be sure to see it at breakfast tomorrow. Rory would make sure. He definitely wouldn't let it go past tomorrow morning.

Rory rubbed his hand over his belly, trying again to tell if it felt different. It didn't, really. He was sure it didn't. And yet...

Well. Beau, and tomorrow night's full moon, couldn't get here soon enough.

Rory sensed a change in Beau across their bond a moment before the got the text message: *On my way!!*

Rory sent back a heart and forced himself to sit down at the kitchen table with the next set of math practice from his study book. He'd already passed the GED test and was all caught up on the classes he was taking through the community college this semester, but math felt enough like work that he could focus on it even when he was too jittery to read or watch TV.

He wound up so absorbed in his problem set that he barely registered Beau walking in, and didn't look up until Beau's hand was on his shoulder. "Oh! I—"

Beau was smiling, and kissed him softly. "My happy, busy, clever husband is all the welcome home I need, baby. Go on and finish."

Rory kissed him again, taking a moment to gauge whether Beau needed his attention, despite what he said—but Beau had already showered at work and changed into clean scrubs, probably before spending the extra hour or two to finish getting all his charts caught up before he left. He didn't seem unduly tired or stressed, just happy to be home, with no secret bitterness underlying his words.

There never was, but Rory had more or less accepted that he would always be looking for it, and noticing the absence. It wasn't such a bad thing to notice, though it was distracting when he was halfway through a proof.

"Go on," Beau repeated, squeezing his shoulder and stepping away. Rory returned to his work, half-listening as Beau located the dinner Rory had prepared, brought it all to the table and poured drinks for both of them.

Rory finished his proof and pushed his papers aside just as Beau sat down—and Beau's gaze went immediately to the little box in the middle of the table, now sitting in the midst of their dinner. Beau looked to him. "Should I..."

Rory shook his head quickly, feeling suddenly unsure. Maybe it was a silly thing to give this way—maybe a jinx, even. "We should eat first."

Beau nodded, accepting that, and moved the box aside before he started serving from the dishes. "So, what were you working on?"

"Geometry," Rory said. "I think maybe I'll take a math class over the summer after all—although there's also that writing class, and art—"

"I'm sure you could manage three, if you wanted to," Beau offered, and Rory carefully did not look at the present as he made a noncommittal noise and launched into yet another rehash of his priorities. Beau reminisced about some of the classes he'd taken when he was getting started; he'd gone to community college, too, before he properly started his undergraduate degree. He seemed confident that Rory could do the same.

If you want to, Beau always said. *It's not necessarily for everyone. Just depends on what you want to do.*

Rory still didn't look at the present, and asked Beau how his day had gone. Beau grinned and launched into a story about Cora, who he had wound up with on this rotation again, to their mutual delight.

But eventually dinner ended, and they were both just sitting there, eyeing their empty plates, and the last of the food, while the present sat just beyond Beau's elbow.

"Oh, Moon, just open it," Rory said abruptly, covering his face with both hands. "It's—it's silly, it's just—"

Beau scooted his chair closer to Rory's and put one arm around his shoulders. Rory leaned into him, peeking through his fingers as Beau tore open the paper one-handed and opened the box.

Rory didn't breathe as Beau reached in, brushing his fingers over the soft weave of the pale yellow cloth, embroidered with dozens of interlocking circles in different colors. Several of them had been done with metallic copper thread, and Beau's fingers gravitated to those. He was quiet a long time, other than the racing of his heart, but finally he said, "Rory? This is... this is a baby blanket."

"Yeah," Rory said softly. "Yeah, it is." Stitched with well-wishes from half the Niemi pack and assorted friends and neighbors, as well as Rory himself.

"But," Beau said, and he finally looked at Rory, and then down at Rory's belly, where there was nothing to see—nothing new at all, except a possibility. "Did you..." His fingers went to the copper threads again.

"Those are just thread," Rory said. "The coil's in a little jar—Casey and I couldn't figure out what exactly to do with it, but it didn't seem like it should just be thrown away."

Beau squeezed him a little. "You know I..." he didn't finish the sentence, just nuzzling at Rory's hair for the space of a breath before he said, instead, "Did it hurt?"

"I, uh," Rory hid his face, and his smile, against Beau's chest. "I wasn't feeling any pain. It was fine."

Beau laughed a little at that. "Well. That's good, then. You, uh... had you planned...?"

Rory shrugged. "I'd been starting to think it was time. I think I've been ready for a while. And then I was talking to Casey about that, and everything, and he mentioned it was a good time to remove it, close to the moon, and..."

Beau kissed his forehead. "There's no rush, you know. Just because it's out, that doesn't mean..."

"I know," Rory said. "And if you think it'll be a bad time to be having a baby—obviously we need to make that decision together. But, you know. It might not even work on this heat—" Or ever, he couldn't help thinking, the fear still lingering that despite everything he was still broken somehow inside, that he could never do what every other omega seemed to do so easily. "But I figured, even if it does, we'll be into your second year by the time a baby could arrive."

He heard the little skip in Beau's heartbeat, the catch of his breath, and then Beau was pulling Rory out of his chair and into Beau's lap, kissing him so fervently that he hardly needed their mate bond singing yes yes yes between them to answer the half-asked question.

Outside the snow had melted from everywhere but the shadowed

422

places, and a few of the tulips were sprouting in the sunniest spots, closet to the house. The moon was waxing, nearly full, and spring was coming, and Rory was laughing and kissing his mate, safe in his arms and ready to try.

THE END

ABOUT THE AUTHOR

Dessa Lux also writes fanfic as Dira Sudis and has one novel published as Dira Lewis through Less Than Three Press. She is a confirmed Midwesterner, a librarian, and a Diet Coke addict, but she does not own a cat.

You can find Dessa on Twitter @DessaLux, or at http://dessa-lux.tumblr.com

Made in the USA
Middletown, DE
25 May 2018